KU-012-452

# BEVERLY BARTON

# COLD HEARTED

**AVON**

AVON

A division of HarperCollins*Publishers*
77–85 Fulham Palace Road,
London W6 8JB

www.harpercollins.co.uk

This production 2011

First published in the U.S.A. by Kensington Publishing Corp.
New York, NY, 2008

Copyright © Beverly Barton 2008

Beverly Barton asserts the moral right to
be identified as the author of this work

A catalogue record for this book is
available from the British Library

ISBN-13: 978-0-00789-966-1

Set in Times New Roman by Palimpsest Book Production Limited,
Grangemouth, Stirlingshire

Printed and bound in Great Britain by
Clays Ltd, St Ives plc

**Mixed Sources**
Product group from well-managed
forests and other controlled sources
www.fsc.org   Cert no. SW-COC-001806
© 1996 Forest Stewardship Council

FSC

FSC is a non-profit international organisation established to promote the
responsible management of the world's forests. Products carrying the FSC
label are independently certified to assure consumers that they come
from forests that are managed to meet the social, economic and
ecological needs of present and future generations.

Find out more about HarperCollins and the environment at
**www.harpercollins.co.uk/green**

# COLD HEARTED

An avid reader since childhood, Beverly Barton wrote her first book at the age of nine. Since then, she has gone on to write well over sixty novels and is a *New York Times* bestselling author. Beverly lives in Alabama.

For further information about Beverly Barton go to her website at www.beverlybarton.com and visit www.Book Army.co.uk for exclusive updates.

By the same author:

*Close Enough to Kill*
*Amnesia*
*The Dying Game*
*The Murder Game*

# COLD HEARTED

# Prologue

Perhaps the best thing he could do for himself and everyone he loved was to commit suicide.

Dan Price stared at the Glock pistol lying atop his desk. He had bought the 9mm automatic for his wife, but she had refused the gift, politely reminding him of her aversion to guns. But at his insistence, she had gone with him to the practice range and learned to use the weapon, only to please him. But to his knowledge, she had never carried the pistol, never kept it in her room or in her car.

If his sweet Jordan had any idea that he was contemplating taking his own life, she would do her best to convince him that no matter what the future held, she would stand by him. It was her basic integrity and loyalty that had first attracted him to the woman who had become his greatest political asset.

Dan lifted the half-full glass of Kentucky bourbon to his lips and finished off the remainder. The liquor burned a path down his esophagus and hit his belly like fire. He coughed a couple of times, then wiped his mouth, picked up the bottle, and poured himself another drink.

If he was going to do this—and he fully intended to end his life tonight—he knew he couldn't do it stone cold sober. He wasn't that courageous. Before he could put the hammer-forged barrel into his mouth and pull the trigger, he needed to be more than a little drunk.

He sipped on the bourbon as he leaned back in the swivel desk chair and let his gaze travel over the room. His private study, as it had been his father's and grandfather's before him. An impressive room inside a 200-year-old antebellum mansion, part of an estate that had been in his family since before the War Between the States. Generations of Price men had served their country, first in wartime and then in local, state, and national politics. In Georgia, the name Price was synonymous with public service.

If he killed himself, how would that affect his family's good name? No Price man had ever taken the easy way out of a bad situation.

But could he continue, knowing what the future held for him? Could he condemn Jordan to such a life? And what about Devon? And his brother, Ryan? They would never desert him, and that would mean great sacrifices for each of them.

*You don't have to do this tonight. You have time.*

But how much time? Six months? A year?

Dan finished off his second drink and poured himself a third.

The grandfather clock in the hall struck twice. Two in the morning.

He unlocked the file cabinet in the bottom drawer of the desk, rummaged through the folders until he found the file he wanted. A copy of his will. His lawyer kept another copy and a third was inside his safe at the house in Bethesda. The contents of his will were not secret to anyone. Everything he possessed would be equally divided among Jordan, Devon and Ryan. Jordan had protested, telling him that she didn't expect such an enormous legacy, but he had quieted her protests with a tender caress.

"I owe you more than I will ever be able to repay," he'd told her.

Dan finished off his third drink.

Minutes ticked by as he contemplated the Glock on his desk. Grandfather Price's antique desk. Family lore claimed the desk had belonged to Jefferson Davis, a contemporary of his ancestor, General John Ryan Price.

Dan poured another glass of bourbon, picked up the bottle and the glass and walked over to the leather Chesterfield sofa. He sat down, placed the bottle on the floor, and considered his options. Death was preferable to the fate that awaited him.


Dan's eyelids flicked open and shut. In the twilight zone of being half-awake/half-asleep, he didn't immediately realize where he was or what had awakened him so abruptly. Woozy from sleep and too much bourbon, Dan recalled that he had contemplated suicide to solve his problems, but in the end, drunk and, oddly enough, thinking more clearly than he had when he'd been sober, he had realized that killing himself would have been the coward's way out.

Dan swatted at something cold against his cheek. His fingertips raked across the metal object. He opened his eyes fully, stared up at the woman leaning over him, and smiled. She did not return his smile. His gaze zipped from her familiar face to his own hand holding the 9mm, its barrel pressed firmly against his head. And it was only when he tried to ease the gun away from his head that he realized her hand covered his, her index finger squeezed tightly over his against the trigger.

"What the—!"

Before he could react, she forced his finger down against the trigger, firing the gun at point blank range directly into his brain.

Dan's last thought was that someone he'd trusted completely had just killed him.

# Chapter 1

Jordan Price was a cold-hearted bitch. Cool, controlled and calculating. If she was a better actress, she would at least show some sign of emotion. She could fake tears or heave a deep, grieving sigh. Anything to indicate she felt at least a modicum of remorse over her husband's death. But the lady hadn't shed a tear. Not during the church funeral attended by hundreds and not at the graveside service for family and close friends.

Rick Carson had met her type before—alluring and dangerous. He hadn't known the late Senator Price personally, but he sure as hell felt sorry for the poor bastard. Every man, even a damn politician, deserved a wife who mourned him.

As the light drizzle increased and quickly turned into a downpour, black umbrellas popped open to shield the small crowd of mourners surrounding the open gravesite. The scalloped edges of the burgundy-red canopy sheltering the immediate family, seated in double rows of four chairs each, flapped loudly as the April wind whipped unmercifully through the nearby trees.

Small town, southern cemeteries were pretty much inter-
changeable, many of the headstones dating back to the
early 1800s and a few graves marked with only large rocks.
Rick figured that, for the most part, his dirt poor ancestors lay in unmarked graves throughout the South, from
Virginia to Kentucky and on into his home state of Mississippi. His father had been the first in his family to ac-
quire a high school diploma and Rick had been the first to
graduate from college. He had about as much in common
with the dearly departed senator as a buzzard has in common with a peacock.

The woman at Rick's side raised her open umbrella
just enough to clear the top of his head, which due to her
being five-ten meant she'd lifted it only a few inches to
accommodate his six-two height. Nicole Powell was his
boss's wife—actually she was Griff's bride of seven months
and co-owner of the Powell Private Security and Investigation Agency. If Griff wasn't out of the country right now,
he'd be here instead of Rick, who had worked for the agency
the past five years.

As the minister uttered the final prayer in the 20-minute
ceremony that had included the mournful wail of a bag-
piper's rendition of "Amazing Grace," Rick shifted his attention from Nicole back to Mrs. Price. She sat ramrod
straight, her chin tilted upward, her teeth clenched, and her
eyelids slowly closing. Reverent enough to shut her eyes,
but not enough to bow her head, the widow took a deep
breath. Was she weary of having to pretend to care and
wishing this day would end? Or was she desperately trying to control any emotion she might feel?

The man sitting beside Jordan Price casually reached
over and grasped her folded hands resting in her lap, then
took one hand in his and clutched it tightly. She didn't
react in any way when he placed their entwined hands between them. Rick sensed these two shared an intimate
bond. Nic had told him that this sinfully handsome guy,

who at the funeral had showed far more emotion than the widow, had been Dan Price's assistant for 12 years. Rumor had it that Devon Markham had been like a son to the senator. So, what did that make him to the senator's attractive, young wife? A friend or a lover?

The minister, a gray-haired gentleman with a kind face and a commanding voice, ended the service by inviting those in attendance to join the family at the Price home for an after-funeral reception. This type of affair was the southern, Protestant version of a wake.

While the others seated stood up and shook hands with the preacher, Markham assisted the widow to her feet, placed his arm around her waist and took a protective stand at her side.

"Let's get out of here," Nicole whispered. "I'll wait and speak to Claire and Ryan at the reception."

"Did they tell you why they were interested in hiring Powell's?" Rick kept in step with Nic's long-legged gait as they made their way toward her Escalade.

"No. All Claire said when she called to tell me about Dan Price's funeral arrangements was that Ryan needed to speak to me after the funeral about hiring Powell's. Considering what she and Ryan were going through at the time, I thought the particulars could wait."

Glancing over his shoulder, Rick took one final look at Mrs. Price. Dry-eyed and rigid, she spoke to the minister. Markham clung to her, not she to him, which implied that she was the stronger of the two and they both knew it.

What was it about the woman that intrigued Rick so? Maybe it was nothing more than her being beautiful. Beautiful, fragile, vulnerable—and heartless. His instincts were usually right on the money and it was highly unlikely he was wrong this time, but for some gut-level reason, he wanted to be wrong about the widow being heartless.

Nicole stopped, turned, and called to him. "What's the matter?"

He realized Nic had walked on ahead of him and he was standing in the rain staring at a woman he didn't know and instinctively didn't like. He caught up with Nic, clicked the OPEN button on his remote to unlock the SUV, and then rushed to open the passenger door for her.

Once seated inside, he started the engine and backed up the car. "What do you know about Jordan Price?"

Nicole shrugged. "Not much really. Counting today, I've met her a total of four times. The first time was Claire and Ryan's wedding. Then again at Michael's christening and the last time was at her wedding, when she married Dan."

Rick drove slowly down the narrow one-lane road that led out of Oak Hill Cemetery. "She's a lot younger than he was. Do you think she married him for his money?"

Nic laughed. "I have no idea." She glanced at Rick. "Why so curious about Jordan Price?"

Rick's grip on the steering wheel tightened. Damn good question. Why was he so curious about the widow? Yeah, sure, he found her attractive. And yeah, her seemingly unfeeling attitude disturbed him. Maybe she reminded him a little too much of his own callous, conniving stepmother, who had sucked his father dry during their marriage and had cheated Rick and his sister out of their meager inheritance.

Rick grunted. "Damn if I know. I just thought it odd that the lady hasn't shed a tear all day."

"Some people cry in private," Nic said. "And the reality of death doesn't always hit a person right away. It often catches up with them weeks later and then they fall apart."

"Yeah, either is a possibility."

"But you're not buying it, are you?"

"Young, beautiful widow buries older, wealthy husband, without any show of emotion whatsoever. And the husband's handsome, young assistant holds her hand and clings to her during the funeral."

"You're painting a really ugly picture, you know. Dan Price committed suicide. He wasn't murdered. Besides, Claire and Ryan like Jordan. And if Jordan hadn't been a good wife to Dan, neither Claire nor Ryan would think so highly of her, would they?"

"Hey, it's nothing to me one way or another," Rick said. "It's not my family, not my concern. I don't know these people."

And he didn't want to know them, especially not Jordan. But if Ryan Price hired Powell's and he was assigned to the case—what then?

She watched from an upstairs window as the hordes descended on Price Manor, Dan's ancestral home.

A gray day, with the heavens weeping, seemed appropriate for the funeral services. Daniel Price had been loved and respected. It was only fitting that the weather reflected the somber mood of the occasion.

We made it through the funeral without breaking down. That's good. The reception won't be as difficult. We'll be able to reminisce about Dan without being morbid. We can laugh about our memories of him instead of cry. In many ways, Dan was a truly good man. A good husband. But if he'd been allowed to live, he would have become a very bad husband, a noose around our necks, a burden we shouldn't have had to bear.

It will take time for us to heal from this tragedy, but eventually, we'll move on, just as we've done in the past.

She hadn't wanted to kill Dan, but she'd had no choice. Not really. If only he had followed through with his plans and had killed himself, he could have saved her the trouble. But apparently, he had lost his nerve at the last minute. As much as she had cared for Dan, she had realized that she couldn't allow him to ruin their lives. If he had lived, they would have suffered along with him each day. It would have been so unfair. Hadn't they already suffered enough? By killing Dan, she had protected them from years of anguish. And in the long run, his early death had been truly merciful for him, too. With Dan and his problems out of the way, they could look forward to raising their baby without the burden of a sick husband.

A baby.

Their baby.

They had wanted a baby for such a long time.

When she was a child, Jordan had dreamed of living in an antebellum mansion, something to equal the splendor of Scarlett O'Hara's beloved Tara. The first time Dan had brought her to his ancestral home in Priceville, Georgia, she had felt an odd sense of homecoming, as if this was where she belonged. For the past three years, she had enjoyed the time they'd spent here far more than their time in D.C. But when she married Dan, she had accepted the fact that she would be a political wife, that she would play the game by the rules. Although she was often uncomfortable with the façade she and Dan had presented to the world, she had never regretted her decision to commit herself to their marriage. He had offered not only security for herself, but for her family whose members depended on her.

Jordan pressed her open palm lightly against her still flat abdomen. Dan was gone, but not lost to her forever. Not as long as the child growing inside her lived, he or she would be a link to her husband. Her son or daughter would carry on the Price name and honor a generations-old heritage. When they had discussed bringing a child into the world, Dan had prophesied that their offspring would one day be president.

*Oh, Dan, why? Why did you do this horrible thing?*

She had found out she was pregnant the day before Dan killed himself and had intended to share the news with him that evening. But after dinner, he had closed himself off in his study and she'd never seen him alive again.

A part of her refused to believe that Dan had taken his own life; but the alternative was equally unbelievable. Yes, Dan had enemies, both personal and political, but no one truly hated him, certainly not enough to kill him.

You have too much to deal with right now without trying to figure out what happened and why. There will be time enough for that later. You have to go downstairs and greet your guests. Dan's friends and enemies, his associates, his family and his constituents.

First and foremost Daniel Price had been a public servant, in one form or another, all his life, just as his father and grandfather had been. The very least she owed Dan was to uphold the family traditions and keep his untainted public image as shiny bright as it had been for the past 55 years.

Jordan felt Devon's presence moments before he reached out and laid a comforting hand on her shoulder. She sighed deeply, then forced a wavering smile and turned to look at her oldest and dearest friend.

"People are asking about you," Devon said. "Do you feel up to facing the mob?"

Jordan nodded. "Almost ready. Give me a couple more minutes."

"It doesn't seem real, does it? Dan gone. You and I left to—" Devon choked down his tears. "Why did he choose such a drastic solution? He should have known once he told us about the diagnosis of early-stage Alzheimer's, we would have been there for him every step of the way. He could have had some good years still ahead of him."

Jordan caressed Devon's cheek, tenderly brushing away his tears. "I don't know. Maybe this was his way of protecting us."

A light tap on her half-open bedroom door alerted them that they were not alone. Devon stiffened as Jordan glanced over his shoulder and her gaze locked with Tobias Harper's dark, penetrating glare.

"Pardon me, Miss Jordan, but Mr. Ryan asks that you come downstairs as soon as possible." The elderly servant, who had been in the Prices' employ since he was a boy, had loved Dan as much as she and Devon. And like them, he had known the real Daniel Price. "Please, ma'am. Mr. Ryan needs you."

"Tell him I'll be down right away."

Tobias nodded, then turned and disappeared up the hall.

Devon offered her his arm.

She shook her head. "No, you should go down first and I'll follow in a few minutes. The last thing we want is anyone speculating about the two of us."

Devon's lips lifted in a sad smile. He took her hand in his and brought it to his lips for a light kiss. Then she stood and watched as he walked away. In private, she and Devon could comfort each other, could share their grief. But in public, they had to be discreet, in honor of Dan's memory as much as to protect themselves from gossip and ridicule.

Squaring her shoulders, taking a deep breath, and steeling her nerves, Jordan marched out of her bedroom suite and hurried down the hall. She paused when she reached the top of the right side of the double curving staircases. The string quartet at one side of the large foyer was all but drowned out by the hum of conversation filling the foyer and both front parlors. No doubt by now, dozens of people were already milling through the dining room to partake of the lavish buffet.

When she descended the stairs, her sister-in-law, Claire, broke away from Ryan in the receiving line and came to meet her. Sweet, lovely Claire, with her bright hazel eyes and warm smile. Her sister-in-law was also her friend. She tried her best not to envy the other woman, who was madly in love with her husband, and also had a strong marriage and an adorable three-year-old son.

Claire circled Jordan's waist with her arm and gave her a quick hug. "Everyone's been asking about you."

"I needed a little time to myself after the graveside service."

"I know, but poor Ryan is on the verge of collapsing. This whole ordeal has simply been too much for him."

Jordan wanted to tell Claire that it had been too much for all of them, not only Ryan, but instead she said, "Why don't you take him back to the kitchen and see if you can get him to eat a bite. I'll take over here."

"Thanks, Jordan. I knew I could count on you. You've been our strength. I don't know what we'd have done without you."

"Go . . . go . . ." She shooed Claire away. "Take care of your husband. I'll handle everything else just fine on my own."

*You've been our strength.*

How many times had Jordan been told that she was always the strong, capable, take-charge person in good times and bad? Her earliest memories were those of being a caretaker. First, when she was only ten, to her sick and dying mother, then afterward to her grieving father. She couldn't remember a time in her life when she hadn't been taking care of others. Perhaps that was her lot in life, her mission, her burden, her duty, the one thing at which she excelled.

After she replaced her brother-in-law in the receiving line, Jordan lost track of time. Eventually, her hand, which had been shaken countless times, became as numb as her emotions. The only way she could make it through this evening without losing her mind was to act and react by remote control. Shake hands. Accept sympathy. Don't cringe when someone she barely knew hugged her. Agree that Dan had been a prince of a fellow and would be sorely missed. Move on to the next person and repeat the process.

Rick hated Price Manor on sight. The antebellum mansion was a relic from the South's notorious past, a plantation house that had been passed down through the generations. No doubt, the Price family could trace their ancestors back to Europe, probably to nobility, albeit some of their predecessors had possibly been born out of wedlock, fathered by kings, princes, dukes and earls. Rick could trace his ancestry back to his hard-drinking, ornery grandpa Carson, whose claim to fame had been that he could whip any man in a fair fight. His father's family home had been a Mississippi shit-shack, with a roof that leaked when it rained and floorboards so wide apart you could see the chickens pecking for worms in the rich soil under the house.

"Looks like something out of *Gone with the Wind*, doesn't it?" Nicole said as they rolled up to the front veranda and stopped.

"Yeah," Rick replied as he got out, handed his keys to the parking attendant and made his way around to the passenger side just as Nicole closed the door. Since it had stopped raining, he'd left the umbrella in the car. "Do your cousin and her husband live here, too?"

"No, they live in downtown Priceville, in an old Victorian house that belonged to Ryan and Dan's maternal grandmother."

"Both sides of the family had money, huh?"

"It seems so." Nic cast him a sidelong glance as they reached the open front doors. "Keep your opinion of Jordan Price to yourself when we speak with Ryan and Claire later. Understand?"

"Yes, ma'am. None of my business. Keep my mouth shut."

Although it wasn't raining, moisture hung in the air, heavy and damp. Rick would have liked to remove his black jacket and rip off his tie, get a little more comfortable and cooler. He definitely wasn't a suit and tie kind of guy. Give him a pair of wash-worn jeans and a cotton shirt instead of fancy duds any day of the week.

Good God, the house was swarming with people, like maggots pouring out of a rotting corpse. The interior temperature had to be a good ten degrees warmer than the humid air outside. Body heat.

Rick and Nicole took their place in the reception line, apparently close to the end since only two couples were ahead of them, one pair offering their condolences to the widow—and to Devon Markham. Two women flanked Jordan, the one on her right, a tall, thin woman with a sharp nose and keen brown eyes, separated her from Markham. The woman on the left was older, but far more attractive. A full-figured blonde who oozed sex appeal. Rick got the distinct impression that both women had stationed themselves there to guard Jordan. Who were they to the young widow? Mother? Aunt? A former nanny?

As the other couples moved on, Nicole stepped up in line and, one by one, offered the foursome in the reception line her sympathy. Jordan reached out and took Nicole's hand.

"I appreciate your driving in from Knoxville," Jordan said. "I'm sure your being here is a great comfort to Claire."

Rick said nothing, simply stuck to Nicole like glue and nodded his head to each of the older ladies. He had intended to pass by as unobtrusively as possible, but suddenly Jordan asked Nicole, "Is this your husband?"

Nic shook her head. "No, Griff is in England. This is Rick Carson, a Powell agent. He offered to drive down with me so I wouldn't have to make the trip alone."

*Smooth, Nic. A little white lie to prevent an awkward moment.*

He looked right at Jordan then. Big mistake. She gazed up at him with blue-gray eyes a shade lighter than the dark gray silk suit she wore, and Rick felt as if he'd been hit in the head with a sledgehammer. The lady took his breath away. Slender, fragile bones, porcelain skin, classically beautiful features. She looked as if she was on the verge of collapse and everything masculine in him wanted to reach out and offer her the support of his strong arms.

Her mouth curved upward in an almost smile. "That was very kind of you, Mr. Carson."

How the hell did he respond to that? "Yes, ma'am. I'm very sorry about your husband."

"Thank you." The soft, sweet sound of her voice wrapped around him like satin cords, pulling him in, threatening to bind him to her.

Not until Nic grabbed his arm and gave it a yank did he realize he was still staring at Jordan, that he hadn't moved an inch and was holding up the line of mourners still waiting to express their sympathy.

Once Nic had ushered him out of the foyer and into the parlor on the left, she said, "I need to find Claire and Ryan and see why he wants to hire Powell's. After that, we can head for home."

"We could split up and go in different directions to look for them," Rick suggested. "Then meet back here in five minutes."

"Okay. Good idea. You start your search in here and I'll go into the other parlor," Nic told him, then just as she turned around, she stopped and said, "Wait up. I see Claire. She's motioning to me."

Rick fell in step beside Nic as she headed toward the foyer again. He caught sight of Nic's cousin, Claire, a leggy brunette almost as tall as Nic.

"Come on," Nic said.

When they approached Claire, she met them at the

pocket doors open to the foyer. "Ryan is in Dan's study. He's waiting for us."

Rick followed the two women down the wide hall and into a dark-paneled room with three floor-to-ceiling windows on the back wall, and two walls covered with built-in bookshelves. Ryan Price stood, with his back to the door, in front of a fireplace topped with an ornately carved mantel. When he heard the door open, he turned slowly.

He moved forward and extended his hand, first to Nicole and then to Rick. "Thank you for coming to the funeral."

"Dan was a good man," Nic said. "I'm so sorry about what happened."

Ryan grimaced. "I don't know how to say this any other way, so here goes—I don't believe Dan killed himself."

"I see." Nic glanced at Claire as if silently asking her if she agreed with her husband. "What makes you think he didn't kill himself? It's my understanding, from what Claire told me, that the local authorities and the Georgia Bureau of Investigation have ruled Dan's death a suicide."

As she rushed to her husband's side, Claire said, "Officially, Dan's death was ruled a suicide. But we were told that it's difficult, if not sometimes impossible, to prove a suicide wasn't murder. Especially when the person supposedly shot himself in the head."

Ryan's gaze settled on the sofa in front of the fireplace. "He was lying there when Jordan found him. The only fingerprints on the gun were Dan's. And there was gunshot residue on his hand from where he had supposedly fired the weapon."

"Then why—?" Nic asked, but Ryan cut her off.

"I knew Dan. Knew the kind of man he was. Under no circumstances would he have killed himself." Ryan slipped his arm around Claire's waist, obviously needing her comfort and support. "I want to hire the Powell Agency to do a thorough investigation and find a way to prove that my brother didn't commit suicide."

Nic glanced at Claire again.

Claire cleared her throat, then said, "I told Nic that we discovered, after Dan's death, that he was in the beginning stages of Alzheimer's."

Ryan heaved a deep sigh. "That information is not to go beyond this room." He glared at Rick. Rick nodded. "Dan might have considered suicide, but I'm telling you that he wouldn't have—" Ryan's voice cracked. Swallowing hard, he turned his head sideways, averting his teary gaze.

"You realize the alternative to suicide is murder," Nic said.

"Yes," Claire answered for both of them.

"Do you have any reason to believe that someone murdered your brother?" Rick asked.

A loud, startled gasp came from the doorway. All heads turned. Jordan Price had opened the door and stood there, eyes wide with shock, her mouth parted and her pale cheeks suddenly flushed.

"Oh, my God, no, no! You can't honestly believe that someone murdered Dan."

# Chapter 2

"Oh, Jordan, I'm so sorry." Claire pulled away from Ryan and took a tentative step toward her sister-in-law. "We wanted to spare you—"

"Exactly what's going on here?" Jordan asked as her gaze quickly flashed around the room, scanning the four people in her husband's study.

Claire, all wide-eyed guilt but genuine concern, halted a few feet from Jordan as if uncertain of what to do or say.

"I wanted to wait until later to speak to you about this," Ryan said. "You have enough to deal with as it is."

With thick auburn hair, the tall, slender Ryan was a younger version of Dan. Only Dan's eyes had been a brilliant topaz and Ryan's were a honeyed brown.

Nicole Baxter Powell remained silent, her compassionate gaze focusing steadily on Jordan. Although Jordan had met the former FBI agent only a few times, she liked Claire's cousin and had no reason to distrust her.

The man at Nicole's side was a stranger, someone she'd never seen before today. His eyes, so dark they appeared almost black, bored into her, his stare intense and hostile. Hostile? Was her imagination working overtime? This man had no reason to be antagonistic toward her. They didn't even know each other.

Jordan looked directly at Ryan. "Answer the man's question. Do you have any reason to believe that someone murdered Dan, that his death wasn't a suicide?"

Ryan frowned, emotional pain etched on his features as he faced Jordan. "I don't believe Dan killed himself. It went against his very nature to take the coward's way out. He was one of the strongest, bravest men I've ever known."

"Dan was also loving and protective," Jordan said. "If he believed that by taking his own life, he might spare us the agony of watching him die by slow degrees, then he might have—"

"No!" Ryan bellowed the one word as he clenched his hands into stiff fists and closed his eyes for a split second.

Startled by her brother-in-law's vehement response, she tensed, every muscle in her body suddenly taut. "There's more to this than just your belief that Dan wouldn't commit suicide, isn't there?"

"Tell her. She'll find out sooner or later." Claire looked from her husband to Jordan and then back to Ryan as if she couldn't decide who needed her comfort more.

"Tell me what?" Jordan asked.

"I spoke to Steve privately the day the autopsy report came in," Ryan said. "You know that Steve and I go way back, that we've been—"

"Yes, I know that you and Sheriff Corbett are good friends, so please stop stalling and just come right out and tell me whatever it is."

"Steve agrees with me that, despite the coroner ruling Dan's death a suicide and the fact he has no solid proof to the contrary, it's possible that Dan didn't kill himself. Steve says that details about a gunshot wound can rule out suicide, but they can't prove it conclusively, that sometimes it's a judgment call."

Jordan felt cold, as if the temperature in the room had dropped a good 20 degrees in a matter of seconds. A chill rippled over her body causing her to quiver.

"You realize what you're saying, don't you? If Dan didn't . . . if he wasn't responsible, then that means someone else . . ." No, she refused to believe that anyone would kill Dan. "But that's not possible. I found Dan lying over there—" she indicated the sofa with a glance "—with the gun still in his hand. The doors were locked and there was no evidence that anyone had broken into the house."

"Who else was in the house other than you and the senator?" Mr. Carson asked.

Surprised by his question and by the fact that he had injected himself into what was a family matter, Jordan snapped her head around and glared at him.

"Rick!" Nicole Powell frowned at her companion.

"No, it's quite all right," Ryan said. "I want Mr. Carson to ask questions. If I hire Powell's to do an independent investigation into Dan's death, then—"

"If you do what?" Jordan felt as if she might faint. Had she heard Ryan correctly? Did he intend to hire an outside agency to dig deeper into the events surrounding Dan's death? What was he thinking? Didn't he realize that if the investigators unearthed too many facts about Dan's life, they might discover a truth that Dan had kept hidden for years, one that could destroy his reputation?

"I know why you're concerned," Ryan told her. "That's why I want to hire Powell's, a firm with a solid reputation for honesty and integrity. Any information they uncover will be kept in strictest confidence." He looked at Nicole. "Isn't that right, Nic?"

"Yes, of course," she replied.

"Do you need a glass of water, Mrs. Price?" Rick Carson asked. "Or maybe something a little stronger. You look as if you're going to pass out."

*I don't like you, Mr. Carson. I don't like the way you*

*look at me, as if you think you know something about me that no one else knows.*

Claire rushed to Jordan, cupped her elbow and said, "Come sit down. Please. Would you like a drink? Ryan can fix you something or I can ring for Tobias—"

"No, I'm all right." Jordan jerked away from her sister-in-law's gentle hold and marched across the room, stopping directly in front of the rough-looking Powell agent. Although he wore a suit and tie, he exuded a raw, rugged masculinity that hinted that beneath the neat façade beat the heart of a primitive male.

"We don't have to do this now, Mrs. Price," Mr. Carson said.

"We had a full house that weekend because of the Easter holiday. The live-in servants were here. Tobias and Vadonna. My stepchildren, Kendra and Wes Brannon, were both home from college. Dan's personal assistant, Devon Markham was here, as was my assistant, Rene Burke."

Rick Carson's gaze met hers head-on. Neither of them blinked.

"Who has a key to the house and knows the code for the security system?" he asked.

"Really, Mr. Carson, now is hardly the time to—" Claire injected.

"No, no, it's perfectly all right," Jordan said. "If Ryan hires the Powell Agency and Mr. Carson heads the investigation, I'm sure he'll ask far more personal questions than that. We might as well get used to being interrogated."

"Oh, please, let's not do this now." Claire slid her arm through her husband's and reached for his hand.

"Claire's right," Ryan said. "This can wait. Jordan's near collapse." He looked pleadingly at Jordan. "I'm sorry. I didn't handle this very well."

"No, let's do this now." Jordan returned her gaze to Rick Carson. "If there is any possibility that Dan was murdered, I want to know. Consider yourself hired, Mr. Carson."

Rick glanced from Jordan to Ryan, then looked directly at Nicole.

"Am I to consider this a firm offer?" Nic asked. "If so, then is Powell's working for you, Ryan, or for Jordan?"

"For both of us," Jordan replied. "Unless Ryan has any objections."

"Of course not," Ryan said. "If you'd like for me to handle the details—"

"And Mr. Carson will be in charge of the investigation, right?" Jordan asked.

"Yes," Nic replied. "Unless you'd prefer another agent, Rick will head the investigation and will have all of Powell's resources at his disposal. If, once he begins the investigation, he feels that more agents are needed, he will make the request to you and Ryan for your approval before contacting headquarters. And since y'all are family—" she glanced pointedly at Claire—"Powell's will offer a discounted rate for our services."

"That won't be necessary." Jordan's jaw tightened. "Spare no expense. You agree, don't you, Ryan?"

"Yes, of course," he replied.

"I'll fax y'all the contract first thing in the morning and Rick will return and begin the investigation tomorrow," Nicole explained, then walked over and offered her hand to Jordan, who accepted it immediately. "We'll find out what happened to Dan. I promise. If he was murdered . . ." She squeezed Jordan's hand, then released it and nodded to Rick. "We should get going."

"I'll see y'all out," Claire said, then followed her cousin and Rick Carson as they left the study.

When she and Ryan were alone, Jordan stared at the new sofa which had replaced the one where only weeks ago she had discovered her husband's lifeless body on Good Friday. On first awakening that morning, she had gone to his room, hoping to share the good news of her pregnancy with him while everyone else was still asleep. But when she saw that his bed had not been slept in, she suspected he had fallen asleep in his study the night before, as he occasionally did. Upon entering the study, she had called his name, but he hadn't answered.

Now, with her eyes wide open, she could still envision the exact moment she realized Dan was dead. Before she noticed the bullet hole in his right temple, a single wound just above his cheekbone, she saw the dark red blood that discolored the gold silk cushion under his head and the gun that he clutched in his hand.

"Jordan?"

Ryan's soft, smooth voice snapped her out of her thoughts and brought her back to the present moment.

He laid his hand on her shoulder. She heaved a deep sigh.

"I don't know which I hate more," Ryan said. "The thought that Dan would actually kill himself or that someone murdered him."

Jordan shrugged off Ryan's hand and walked away. Pausing as she reached out to open the door, she glanced over her shoulder. "If Dan was murdered, I want his murderer found and punished. But I do not want Dan's good name sullied. I'll hold you personally responsible for making sure of that."

"God, Jordan, do you think I want anyone to find out the truth about Dan or about his relationship with you?"

"Then see to it that what was our personal business remains just that." She narrowed her gaze, issuing her brother-in-law a gentle warning. "And from now on, no more secret meetings with the Powell Agency. I'm to be included in any discussions with Mr. Carson. Is that understood?"

She didn't give Ryan a chance to reply. She'd made her point. Her brother-in-law's motives had been admirable—he had wanted to spare her more anguish, especially today. But he had underestimated her as so many people did. Even after knowing her for several years, he saw only the façade that she presented to the world. Few people knew the real Jordan Harris Brannon Price. Sometimes, she wasn't sure she knew herself. She had buried her true self beneath so many protective layers in order to survive that very little, if any, of the sweet, innocent, somewhat naïve girl she'd once been still remained.

Nothing in her life had turned out the way she had hoped it would. None of her youthful dreams had come true. The girl who had been engaged to Robby Joe Wright, who had longed to be a grade school teacher and the mother of at least three children, was only a vague, melancholy memory.

Twice before, fate had given her two choices: let tragedy defeat her or make her stronger. She had that same choice now. And if she knew nothing else about herself, she knew one thing—Jordan Price was a survivor.

Rick kicked back in Nicole's Cadillac Escalade and relaxed as they flew along Interstate 75, halfway between Priceville and Chattanooga. The lady drove like a bat out of hell, slowing down only when absolutely necessary. Right now she was speeding along at 85 and the limit was 70.

"If you don't want to head this case, I can assign someone else." Nic cast a sidelong glance his way.

"What makes you think I don't want the case?"

Nic chuckled softly. "Oh, maybe your obvious animosity toward Jordan Price for one thing. You can't go into an assignment with an open mind if you've already found the client guilty."

"You think I believe Mrs. Price killed her husband?"

"Do you?"

"Do I think the lady is capable of murder? I'm not sure. Maybe. She's one cool customer."

"Just because she wasn't hysterical with grief today doesn't mean she didn't love Dan."

"You're right, it doesn't," Rick agreed. "But look at the facts. He was twenty years older, rich and powerful, and his death may not have been suicide. What's the first rule of thumb in a case such as this?"

"Suspect the wife."

"Right. And add to that scenario a young lover and you've got a recipe for murder."

"You're assuming that Jordan and Devon Markham are lovers," Nic said. "I think you're wrong about that."

"Why do you think I'm wrong?"

"Woman's instinct."

Rick laughed. "Care to elaborate?"

"Yes, I think they love each other, but they're not in love. They don't look at each other or touch each other the way a couple in love does."

"You can tell if a couple is in love from watching the way they look at each other?"

"I told you that my theory is not based on scientific facts, just good old-fashioned woman's intuition."

"Okay, say I buy your theory. That doesn't rule out Jordan Price as a suspect."

"Jordan is not a suspect. She's our client," Nic reminded him. "She hired us, remember?"

"Ryan Price hired us. She jumped on the bandwagon when she realized that we were going to do an investigation. After all, if she had put up a protest, it would have made her look guilty."

"I think maybe I should put Holt Keinan or Maleah Perdue on this case."

"Don't."

Nic gave him another sidelong glance, her gaze questioning him. "Give me one good reason why I should hand this case over to you, all things considered?"

"Because I want to be proven wrong," he admitted. "I don't want Jordan Price to be guilty."

"Hmm . . . You surprise me. I never suspected—"

"That I find the lady intriguing? That I'm as suscepti-ble as the next guy to a beautiful, vulnerable woman?"

"Okay, the case is yours," Nic told him. "But if I get one complaint from either Jordan or Ryan, I'll jerk your ass off the case and put another agent in charge. Under-stand?"

"Yes, ma'am. I understand."

By seven that evening, the house had cleared, the string quartet had left and the caterers had cleaned up and gone. Only family and close friends remained, only those to whom Dan Price had been far more than a colleague, an ac-quaintance, another good old boy, or just their senator. The numbness that had encompassed Jordan for the past few weeks, from the moment she discovered Dan's body until this evening, began to fade. She wished that she could re-main in the semi-frozen emotional state, acting and reacting with control and logic. But sooner or later, she would have to confront the truth and deal with her personal grief.

"Do you want us to stay here tonight?" Claire asked. "I can call my mother and ask her to either keep Michael until tomorrow or bring him here."

Jordan tried to smile at her sister-in-law, but the effort failed. "No, please, you and Ryan should go home. You're less than five miles away, if I were to need you. Besides"— she glanced over her shoulder into the parlor—"I have more than enough company."

"How is Devon holding up?" Claire whispered.

"In public, he's holding it together. In private . . . he'll make it through this somehow. I'll take care of him."

"You always have, haven't you?"

Jordan nodded. "Making plans for the baby will help us both. I just wish I'd had the chance to tell Dan . . ."

"You're thinking that if he'd known about the baby, he wouldn't have . . . that he might still be alive."

Jordan's gaze connected directly with her sister-in-law's. "Claire, do you believe that Dan was murdered?"

Claire sighed heavily. "I don't know. Ryan is convinced that Dan didn't kill himself. It definitely wasn't an accident, so that leaves only murder."

"I can hardly bear the thought that Dan committed suicide, but the thought that someone murdered him is almost more than . . ." Jordan paused and took a deep breath. "Whatever happens, we'll face it together, the family, those of us who loved Dan."

Ryan came up to them and draped his arm around Claire's shoulders. "Ready?"

"Yes, whenever you are."

He looked at Jordan. "I'll let Nicole know that Mr. Carson can stay with us during the investigation. And I apologize again for not consulting you first."

"I understand your motives," Jordan said. "And as for Mr. Carson staying with you and Claire—that won't be necessary. We have more than enough room for him here, far more room than y'all have."

"Are you sure?" Ryan asked. "I got the feeling that you didn't especially like Mr. Carson."

"I don't know Mr. Carson. But if Nicole thinks he's the best agent to spearhead the private investigation, then I have no objections. After all, she's the expert, not you or I."

"Believe me, I don't want to think that someone murdered Dan, but it's the only explanation that makes sense to me."

"You mean that it's the only explanation you will accept."

"Yes, it is the only explanation I'll accept," Ryan agreed. "I refuse to believe that Dan would commit suicide, not even after being diagnosed with Alzheimer's." His face flushed with aggravation. When Claire leaned into him, he tightened his hold around her shoulders and gave her a reassuring hug. "I'm okay, honey."

"You should both go home and try to get some rest," Jordan said. "I'll contact Nicole and inform her that we decided Mr. Carson will stay here at Price Manor during the investigation. And I'll tell the others tonight that we have hired the Powell Agency to look into the circumstances surrounding Dan's death."

Claire offered her a wavering smile, and then she ushered Ryan out the front door. Jordan closed her eyes and prayed for strength. The very last thing she and this family needed right now was a private detective sticking his nose into matters that were highly confidential.

But if Dan really had been murdered?

"Jordan, are you all right? You're as white as a sheet." The country twang to Roselynne's voice was quite distinctive. Her stepmother had been raised on a farm on Sand Mountain in the northeastern tip of Alabama and had lived a rather hard life before marrying Jordan's father. Jordan had been twelve years old. Her own much-adored mother had been dead for less than two years and in the beginning, Jordan had despised Roselynne.

She turned to face her stepmother, a voluptuous blonde whose clothing tastes ran to animal prints, four-inch heels, and oversized jewelry. Today, even though her hair was teased and her makeup was heavy, she wore a simple black dress, albeit one that hugged every generous curve of her 58-year-old body. Trailing along behind Roselynne, her daughter Tammy paled in comparison, like a little brown wren alongside a red bird.

"I'm all right. Just tired."

"Well, of course, you're tired. Who wouldn't be after the day you've had. Good God, I think the whole damn state of Georgia tramped through this house and probably half of Tennessee to boot." Roselynne placed her fleshy arm around Jordan's shoulders. "Are you hungry, honey?" She snapped her fingers at Tammy. "Go get your sister a plate of food and some iced tea."

"No, please, I couldn't eat a bite." Jordan looked at her stepsister, their gazes meeting for a millisecond before Tammy bowed her head shyly and clasped her hands together in front of her.

"Lord help you, girl," Roselynne hugged Jordan to her side. "You're going to waste away to nothing."

"I'd be more than happy to fix something for you," Tammy offered, her voice not much more than a whisper.

Before Jordan could reply, Darlene Wright came into the foyer and eyed Roselynne and Tammy with her usual disdain. "Will you please leave her alone and stop nagging her. What Jordan needs is peace and quiet." She shooed Roselynne aside. "Why don't we go up to your room? I'll draw you a nice warm bath and if you'd like, I'll have Vadonna bring up a tray later."

"Jordan doesn't need to be alone." Roselynne squinched her face in a sourpuss frown directed at Darlene. "She needs to be surrounded by family." She emphasized the word family.

Jordan closed her eyes for a moment, wishing that just this once her stepmother and Darlene could put aside their personal differences. From the moment the two women first met, more than a dozen years ago when Jordan became engaged to Darlene's son, Robby Joe, they had disliked each other. During the years since, nothing had changed. Each laid claim to being Jordan's surrogate mother, each loving Jordan in her own unique way, each adding immensely to the burden of family responsibility that weighed heavily on Jordan's shoulders.

Within those brief minutes when Jordan gathered her thoughts before she took charge of the situation, the other members of her family-and-friends entourage migrated from the two parlors into the foyer. She had hoped to find a few moments alone with Devon to tell him about hiring the Powell Agency before telling everyone else. But with all those eyes focused on her, everyone waiting expectantly for her to say or do something that would put them at ease, she decided that there was no point in putting off the inevitable.

"Please, everyone, I need to share some information with y'all," Jordan said. "Afterward, I'll need a few moments alone with Devon and then I plan to go to my room—alone—and I'd appreciate no one disturbing me tonight."

"Oh, Jordan, honey, you shouldn't be alone," Roselynne said.

"Good God, Mother, leave her alone," J.C. called from the other side of the foyer. "Jordan doesn't need you smothering her with your show of motherly affection."

"Johnny Cash Harris, my affection for your sister is genuine and you damn well know it!" Roselynne glared at her son, who stood lounging insolently against the door-frame, a glass of his usual scotch and soda in his hand.

"Will all of you please listen to what I have to say." Jordan spoke louder than she had intended, but her tone and volume achieved the effect she had wanted. To a person, everyone quieted and looked right at her.

"We're listening," Devon told her as he came forward, pausing a few feet away, his sky-blue eyes focused on her.

Jordan cleared her throat. "Y'all know that the GBI coroner ruled Dan's death a suicide." She took a deep breath. "But I'm afraid there is some question as to whether or not it's possible that Dan didn't kill himself."

When rumbling noises spread through the foyer, Jordan held up a restraining hand. "Please, hush . . . right now. Ryan and I have hired the Powell Private Security and Investigation Agency to conduct an investigation into Dan's death. Tomorrow, a Powell agent, Mr. Rick Carson, who was at the funeral today with Claire's cousin, Nicole Powell, will arrive here at Price Manor. Mr. Carson will be staying here during the course of the investigation. I want y'all to treat Mr. Carson as our guest and cooperate with him fully."

"Are you saying what I think you're saying, that there is reason to believe that Dan was murdered?" Rene Burke, Jordan's assistant and longtime friend voiced the question that no doubt was going through everyone's mind.

"Yes." Jordan held her hands open at either side of her body in a defensive stance, a silent warning for the others to keep their distance. She'd had as much sympathy and comforting today as she could endure. "Any questions or concerns you have will have to wait until tomorrow. I'll see all of you in the morning." She held out her hand to Devon. "I need to speak with you a moment. Alone." Her gaze traveled around the room issuing a silent order to everyone present.

Within two minutes, the foyer had cleared, leaving Jordan and Devon completely alone.

"Hiring the Powell Agency wasn't your idea," Devon said, keeping his voice low and quiet.

"No, it was Ryan's idea. I just happened to walk right into the middle of a secret meeting he and Claire were having with Nicole Powell and Mr. Carson."

"Does Ryan really believe that Dan was murdered?"

"Yes, I think he does."

"You realize what might happen, don't you? If the investigator digs too deeply into Dan's personal life—"

"I wish we could find a way to prevent him from finding out the truth," Jordan said. "But I don't know if that's possible. I have the distinct impression that Mr. Carson already suspects something."

"Suspects what?"

"I think he believes that I killed Dan or perhaps that you and I killed him because we're lovers."

# Chapter 3

Robby Joe smiled and held open his arms. She went flying into his loving embrace, feelings of pure happiness enveloping her. He was the most important person in the world to her. He was the man she loved, her future husband, the father of the children she would have one day.

When she was with Robby Joe, she felt that nothing bad could ever happen to her again, that all the bad things in her life were behind her forever. Their June wedding was only a month away, an elaborate affair that his mother had insisted on paying for, even down to helping Jordan pay for a beautiful wedding dress that she otherwise couldn't have afforded.

With her arms wrapped around Robby Joe's neck and her head resting against his shoulder, Jordan sighed with deep contentment. Sunlight struck the one-carat diamond on her finger. Gazing at her engagement ring, she thought about the night this past October when Robby Joe had proposed. A starlit night, a carriage ride, a declaration of love.

*"I love you," she whispered in his ear. "I love you so much."*

*"I love you, too," he told her.*

*Jordan closed her eyes, savoring this moment of pure joy.*

*Suddenly, she could no longer feel Robby Joe's arms around her, couldn't feel his warmth and his strength.*

*"Robby Joe?"*

*When she opened her eyes, she found herself all alone. She held up her left hand. Her engagement ring sparkled on her third finger.*

*She heard someone weeping, soft, mournful sobs. Who was crying and why? Something terrible must have happened. Someone was very sad.*

*"Robby Joe, where are you? Do you hear that woman crying? Why is she crying?"*

Jordan woke with a start, gasping for breath, her heart racing and perspiration dampening her skin. She opened her eyes and tossed back the covers. Her bedroom lay in semi-darkness, the only illumination coming from the mellow glimmer of moonlight shining through the French doors leading to the balcony. She swung out of bed, slipped her feet into the quilted satin house shoes in front of the nightstand, and reached for the satin robe lying across the antique cedar chest at the foot of the mahogany sleigh bed.

The pain radiating from deep inside her seemed as immediate and potent as it had the day she and Darlene buried Robby Joe. Twelve years ago.

Jordan unlocked the French doors, opened them, and stepped out onto the balcony that overlooked the back courtyard and the rose garden. After yesterday's heavy rain, the earth smelled rich and fresh, and a hint of gold overspread the dark sky, a prelude to the approaching dawn.

She hadn't dreamed about Robby Joe in a long time,

not in years. But she supposed that Dan's recent death and funeral had reawakened long-buried memories in her subconscious. Like so many of her memories, those of Robby Joe were memories of happiness that had ended in sorrow. Sometimes it seemed that her life had been little more than a series of tragic events.

Watching her mother dying a little each day with the cancer that ravaged her body would have been traumatic for anyone, but for a child of ten, it had been devastating. During that final year, she had been the glue that held her family together. She, a mere child, had been the one who had comforted her dying mother and consoled her grief-stricken father.

And then less than two years later, when Daddy had brought home a new bride, a woman as different from her own mother as night is from day, Jordan had withdrawn into a secret place inside herself. She had been polite to her stepmother, even though in the beginning she had intensely disliked the loud, flashy, bleached blonde. She had shared her room with her shy little stepsister without complaint and endured her teenage stepbrother, who at the age of fourteen, smoked, cursed, drank beer and claimed he was screwing their 17-year-old neighbor.

Meeting Robby Joe her sophomore year of college had changed her life. He was such a dreamboat: good looking, smart, kind and caring. And he came from a good family. They dated on and off for over a year, falling in love slowly. Their junior year, he had invited her home with him for Thanksgiving. Since Robby Joe was an only child, Jordan had been afraid his widowed mother would resent her, perhaps even dislike her. But nothing could have been further from the truth. As it turned out, Darlene Wright and Jordan's mother had been sorority sisters at Ole Miss. And Darlene's genteel, cultured persona reminded Jordan of her mother. By the time she and Robby Joe had become engaged, she thought of his mother as her second mom. They had far more in common than Jordan would ever have with her stepmother.

Everything had been so perfect, perhaps too perfect.

If only Robby Joe hadn't died. How different her life would have been if—

*Damn it, don't do this to yourself!*

She had stopped playing the "what if" game years ago. She had given up all her foolish young dreams of passionate love, of children born from that love, of a happily-ever-after. Harsh reality had slapped her in the face repeatedly, knocking all romantic notions out of her head.

She had cared for Dan and had respected him. But she had not been in love with him. She had lost a dear friend and she would miss him terribly. But her heart wasn't shattered. She didn't feel as if she, too, had died. It wasn't the same as it had been when she lost Robby Joe.

Jordan laid her open palms on her still flat belly. She was barely six weeks pregnant. Only her family and closest friends knew, but sometime soon, she would have to share her news with the world. She wanted this baby, who would be raised as Dan Price's child and would be Dan's heir. But she wouldn't have to raise her son or daughter alone. Devon would be a father to the child, loving it for so many reasons.

Rick parked his Jeep Wrangler down the street from the Dade County Courthouse. After getting out, locking up, and stuffing his keys into the pocket of his jeans, he jaywalked across Case Avenue. He located the sheriff's department without any trouble since he'd called ahead this morning and asked for exact directions. Trenton, the county seat, with a population of less than 2000, was located south of Priceville, so after he finished his business here, he'd have to backtrack a few miles.

Although the Powell Agency would do in-depth re-
search during the course of this case, an agent always began
an assignment with basic info. While compiling barebones
information about Priceville and the Price family, Rick
had looked up Sheriff Steve Corbett. The guy had been
sheriff since the late nineties and had worked as a Trenton
policeman for a number of years before running for elected
office. He had a spotless reputation, was known as a straight
arrow kind of man with a wife and two kids, and he
taught Sunday school.

Rick had spoken to Sheriff Corbett personally on his
drive from Knoxville. He had set up an appointment for
11:30 to meet with the sheriff and the two officers in
charge of the investigation into Dan Price's death: Lt. Nolan
Trumbo and Lt. Haley McLain.

The minute he announced himself, he was shown into
the sheriff's office. A broad-shouldered, heavy-set man with
a thick, dark mustache and military-short graying hair came
from around the desk and offered Rick his hand. In his
peripheral vision, Rick noticed a female officer immediately stand at attention.

Sheriff Corbett pumped Rick's hand in a cordial, good
old boy way. "Come on in, Mr. Carson, and meet Lt. McLain.
I'm afraid Nolan Trumbo had a family emergency this
morning. You'll meet him later."

They exchanged a strong cordial handshake; then Rick
turned to the lieutenant. "Ma'am."

She nodded and offered him a hint of a smile, responding in a friendly manner without being flirty. The deputy,
probably in her mid-to-late thirties, filled out her uniform
quite nicely, with curves in all the right places. She wore
her light brown hair cut short with wispy curls framing
her heart-shaped face.

"Take a seat." Sheriff Corbett indicated a chair to the
right of his desk as he sat down in his leather swivel chair

behind the desk. "I've spoken to Ryan and assured him that this office will cooperate with the Powell Agency's independent investigation."

"We appreciate that," Rick said as he lowered himself onto the metal folding chair.

"You understand that the Georgia Bureau of Investigation took over and it was their medical examiner who did the autopsy on Dan, so, in a way, my hands have been tied," Corbett explained. "Officially, Dan's death has been ruled a suicide, but with Ryan's doubts and Haley here not a hundred percent convinced, I'm glad Ryan hired your outfit to dig around and see what y'all can find."

"I'm working for Jordan Price, too," Rick said. "She and her brother-in-law hired Powell's."

"Yeah, that's what Ryan told me. He sure hated to upset Jordan so soon after the funeral." Corbett made a clicking sound with his tongue as he shook his head. "It was hard enough for her to have to accept that Dan killed himself, but if Ryan's right, it's going to be even more difficult for her to know somebody murdered her husband. She's been a pillar of strength for Ryan and Claire. I don't know what they'd have done without her to step in and handle all the details. She's a mighty fine lady and Dan was as lucky as a man could be to have had her for his wife."

How could he reply to that comment? Obviously Sheriff Corbett had fallen under the Jordan Price spell. Rick glanced up at the deputy, who stood rigid and silent. "Do you agree with Ryan Price that his brother didn't kill himself?"

She looked to the sheriff for permission to speak, and answered only after he nodded. "I have my doubts."

"Care to elaborate?"

"The evidence points to suicide," Lt. McLain said. "Senator Price's right hand showed evidence of firearms residue and trace metal indicating he was holding the gun when it was fired. Also, the skin around the wound showed a powder tattoo, which indicates—"

"That the weapon was fired from no more than two feet away," Rick completed her statement.

"That's right." She nodded. "The GBI ballistics lab did a test firing, and their findings, along with one other fact— that there was a contact wound and an impression of the muzzle on the senator's head, indicating the weapon came in direct contact—suggest suicide."

"What makes you think it wasn't suicide?" Rick looked her right in the eye. "Nothing you've told me indicates that the senator's death wasn't—"

"You're right," she replied. "On the surface, the evidence points to suicide. But since this was my case, I made a point of thoroughly studying the autopsy report— even reading between the lines, if you want to call it that. A few things seemed a bit off to me, but I dismissed them as nothing but my investigator's curiosity and possibly my imagination. But the more I thought about it, the more I knew I couldn't let it go. So, I told Steve . . . uh, Sheriff Corbett and he agreed with me."

"Exactly what seemed 'off' to you?" Rick asked.

"For one thing, the autopsy report showed arthritis in the senator's hands, including the fingers of his right hand, which might have made pulling the trigger painful."

"Painful but not impossible," Rick said. "The evidence clearly showed that his finger pulled the trigger, right?"

"Right. He could have pulled the trigger. But there was something else—the senator's trigger finger was broken and there was bruising on the top of his hand."

*Son of a bitch!*

"You think that somebody grabbed the senator's hand, forced the gun into it, and squeezed their hand over his hard enough to bruise his hand. And this person pressed down so hard when they forced his finger against the trigger that it broke the bones."

"It's all speculation," Sheriff Corbett said. "But coupled with Ryan's sincere conviction that his brother would never have killed himself, it's enough to question if the senator might have had a little assistance in shooting himself."

"The senator wasn't a small or weak man," Lt. McLain said. "Either he would have had to have been drugged or the person who forced the gun into his hand had to be quite strong. The autopsy showed no evidence of drugs, but I found evidence at the scene that he'd been drinking."

"Apparently the GBI didn't think this info was significant proof of murder or they wouldn't have ruled the death a suicide."

"Apparently," Lt. McLain said. "And you do realize that it's highly unlikely that we can prove it was murder."

"But if we work under the assumption that it was murder and not suicide, we can look for a killer. In order to prove our theory, we will have to find the murderer and if possible, get a confession."

"Then you believe I might be right to question the GBI's Medical Examiner?" she asked.

"Yeah, I think there's a good possibility you're right and he's wrong."

"I know what we've got isn't much," the sheriff said, "but it's a start. Anything you need from us, just let us know. You can contact Haley day or night while you're on this case. She'll be available."

When Corbett glanced at her, Haley McLain said, "Yes, sir." Then she looked at Rick. "Our department doesn't have the budget or the manpower—or for that matter, the authority—to investigate further. The M.E.'s official decision was suicide, but if Powell's can prove otherwise, then we can reopen this case."

"I don't suppose you've got a list of possible suspects, do you, Lieutenant?"

Haley cleared her throat. "No, I'm afraid I don't."

Rick figured by the nervous way she cut her eyes toward Corbett and then cast her gaze to the floor that the deputy did have a list, even if it was just a mental tally of who might have had a reason to murder Senator Daniel Price.

"I'd like to take a look at the case files, including the autopsy report," Rick said.

Corbett nodded. "Haley, why don't you walk Mr. Carson out and see that he gets copies of whatever he needs."

"Yes, sir."

Rick fell into step behind the curvy brunette, his gaze settling on the sway of her trim hips, noting how her slacks cupped her firm buttocks, not a panty line in sight. That meant one of two things: either she wasn't wearing panties or she was wearing a thong. Either was damn sexy. And the thought intrigued him.

While they waited for the sheriff's secretary to copy the files on the Price case, Haley offered Rick a cup of coffee, which he accepted.

"If Dan Price was murdered, who heads your suspects list?" Rick asked.

"I told you that I don't have a—"

"A political adversary? A disgruntled constituent? The loyal assistant? The grieving widow?"

Haley eyed him over her half empty coffee cup and took a sip before responding. "The husband or wife is usually the chief suspect until he or she is ruled out. But from what I know about Mrs. Price, people believe she's practically a saint."

Rick grunted. "I guess I'll find out for myself pretty soon. I'm going to be staying at Price Manor for the duration of this investigation."

"And whose idea was that?"

"Mrs. Price invited me to stay."

"And naturally you agreed."

Rick shrugged.

"There's something else I've heard about Mrs. Price."

"What's that?" Rick asked.

"That the lady can be very persuasive."

She watched from the upstairs window while the Pow-ell agent parked his Jeep in front of the house. They didn't want him here. He was not welcome, but he mustn't know that, just as no one must ever find out that Dan had told her about the Alzheimer's diagnosis. How fortunate that he had trusted her so completely, enough so that she was able to plant the idea of suicide in his mind. If only he had followed through . . . Water under the bridge. She had to accept the reality of their situation and deal with it ac-cordingly.

They would have to be polite to Mr. Carson; however, there was no reason for them to be friendly.

Ryan had done what he thought best and the rest of them had to live with his decision. She'd had no idea that Dan's brother would refuse to believe he had killed him-self, especially not after the medical examiner ruled his death a suicide. Why couldn't he have accepted their find-ings? If he had, they could all move on and put the unfor-tunate incident behind them.

But now we have to be very careful not to give Mr. Carson any reason to suspect us. He has no proof that Dan did not commit suicide and unless we slip up and do or say something suspicious, Mr. Carson can in-vestigate as long as he'd like and in the end, he'll still have no proof. We didn't make any mistakes that night.

Tobias met Mr. Carson in the middle of the driveway. She couldn't hear what they were saying, but after only a few moments, Tobias took the man's suitcase and he returned to his Jeep. Apparently he was taking the vehicle around to the garage at the side of the house.

She stepped away from the window, turned, and walked into the bathroom. She studied her reflection in the mirror. Pale. Dark circles under her eyes. She was a woman in mourning. That's what she wanted Mr. Carson to see.

Jordan met Tobias as he entered the foyer, a black suitcase in his hand. He paused and said, "Mr. Carson has arrived, Miss Jordan. I had him park in the garage. I told him that you would be waiting for him in your study."

"Yes, thank you."

"In which room should I put his things?"

"I had Vadonna air out Mr. Ryan's old room. It's one of the larger bedrooms and is quite masculine. I believe it will suit Mr. Carson, don't you?"

"Yes, ma'am. It should."

Jordan took a deep breath. She dreaded having a stranger living in her home almost as much as she hated the thought that he would be trying to prove that someone had murdered Dan. But by keeping Mr. Carson close, she would be able to oversee his investigation on a day-to-day basis and all information would come to her before it reached Ryan.

Instead of going directly to her study, she made a detour through the kitchen. Vadonna lifted her head and turned from where she was loading the dishwasher.

"Yes, ma'am, is there something you need?"

"I'd like a fresh pot of decaf coffee for two delivered to my study in about ten minutes, please. Until then, I don't want to be disturbed. I'll be speaking privately with Mr. Carson."

"Yes, ma'am, coffee in your study in ten minutes." Vadonna closed the dishwasher and hit the START button. "Oh, Miss Jordan, have you seen Mrs. Wright in the past few minutes? She was concerned that you hadn't joined them for lunch and said she might take you up a tray."

"No, I haven't seen Darlene, but if you do, please tell her that I'm fine and I don't want anything to eat."

Vadonna nodded.

Jordan left the kitchen and made it halfway to her study before Rick Carson entered the house. She looked down the long hall to where he stood in the foyer, his head tilted upward as he scanned the open staircases leading to the second level. Yesterday, she had paid little attention to the dark-haired man who had attended Dan's funeral with Claire's cousin. But today, as she studied him while he was unaware of her presence, she realized that he was the type of man who wouldn't ordinarily be overlooked. It wasn't because he was tall, muscular and attractive in a rough and rugged sort of way, but because he exuded a raw masculinity that disturbed her as it probably did every woman he met.

*Don't just stand here gaping at the man. Meet and greet. Put a pleasant expression on your face and welcome him.*

Jordan walked down the hall. Rick looked directly at her as he waited for her to come to him.

"Good afternoon, Mr. Carson." She held out her hand. "Welcome to Price Manor."

He hesitated for a millisecond before he clasped her hand. His grip was strong yet gentle and his hand was warm and hard. She was suddenly acutely aware of him in that age-old way a woman is aware of a virile man.

She jerked her hand away, hating how his touch had made her feel. But she managed to keep a pleasant expression on her face.

"Before I show you up to your room so that you can settle in, will you please come into my study for a few moments. I'd like to speak to you privately." Jordan indicated the direction with a sweep of her right hand.

When she glanced at Rick Carson, she noticed that he

was staring at her left hand. She looked down and realized the afternoon sunlight streaming in through the windows had hit her engagement ring and wedding band, making the diamonds sparkle with brilliant fire. She dropped her left arm to her side and pressed her palm against her thigh.

She knew what this man, this trained investigator, was thinking. The three-carat diamond flanked by two smaller half-carat diamonds and coupled with a diamond-studded platinum wedding band all but screamed rich widow. He no doubt believed that her husband had spoiled her with outrageously expensive jewelry. But the rings, as with the other jewelry Dan had given her, had been for show. At the time, she had tried to dissuade him from buying her the gaudy rings. But he had insisted, telling her that it would be expected for a man with his wealth to buy his second wife rings that would equal or exceed the value of those he had bought his first wife.

Jordan and Rick Carson exchanged heated glances before she turned and headed for her small study at the rear of the house. She didn't look over her shoulder to see if he was following, but she knew he was. Not only could she hear his heavy footsteps, but she could feel his presence as if it were a shadow hovering over her. Watching her. Examining her.

The man made her nervous.

She didn't pause when she reached the open door that led into her private sanctuary. This room had once been part of a back porch that had spanned the length of the house, but sometime in the past 50 years, a section of the porch had been enclosed and divided into two rooms. A glass encased sunroom filled with antique white wicker lay on the right side and her study on the left. A wall of windows faced the back courtyard. The ceiling and two walls boasted old beaded board painted a pale peach and what had once been the exterior wall was white-washed brick.

She had decorated the room herself and had chosen each item, each piece of furniture, with great care. This was the only room in the entire house that was hers alone. Even though she had not shared a bedroom with Dan, her room, like the others in this old mansion, held priceless antiques and had been professionally decorated.

Jordan paused in front of the beige-and-brown striped settee, then turned slowly to face her guest. Their gazes clashed. Jordan swallowed.

"Please, take a seat," she told him as she eased down onto the settee.

"Yes, ma'am." He took the rust-colored easy chair across from her. "Is there some kind of problem?"

"I hope not, but if there is, I think we need to resolve it as soon as possible. Agreed?"

"Yes, ma'am."

"Ryan trusts you because you're employed by Nicole and Griffin Powell and normally I trust Ryan's judgment. But I need to be certain that I can trust you to keep any personal information you uncover during your investigation completely private and never reveal it to anyone other than Ryan and me."

"I can assure you that, unless I uncover something that directly incriminates either you or Ryan in your husband's death, all information will be kept in strictest confidence."

Jordan's heart stopped for a millisecond. Was this man saying what she thought he was? Was he implying that— No, surely he wouldn't dare suggest that either she or Ryan might have been responsible for Dan's death.

"Mr. Carson, are you actually suggesting that Ryan or I might have—"

"Look, let's lay our cards on the table right now. I'm a straightforward kind of guy and since you're paying for my services through the Powell Agency, you have a right to know that my only goal is to find out if your husband was murdered and if he was, who killed him. Do you understand?"

"Yes, I understand. That's why Ryan and I hired you."

When he leaned forward, Jordan instinctively withdrew, pressing back against the sofa, her body unconsciously trying to escape from the threat she sensed he posed.

"Then you won't object if I ask you one simple question, will you?"

Her heart raced at breakneck speed.

"Ask your question," she said.

He looked her square in the eye, his dark, penetrating stare pinning her to the spot. "Mrs. Price, did you kill your husband?"

# Chapter 4

Rick could tell that his question had not surprised Jordan Price. She glowered at him with those cool blue-gray eyes, her expression an odd mixture of hurt and anger. But she stayed perfectly calm. Only the telltale clenching of her jaw and the hard glare revealed any emotion.

"Would you believe me if I told you that I did not kill my husband and that I cared deeply for him?"

"Cared deeply? Odd choice of words, Mrs. Price."

"Honest choice of words," she said. "I loved Dan, but not in some silly, youthfully passionate way. Our marriage worked for both of us. In our own fashion, we were quite content."

"Another odd choice of words."

"But once again an honest choice."

"You're not much for deep, passionate feelings, are you?"

She stared at him, a glimmer of something unsettling bubbling just below the surface, a hint of fury, a tinge of inner fire.

*Don't go there, Carson. Do not for one minute believe*

*that she hasn't used this feminine trick on other men. What she wants is for you to believe that you're the one man on earth who could bring her dormant passion to life. Don't be a fool. Don't fall for her oh-so-smooth act.*

He gave her a thorough once-over, not subtle in the way he appraised her physical assets. Yeah, so his manner was a bit on the crude side, not the least respectful. But in his book—the Rick Carson book of rules and regulations—a person had to earn his respect.

Jordan was willowy slender, but not skinny. Her hips rounded nicely and her breasts were large enough to fill a C-cup bra. He surmised her height and weight: five-four, a hundred and twenty pounds. Her creamy skin was like fine porcelain, unmarred by the sun or a tanning bed. She possessed an almost ethereal quality, like an angelic statue brought to life.

"You're staring," she told him, her voice slightly breathless.

Yes, he was. He was staring at a beautiful woman, but one he suspected was deadly. Was Jordan Price a black widow? Or was she what she appeared to be—sad, vulnerable, and in need of a strong shoulder to lean on?

Rick shook off the latter thought. He wasn't here to give comfort. His job was to investigate a murder.

"Let's say for the sake of argument that I believe you, that you didn't kill your husband. Do you have any idea who did?"

She lifted her slender hand and smoothed back an errant strand of ash blonde hair. The thick mass was pulled loosely away from her face and secured with a silver clasp into a broad bun at the nape of her neck. Other than the ostentatious set of rings on her left ring finger, her jewelry was minimal, only a silver-and-gold watch and a pair of small, discreet diamond earrings.

Goddamn, why did she have to be so beautiful?

"I have no idea who killed Dan, if indeed he was murdered," Jordan said. "He had political enemies, of course, but certainly none of them would have killed him."

"What about personal enemies?" Rick tried his best not to skim his gaze over her body again, but his best wasn't good enough. Sitting there in a pair of navy blue slacks and a white cotton sweater, she was hardly dressed for sex appeal, but he found her sexy as hell. When he returned his attention to her face, his gaze collided with hers.

"I don't know of anyone who would want to kill Dan."

He sensed that she might be withholding something. But why? Did she suspect Devon Markham and was protecting him because they were lovers?

"You do realize that if there was bad blood between your husband and another person, I'll find out while I'm investigating. So, why don't you save me some time and just tell me."

She drew in a deep breath and released it slowly. He noted the rise and fall of her breasts. Damn it, he had to stop lusting after Jordan. First and foremost, it was hardly professional to have the hots for your employer. And second and probably even more important, it would be stupid to become emotionally involved with a woman he suspected of murder.

"Dan and his ex-wife, Jane Anne, were not the best of friends, but I don't think she's capable of murder." Jordan paused for a moment and glanced toward the closed door to her study. "My stepbrother, J.C., and Dan have had a few arguments. J.C. is a gambler and last year, he got himself into deep debt. Dan helped him, but when he went to Dan again this year, Dan turned him down."

Rick nodded. "And that's it. His ex-wife and your stepbrother?"

"As far as I know. Dan was highly respected and people in general liked him. He was a man with a good heart."

She clenched her teeth and swallowed. If she was faking emotion, she was doing a really good job. Unable to stop himself, Rick reached out and clasped her hand. Their gazes met and God help him, it was all he could do not to pull her into his arms to comfort her.

He gave her hand a reassuring squeeze, then abruptly released her. "I'll need office space of some type while I'm here." *That's it, Carson, stick to Powell Agency business and steer clear of any monkey business.* "Access to high-speed Internet, a fax machine, a copier and printer. Could that be arranged in whatever room you've—?"

"All of it is available in Dan's study. He used that room as his home office. Feel free to arrange things any way you'd like. I'll inform Tobias and Vadonna that the room will be yours to use while you're here."

"Are you sure you want me using your husband's study? I mean, considering that's where he died."

Jordan clutched her hands together and moistened her lips with a quick, light lick.

Did she have any idea what kind of an effect she had on him? Sure she did. She was playing him and he'd damn well better not forget it.

"Yes, I'm sure you may use Dan's study. I—I hadn't been back in there until yesterday when I interrupted your private conversation with Ryan."

"Everyone is a suspect until I rule them out, including you and Ryan. If you have a problem with that, I need to know now."

She almost smiled. Her lips curved upward ever so slightly and he noted a faint trace of laughter in her eyes. "Please, call me Jordan. And may I call you Rick?"

He nodded. What sort of game was she playing? *Please, call me Jordan. And may I call you Rick?*

A soft rap on the half-open door interrupted them.

"Yes, come in, please," Jordan said, as if she was expecting someone.

A plump, middle-aged woman entered the room, a silver tray in her hands. She set the tray on Jordan's desk.

"Thank you, Vadonna," Jordan said.

"Yes, ma'am. Will there be anything else?"

"No, thank you, that will be all."

While the woman exited, Jordan indicated the silver pot and accessories on the tray. "Would you care for coffee?"

Rick shook his head. "I don't think so."

Jordan focused on him. "You laid your cards on the table, Rick, and asked me point blank if I killed my husband. Now it's my turn to be brutally honest. I don't like you. I don't want you here invading my home and my grief, taking away my privacy and questioning my integrity. But if my husband was murdered, I want his killer found and brought to justice. I want you to do your job. However, if you do anything to sully Dan Price's reputation, I'll see to it personally that you regret it. Do I make myself clear?"

"Yes, ma'am. Crystal clear. Any skeletons your husband had in his closet will remain there."

She sighed heavily. "I expect to be kept up-to-date on the investigation. For now, a daily report will suffice."

The lady was accustomed to giving orders and having them obeyed. The privilege of wealth—her dead husband's wealth. "Will every morning right after breakfast be suitable for my daily report or do you prefer for me to report right before bedtime?"

"Every morning works for me." A cool, succinct reply.

When she stood, he stood.

"I'll have Tobias show you to your room. If there's anything you need, please let us know." As she walked toward the door, he followed. "Dinner is at seven."

She opened the door and ushered him out of her study, effectively dismissing him. "If you'll wait in the foyer, I'll find Tobias."

He watched her as she walked away. She moved with a fluid grace that came as naturally to her as breathing. Jordan Price's kind of class couldn't be learned. It was innate.

If he didn't watch his step, the lady would have him wrapped around her little finger in no time at all.

Rene washed hurriedly, removing the smell of sex from her body, then not bothering to dry off, she yanked on her thong and pulled up her slacks. As she hooked her bra, she noticed a bruise on her left breast. J.C. liked to bite, not forcefully enough to bring blood to the surface, but hard enough to bruise. While slipping on her blouse, she returned to the bedroom and found J.C., still naked, sprawled in the center of the bed, a rakish smile on his too-handsome face.

"What's the hurry, babe? Sister won't need you this afternoon. She's got that stud Powell agent to keep her company." J.C. chuckled.

"Will you shut up! What a thing to say, to imply that Jordan would find Mr. Carson sexually appealing and poor Dan not cold in the ground."

"Dead's dead. Dan's as dead now as he will be six months from now. Besides, you and I know that she wasn't getting any from old Danny boy."

"Hush! You say the most awful things. Have you no respect for your sister and Dan?"

"I respected my brother-in-law's power and money. And I respect the hell out of Jordan, frigid bitch that she is."

"Get up, take a shower and get dressed," Rene told him, hating herself for having succumbed to J.C.'s immeasurable charm once again. The guy could be a real jerk, but he was dynamite in bed. At least she thought so. Maybe the fact that she was halfway in love with him colored her vision.

"The only reason you think Jordan is frigid is because she can so easily resist you." Picking up a comb from the vanity, she raked it through her short black hair. "For God's sake, she's your sister and you still hit on her. You're a real ass, you know that?"

J.C. slithered out of bed like the snake he was, and stood to his full five-eleven height. Lean, lightly muscled, his skin appearing darker than it actually was because of his sandy hair and pale blue eyes, the man was gorgeous.

As his gaze glided over her sensually, he moved toward her, then reached out and jerked her up against him. "She's my stepsister. Technically, if I screwed her, it wouldn't be incest."

"You're a worthless shit."

He grinned, rubbed his semi-erect penis against her and grabbed her butt. "Yeah, but I'm *your* worthless shit, aren't I?"

Rene pulled away from him. "I'm not fool enough to think you're exclusively mine. Not when I know you'll fuck just about anything with a pussy."

J.C. laughed. "Honey, you know you're my favorite pussy."

Ignoring him as he turned and headed for the bathroom, Rene inspected herself in the mirror. She needed lipstick. Otherwise, she'd do.

She hadn't seen Jordan since breakfast this morning and it was past time she checked in with her boss. It had taken her a while to adjust to working for Jordan instead of with her. They had met when they'd been in college, both working two jobs to pay their tuition. A few years after graduation, Jordan had called her out of the blue and offered her a position at the Atlanta PR firm where Jordan had just received a promotion. They had remained friends ever since and when Jordan married Senator Daniel Price and needed a personal assistant, she'd offered her the job. She had snapped it up posthaste.

Halfway along the upstairs hall and lost in her thoughts, Rene almost ran over Darlene Wright, who stepped aside just in time to prevent being hit head-on.

"Good afternoon." Rene spoke to the old biddy simply out of courtesy.

Turning up her sharp, birdlike nose, Darlene gave Rene a condescending glance. "Have you seen Jordan?"

"Not since breakfast. Why?"

"I know she was expecting Mr. Carson, the Powell agent, and I wanted to make sure she's all right and that his arrival didn't upset her."

"Why should his being here upset her? After all, she hired him, didn't she?"

Darlene snorted. "I suspect that Ryan gave her little choice. If he had simply accepted the medical examiner's findings, it would be unnecessary for Jordan to suffer more than she already has."

"You're right." As much as she hated to agree with this snooty old bitch, she, too, didn't want to see Jordan put through the wringer. "But all we can do is stand by and try to help her as much as we can. And pray that Dan wasn't murdered."

"I'm sure he wasn't. After all, who would want to kill a lovely man like Dan?"

"He *was* a sweetie, wasn't he?" Rene sighed. "Our poor Jordan. She has the damnedest luck with men."

Darlene gasped. "What a terrible thing to say!"

"Oh, crap. You know I didn't mean anything by what I said. I just meant if anybody's had enough tragedy for two lifetimes, it's our Jordan."

"If my Robby Joe had lived . . ." Her voice trailed off on a fragile, whispery moan.

Damn, she didn't want to hear about Robby Joe being the love of Jordan's life. Not again. Not today. If Darlene had spouted off that tale of woe once, she'd done it a million times.

"Look, if I see Jordan, I'll tell her you're looking for her." Rene eased around Darlene and headed straight for the back stairs.

"She's not in her study," Darlene called. "And she's not in her room."

"Okay. Thanks for telling me."

Two places not to look for Jordan: her bedroom and her study.

She'd search for her boss, and if she didn't find her soon, she'd try calling Jordan on her cell phone. But she doubted that would do any good. Jordan's phone was probably turned off to prevent taking unwanted calls.

After scouring the downstairs, even the kitchen and bathrooms, Rene stepped out the back door, pulled a pack of cigarettes and a lighter from her pants pocket and lit the cigarette. She had all but given up smoking, but in dealing with Dan's death, she had reverted to an old bad habit for solace. Drawing in deeply, she sighed with contentment as she paced back and forth on the porch.

Suddenly she heard soft weeping. The sound came from behind the hedges that screened the small back porch from the patio surrounding the pool. She took another draw on the cigarette, stepped off the porch and walked out into the yard. As she turned the corner of the tall hedgerow, she felt a prickle of apprehension and sensed she was being watched. After looking right and left, she glanced up, her gaze scanning the second-story windows. A dark shadow stood at one of the windows.

Rick Carson stared down, but not at her.

She followed his line of vision and gasped. Holy shit!

Rene made a beeline to where Devon stood on the patio, Jordan wrapped in his arms. When she approached, Jordan lifted her head from Devon's chest.

"Is something wrong?" Jordan asked.

"You two are putting on quite a show for our resident detective," Rene told them. "Don't look now, but Rick Carson is watching you two from his bedroom window and God only knows what he's thinking."

# Chapter 5

Rick was definitely a fish out of water with this bunch. To start with, he was underdressed for dinner. But how was he to know the other three men would be in suits and ties? He supposed it didn't matter. After all, he wasn't really a guest, just another employee and he wouldn't have been surprised if he'd been asked to eat in the kitchen with Tobias and Vadonna. As he entered the dining room, he ran his hand over his face. He should have shaved again since his beard grew fast and despite having shaved this morning, he already sported a five o'clock shadow. As for his clothes: he wore jeans, a blue chambray shirt and a lightweight brown twill jacket. He had dropped the only suit he owed, the one he'd worn to the funeral yesterday, by the cleaners on his way out of town this morning.

Passing his gaze over the room's occupants, he immediately noticed that Jordan was missing. As he surveyed the large dining table set for ten, he got a whiff of an overly sweet but probably expensive perfume.

"Well, honey, you stick out like a sore thumb, don't you?" The woman's voice whispered in his ear. When he turned to his left, he glanced down at the overblown bleached blonde who was grinning at him as if she knew all his secrets. "Of course, some of us prefer our meat raw." Her laughter radiated from deep in her throat, a husky, lifetime smoker's rumble.

He cocked one brow and smiled at the woman who was a good 20 years his senior. "I believe we met briefly yesterday. I'm Rick Carson. I'm from the Powell Private Security and Investigation Agency."

She took his hand in hers and held it. Her smile accentuated the wrinkles around her eyes and mouth. Laugh lines. He'd bet this woman had done a lot of laughing in her life.

"I'm Roselynne Harris. Jordan's mama." When he looked at her questioningly, she amended her statement. "Well, stepmama, actually. I married her daddy when Jordan was twelve. But I love that gal as if she were my own, love her just like I do Tammy and J.C."

"Tammy and J.C.?"

"My other kids. Jordan's Daddy adopted my boy and girl. He was a good man. Jordan takes after him." She pointed first to the petite brown-eyed, brown-haired woman standing in the corner alone. Sad-faced and plain, Tammy apparently sensed her mother's scrutiny and turned to stare wide-eyed at Roselynne. "I named her after Tammy Wynette. You know she was the queen of country music. 'Stand by Your Man' was one of her big hits." Roselynne's gaze traveled around the room, lighting on the lanky, blond guy who was talking to the two teenagers. From their strong physical resemblance—dark hair and eyes, tall and slender—the teens could easily pass for twins.

"That's my boy there." Roselynne pointed at the blond. "That's my J.C., my pride and joy. Named him after Mr. Country Music himself, Johnny Cash. I was on my way to a career as a country singer when I met my first husband." She lowered her voice back to a whisper. "Got myself knocked up and married the good-looking, worth-less bum."

"It happens," Rick said. "Who are the twins talking with your son?"

"Oh, them? That's Kendra and Wes Brannon. But they're not twins, just brother and sister. She's eighteen and he's twenty. They're Jordan's stepchildren."

"Hmm . . . They were here Easter weekend when Senator Price died, weren't they?"

"Uh, yeah, I guess they were. That was that weekend. We were all in and out. The kids were in from college. He goes to Auburn and she's over at the University of Georgia, where Jordan went."

"You said that y'all were in and out during that weekend. Do you know if everyone here tonight was in and out of the house when Dan Price died?"

Roselynne paused before she spoke, something Rick figured she didn't do all that often. He had her pegged for the type who seldom wasted time thinking about what she said. "Devon is—was Dan's assistant. He lived wherever Dan and Jordan lived. And Rene—" she pointed to the attractive brunette deep in conversation with Devon Markham "—is Jordan's assistant and lives here, too, when they're in Georgia. I believe she has her own place in D.C."

"What about you and your children, where do y'all live?"

"Playing investigator?"

"Not playing, Mrs. Harris. Just doing my job."

She grinned. "Call me Roselynne. Everybody does."

Yeah, he'd bet everybody did. Every man she'd ever met. "Okay, Roselynne, so where do you—?"

"J.C. travels quite a bit, but when he's in town, he stays with me part of the time. Tammy's got some health issues, needs some looking after, if you know what I mean." Roselynne tapped her right temple. "My girl's high strung and nervous."

Was that Roselynne's motherly way of saying her daughter was mentally unbalanced?

"Jordan's kids are away at college, but home to them is wherever Jordan is. They adore her, just like we all do."

"I hear the lady is practically a saint."

"As far as I'm concerned she is." Roselynne's eyes misted. "To know Jordan is to love her. Take my word on that. You won't find a single solitary soul who'll say one word against her."

"I find that hard to believe. Even saints have enemies."

"Not our Jordan," Roselynne said emphatically.

"What are you telling this man about Jordan?" The woman who had just walked up in front of them glared at Roselynne, contempt in her gaze.

"Mrs. Harris was just telling me what a saint Jordan is," Rick said.

The woman turned her sharp stare at him, her eyes small and dark. She looked down her thin, hawkish nose at Rick, dismissing him as an inferior being.

"I'm Rick Carson, the Powell agent that Mrs. Price and her brother-in-law hired to investigate Senator Price's death." Rick offered her his hand.

She glowered at his hand for a good half minute, as if considering the possibility that he was somehow contaminated. Finally she grasped his hand in a firm, confident shake.

"I'm Darlene Wright. Jordan's—" she hesitated, as if uncertain of their relationship "—Jordan's friend. Jordan's mother, Helene, and I were sorority sisters and friends. I think of Jordan as my daughter and she thinks of me as her mother." Darlene cast Roselynne a sidelong glance, her expression daring the other woman to contradict her.

"So it seems that Mrs. Price is a fortunate woman—she has two mothers."

Before either woman could respond, the room fell into an instant hush and all eyes turned to the doorway. Jordan entered the dining room quietly. But her presence captured everyone's attention, their reaction to her entrance as reverent as if she were the Queen of England, or maybe an angel come down from heaven.

How did one small, fragile woman command such devotion?

Had he pegged her all wrong? Was she the cold-hearted bitch who hadn't shed a tear at her husband's funeral? Was she the beautiful, vulnerable widow he instinctively wanted to comfort? Was she the adulterous wife who was having an affair with her husband's assistant? Was she the much adored daughter to two women? Was Jordan Price really a candidate for sainthood or was she a heartless murderer?

Rick watched as, one by one, Jordan's admirers swarmed around her. Although they showed concern for her, and it was obvious that they all cared about her and she them, Rick got an odd vibe. It was almost as if they fed off her, draining her of her strength and energy, absorbing her light into their darkness.

*Hell, where had that weird thought come from? Absorbing her light into their darkness. Getting a little deep there, Carson. Next thing you know, you'll need some hip boots to wade through the crap.*

Jordan parted her sea of devotees and came to him, pausing when she was within arm's reach. "Good evening, Mr. Carson . . . Rick."

"Jordan." He nodded.

"I hope your accommodations are satisfactory. If not—"

"The room is fine. Thanks."

"I apologize for keeping y'all waiting," she said. "I was on the phone with the governor. He wanted me to know that he's appointing Gary Werneth to complete Dan's term. He—" Her voice trembled. She closed her eyes and bowed her head.

Everyone in the room seemed to move forward, as if

ready to envelop Jordan with comfort or catch her if she fell. But it was Kendra Brannon who actually wrapped her arms around her stepmother and hugged her.

Jordan returned the hug, then pulled free and announced, "Please be seated, everyone. I'll let Vadonna know we're ready for dinner to be served."

During the hour and a half it took to complete the four-course meal, Jordan made a great effort to put everyone at ease. Rick had been placed between Rene Burke, Jordan's assistant, and Darlene Wright. Both women treated him with cordial respect, but neither was actually friendly. Across from him, Tammy Harris spoke only when spoken to, and eyed Rick shyly when she thought he wasn't looking. Jordan included Rick in the conversation whenever possible, as did her stepmother, Roselynne, but for the most part, everyone ignored him. They probably thought of him as the proverbial white elephant in the room. No one was openly rude to him, but he sensed a mixture of antagonism and curiosity from Jordan's family and friends.

After dinner, as everyone rose to their feet and milled around the room, Jordan made her way to him, pulled him aside, and asked, "Would you join Devon and me in my study?"

"Sure."

She motioned to Markham who stood halfway across the room, watching and waiting. She snaps her fingers and he comes running, Rick thought. How many poor bastards had been at her beck and call the way her husband's handsome young assistant was?

Both Rick and Markham fell into step behind Jordan as she led them away from the others, down the hall and into her private sanctum. After closing the door behind her, she reached out and took Markham's hand in hers. Rick looked from their clasped hands to their faces. Whatever this was about, they were presenting a united front.

"I want to clear something up right now," Jordan said.

"There is no need for you to try to find out what my relationship with Devon is. Don't waste your time when it's better spent trying to find out if Dan was murdered and if so, who killed him."

"Are you ordering me not to—"

"Jordan and I are not lovers," Markham said.

*Yeah, tell me another one and maybe I'll believe it.* "If you say so."

"Devon and I have known each other since we were children," Jordan said. "He's been my best friend for as long as I can remember, in grade school and in high school. But we are not lovers. We've never been lovers."

"Okay. You're not lovers, just good friends. I got it."

"And if you're concocting any other scenarios where Jordan and I killed Dan, then erase those from your mind," Markham told him. "We both loved Dan. Neither of us would have ever done anything to hurt him."

"Who do you think would have had a reason to hurt him?" Rick asked. "Mrs. Price claims that she can't think of anyone who might have had a motive to kill Dan. She doesn't think that the senator's disgruntled ex-wife or her money-grubbing stepbrother is capable of murder. What do you think, Mr. Markham?"

Devon Markham's movie idol handsome face flushed, but other than that he kept his feelings completely under control. "I agree with Jordan. The divorce was difficult for Jane Anne, but eventually she and Dan moved beyond what had happened in the past. I can't say they were friends, but they certainly weren't enemies. As for J.C.—he's a charming good old boy, but—" Markham glanced toward Jordan and shrugged "—but despite the fact he is part of Jordan's family, the man isn't worth shooting. It would be a waste of good lead."

"Well, thanks for the information," Rick said. "Nobody wanted Dan Price dead, but the man's dead nevertheless. Possibly, somebody went to a great deal of trouble to make his death look like a suicide." Rick swung his right index finger back and forth, pointing at Jordan and Markham. "And you two are really good friends, but not lovers, so I shouldn't waste time suspecting that either of you or the two of you together might have killed the senator for reasons unknown. Have I got all that right?"

"See here, Mr. Carson." Markham released Jordan's hand and confronted Rick face-to-face. "There's no excuse for such insulting behavior. Jordan has endured more than enough these past few weeks without having to deal with attitude from you."

Rick looked directly at her. Big mistake. She had that woeful look of a sad, vulnerable creature greatly in need of solace. And God help him, he wanted to give the widow a lot more than solace.

She laid her hand on Markham's arm. "It's all right, Devon. Really. I believe Mr. Carson . . . Rick . . . was simply playing devil's advocate. He didn't mean to be insulting." She gave Markham's arm a tender, loving squeeze. "Would you mind leaving us alone? Rick and I have a few other matters to discuss."

Markham looked at her questioningly, evidently hesitant to leave her alone with Rick. "If you're sure."

"I'm sure."

Markham glowered at Rick, issuing him a silent but definite warning before he reluctantly walked out of the room.

The moment they were alone, Jordan closed her eyes and sighed.

*Very effective. Sweet and helpless. And here I am, a big, strong shoulder to lean on. God, how stupid did she think he was?*

"From here on out, take all the pot shots at me you want," Jordan said. "But Devon is off limits. I can take whatever is dished out, by you, by anyone, by life in general. But Devon can't. Dan's death has hit him hard. I know someone like you can't possibly understand another man being emotionally fragile, but that's exactly what Devon is right now. If you hurt him, I'll—"

"What do you mean, someone like me?"

"A tough guy. All macho rough and proud of it."

"It seems I'm not the only one who's made a gut reaction judgment call. Yesterday, you pegged you for a cold-hearted bitch and today you've decided that I'm a Neanderthal, all brawn with no brains or feelings." When he moved toward her, she took one step back, then halted and stood her ground as he approached. When only a hairsbreadth separated them, he looked down at her and asked, "If you're wrong about me, maybe I'm wrong about you."

"Am I wrong about you, Mr. Carson?"

"Partially. Am I wrong about you, Mrs. Price?"

"I'll leave that for you to decide when we become better acquainted."

It was all he could do to keep his hands off her. The only problem was, he wasn't sure if he wanted to kiss her or shake the living daylights out of her.


After Rick left her study, Jordan locked the door and turned out all the lights, except the one on her desk. She walked to the windows and looked out into the darkness. A powerful, almost unbearable ache welled up inside her and for the first time since Dan's death, she allowed the pain freedom. She stopped trying to control it, temporarily succumbing to her grief. Standing alone in the shadows, unable to cry, she trembled as the sadness engulfed her. She grieved for Dan, for a future that would never be, and for a past that she could not change.

She closed her eyes and moaned quietly. She wanted to

scream, to rant, to curse the heavens. If it were within her power to go back a few short weeks and change things, would she? For her child's sake?

How many more good years might Dan have had? One? Five? They would never know. His untimely death had saved all of them and at the same time had cheated them. Even if Devon could not see both sides of the issue, she could. If that made her the cold-hearted bitch that Rick Carson had accused her of being, then she accepted the condemnation. Life was never all black or all white; instead it was shades of gray. People were never all good or all bad, but myriad combinations.

Had life and circumstances taken away all that was pure and good and loving inside her? Had she truly become cold hearted, so much so that she could admit, if only to herself, that perhaps Dan's death would free her from the lie her life had become?

*Forgive me, Dan. Please forgive me.*

*We both deserved so much more than what we had to settle for, a marriage without passion, living two separate lives, one in public and the other in private.*

Jordan slumped down into the nearest chair, bent over and covered her face with her hands, effectively muffling her moans. She wanted to cry, wished she could weep cleansing tears, allowing them to flow freely until she was spent. Crying would be such a relief. She curled up in the large, overstuffed chair, pulled the folded afghan from the arm, opened it, and wrapped it around herself.

Tomorrow morning she would face what lay ahead: the reading of Dan's will, the private investigation into his death, Gary Werneth taking Dan's place in the senate, holding together and providing for her hodgepodge of a family, bringing her child into the world without his or her father, accepting the fact that she was destined to live the rest of her life without love.

But tonight, she didn't have to be strong and brave.

She didn't have to carry the weight of the world on her shoulders. She didn't have to feel guilty or blame herself for what had happened.

All she had to do was survive one more night.

She tapped softly on the door. She was concerned about Jordan. Devon should have stayed with her. He had always been such a comfort to her, had been at her side through all her tragedies. But perhaps this time, Devon couldn't give her what she needed because he, too, was grieving a personal loss. He had loved Dan, as they all had loved him. What would happen to them now that Dan was gone? Unless he had changed his will without informing anyone, Jordan stood to inherit a third of his vast fortune. If only she'd been able to tell him about the child she was carrying, he might have divided things up differently. Even now, it was possible that a clever lawyer could protest the will and claim a portion of Dan's wealth for his son or daughter. But no matter what Jordan decided to do about the inheritance, there was no need to worry. Jordan would take care of her. She'd take care of all of them, just as she'd been doing for years.

"Jordan . . . Jordan, are you all right?" She tried the handle and found the door locked. *Oh, my, that wasn't a good sign.* "Please, Jordan, let me in. We'll talk. Please, Jordan . . ."

Silence.

"If you need anything . . . Oh, Jordan, I'm so very sorry about Dan."

Why wouldn't she answer? It wasn't like Jordan to shut her out of her life this way.

"I love you, Jordan, so very much. You know I'd do anything for you. Anything."

No reply. No response of any kind.

She pressed her forehead against the closed door and

laid both hands, palms open, flat against the doorframe on either side. "I'll never leave you. I promise that you can depend on me as long as I live."


Rick took the call from fellow Powell agent, Maleah Perdue, at nine-thirty that night.

"I'll fax you everything we've got in the morning," Maleah told him. "But I thought I'd fill you in on some information I found more than interesting."

"Shoot," Rick said.

"I've formed a theory based on the preliminary info we've gathered. Let's see if you agree after I present the evidence."

"Evidence? You sound like you've decided who our killer is."

"We aren't a hundred percent sure Senator Price was killed, are we?"

"Not a hundred percent," Rick said.

"If he was murdered, at this point in the investigation, I'll give you odds that the wife killed him."

Rick's gut tightened. "Based on what evidence?"

"You already know that Daniel Price was not Jordan Price's first husband, don't you?"

"Yeah. So what?"

"She was a widow when she married the senator, so now at the ripe old age of thirty-four, she's been widowed twice," Maleah told him. "Actually, she was almost widowed three times."

"Explain."

"When she was twenty-one, she was engaged to a man named Robby Joe Wright. Three weeks before their wedding, he died in a one-car accident. Then a few years later, when the lady was in her late twenties, she lost husband number one, Boyd Brannon, in a hunting accident, and now her second husband supposedly committed suicide. Odd, don't you think, that three men who loved Jordan Price have died?"

"Are you saying you think she killed all three men?"

"Maybe. Possibly. I'm going to dig deeper and find out if she gained financially from Robby Joe Wright's death or Boyd Brannon's death. Want to bet me that she did? Let's say fifty bucks?"

A sick feeling hit Rick in the pit of his stomach. "If I was sure the lady was innocent, I'd take you up on that bet."

"But you're not sure, are you? You're wondering, just like I am, if maybe Jordan Price is a black widow."

# Chapter 6

Rick spent his first night at Price Manor alternating between a restless sleep riddled with odd dreams and episodes of wide-awake floor-walking. There was something about staying in this old mansion that didn't set right with him. He didn't believe in ghosts, but if he did, he would be on the lookout for the late senator. He'd sure like to ask Dan Price who had killed him.

A couple of times during the night, he could have sworn he'd heard footsteps in the hall outside his door. And then once, he woke up because he was dead certain he'd heard someone scream. But when he had checked the hall, it had been empty and silent. Apparently, he'd been suffering from some really weird nightmares.

It didn't help that he hadn't been able to stop thinking about what Maleah had told him about Jordan. The lady had lost two husbands and a fiancé in the span of twelve years, each man having met an untimely death. Okay, so it was possible that she was simply very unlucky in love. But what were the odds that a woman who hadn't even celebrated her thirty-fifth birthday would have buried three men who had loved her?

While Rick shaved and showered, he listed all the reasons he should not jump to conclusions, reasons he should not assume Jordan was guilty of murdering her husband. Then he listed the logical reasons why she could have murdered three men. By the time he had dressed and was ready to go downstairs for breakfast, he had come to one conclusion—he should call Nic and ask her to replace him on this assignment. The bottom line was simple: he suspected his employer of murder. Before he phoned Nic, he needed to speak to Jordan. She would be expecting his first report this morning and the least he could do was confront her with the information and give her a chance to defend herself.

Once downstairs, Rick caught a glimpse of Tobias as he entered the dining room.

"Good morning, Mr. Carson." Tobias nodded, then carried a silver coffee pot into the dining room and placed it on a silver tray atop the sideboard.

Rick paused in the open doorway. "Has Mrs. Price come down yet?"

"Yes, sir. Miss Jordan is in her study."

"Thanks."

Rick checked his wristwatch as he headed toward Jordan's study at the back of the house. Seven-thirty. Apparently, she was an early riser, just as he was. Except for the servants, the downstairs appeared to be empty of other inhabitants. He wondered just how many people had actually spent the night here and how many had finally made their way home.

When he neared Jordan's study, he heard voices coming from inside, but he couldn't make out the conversation. The door stood ajar, more than halfway closed, so he paused and listened without making his presence known.

"You don't have to do this today," a female voice said.

Rick thought it sounded like Rene Burke, but he wasn't a hundred percent sure.

"The sooner the better," Jordan said. "The longer we wait, the more speculation there might be about who the father of this child is."

*Child? What child?*

"You make a valid point," Rene replied. "I'll put together a press release, that is, assuming you don't want to make the announcement yourself."

"No, I think it would be in poor taste for me to speak publicly so soon after Dan's death. But please express how happy I am about the baby and how much Dan and I wanted this child."

The news hit Rick like an anvil dropped on his head. Jordan Price was pregnant!

"Oh, sweetie, if Dan had only known . . . ," Rene said. "At least this way, you'll always have a part of Dan with you. We all will, all of us who loved Dan. And anyone who knows you would never question your child's paternity."

"Thank you for saying that," Jordan told her assistant. "From now on, the most important thing in my life is my child. He or she comes first. I will do whatever it takes to protect my baby and give him or her the best life possible, even without Dan here to help me."

"He will have Devon and his Uncle Ryan for male role models and all of us to love him. And he'll grow up knowing what a fine man his father was."

After knocking on the partially closed door, Rick swung it open all the way. "Am I interrupting anything? If so, I can come back later."

The two women turned quickly to face him, both obviously surprised by his intrusion.

"No, please, come in," Jordan said. "Rene was just

leaving." She turned to her assistant. "I'd like to read over the press release before you contact the media."

"Certainly." Rene offered Rick a forced smile as she walked past him and out of the room.

"Would you care for coffee?" She indicated the carafe on her desk. "I'm afraid it's decaf. Or if you prefer hot tea, I can—"

"Coffee's fine, but it can wait. I'm here, as promised, to report to you."

"Yes, of course. I suppose I wasn't expecting anything this soon."

Rick looked her over, from head to toe. She didn't look pregnant. No tummy bulge, not even a slight one. She was slender and pale. Too pale. Weren't pregnant women supposed to glow?

How could he confront a pregnant woman with his suspicions? He had already asked her if she'd killed her husband and she'd told him that she hadn't. What if he pointed out that she'd lost two husbands and a fiancé and implied how unlikely that all three died of natural causes and it upset her? He didn't like the idea of upsetting Jordan, especially considering her condition.

"Look, I think you should know that I overheard your conversation with Ms. Burke," Rick confessed. "At least enough to know that you're pregnant."

Sighing, she nodded slowly. "My pregnancy isn't a secret. Everyone in my family and close circle of friends already knows. And after the press release later today, the whole world will know."

Rick glanced at her flat stomach. "You're not showing. You must not be very far along."

"About six weeks."

"And the senator didn't know you were pregnant?"

"No. I had planned to tell him that morning when I found him in his study."

"You want this child, don't you? I heard you say that your child was the most important thing in your life."

"We wanted a child. Dan and I. I just wish he could have . . ." She swallowed hard.

Rick gritted his teeth. She seemed so sincere, so genuinely sad.

"Dan would have been such a good father. He was a good man. Kind and caring. He would have loved this child so much."

When she unconsciously laid her hand over her belly in such a gentle, protective movement, Rick sensed how much this child meant to her. She wasn't faking the depth of her feelings. And if she loved his child, didn't it stand to reason that she had loved Dan Price?

"Look, is there anything I can do for you?" Rick took a tentative step toward her, desperately wishing he could erase the pain he saw in her eyes.

"I'm sorry, Mr. Carson . . . Rick." Jordan tried to smile. "I'm all right. Really I am." She changed the subject quickly. "You're here to give me a report, aren't you?"

He watched while she poured herself a cup of decaf from the carafe on her desk. She took a sip of the black coffee.

"I really don't have anything to report," he said. "Nothing you don't already know."

She took several more sips of coffee, then set the cup and saucer on her desk and glanced at Rick. "I sense there's something you wanted to say to me."

"It can wait."

"Please, won't you sit down? Have some coffee and tell me whatever it is."

His experience with pregnant women was very limited. He'd never been married or fathered a child. His sister was older than he, so he hadn't seen his own mother pregnant. And after devoting most of her life to her career, his sister had married only a couple of years ago and she and her husband had adopted a ten-year-old last year.

Rick didn't sit. Instead, he walked over to Jordan and looked her right in the eyes. "I received a report from Powell's last night."

"A report on what?" she asked, her expression one of total innocence.

"A report on you."

Her expression didn't alter except for a slight flickering of her eyelashes that hinted surprise. "You requested a report on me?"

"It's standard procedure. I'll get one on Ryan, too, probably later today."

"Did you find anything of interest in the report, something that adds to your suspicions?"

"You've had several tragedies in your life."

"I'd say that's an understatement."

He suspected that she was forcing herself not to break eye contact, to continue looking directly at him. "It's no secret that Dan is the third man that I've loved and lost. My fiancé died in a one-car accident shortly before we were to be married. I was twenty-one. My first husband was killed in a hunting accident when we'd been married only two years. And now, Dan . . . Neither Robby Joe nor Boyd was murdered, if that's what you're wondering."

"Murder can be made to look like an accident," Rick said and when her face went chalk white and her eyes widened in shock, he wished he'd kept that assessment to himself.

Jordan slumped into the chair behind her desk, her movements indicating that she could barely manage to stand on her own two feet. Rick took several tentative steps toward her, concerned about her welfare.

She held up a restraining hand. "No, please. I'm all right. Just shocked that you would even consider such a thing was possible."

"Look, I was hired for a specific reason and I have to consider every aspect of the situation, which means looking into the past. The senator's past, your past, and the past of anyone who had an opportunity to kill Dan Price."

"I know you're just doing your job, but the very idea that Robby Joe's death or Boyd's was anything other than an accident is ludicrous."

"Look, I'm sorry if I upset you, especially since you're pregnant," Rick said. "I think maybe we should discuss Powell's sending in another agent to replace me, all things considered. I'm probably not the best man for this job."

"No! I don't want another agent," Jordan said vehemently. "I—I don't want to start all over again with someone else. You're here. You're qualified. If you weren't, Nicole wouldn't have sent you. Am I right?"

"Yes, ma'am, you're right. But I thought that since—"

"I'm not offended that you think I might have killed Dan. In your place, I might question my innocence, too, especially after learning that Dan was not the first man in my life who died unexpectedly. But I didn't kill Dan anymore than I killed Robby Joe or Boyd. I'm not afraid of the truth and the truth is that Robby Joe's death and Boyd's death were terrible accidents. And if Dan really was murdered, I'm not his killer."

Damned if he didn't believe her. At least for the moment. She looked so sincere, sounded so sincere, and sent out strong I'm-sweet-and-innocent vibes. Everything in him wanted to believe her without question. He wanted her to be just what she seemed, a grieving, pregnant widow who really had cared deeply for her husband and wouldn't have harmed a hair on his head.

Maybe he should stick around, stay on the job and prove to himself that Jordan was innocent of any wrongdoing. Wasn't that what he wanted?

"Will you please reconsider leaving, Mr. Carson? Please stay and continue to investigate Dan's death." She gave him a pleading look that had him all but dropping to his knees and begging her to forgive him for ever doubting her. Damn, she was good. Either that or he was far too susceptible to her charm.

"Yeah, sure, I'll consider staying, if that's what you really want."

"It's what I want, someone impartial who will find out the truth about Dan's death." She offered him a fragile, seductive smile.

Hell, he was reading far more into her delicate smile than she intended. He wanted it to mean something personal. It didn't and he damn well knew it didn't.

*You can't stay here. You're too vulnerable to Jordan's charm to remain impartial. You know she could be guilty of three murders, but you want her to be innocent because you want to screw her.*

There, he'd said it. He had admitted that he was thinking with his dick and not his brain. And he suspected he wasn't the first man who'd let his libido take over and his good judgment go out the window where Jordan Price was concerned.

Before he had the chance to refute his agreement to stay on as the Powell agent investigating her husband's murder, they both heard a loud ruckus, the sounds of shouting, screaming and running feet coming from somewhere nearby.

*What the hell?*

Jordan shot up out of her chair and muttered under her breath, "Oh, Lord, what now?"

When they both headed toward the door, Rick falling into step behind Jordan, Tammy Harris came flying into the room, a wild-eyed expression on her face. Tears streamed down her cheeks as she rushed to Jordan. She wrung her hands together, all the while gulping for air.

Jordan grabbed Tammy's trembling hands. "What's wrong?"

"Help, please help," Tammy blurted out, her voice shaky.

Jordan squeezed Tammy's hands. "Calm down. Everything will be all right. Just tell me what's wrong."

A loud thump followed by another and then another gained their attention. Tammy glared through the open doorway, sheer terror in her eyes.

"You have to stop them before they kill each other," Tammy finally managed to say on one long, hurried breath.

"Who?" Jordan asked.

"J.C. and Wes," Tammy told her. "They're fighting."

"What happened? Why are they fighting?"

"Stop them, please." Tammy jerked her hands free of Jordan's tenacious hold. "I can't stand it. I can't. You have to stop them before they kill each other."

"Okay, okay. Just calm down."

Kendra Brannon's appearance halted Jordan outside her study.

"Jordan, you have to do something," Kendra said. "Wes and J.C. are fighting and it's all my fault. J.C. was sort of flirting with me and Wes went berserk. You know how protective he is. He thinks J.C. is too old to be flirting with me."

"Damn!" Jordan huffed loudly. "J.C. *is* too old to be flirting with you. But Wes shouldn't have started a fight over it. Come with me. Now." Jordan glanced from Kendra to Tammy. "We'll put a stop to things before someone gets hurt."

Kendra eyed Rick, who stood inside the study. "Shouldn't he come, too? He looks like he could handle J.C. and Wes."

"Want me to take care of this for you, Mrs. Price?" Rick asked, dreading the thought of breaking up a fist-fight.

"Please, come with us," Jordan told him. "But let me handle things. I'm used to playing referee and peace-maker in this family."

By the time they made their way to the scene of the

brawl, the fight that apparently had begun inside the house had moved out onto the veranda. Just as Jordan opened the front door, Wes knocked J.C. down the steps and onto the lawn.

"I want you two to stop this stupid fighting right this minute!" Jordan shouted in an I-mean-business, authoritarian voice.

J.C. came up from the ground swinging, his face bloody and sweat dampening his silk shirt. Taking a stand, Wes prepared to defend himself, a look of pure hatred on his face.

"Enough!" Jordan ran across the veranda and down the steps.

Shit! She was heading straight toward the two battered fighters and neither one seemed aware of her presence.

*Don't do it, honey. Don't step between them.*

But that's exactly what Jordan did, walked right between J.C. and Wes, with both men ready to continue clobbering each other. Rick went after her, but didn't reach her in time to prevent her from putting herself in harm's way.

"Don't interfere, Jordan," Wes said. "I'm going to beat the crap out of him, so help me God. After I finish with him, he'll think twice before he touches Kendra or any other girl young enough to be his daughter."

"Oh, for goodness sake, Wes, all he did was kiss me," Kendra shouted. "And I didn't try to stop him!"

Jordan glowered at J.C. "Leave. Now. Go home and stay there. We'll talk later."

J.C. wiped the blood from his mouth. He smirked at Jordan. "Just keep the kid away from me." He glanced at Kendra. "Hell, keep both of those brats away from me."

When he started to walk off, Wes lurched for him, but Jordan grabbed Wes by the shoulders and shook him. J.C. meandered away, around the house, whistling to himself. Wes threw off Jordan's hold, obviously intending to go after J.C.

In his peripheral vision, Rick noted that the entire household had come out on the veranda—Roselynne, Darlene, Rene, Devon and both servants—just as Wes shoved Jordan's hands off his shoulders. Rick realized that Wes had pushed Jordan harder than he'd intended and she was falling backward. Only when Rick dashed straight to her and caught her just before she hit the ground did Wes realize what he'd done. That realization stopped him cold.

"Oh, God, Jordan, I'm sorry," Wes said.

Rick swooped a dazed Jordan up in his arms, something primeval inside him wanting to protect her, needing to keep her safe from this swarm of vultures hovering around her.

# Chapter 7

Jordan grabbed hold of Rick by instinctively throwing her arm around his neck. Momentarily stunned by what had happened, she stared into his eyes. Their gazes connected and instantly locked. Knowing she had to remove herself from such intimate contact with this man, she inhaled and exhaled a deep, steadying breath before saying, "Please, put me down."

Rick hesitated for a split second, then eased her onto her feet.

"Thank you," she mouthed the words quietly.

He didn't get a chance to say anything before the adoring Jordan Price tribe swarmed around her, each person professing their concern. But Devon Markham cut through the other groupies and all but pushed Rick aside.

"Are you okay?" Devon asked, genuine worry marring his handsome features.

"I'm fine." She patted him on the arm and then turned to the others. "The show's over. Everything is going to be fine. Please, all of you, go back inside."

Tobias and Vadonna returned to the house immediately,

while no one else hurried back inside; instead they began mumbling among themselves.

"Wait up, Wes," Jordan called to her stepson. "We need to talk." She looked from Wes to his sister. "You, too, Kendra. Both of you go sit down. I'll be there in a minute." She turned to Rick. "Please, go eat breakfast and get your day started. I have to do my job as their stepmother and sort things out with them before I send them both back to school."

"I don't mean to interfere, but shouldn't you confront your stepbrother about making advances to a teenager first?"

Jordan grimaced. "No, the children first. I'll deal with J.C. later."

Rick nodded, then left her to handle the family situation on her own. She squared her shoulders and walked across the lawn, up the steps and onto the veranda. Wes sat in one of the big wicker chairs, his legs spread, his shoulders and head drooped, and his hands clutched together between his knees. Kendra paced back and forth. Pausing when Jordan approached, she looked at her in a wide-eyed, pleading manner.

"Wes overreacted to something that was none of his business in the first place," Kendra said.

Pointing her index finger in Kendra's face, Jordan gave her a stern, disapproving, maternal glare. "J.C. kissed you, right?"

"Yes."

"Did anything else happen?"

"No."

"Has he kissed you before?"

"Once."

"Kendra Diane Brannon, you are eighteen years old. J.C. is thirty-six. Do the math. He's twice your age and has had five times more experience. He is a sweet-talking womanizer who uses and discards women as if they were Kleenex."

"But—"

"No buts," Jordan said. "Whatever he's said to you, whatever you think you feel for him, forget it."

"You're not being fair," Kendra whined, reminding Jordan of just how immature her stepdaughter was.

Maybe it was her fault that Kendra still saw the world through rose-colored glasses, but she had so wanted to protect her from life's harsh realities as long as possible. When Jordan had married Boyd, Kendra had been a shy, starved-for-motherly-affection little girl of ten, the same age Jordan had been when she'd lost her own mother. She had reached out to Kendra immediately, offering her the love and attention she had so desperately needed.

"I'm being sensible. I am protecting you because I love you. And in case you have any doubts, let me spell this out for you. This subject is closed. After breakfast, I want you to go upstairs and pack your bags. You're going back to university today instead of this weekend."

"Oh, Jordan, do I have to . . ." Kendra stopped mid-sentence, heaved a deep, overly dramatic sigh and said, "Okay, I'll go."

"You know I'm doing what I believe is best for you under the circumstances."

"Yes, ma'am. I know."

"Go on inside. I need to talk to Wes. Alone."

As soon as Kendra left, Jordan turned to Wesley. He wouldn't look at her. Instead, he stared at the floor. Even though he was now a young man of twenty, broad shouldered and six feet tall, she would always see him as he'd been when she first married Boyd, a hostile twelve-year-old who was determined to hate his new stepmother. It had taken her a year of hard work to win him over and make him realize that she didn't expect to take his mother's place, that she wanted her own place in his life and his heart.

"Look at me, Wes."

He hazarded a quick glance up at her.

"You should have come to me when you saw J.C. kiss Kendra and let me handle the problem. All you achieved by physically attacking J.C. was to bruise and bloody both of you and create a hullabaloo within the family."

"Yeah, well, it did more than that," Wes told her. "It made me feel damn good to hit him."

Barely managing not to smile, Jordan laid her hand on Wes's shoulder. "I suppose it did. There have been a few times when I've wanted to knock some sense into J.C."

"I don't see how you can stand having that sleazeball around. He's worthless and everybody knows it. Even Devon, who likes just about everybody, has no use for J.C."

"J.C. is my stepbrother. He's family."

"Have you considered the possibility that he killed Dan?"

The question genuinely startled Jordan. "No, I haven't because despite all of J.C.'s faults, he's not capable of murder."

"Yeah, he is," Wes said. "Everyone is. He kept hitting up Dan for money and when Dan didn't come through the last time, J.C. got really pissed. What if he thought by killing Dan, you'd inherit and—"

"J.C. did not kill Dan. We don't even know for sure that Dan was murdered."

Wes shrugged. "Just don't trust him, okay? You're too smart for that, but at the same time, you've got a really soft spot when it comes to taking care of friends and family." Wes rose to his feet. "Please, be careful around him."

"I appreciate your concern."

"I'll go pack, too." Wes grinned. "I figure you'll want me to leave when Kendra does."

Jordan slipped her arm around her stepson's waist. "It's

for your own good. You two have missed more than enough school this semester and I know y'all stayed on because you're concerned about me. Don't be. I'm going to be all right. Devon's here, as is Roselynne and Darlene, not to mention Rene."

"Gee, that makes me feel a lot better," he said sarcastically. "Devon's a basket case since Dan died, and Roselynne and Darlene both need keepers, so Rene's the only person left you can actually count on. Her and that Carson guy. I know you don't like him, but I have a feeling he's okay."

"Yes, I have the same feeling. If I can ever convince him that I'm not some black widow who's killed two husbands and a fiancé—"

"You're joking? He can't possibly think you whacked Dan or that you killed Dad or—"

"It's his job to find out the truth," Jordan said. "And that's what I want, what we all want."

Wes hugged her and kissed her cheek. "If you need me, I'll just be a phone call away. I wish . . ."

"What do you wish, honey?"

"I wish you had someone to take care of you the way you take care of all of us. More than anyone I know, you deserve to be happy."

A knot of emotion tightened Jordan's throat, making it impossible for her to respond. She and Wes exchanged a tender mother-son moment that needed no words.

Tammy yanked open the front door to the home she shared with their mother and marched into the living room. J.C. took a puff on his cigarette, then blew out a spiral of smoke. His little sister looked spitting mad.

"What's up, buttercup?" he asked, trying to lighten the mood.

"How could you? Are you out of your mind?"

"Me? Nope. You're the sibling with a few loose screws, not me." He twirled his index finger beside his temple to indicate she was crazy.

Tammy bristled at his attempt to be funny. "Kendra is Jordan's stepdaughter so that makes her off limits to you."

"No woman is off limits to me if I want her and believe me I want Kendra. I'd like to pop her cherry if one of those college boys hasn't already done it. And if they have, then I could show her the difference between being diddled by a boy and fucked by a man."

"You're disgusting. You know that, don't you? Mama should have put you in a sack and drowned you in the river when you were born."

J.C. chuckled, then took another draw on his cigarette. "Sugar, you're the one who should have been put down like a rabid dog. You're nothing but a burden on Mama and on Jordan." He placed his cigarette in the ashtray on the side table. "Poor, pitiful, little Tammy."

She came at him with teeth bared and claws out, lunging on top of him like the wild creature she was. She managed to rake his cheek with her fingernails before he manacled both of her wrists and forced her to her knees.

"You're hurting me," Tammy cried.

He increased the pressure, making her scream for mercy.

"Johnny Cash Harris, what the hell do you think you're doing?" Roselynne yelled as she came through the door. "For pity's sake, let her go."

He loosened his tight hold, but didn't release his sister. "She's gone loco again. If I hadn't grabbed her, she'd have done worse than scratch my face. She's crazy and it's time you put her away someplace where she can't kill anybody else."

Roselynne stomped toward them, hellfire and damnation in her eyes. J.C. jerked Tammy to her feet as he stood and then he shoved her toward their mother. Tammy went running into Roselynne's open arms.

Soothing her child with comforting strokes, she murmured endearments. "Now, go to the bathroom and wash your face while I talk to J.C."

"Yes, Mama," Tammy said, meek as a lamb.

J.C. had never understood how their mother could so easily control Tammy with a few words and a tender touch. The only other person who came close to controlling his crazy little sister was Jordan. But Jordan had a way with people in general, not just Tammy.

As soon as Tammy disappeared into the bathroom, their mother turned on him. "Damn it, boy, what am I going to do with you? Manhandling your sister is not allowed. How many times do I have to tell you? And as for the other, about her killing somebody—I don't want to hear you spouting off such nonsense ever again. You hear me?"

"It's not nonsense and you know it. Don't tell me that it hasn't crossed your mind that Tammy might have killed Dan."

"Shut your mouth! Nobody's proved that Dan didn't kill himself."

"Ryan Price thinks Dan was murdered. And so does that Powell agent who's snooping around."

"Everybody's got a right to their opinion. Just because Ryan can't accept the fact that Dan committed suicide doesn't mean he didn't do it. And Rick Carson is being paid to be suspicious, to snoop around and find out what's what."

J.C. laughed. "I'd like to be a fly on the wall when he unearths the truth about Dan and Jordan's marriage."

"Whatever he finds out, he'll keep to himself. It's a rule of some kind that private eyes have."

"Aren't you the least bit curious about the baby?" J.C. asked. "It's kind of difficult for a woman to get pregnant if her husband isn't screwing her."

"I don't want to hear anymore talk like that either. The

baby Jordan is carrying is Dan Price's kid, Dan's heir. You got that?"

J.C. winked at his mother. "Yeah, I got it. And if she gets more of Dan's money for that kid, then it'll mean more for all of us, right?"

"You're a greedy, ungrateful—"

"I just tell it like I see it." He narrowed his gaze and studied his mother for a couple of seconds. "You didn't by any chance know, before Dan killed himself, that he had Alzheimer's, did you, Ma?"

J.C. was creating problems they didn't need. She'd probably have to deal with him sooner rather than later. The very thought of disposing of him was abhorrent to her since he was part of the family. She had put up with his bad behavior, excused his misdeeds, and refrained from killing him because he had not posed a real threat to them. Not until now. He had become a liability. Even before she'd killed Dan, she had known it was only a matter of time before J.C. would have to be eliminated. His actions were hurting them more and more all the time. She couldn't allow him to continue upsetting them, not with a baby on the way. Nothing and no one was more important than their child.

She would simply have to wait for the right moment and then strike. And it had to look like an accident. If only she could have found a way to have made Dan's death look accidental instead of like suicide, as she had some of the other deaths.

Killing J.C. immediately was out of the question. First of all, she never eliminated someone without reason and that required her to consider all sides of a situation. Once she had made her decision, as she had with J.C., she formulated a plan. That took time, days, even weeks. She couldn't do anything to bring suspicion on herself, especially this soon after Dan's death. And she certainly couldn't take any undue chances with a private detective living here at Price Manor.

But when the time was right, she would remove J.C. from their lives, just as she had removed all the others who had betrayed them, either intentionally or simply by an act of fate.

Jordan waved goodbye to Kendra and Wes as they drove away. As much as she would have loved having them here until Sunday, sending them off today had been the right decision. She couldn't risk what might happen if they stayed and Kendra disobeyed her and encouraged J.C.'s attention. Her stepbrother couldn't be trusted around any woman who appealed to him, and young, inexperienced girls like Kendra appealed to him greatly. She remembered all too well how he'd come on to her more than once when she'd been in her teens. For years, she was able to fend him off without any real harm done, but eventually, she'd had to go to Roselynne. She never knew what her stepmother had said or done, but whatever it had been, Jordan had never had to fight off J.C. again.

"We'll miss them, won't we?" Darlene came up beside Jordan so quietly that Jordan jumped.

"Oh, dear, I didn't mean to startle you. I'm so sorry."

She smiled at Darlene. "It's okay. I guess I'm a little edgy this afternoon." She draped her arm through Darlene's and smiled. "Yes, we will miss them, but sending them back to school will save us from having any more problems for the time being."

"You should send J.C. packing," Darlene said. "That man . . ." She sighed. "I hate to speak ill of anyone, but J.C. is nothing but trouble."

"I know, but we'll give Roselynne a chance to deal with him first and if that doesn't work, I'll ask him to leave. He's stayed longer than he usually does when he visits. I really didn't expect him to stay this long."

"He's waiting for the will to be read, hoping when you come into your inheritance, you'll be generous with him and Roselynne and Tammy."

"I suppose you're right about his reasons for staying. Maybe I should tell him that although I'll take care of Roselynne and Tammy, I've washed my hands of him. He won't have any more luck getting money from me than he did getting it from Dan."

"I . . . uh . . . really shouldn't say this, but . . . well, have you ever considered the possibility that J.C. killed Dan?"

"Let's walk." Jordan tugged gently on Darlene's arm.

Darlene nodded agreement and the two women strolled down the long drive that led from the house to the county road half a mile away.

"Are you upset with me for—?" Darlene asked.

"No, of course not," Jordan replied. "It had never entered my mind that J.C. might have killed Dan. But you're the second person today who has suggested that J.C. could be a murderer."

"Was Wesley the other person?"

"Yes."

"Wesley is a very bright boy. I know that Roselynne and her children are family, but if it turns out that Dan was murdered, I think Mr. Carson and the sheriff should look to those three first. I've seen Tammy throw some hysterical hissy fits over the years. There's no telling what she might do. And Roselynne . . . well, if there's any money involved . . ."

"Mr. Carson suspects that I might have killed Dan," Jordan said.

Darlene gasped. "That's the most preposterous thing I've ever heard."

"No, it isn't. Not really. When you look at the facts,

that my fiancé, my first husband and now my second husband have all met untimely deaths—"

"Robby Joe's death was an accident, a tragic accident that almost destroyed us. How could anyone think that you killed him when you loved him with all your heart?"

Jordan stopped, took both of Darlene's hands into hers and smiled warmly at Robby Joe's mother, a woman who was as dear to her as anyone on earth.

"Robby Joe was the love of my life." Jordan kept her smile in place even though she wanted to cry. She had to stay strong, for Darlene's sake as well as her own.

"If the baby is a boy, I wish you could name him Robby Joe, but I know that's out of the question." Darlene laid her open palm over Jordan's flat belly.

"I haven't thought about names. Besides, this may be a little girl." She laid her hand over Darlene's on her stomach.

"If it is, you should name her after your mother."

"My mother and Dan's mother—Elizabeth Helene."

"And Daniel, Jr., if it's a boy?"

A cold chill rippled through Jordan. No, she couldn't name her son Daniel, Jr. "There's plenty of time to decide on a name. I'm sure that in seven months, we'll come up with something perfect for our baby."

Darlene sighed as she removed her hand from Jordan's stomach. "You are so generous to share your child with us, with me and Devon and the others. Your son or daughter will be the closest thing to a grandchild that I'll ever have."

"He will be a very lucky child to have so many people to love and care for him—or her. My family and friends and Dan's family and friends."

Jordan glanced toward the sky and noted the swirling dark clouds. "I believe it's going to rain. Maybe we'd better head back to the house."

Darlene gazed skyward. "You're right. It looks like a springtime storm is brewing."

They walked hurriedly up the drive, barely making it onto the veranda before the first raindrops hit the ground. By the time they were inside, the bottom fell out and distant flashes of lightning zigzagged through the sky.

"Excuse me, Miss Jordan, but there's a phone call for you." Tobias stood at the back of the wide foyer, the portable phone in his hand.

"Who is it?" Jordan asked.

"It's Mrs. Price," Tobias said. "Mrs. Jane Anne Price."

Jordan exchanged a why-is-she-calling? look with Darlene, then held out her hand for the phone. She met Tobias in the middle of the foyer.

"Hello, Jane Anne," Jordan said.

"Hello, Jordan."

"Is there a specific reason why you're calling?"

"I just heard the good news about your being pregnant. I wanted to congratulate you for achieving such a miraculous conception."

Jordan's heartbeat accelerated. "I'm very happy about the baby, as Dan would have been. He wanted a child as much as I did."

"Yes, I know how much Dan wanted a child. I regretted that he and I were never able to have a baby of our own," Jane Anne said. "And considering the fact that the doctors told us Dan was sterile, think how surprised I was to hear that you're now carrying Dan's baby."

Jordan swallowed hard. "What do you want, Jane Anne?"

"I want a piece of the pie. I seriously doubt that Dan mentioned me in his will, but I'm sure you will inherit a sizeable fortune."

"Dan was a generous and caring man. I'm sure he provided for me."

"You and Devon and Ryan, no doubt."

"How much?" Jordan asked.

"Keeping a secret as potentially damaging to Dan's reputation and to yours should be worth at least a million, don't you think?"

Damn, damn, damn! Dan had been wrong about Jane Anne no longer being vindictive. He had paid her off—or so he'd thought—with an astronomical divorce settlement years ago. Apparently, she felt she was entitled to a great deal more.

"I can't get my hands on that much money," Jordan said

"I'll be happy to take it in payments. Say, a hundred thousand now and another hundred thousand once the will is probated."

"And if I refuse to pay your blackmail money?"

"Then I'll go to the press and tell them that the child you're carrying can't possibly be Dan's baby because not only was he sterile, he was also—"

"I'll have the money for you within forty-eight hours."

# Chapter 8

Wallace McGee IV had followed in his father's and grandfather's footsteps as the Price family lawyer. Since Wallace McGee, Jr. had married one of Dan and Ryan's great-great aunts, both families considered themselves related. And in old southern families, blood was indeed thicker than water. Family came first.

She studied Wallace while he read Dan's will with a theatrical flair worthy of an amateur thespian, pausing at certain intervals for dramatic effect. As broad as he was high, rosy cheeked, and bald, except for puffs of unruly white hair above his ears and around the back of his neck, Wallace resembled an aging Pillsbury Dough Boy. But his keen dark eyes hinted of the sharp wit and shrewd mind behind the fat, congenial, good old boy façade.

They liked Wallace well enough and trusted him as much as they trusted anyone. Dan had certainly thought the world of his old friend and Dan had been a fairly good judge of character.

As they had expected, there were no surprises in Daniel

Price's will. He hadn't made any last-minute changes, hadn't added a codicil to include or eliminate anyone or alter the way he wanted his fortune divided. Several million had been donated to various charities and generous pension funds had been set up for Tobias and Vadonna. The bulk of Dan's fortune—$57 million—had been divided equally among his brother Ryan, his wife Jordan, and his assistant Devon Markham. Price Manor would belong to Jordan during her lifetime and upon her death would become the property of Ryan's heirs.

Considering the fact that there was now a child involved—Dan's son or daughter—she felt certain that they could go to court and obtain a larger portion of the estate and sole ownership of Price Manor. But if they took that type of action, wouldn't it cast suspicion on them since the cause of Dan's death was in question?

Ryan Price looked at his wife before he spoke and the two exchanged a silent agreement. "I feel that, considering the fact that Jordan is pregnant, perhaps all three of us should agree to put a portion of our inheritance into a trust for the baby."

"Oh, Ryan, that's not necessary," Jordan told him. "I intend to put most of the money Dan left me in trust for our child."

"Are you sure?" Ryan asked. "You know that I'm financially secure without Dan's money and I feel certain that if Dan had known about the baby, he would have—"

"You don't have to worry about the baby's future," Devon assured Ryan. "Like Jordan, I plan to put a large portion of my inheritance into a trust for him or her."

"All right, if that's what you both want." Ryan glanced at Darlene, and then moved on, briefly scanning the others in the room: Roselynne, Tammy, Rene, and both servants. "You haven't forgotten that you have this house to keep up, servants to pay, and several other people depending on you for their support."

"I believe I'll be able to do all that with nothing more than the interest from nearly twenty million dollars," Jordan said.

"Well, that seems to settle that," Wallace announced. "Now, if no one has other questions or comments, I'd like to drink a toast to Dan." He looked at Tobias, who stood in the back of the room. "Some of Dan's Napoleon brandy is in order, wouldn't you say?"

"Yes, by all means," Jordan agreed. "Please, Tobias, bring out a bottle for Mr. McGee. And serve anyone who'd like a glass. Of course, I won't be drinking."

None of Dan's Raynal VSOP for the little mother-to-be. They knew the importance of prenatal care, which included no drinking. Their baby's health was their first priority.

"Jordan?" Claire slipped her arm around Jordan's shoulders. "How are you doing . . . really?"

"I'm all right."

"At least we have this over with now," Claire said. "One more thing out of the way." She gasped. "Oh, dear, that sounded horrible, didn't it? But you know what I meant. The sooner all the legalities are settled, the sooner we can all try to get back to our normal lives."

"Yes, you're right. Unfortunately, my normal life included Dan."

"I'm saying all the wrong things, aren't I?"

"No, of course not. I understand what you're trying to say. I know you, Claire. I know what a caring person you are."

"Thank God. The last thing I'd want to do is make light of how much you've lost or belittle your relationship with Dan."

Ryan interrupted, sparing Jordan the need to reassure Claire once again. "Everything all right here?"

"Yes, of course, darling," Claire said.

"As soon as we share a toast to Dan, we'd better head home. The weather has turned nasty out there. The springtime shower has turned into a storm."

"Why don't y'all stay for dinner?" Jordan said.

"Some other time?" Claire asked. "Michael has the sniffles and he's a handful when he's sick. I'm afraid he's worn my poor mother to a frazzle."

"Of course, some other time."

Tobias brought in the bottle of brandy. He opened the bottle, poured a liberal amount into a snifter and handed it to Wallace, who swirled it around and around before taking the first sip.

"Ah, delicious," Wallace said.

Within minutes, everyone had a glass of brandy, except Jordan. Wallace lifted his glass.

"Here's to one of the finest men I ever knew, my good friend and dear cousin, Dan Price."

She agreed. Dan had been a fine man. Such a pity that she'd had to kill him. But she had done what was necessary, just as she had in the past. She had to protect them, didn't she? In the future, they wouldn't need a man in their lives. They would have the baby. That would be more than enough to make them happy. And they deserved to be happy. And if anyone else stood in the way of their happiness, she would take care of them, just as she planned to take care of J.C. if he caused them any more trouble.

"You are not going alone to meet her," Devon said, his usually smooth brow wrinkled with worry. "I'm coming with you."

"No, you're not. I'm meeting her alone on Old Pine

Creek Road tomorrow at four. I'll make some excuse to everyone about needing some time alone to think."

Devon rubbed the back of his neck. "I tried to tell Dan that Jane Anne had never forgiven him, that despite her act of we-can-be-friends, the woman wasn't to be trusted."

"You know how Dan was, he wanted to think the best of everyone and that included his ex-wife."

"How someone as genuinely nice as Dan survived in the dog-eat-dog world of politics still amazes me, but he did what he had to do to continue his family's legacy of service to the country. You and I know better than anyone else what lengths he would go to in order to keep his seat in the senate."

Jordan caressed Devon's arm tenderly. "His personal life was a lie and you and I helped him deceive the world. Now, it's up to us to keep his secrets safe, no matter what we have to do and that includes paying his ex-wife a million dollars."

"Do you think she'll be satisfied with only a million? The lady has expensive tastes. She's gone through the ten million divorce settlement in the past twelve years."

"What choice do we have but to pay her? I'm not thinking only of Dan's reputation, but of my baby. If the truth comes out, the press will have a field day with the news. We'll be hounded for months, Dan will be vilified and made fun of and our child will be ridiculed for the rest of his or her life."

"I swear I could strangle that woman for putting you through this now, just after our losing Dan and with you pregnant, not to mention our having to deal with that private investigator trying to prove that Dan was murdered." Devon ran his hands together, his slender thumbs rubbing against his open palms as he switched from his right hand to his left and back again.

Poor, sweet Devon. He'd been a nervous little boy, shy and hesitant, with big blue eyes that looked at the world with wonder and uncertainty. She remembered the first time she saw him peering around his mother's hip where he was half hidden from view. It had been the first day of school, Mrs. Coker's second-grade class. Within a week, they had made friends. Within a month, they were good friends. By the year's end, they had become best friends for life.

There wasn't anything they wouldn't do for each other.

Jordan clutched his hands to steady them. "Don't worry. I'll take care of everything, just as I always have. I'll deal with Jane Anne and make sure she knows that this million-dollar payoff is a one-time only deal and if she tries to extort more money from me, I'll contact the police. If I can get my bluff in on her now, we might not have to deal with her for a few years.

"As for Rick Carson—he's simply doing the job that Ryan and I hired him to do." Not even to Devon, her oldest and dearest friend, would she admit that she was afraid of Rick. Afraid of him because he suspected she was a murderer. And afraid of the unwanted attraction she felt for him.

"You were practically forced to go along with Ryan's wishes. If you hadn't agreed to hire an investigator, what—?"

Jordan framed Devon's face with her hands and looked up into his eyes. "Sweetie, you have to stop doing this to yourself. If you don't, you're going to have a nervous breakdown. I know that you've been barely holding it together since Dan died and worrying about me has only made matters worse. Everything is going to work out. I promise."

Devon grabbed her hands that were on his face, clasped them together and kissed the tips of her entwined fingers. "Do you know how much I love you?"

"Yes, I know. I love you, too. And I'll take care of you. I'll find a way to make things right again."

She slid her arms down across his shoulders and opened them to embrace him. When he laid his head on her shoulder, she felt the dampness of his tears through her thin silk blouse.

Not wanting either Jordan or Devon to realize that he had overheard their confessions of love just as he arrived outside the partially open door, he turned and walked away. He had intended to speak to Jordan before he met with Ryan Price. The updated info on the men in Jordan's past that Maleah had e-mailed him only increased his suspicions. Good thing he'd happened upon the lovers; otherwise, Jordan might have hoodooed him and convinced him that she had been a devoted wife to Dan Price, as she had been to Boyd Brannon. Rick had wanted to believe she was what she represented herself to be. But the grieving widow bit was just an act. In reality, she was in love with her husband's handsome young assistant and he with her. That information alone made the two of them prime suspects in the senator's murder.

Rick hurried through the house and went outside on the back porch. The late afternoon thunderstorm had moved through, leaving behind a slow, steady drizzle. Although it was not quite five-thirty, with the sunlight obscured by gray clouds, twilight was approaching early today.

He removed his cell phone from his pocket and dialed Ryan's number. "Mr. Price, this is Rick Carson. I need to speak to you. I have some information I believe you will find interesting. I'd like to drop by your house after dinner this evening."

"Yes, of course," Ryan replied. "Would seven-thirty be okay with you?"

"Seven-thirty's fine."

One call down and another to go. He dialed again and

when he heard the woman's no-nonsense voice say "Lieutenant McLain here" he smiled.

"Lt. McLain, this is Rick Carson."

"Hello there." Her voice softened.

"Have you had dinner yet?"

"It's a little early for dinner, isn't it?"

"I'd like to talk to you and I thought we might have an early dinner, maybe in downtown Priceville. I'm buying."

"There's a nice Italian restaurant on Main Street," Haley told him. "I could meet you there in about twenty minutes."

"Twenty minutes it is."

"Rick?"

"Yeah?"

"Want to give me a hint about what we're going to be discussing over dinner?"

"Sure. Powell's has unearthed some information that has me halfway convinced I know who killed Dan Price. I need somebody smart, savvy and unbiased to tell me that either I'm right or that I'm reading this all wrong."


They finished their salad before Haley put down her fork and looked directly at Rick. "Okay, let's hear it."

"You don't want to wait until after the lasagna?"

"Nope. I've waited long enough. My curiosity is driving me nuts."

Rick grinned. He liked Haley. He liked her up-front, in-your-face personality, her air of self-confidence, her sexy voice, and her big boobs. She wasn't classically beautiful, but she had an earthy quality that appealed to him. Haley McLain was as different from Jordan Price as day is from night. Haley was like good everyday earthenware, sturdy and reliable, that could withstand the rigors of daily use and was dishwasher friendly. Jordan was like fine china, easily broken, meant to be taken out and used only on special occasions, and that required hand washing.

"Dan Price isn't the first man in Jordan's life who died under mysterious circumstances," Rick said.

Haley's brows lifted. "I know she was a widow with two stepchildren when she married the senator."

"Her first husband died in a hunting accident, but the authorities never discovered who the other hunter was, the one who shot Boyd Brannon."

"And you find that suspicious?"

"Not if that's all there was to it, but it is when added to the other information."

"Which is?"

"Boyd Brannon had a half-million-dollar life insurance policy. His beneficiary was his wife, Jordan Harris Brannon."

"There's nothing unusual about a husband naming his wife as his beneficiary," Haley said.

"Six years earlier, Jordan's fiancé died in a one-car wreck. Robby Joe Wright had inherited several hundred thousand dollars worth of stock from his grandfather. He left that stock to Jordan.

"Two years before her fiancé's death, Jordan lost her father. Supposedly, he died from a heart attack. Even though he was married at the time to his second wife and he did leave her the house and their joint bank account, his insurance went to Jordan. A hundred thousand."

"Very interesting."

Haley lifted her glass to her lips and took a sip of iced tea. Their waitress brought two plates piled high with delicious-smelling, steaming-hot lasagna and set their meals in front of them.

"Will there be anything else?" the waitress asked. "More tea or more bread sticks?"

"I'm good," Rick said.

"Me, too," Haley said. "Thank you."

As soon as the waitress left, Rick asked, "Don't you see a pattern?"

"Are you saying that you think Jordan Price killed her father, her fiancé, and her first and second husbands?"

"And a former boss."

"What?"

"When she worked for a PR firm in Atlanta, her boss accidentally fell down a flight of stairs and broke his neck. Who do you think stepped into his shoes and got a major promotion and pay raise?"

"Jordan."

"Whether or not she killed all those men, a relationship with the lady seems to be deadly for the guys in her life."

"Do you have any proof that she killed even just one of them?"

"No proof," Rick admitted. "But what are the odds of a woman having that many men in her life die suddenly, one right after the other?"

"Stranger things have happened. But I have to admit that that many accidental deaths are unlikely and would be a really odd coincidence. And since Jordan profited from each of their deaths, that does make her look guilty. I hear that Senator Price was worth in the neighborhood of sixty million. Even if she doesn't get the whole bundle, I'd say that this time, the lady hit the jackpot."

"So you agree with me?" Rick asked. "You think it's possible that Jordan Harris Brannon Price is a killer."

"Sure, it's possible, but how can you prove it? All these deaths were years ago, except the senator's. And I assume each of the accident victims underwent an autopsy and nothing suspicious showed up."

"No one was looking for evidence of a murder in any of the cases," Rick said. "Give me some advice, lieutenant. The Powell agent who gave me the info on Jordan suggested that I tread very carefully because, technically, the Powell Agency is working for Mrs. Price. I have an appointment with Ryan Price at seven-thirty this evening. Do I tell him that I suspect his sister-in-law, Saint Jordan, may have killed not only his brother, but her first husband, her fiancé, and possibly her father and a former boss? Would he or anyone else believe that someone who appears to be so genteel, so kind and so very vulnerable could be a murderer?"

Haley studied him quietly for a couple of minutes, long enough to make him uncomfortable.

"What is it?" he asked.

"Despite the evidence staring you in the face, you don't want her to be guilty. You want me to talk you out of it, don't you? You want me to convince you that you're wrong, that Jordan is all those things—genteel, kind and vulnerable. You want to be convinced that she isn't a murderer."

He opened his mouth to deny her accusation, but his denial died on his lips. "Okay, let's say you're right and I don't want her to be guilty, that my gut is telling me I'm wrong, that there's no way in hell she could kill anybody."

"Is it your gut talking to you or is it your dick?"

Rick clenched his teeth, totally pissed by her question and by the fact that Haley was right. If he didn't have the hots for Jordan, he wouldn't question the hard, cold facts. He wouldn't second guess his usually sound judgment.

Rene watched Rick Carson and Lt. Haley McLain as they left Gino's Restaurant in downtown Priceville. She had followed the Powell agent when he left Price Manor this evening because she had accidentally overheard his cell phone conversations with Ryan and with the lieutenant. She hadn't meant to eavesdrop, but she'd been outside for a smoke break, and a hedge barrier between the back porch and the patio had prevented Rick from seeing her. She heard him tell the sheriff's deputy that Powell's had unearthed some information that halfway convinced Rick he knew who killed Dan. Rene realized then and there that she had to find out what he knew.

Wearing a hat and sunglasses, she had arrived at Gino's before Rick and Haley McLain and as luck would have it, they'd been seated in a booth in front of her. Wanting to get closer to them, she had quietly asked her waitress if she could move to the booth right behind Rick and the lieutenant. She hadn't been able to hear their entire conversation, but she'd heard enough to know that Rick suspected Jordan of not only murdering Dan, but Boyd, Robby Joe, Mr. Farris, her old boss, and even her own father. And now, Rick would go to Ryan and tell him about his suspicions. The question was, would Ryan believe him? And if he did, what would he do about it?

# Chapter 9

Ryan Price hadn't laughed in his face. Rick supposed that was something. Jordan's brother-in-law had listened patiently while Rick explained the information that Powell's had dug up about his brother's wife. Then he had calmly defended her.

"Jordan is no more capable of murder than I am," Ryan had said. "She is one of the kindest people I've ever known. Believe me, she did not kill Dan. And if any of the other men in Jordan's life were murdered, you'll have to look elsewhere because someone else killed them."

So, here Rick was, coming back to Price Manor and back to square one in the investigation. Could someone like Ryan Price who had known Jordan for several years be totally wrong about her? Wouldn't he be a better judge of the woman's character than Rick, who had met her only a few days ago?

But evidence was evidence.

Yeah, but exactly what evidence did he have against Jordan? Totally circumstantial, just as Haley had said.

Was it possible that the deaths of the four other men

weren't murder? Could it simply be a strange coincidence and Jordan was one of the unluckiest women in the world as far as the men in her life?

So, what did he do now? He couldn't dismiss this information as if it were useless. On the other hand, he couldn't assume Jordan was guilty and not look elsewhere for Dan Price's killer.

If Jordan killed her husband, why had she insisted he stay on as the investigator for Powell's when she had to know that he would eventually find out everything about her past?

But that was just it—he didn't know everything about her past. All he had were some basic facts. Four men, five counting Dan Price, in Jordan's life had died and she had benefited financially from each death. Those facts did not make her guilty of murder. It was possible her father's death really had been nothing more than a heart attack. And the other three deaths could have been accidents.

He probably needed to call Nic and fill her in on what had happened, assuming Claire Price hadn't already gotten in touch with Nic. If she had, then he'd have some major explaining to do. After all, it wasn't an agent's job to dig up evidence that implicated the client in five murders.

Rick headed for Dan Price's study, which he had converted into his temporary office. He'd pour himself a drink from the senator's stocked bar, then telephone Nic. Maybe she'd take him off this case. All things considered, that might be best for everyone involved.

Halfway to the study, he heard footsteps tapping hurriedly along the hall that led from the back of the house. Someone in high heels was running. Curiosity and a desire to postpone calling his boss prompted Rick to search for the source of the footsteps. Just as he rounded the corner that led away from the den, he saw Jordan hurrying into the powder room located at the rear of the house.

From the stricken look on her face, he assumed she was sick.

Should he get someone to help her? Should he check on her himself?

The lady was pregnant. Morning sickness was par for the course, right?

While he considered what to do, he continued walking toward the powder room. The door stood ajar giving him a full view of Jordan on her knees, her head bent over the toilet bowl, her hands clutching her stomach.

She moaned a couple of times, then retched violently and threw up. After wiping her mouth with the back of her hand, she groaned and quickly threw up again.

Rick stepped into the bathroom, intent on helping her, but instead he unintentionally frightened her. She gasped, jerked around and glared at him.

"What are you doing in here?" she asked.

God, she looked like death warmed over. Pale and weak and so very sick.

"I'm sorry I scared you," Rick said. "I heard you running down the hall and I came to see what was wrong."

"I'm nauseated," she told him. "Morning sickness at night. I've had a few mild episodes the past few days, but nothing like this."

"How can I help?"

She shook her head. "You can't—"

Before she managed to finish her sentence, another wave of nausea hit her and she vomited again.

Damn, was this what it was like for all pregnant women? If so, he couldn't imagine anyone having more than one child.

Vaguely recalling a couple of times when he'd had stomach viruses as a kid, he remembered how tenderly his mother had taken care of him. Rick went over to the sink, yanked the fancy hand towel off the rack, turned on the faucet and dampened the towel. When Jordan eased her head up and away from the toilet bowl, Rick knelt down beside her and gently wiped her face with the cool cloth. Instinctively, he lifted his other hand and caressed her back.

"Feeling any better?" he asked.

"Some. Thanks."

When she looked at him, her blue-gray eyes filled with gratitude, he wanted to wrap his arms around her. She was pregnant and alone and needed someone to look after her.

"Are you finished or do you think you need to stay here a little longer?"

"Give me a few minutes," she said. "I think the nausea has passed, but I'm not sure."

He wiped her face again, then tossed the towel into the sink as he stood. "Want to get up?" He held out his hand.

She took his hand and allowed him to help her to her feet. Unsteady on her wobbly legs, she swayed toward Rick. He slipped his arm around her waist as she leaned against him, her breasts brushing against his chest. Their gazes met and held for a split second, then she moved back, putting a couple of inches of safe space between them.

"Would you mind walking with me to my bedroom?" Jordan asked. "I feel a little woozy and—"

"I can carry you if you think you can't walk."

She smiled. "That's very kind of you, but I believe I can walk. I just don't want to be alone in case I faint. I'm one of those silly women prone to fainting when I get sick."

"Would you like for me to get someone else to help you? Your stepmother or Mrs. Wright or—"

"No, please." She grabbed his arm. "Don't disturb them. I don't want to upset either of them. Roselynne and Darlene are already worried about me and all the stress isn't good for either of them. Both of them have health issues. Roselynne has high blood pressure and Darlene has dealt with colitis for years. I'm afraid they'll overreact to what is nothing more than normal morning sickness."

"Are you sure that's all it is?" Rick asked. "Not that I know anything about being pregnant, but you were pretty sick."

"I'm sure. If you will just help me upstairs, I'll be fine."

Rick kept his arm around her waist, which he could easily span with his two hands. As they made their way up the stairs, he felt her leaning into him, depending on his strength to keep her steady. For her sake, he took the steps slowly and carefully, mindful of the fact that she might either faint or throw up at any moment.

At the top of the stairs, he sensed that she needed to pause, so he stopped and waited for her to signal to him when she was ready to go on.

"Are you sure you're okay?" he asked.

She nodded, but didn't speak.

She looked white as a sheet, all color drained from her face. Her hand on his trembled. Without asking permission, Rick scooped her up in his arms and carried her down the hall. She didn't complain, didn't protest his actions in any way. When they reached her bedroom door, he maneuvered her in his arms in order to turn the doorknob. Once inside her semi-dark room, he carried her straight through the sitting area and directly to her antique sleigh bed. He set her on the edge, atop the thick comforter, then reached out and turned on a bedside lamp.

"I'm going to get Mrs. Wright. You need—"

She grasped his arm. "No, please. I'll be fine. Just stay with me a few minutes. Please."

She needed him. Wanted him.

He wasn't going anywhere.

"Is there something I can do?" he asked.

"I have a mini-refrigerator in my dressing room—" she

indicated the direction "—and there are colas in it. Would you mind getting one for me?"

"Sure thing. Do you want ice?"

"No. Just open the bottle for me, if you would, please."

He found the mini-fridge tucked neatly under the wall-to-wall vanity in the large dressing room. The refrigerator was stocked with a variety of items, including several small bottles of cola. He retrieved one of the bottles, closed the fridge and twisted off the easy-open cap. As he walked across the room, he caught a hint of Jordan's delicate perfume where it lingered on the upholstered vanity stool and on her robe hanging on the back of the door. Subtle, flowery, and no doubt outrageously expensive perfume that probably cost more per ounce than a week's pay for the average Joe.

When he returned to the bedroom, he found Jordan lying on the bed, her head resting on several pillows that she had propped against the headboard. He handed her the cola. She smiled at him as she accepted the bottle.

*That's a Helen of Troy smile. A smile that could launch a thousand ships. A smile that could send an army of men to their doom.*

Her fingers touched his in the exchange, a momentary brushing that ended before it had begun. She lifted the cola to her lips and took a couple of quick sips, then sighed.

"Thank you."

He shrugged. "Yeah, sure."

"This being pregnant is quite an experience," she said. "I've heard other women talk about what it's like, but . . ." Her smile wavered. "I've wanted a child for a long time and I'd almost given up hope. I never thought I'd be going through this without Dan."

She seemed genuinely sincere, but if this child was Devon Markham's . . . If? Did he have any doubts? Yeah, he did. Far too many doubts where Jordan was concerned. His opinion of this woman vacillated practically minute by minute. Right now, he tended to think she just might be the saint that so many people thought she was. Half an hour ago, he'd been convinced she was a cold-hearted murderer.

"You have family and friends," Rick reminded her. "I know that no one can take a husband's place, but you have Ryan and Devon Markham who can step in and act as substitute fathers."

"My child will be fortunate to have so many people love him or her."

She drank more of the cola, quickly emptying half the bottle, then she set the bottle atop a decorative coaster on the nightstand.

"Feeling better?" Rick asked.

"Much." She reached out and took his hand. "You've been very kind to me, Rick. I appreciate your taking such good care of me. I'm not accustomed to being . . . uh, let's just say that usually I'm the caretaker, the one looking after someone else."

"Then it's time somebody looked after you, isn't it, considering you're pregnant and that you recently lost your husband."

She squeezed his hand, then released it. "I'll be all right now, if you want to go."

"I can stay for a while longer, if you'd like."

She patted the side of the bed. "Sit and talk to me. Just for a little while. Talk to me about anything except Dan's death and the investigation. Tell me about yourself. Your family. How you became a Powell agent."

Rick hesitated before sitting down on the bed. Being alone with her, within easy touching distance, might be a really bad idea. After all, she was a beautiful woman and even if her husband wasn't cold in the ground, Rick sensed an attraction between them, on her part as well as his.

"I was in the military for a few years," he told her. "Then I bummed around the world, took odd jobs here and there, and finally settled back in the U.S. An acquaintance mentioned that the Powell Agency was hiring. I filled out an application, went for an interview and now I've been with them for nearly five years."

"Do you like your job?"

"Yeah, I like it well enough. It pays the bills."

"I worked for the Peachtree Agency, a PR firm in Atlanta, before I married Dan. I'd worked for them before and during my marriage to Boyd."

"You gave up your career for the senator?"

"When I agreed to marry Dan, I knew that he would need me at his side in Washington as well as when he came home to Georgia." She stared at Rick. "Are you married?"

"No."

"Ever been married?"

"No."

"Is there someone special—?"

"No. I fly solo. No emotional baggage. I hook up with somebody occasionally. Nothing serious for either of us. It's the way I like my life. Simple and uncomplicated."

"And lonely."

"Being alone and being lonely are two different things," he told her.

"Yes, of course, you're right." She looked down at her hands folded in her lap. "I've seldom been alone and yet I'm often lonely."

Okay, time to leave. He was on the verge of making a fool of himself over this woman. If he stayed much longer, he'd kiss her and that's the last thing either of them needed.

He eased off the bed and stood. "If you think you'll be okay, I guess I'd better head for my room."

She scooted to the edge of the bed. "I'll be fine. I think I'll take a long, relaxing soak in the tub and maybe afterward read for a while."

He walked backward a few feet, making his way to the door. "If you need me . . ."

"I won't. Not tonight."

*Stop staring at her as if she were your favorite dessert.*

Rick smiled. She smiled. He turned and all but ran out of her bedroom.


Dan had come to her after dinner that evening more than three weeks ago and asked to speak to her for a few moments. He'd taken her to his study and closed the door.

"I need you to help me," he'd said.

"Yes, of course. You know I'll do anything you need for me to do."

"Dr. Carroll has diagnosed me with the early stages of Alzheimer's."

Amazed at how calmly he'd told her, she had tried not to burst into tears. He had put his arm around her shoulders. So like Dan to comfort her when he was the one who had been diagnosed with an incurable disease that would take his life away from him by slow, humiliating degrees.

She had been shocked at first, then as the reality of the situation set in, she had been deeply saddened. During their years with Dan, they had been very content. He was a good man who had made a reasonably good husband and his great wealth afforded them a life of true luxury. And he wanted a child, just as they did, something Boyd Brannon had not wanted. Boyd had two children of his own and at forty-five, he hadn't wanted to start a second family. Although they'd been disappointed, they accepted his decision because they believed he was a good man. And they'd had his children to love. But Boyd had proven a great disappointment. He had done something unforgivable. He had committed adultery. They couldn't forgive him for such a grievous sin. He had sworn it was only once. A one-night stand that had meant nothing. But they knew that if a man cheats once, he'll do it again.

She'd had no choice but to kill him. He hadn't deserved to live.

And Dan hadn't deserved to die, but she'd had no choice but to kill him, too. She supposed she could have waited until his disease had progressed, but dealing with the news of Dan's Alzheimer's diagnosis would have added undue stress to their lives and might have affected the pregnancy. She couldn't risk anything happening to the child they had wanted for such a long time.

When she had left him that night, alone in his study, she'd thought for sure she had convinced him that suicide was his only course of action. Oh, she hadn't come right out and suggested that he kill himself. No, she was smarter than that. But she had made subtle references to how a man in his position might want to spare those he loved from going through hell with him, day after day, year after year.

She had gone back to check on him later and found him passed out drunk. Everyone else had been upstairs asleep, so no one had seen her reenter the study. She had sat there, waiting for the right moment, watching Dan as he slept. As soon as he began to stir and mumbled in his sleep, she had slipped on her gloves and picked up the gun from the desk. It had been relatively simple to lift his hand and put the gun in it, then hold his hand in place and raise the gun to his temple. His eyes had opened for just a second before she pressed his index finger down on the trigger.

He had smiled at her.

She hadn't smiled until later, after she had left the

study and knew that she had solved all their problems once again.

Nicole Baxter Powell hung up the phone after a brief conversation with her cousin Claire, then rolled over in bed and snuggled against her husband who had just tonight returned from his trip to England. It had been the first time they'd been apart more than a couple of days since they married last year and she had missed him terribly.

Griff slid his arm under her shoulders and pulled her close as he lowered his head and kissed her. "From the frown on your face, I'd say that was business and not chitchat with Claire."

Nic sighed. "You'd be right."

"What's wrong?"

"You know that Ryan and his sister-in-law Jordan hired Powell's to do a private investigation, to look into the circumstances surrounding Dan Price's death."

"Yes, you explained all of that during one of our daily phone calls. Ryan doesn't believe his brother would commit suicide."

"Well, it seems that Rick, just doing his job, asked Maleah to have Powell's do a thorough background check on Jordan Price and he discovered some info that helped him form a theory about who might have killed Dan Price."

"And this is bad? Having a suspect has upset Claire?"

"It's not having a suspect that has upset her and Ryan, it's who the suspect is that has them both very concerned."

"Well, don't keep me in suspense."

Griff grinned at his wife. His sexy, irresistible smile issued her an invitation she wanted to accept immediately.

"Oh, Griff, the last thing I want to do is talk business on your first night home."

"Then just spit it out. The sooner we deal with the

problem, the sooner you can get down to giving me my welcome home present."

She punched him on the arm. "Did you miss me as much as I missed you?" She planted kisses all over his face.

He grabbed her shoulders and shoved her to arm's length, holding her securely. "Who does Rick think killed Senator Price?"

"His wife."

"Jordan Price?"

"It seems he thinks she might be some kind of black widow because her first husband and a former fiancé and a former boss all died accidentally and she profited monetarily from each death."

"Sounds like a motive to me. What do Claire and Ryan think?"

"They're ready to fire Rick. They're a hundred percent sure of Jordan's innocence. Claire said that Jordan could no more have killed Dan than she could have."

"So call Rick in and send out another agent to replace him."

"But what if Rick's right?"

"If he is, another agent will come to the same conclusion and if that happens, maybe Claire and Ryan will change their minds."

Nic lifted her arms up and around Griff's neck. "I'll call Rick in the morning. Right now, I have something far more important to do."

Griff's smile widened. "And just what would that be, Mrs. Powell?"

She unbelted her robe, slipped it off her shoulders and tossed back the covers. Then she crawled on top of him, naked body on naked body.

"Welcome home, husband."

# Chapter 10

Rick's cell phone rang at five forty-five, waking him from a deep sleep. It took him a full minute to realize where the noise was coming from and to react accordingly. He rolled over, tossed his arm out and grabbed the phone off the nightstand. First he glanced at the time and then the caller ID before answering.

Griff Powell.

Something had to be wrong for his boss to call him this early in the morning.

"Rick Carson here," he said and braced himself for bad news.

"Tell me how the Priceville *Daily Gazette* got hold of the information that Jordan Price has lost one husband to suicide and another husband, a fiancé, and a former boss to accidents, and even a father to a supposed heart attack."

Holy shit! "I have no idea," Rick said as his mind tried frantically to assimilate this news.

"I just got off the phone with Ryan Price. It seems the *Daily Gazette*'s publisher is an acquaintance and the man had the decency to forewarn Ryan what today's front page headline would be. Want to take a guess what it says?"

Rick reacted by immediately going into defensive mode. "I did not leak any information to the press."

"I didn't think you did," Griff told him. "Who, other than Mrs. Price and Ryan, did you talk to about Jordan's past?"

Crap! He'd told Lt. Haley McLain. But why would she go to the press with the info? What possible reason would she have to betray his confidence? Maybe it wasn't Haley. But who else could it have been?

"I spoke to a member of the Dade County sheriff's department and asked her opinion about how she interpreted the info about Jordan Price's past. I needed someone outside of Powell's I could trust to use as a sounding board."

"Maybe you trusted the wrong person," Griff said. "Find out and report back to me. But first, tell Mrs. Price what's happened. It will be better if she hears it from you. If she believes that you are the source of the leak, I'll have no choice but to replace you. Ryan is spitting mad and ready to fire you, but I assured him that the *Daily Gazette* did not get their info from you."

"Did he believe you?"

"He's keeping an open mind for the time being."

"I'll call you when I have something to report."

"You have to know that once this information runs in the local newspaper, the media will bombard Jordan. I suggest securing Price Manor immediately. Get in touch with local law enforcement ASAP. Maleah and Holt will arrive by noon today. If you find that you need more agents, I can have half a dozen there by tomorrow."

Conversation over. The End.

Rick flung off the covers, got up, and went straight to the bathroom. He shaved with his electric razor, something he did only when he was pressed for time, took a three-minute shower, and dressed hurriedly.

No matter whether Haley leaked the news or someone else did, the end results would be the same. All hell was about to break loose. Jordan Price would be caught in the middle of some nasty accusations. And it was his fault.

Someone called her name. Her eyelids flickered as she tried to wake. Suddenly bright sunlight poured into her room and even with her eyes partially closed, she realized someone had opened the blinds.

"What's wrong?" she asked, still half-asleep.

"Wake up, Jordan." Devon approached the bed.

As she sat up, the covers dropped to her waist, revealing the top of her blue silk pajamas. She looked at Devon and gasped. The expression on his face told her that something terrible had happened.

"Take a look at this." He handed her a folded newspaper. "It's unbelievable that anyone could be so vicious."

Jordan took the newspaper, unfolded it, and looked at the front page.

The headline read: IS JORDAN PRICE A BLACK WIDOW?

Her entire body went numb. Even though Devon was talking to her, all she heard was the roar of her own heartbeat. She scanned the article quickly. Her past tragedies were laid out like a blueprint of murder and mayhem despite the fact that not one accusation had been made against her. But if she were John Q. Public, she would read this article and believe that the woman who had lost almost every important man in her life and had profited from each death was probably a cold-blooded murderer.

"How did this happen?" she asked. "Who would have given this information to the *Daily Gazette*?"

"It had to have been Rick Carson," Devon told her. "He's the one who had the Powell Agency dig up all your ancient history. And he's the one who suspects you and I killed Dan. Who else could it have been?"

Rick Carson? No, she refused to believe that he would deliberately hurt her this way. And it was apparent that whoever had leaked this info intended to harm her.

*Get real, Jordan. You hardly know Rick. You have no idea what he's capable of doing.*

But he had been so caring last night, so gentle and considerate. She had sensed the goodness in him. Had it all been an act? Had there been an ulterior motive behind his kindness? Had he hoped she would trust him enough to confess her sins?

"I don't think Mr. Carson would betray a client," Jordan said, trying to convince herself as well as Devon. "He has to know that if he did such a thing, he would lose his job."

Devon nodded. "Yeah, okay, that makes sense. But if not Mr. Carson, then who? No one in the family and certainly none of your close friends would ever go to the press with such a ludicrous story."

"Did you read the article?" Jordan asked. "It's not a ludicrous story. From what I read, it simply states the facts as they are and leaves the rest up to the reader's imagination. Only the headline implies that I murdered both of my husbands and my fiancé."

"Oh, God, Jordan, this is bad. Really bad."

"Don't fall apart on me," she told him. "Not now."

Her poor, sweet Devon. So sensitive, so highly emotional, so easily hurt. Losing Dan had nearly destroyed him. As his best friend, she always tried to protect him, but sometimes it just wasn't possible. Now, with this new development, how was she going to keep the vultures at bay and protect not only Devon, but herself and her unborn child?

She threw back the covers, got out of bed, and hugged Devon. He clung to her, doing his best to offer her his support while he drew strength from her.

A loud rapping noise gained their immediate attention and both turned just as the door opened. Rick Carson stood in the doorway glaring at them. Devon tried to pull away from her, but Jordan slipped her arm around his waist. She had nothing to hide, nothing to be ashamed of, certainly not her relationship with Devon.

"Please, come in," Jordan said.

Rick entered the room and closed the door behind him. He glanced at the newspaper lying on the bed. "You've seen it."

"Yes," Jordan said. "I take it that you know all about the front page article. A rather damning headline, don't you think?"

"I haven't seen the newspaper." Rick crossed the room, reached out, and picked up the Priceville *Daily Gazette*. He cringed when he read the headline. "Son of a bitch," he murmured under his breath.

"If you hadn't seen this morning's paper, then how did you know about the article?" Devon asked.

"My boss, Griffin Powell, telephoned me. It seems that the publisher of the *Daily Gazette* contacted Ryan earlier this morning to warn him about the article, and Ryan called Griff."

Jordan looked him square in the eye, hoping that she could tell if he was lying to her. "I'm going to be as brutally honest in asking you a pointed question as you were with me a couple of days ago."

He nodded.

"Did you leak the information about my past to the press?"

"No, I did not."

She released a breath she didn't even know she'd been holding and then swallowed the lump of tension in her throat. Heaven help her if she was wrong, but she believed him. "It's only a matter of time before the phones will start ringing off the hook and the media swarms the house. We have to do something—"

"It's being done," Rick said. "I've ordered the gates at the front entrance to be closed and no one allowed onto the private drive without permission from either you or me. I've put in a call to Sheriff Corbett. We'll need some deputies to keep order at the gate. Two more Powell agents will arrive by noon today. And I woke your assistant and told her what's happening so she can take care of the phone calls."

"I need to see Ryan and Claire." Jordan pulled away from Devon and took a tentative step toward Rick. "I have to explain that—"

"Ryan is ready to fire me because he thinks I leaked the information. Your brother-in-law seems to have complete faith in you, so you shouldn't be concerned about what he and his wife might think. Apparently, they're a hundred percent on your side."

Of course, she should have known that she could count on Ryan and Claire's support. Over the past three years during her marriage to Dan, they had learned to trust one another. They had become as dear to her as the other members of her adopted family.

"Oh, mercy! Darlene and Roselynne will both go ballistic and worry themselves sick about me. And when this information spreads to the state and then national news media, Kendra and Wes will have to deal with their classmates' taunts about their stepmother."

"Try to stay as calm as you can." Rick came toward her, but stopped short of touching her. "Your getting upset isn't good for you or your baby."

"Don't you think I know that?"

"Yes, of course you do." Rick looked at Devon. "Why don't you gather the family downstairs in the parlor so we can tell everyone at once about what's happened and how we're going to handle the situation. Do you think you can do that for Jordan?"

Devon's misty eyes widened as if uncertain how to react to Rick's request. He glanced at Jordan before replying. "If that's what Jordan wants me to do."

"Yes, please," she replied.

"I need you to trust that I can and will handle things," Rick told her. "But in order for me to do some damage control and keep you safe and away from the press, I have to ask that you allow me to be in complete charge, to make the decisions and issue the orders."

"I'm not sure that's such a good idea," Devon said. "After all, how do we know for sure that you're not the one who leaked this information about Jordan to the *Daily Gazette*?"

With her gaze glued to Rick, Jordan placed her hand on Devon's arm. "It's all right, Devon. I trust Rick." She pivoted and smiled at Devon. "Round up the herd and corral them in the parlor. I'll be down shortly."

Hesitantly, Devon nodded, returned her smile, and headed for the door. He gave Rick an if-you-hurt-her-you'll-answer-to-me glower.

Once alone in her bedroom with Rick, Jordan suddenly realized that she was standing there in front of him wearing nothing but her silk pajamas. She shifted uncomfortably on her bare feet.

"I—I need to get dressed," she said.

"Do you really trust me?" he asked.

She breathed deeply, steadying her nerves, and then answered. "Yes, I do." Oddly enough, she really did trust him. She felt certain that Rick had not leaked the info about her past and she had no qualms about him being in charge. "I trust you enough to put myself in your capable hands."

"Thank you. I'll do my best not to let you down."

"I . . . uh . . . should put on some clothes," she told him.

They stood facing each other for a full minute before Rick broke eye contact and said, "I'll just let myself out and wait for you in the hall. Take your time. I'll make sure no one bothers you."

"Thank you."

Why was it that she felt as if Rick truly could protect her from everything and everyone? Something deeply primitive and totally feminine urged her to run into his arms.

Instead of acting on impulse, she said, "I won't be long," as she rushed into her dressing room.

Ryan and Claire arrived at Price Manor shortly after Rick escorted Jordan downstairs to alert her family of the upcoming media frenzy that would soon consume Jordan and everyone associated with her. Sheriff Corbett arrived at Price Manor before nine, accompanied by Lt. Haley McLain and two male deputies, Wilson and Burgess. The deputies were posted at the closed gates at the end of the long drive where news crews from area newspapers and television stations had begun congregating by seven that morning.

Steve Corbett spoke to Jordan and then to Ryan, reassuring both of them that, as sheriff, he would see to it that his deputies took care of crowd control, .

"And we'll cooperate with the Powell agents," Corbett told Ryan. "We can coordinate this any way y'all want us to."

While the sheriff continued his conversation with the Price family, Rick went over to Haley and as inconspicuously as possible, grabbed her arm and dragged her out into the hall. She huffed and glared, but didn't utter a word of protest until they were alone.

"What's the manhandling all about?" she demanded.

He released her. "Want to tell me how the Priceville *Daily Gazette* got hold of the information about Jordan's past?"

Taking a defensive stance, she glared at him. "If you're implying what I think you are, then—"

"I'm not implying anything. I'm point blank asking you if you contacted someone at the *Daily Gazette* and gave them the information I shared with you last night."

"Why would I leak the information? What possible reason would I have to do such a thing?"

"You think Daniel Price was murdered," Rick said. "And after what I told you last night, you're probably convinced that Jordan killed him."

"Like you're not."

Ignoring her comeback, he outright accused her. "You leaked the info in the hope you could get the case reopened and the senator's death ruled a homicide. Am I right?"

"Yes, you're right about my wanting the case reopened, but you're wrong about my betraying your confidence and deliberately leaking info about Mrs. Price."

Rick didn't believe her. Logic dictated his certainty that she was the guilty party. "If you didn't do it, then who did?"

She relaxed a little, lowering the protective barrier she had erected between them. "I have no idea. Maybe someone overheard us talking last night at the restaurant. Or maybe someone at the Powell Agency—"

"It was not a Powell agent."

"Then I don't know."

"If I find out that you're lying to me—"

"You'll do what, big man?" With her protective barrier in place again, Haley shot him an eat-dirt-and-die glare. "I've told you I wasn't the one who leaked the info. You can believe me or not. Your choice." Without a backward glance, she whirled around and went into the parlor.

Usually, his gut instincts were pretty accurate, but lately they seemed to be off. Way off. He should believe Haley. She was a law enforcement officer, someone sworn to protect and defend. He had no reason not to trust her. On the other hand, Jordan Price's background all but proclaimed her to be a killer, a woman who had murdered at least four men. So why was it that his instincts told him that Haley was lying and that Jordan was innocent?

When Rene informed Jordan that Jane Anne Price had been one of the numerous callers who had left a message for her to get in touch, Jordan excused herself from the parlor where she'd been trapped since early morning. The entire family was here, except for her stepchildren, and she had begun to feel smothered with so much loving support. Although she dreaded speaking to Dan's ex-wife, she found that she would gladly use any excuse to get away from the inter-family chaos the news headlines had created. When she shut the study door behind her, she leaned back and closed her eyes, wishing she could blot out the nightmare her life had become as easily as she shut out the light. She was tempted to lock the door. But what was the use? If anyone wanted her, they would knock until she let them in. There was no privacy in this house, no privacy in her life.

Although she'd had more than enough people hovering around her, each one doing his or her best to comfort her, Jordan realized that the person she had wanted to turn to for understanding, to lean on for support, had been busy doing his job, doing what needed to be done.

Of course, her desire to seek comfort from Rick wasn't logical. He was little more than a stranger, a man who doubted her innocence, the person others thought might have betrayed her. And yet her feelings were what they were. Maybe it was nothing more than foolishness to want a strong shoulder to lean on, to long for someone to take care of her instead of her carrying the burden alone. She felt as if she'd spent a lifetime looking after everyone else's needs and neglecting her own.

Except for when she was engaged to Robby Joe.

He had been her rock. A strong, gentle, caring man who had loved her as much as she had loved him. Her one true love. Her only love.

Releasing a cleansing breath, Jordan opened her eyes. The plantation blinds that covered the windows were closed, blocking the outdoor light. Her study caught the afternoon sunshine since the back of the house faced southwest. With a frantic rush, she opened one set of blinds after another, flooding the room with the light and heat.

If only she hadn't lost Robby Joe . . .

But she had. He was dead and buried. Lost to her forever.

Boyd Brannon had been a decent man and she had cared for him, but neither he nor she had gone into their marriage expecting grand passion. He'd been a widower more than fifteen years her senior, with two young children he was raising on his own. They had met when his company had hired the Peachtree Agency as their PR firm. Their relationship began as friendship and in all honesty that's what it had remained, even after they married. He had wanted a mother for his children, a congenial companion, and a wife who would be an asset to an ambitious executive. Looking back, she realized she shouldn't have married him, but she had thought she could find fulfillment in motherhood. At first Boyd had suggested they wait to have a child of their own, but after a year of postponements, she had confronted him.

"I'm sorry, Jordan, but I don't want another child. Why can't you be satisfied with helping me raise Wes and Kendra? They've grown to love you like a mother."

Boyd's decision for them not to have a child had broken her heart, but she had accepted the hand she'd been dealt and tried to make her marriage work. Even when she had discovered he'd been unfaithful to her, she hadn't left him because of the devastating effect it would have had on Wesley and Kendra.

When Boyd was killed in a senseless hunting accident, she had mourned the loss of the children's father, but not the loss of her husband.

Jordan sat down at her desk. She couldn't use the landline because Rene had been forced to disconnect the phone. The calls had poured in, one after another, keeping the phone ringing off the hook all morning.

She slipped her hand into her pocket, pulled out her cell phone and laid it atop the desk. She had turned it off, per Rick's instructions, earlier today.

*Call Jane Anne and get it over with.*

There was no way she could leave Price Manor today or tomorrow or possibly even the day after to meet Jane Anne. She would be followed everywhere she went, her every move scrutinized.

She wondered if Dan had ever loved Jane Anne, even in the beginning of their marriage? Maybe she'd been a different person then, a better person, or at least Dan must have thought so or he wouldn't have married her. In a way, Jordan supposed she understood why Jane Anne had been so bitter about the divorce, why she had reacted as she had. But if she had loved Dan, truly loved him, she would have forgiven him and accepted the truth without seeking revenge. Even now, twelve years later and with Dan dead, Jane Anne posed a threat to his good name, his unblemished record, his part of the Price family legacy, and to the future of the child Jordan carried.

She turned on her cell phone and the moment it picked up a signal, she dialed Jane Anne's number.

"It's about time you returned my call." Jane Anne laughed. "But I suppose you've been busy trying to convince everyone that you really aren't a black widow who has killed two husbands."

"Is that why you called, to ask me if I killed Dan?"

"Hell no. I don't give a damn if you killed him. The son of a bitch deserved what he got, don't you agree?"

"No, I don't agree, but then I loved Dan and apparently you never did."

"Jesus! You're such a liar."

"I assume your reason for calling has to do with the arrangement we made for us to meet," Jordan said. "I'm afraid that will be impossible right now. I'm virtually trapped here at Price Manor. I need a few more days, maybe a week—"

"You can't get out, but I can get in. All you have to do is add my name to the Please Admit list and I can come to you."

"I don't have the amount we agreed on here at the house."

"That's all right. I'll take a check."

"Do you think that's wise?"

"Look, you can't talk me out of this," Jane Anne said. "I want my money and the sooner the better. I'm doing you a favor taking a down payment instead of demanding the entire million up front. Now more than ever, you certainly don't want me telling the world about your arrangement with Dan, do you?"

"You know I don't."

"Then see to it that I can get past the front gates this afternoon and have my check ready."

"Please, can't this wait a few days?"

"Each day you delay means the price goes up. In a few days, I may want two million. Or maybe I'll just contact Devon and see if—"

"Leave Devon alone!"

Jane Anne's self-satisfied laughter angered Jordan. The woman was deriving pleasure from taunting her.

"So protective. Like a mother hen. You'd do just about anything for Devon, wouldn't you? You must love him a great deal."

"Be here at five. Go to the back gate. You know where it is. I'll meet you there and let you in."

"You don't want anyone to see me, do you? That's fine by me. I'm willing to stay completely in the background as long as I get my money."

"You'll get it. I promise."

Rick hadn't gotten a chance to talk privately with Jordan again and it was probably better that he hadn't. Whenever he had glanced her way during this long, exhausting day, she had looked at him with an expression of longing in her cool blue-gray eyes. He'd told himself that it was his imagination, that he'd seen what he wanted to see. He wanted her to need him, wanted her to depend on him, and he wanted to be her champion. God knew she didn't have anyone else, not really. Yeah, sure, she had a bunch of people smothering her with attention, but their actions simply masked their own need for Jordan to soothe their worries. Except for Ryan and Claire, the rest of them depended on Jordan for either financial or emotional support or for both. But who could Jordan depend on?

*At the end of the day, maybe she turns to Devon Markham. Maybe he holds her in his arms and comforts her. Maybe he tells her that he'll take care of her.*

*Maybe, but not likely.*

Rick sensed that, whatever their relationship might be, Jordan and Devon were not equals. She was the stronger of the two by far, and a woman such as Jordan needed a man who was her counterpart in every way.

What was there about her that made a guy go all goofy in the head? He had to question his own common sense. He knew damn well there was a definite possibility she was a ruthless killer, and yet he couldn't control some gut-level need to take care of her.

Right this minute, his first impulse was to look for her, just to check on her and see how she was holding up. With Maleah and Holt here at Price Manor, he had been able to relinquish some of his duties to them, but that didn't mean he had time to search for Jordan. He had spent part of his day working with Rene Burke to formulate a game plan, one they had already set in motion. Rene had cleared the press release with Jordan, a simple statement from Ryan Price saying emphatically that he had complete confidence in his sister-in-law and supported her without question.

What Rick really needed about now was some fresh air. Dinner this evening was bound to be a three-ring circus. He hated the thought of watching Jordan try to force down food she didn't want simply to keep others from worrying about her. He'd speak to her before dinner and suggest she request her meal be sent to her room.

A long walk around the grounds should help him let off some pent-up steam and clear his head. He was torn between wanting to take Jordan away from all this madness, to keep her safe, and simply walking away before she enticed him even deeper into the quagmire her life had become.

He went out onto the side porch and walked to the back of the house. The sun rested low in the western sky, a yellow-orange globe of brilliant springtime light and warmth. The country air was crisp and clean, the scent of flowering trees, shrubs and flowers in the air. As he gazed out over the grounds, he caught a glimpse of someone entering an archway of trees that led to one of the two ponds on the property. The lone figure moved quickly, almost running. A woman. Small and slender. Wearing brown slacks and a beige sweater. Jordan?

Rick decided to follow her. If it was Jordan, and he was pretty sure it was, where the hell was she going? Could it be that she, like he, needed some time alone and had decided to take a brisk walk in the fresh air? He'd follow, but keep a discreet distance behind her.

As he drew closer, he was able to see that it was Jordan and she was carrying something in her hand, something that looked like a rectangular piece of paper or maybe an envelope. When she walked past the pond and straight toward the vine-covered fence at the back of the estate, Rick watched from behind a large oak tree, making sure she remained unaware of his presence.

She went directly to the electronic gates, ones that were kept locked at all times and required a security code to open. The gates faced an old dirt road that hadn't been used in years. The back entrance from that road to Price Manor had long ago become overgrown with grass and weeds, leaving only scattered patches of gravel from the unpaved drive.

Jordan pushed aside the vines that partially covered the security pad and punched in the code. Rick crept closer, quietly and carefully. He slid behind another tree, a towering poplar. After opening the gate, Jordan stood there as if she was waiting for someone. What the hell was going on?

Although it couldn't have been more than three or four minutes, it seemed much longer before he heard a car approach the back entrance to the estate. From his vantage point, he saw a small red sports car pull to a stop, then a petite brunette in jeans and boots, with large sunshades hiding her eyes, met Jordan at the gate. He was too far away to understand their conversation, hearing only the hum of their voices. They didn't talk long before Jordan handed the other woman the envelope she'd been clutching. When she shoved her sunglasses up and onto her head, Rick recognized the woman—Jane Anne Price, the senator's ex-wife.

She opened the envelope and removed its contents, then smiled. From the best he could tell from this distance, the first Mrs. Price held a check in her hand.

Shit! Was Jordan paying off her husband's ex-wife? Blackmail? Just what did wife number one know that wife number two wanted kept secret?

The women talked for a couple more minutes, and then Jordan turned and walked away. Jane Anne opened the small shoulder bag she carried, dropped the check inside, and snapped the purse closed.

Rick had every intention of confronting Jordan. If she was being blackmailed, she should have come to him and let him handle things. But maybe she couldn't. Maybe the information the first Mrs. Price had implicated Jordan in the senator's murder.


Jane Anne smiled. The hundred thousand in her purse was only the first payment. There would be much more to come. She wouldn't be greedy. A million was enough—for now. Later on, when she needed it, she could ask for a little more. After all, Jordan would soon come into a sizeable fortune, even if she had to share part of Dan's wealth with Ryan and Devon. And apparently Jordan was smart enough to know she wasn't bluffing about revealing all of Dan's ugly little secrets to the world, so she was willing to pay for her silence.

No need hanging around here now that she'd gotten what she came for. Only a handful of people knew about the old dirt road behind the Price property or that there was a back entrance to the estate. All she had to do was close the gates behind her and they locked automatically. Of course, she could easily get back in anytime she wanted because she remembered the code from when she'd been married to Dan. His mother's date of birth. There would have been no reason for him to change it.

Just as she approached the gate, someone called her name. She looked over her shoulder, but didn't see anybody.

The wind ruffled through the nearby trees, a barely noticeable caress. One squirrel scurried through the underbrush while another swung out of a high tree branch and onto another.

"Who's there?" she asked.

No reply, the only sounds the soft whisper of the wind and the gentle heartbeat of the woods.

She shoved the partially open gate wide enough for her to get through. Once again someone called her name.

Her heart stopped for a millisecond. Whirling around she thought she'd catch the person taunting her, but she still didn't see anyone. "I know somebody's there. What do you want?"

Silence.

One thing that Jane Anne knew for sure—the voice had been feminine.

"Leave me the hell alone," she called, then ran through the open gates and toward her Porsche. She wasn't going to hang around while someone played silly mind games with her.

Just as she grasped the driver's side door handle, someone came up behind her. Before she could turn and face her stalker, the person wrapped a silk scarf around her neck and quickly tightened it. Jane Anne clutched at the scarf, but her attacker rammed a knee between her legs and toppled her to the ground. She tried to fight off the madwoman, but she settled on top of Jane Anne, using the weight of her body to hold her down.

"You're a threat to us. You have to die."

Jane Anne felt the scarf tightening around her neck cutting off her air. Desperate to breathe, she struggled to loosen the scarf, inadvertently scratching her neck with her own fingernails.

*I won't let you do this. I won't let you kill me. I won't!*

*    *    *

Jane Anne might be petite, but she was a fighter. She struggled against the scarf tightening around her neck, clawing at her own skin in an effort to survive. Fresh blood oozed from the scratches her hot pink acrylic nails had made.

You aren't going to win this fight. In a few minutes, you will realize that you're going to die and there's nothing you can do to save yourself. You made a mistake thinking you could blackmail us. I watched you smiling, so self-satisfied and smug, after Jordan gave you the check. You were probably thinking about all the ways you were going to spend our money and how often you would come back to us for more.

I hate you, you stupid bitch! I hate you for creating more problems for Jordan. I will not allow you or anyone else to hurt her. I've always protected her and I always will.

Jordan might be willing to pay you for your silence now and in the future, but killing you is a much simpler and more satisfying way to deal with the situation. Doing things my way means you'll never bother us again.

She drew the scarf tighter and tighter, her anger fueling her strength.

Die, bitch, die!

*Help me, dear God, please. Let me live. I promise that I'll give back the money. I'll leave Jordan alone and never bother her again.*

The woman strangling her seemed to possess superhuman strength. The harder Jane Anne struggled to free herself, the more furious her attacker became. As the woman pressed her lower body harder against Jane Anne, affectively trapping her on the ground and all but immobilizing her, her rage increased with every passing second.

Jane Anne gasped, fighting for every breath, but there was no air. She couldn't breathe. Oh, God, she couldn't breathe! *No, please . . . please . . .*

Giving one final convulsive gulp, she realized she was dying.


Jane Anne went limp as the life drained from her body. Even when she felt fairly certain that the woman was dead, she squeezed the scarf tighter and tighter until there was no doubt in her mind that the greedy, conniving bitch was truly dead.

She rose slowly to her feet and stared down at her handiwork. Her victim's face and neck were dark red, congested with blood. Her eyes were wide open, staring heavenward. Too bad she would never actually see heaven. Women like Jane Anne always went to hell. Her mouth gaped wide open from her desperate, futile attempts to draw air into her lungs.

She smiled to herself as she wiped her sweaty palms off on the front of her slacks.

Mission accomplished.

Well, almost. She needed to get rid of the body as quickly as possible.

Hmm . . . What to do? What to do?

She snapped her fingers.

There was a pond not far from the back gate. She eyed the woman's body, surveying her from head to toe. Jane Anne probably didn't weigh more than a hundred pounds; surely, she could manage to drag the corpse from here to the pond.

She leaned down, grabbed Jane Anne's ankles and tugged. Dead weight. She sighed. Put your back into it, she told herself. She tried again and managed to get a stronger hold on the ankles. After glancing around to make sure there was no one nearby, she pulled Jane Anne along the ground, over the gravel, through the open gates, and onto the grass.

Once she dumped the body into the pond, she would go back to the house as quickly and quietly as possible. She couldn't let anyone see her.

But what about Jane Anne's car? If she left it where it was, wouldn't someone see it? Maybe not today, since the back gate was never used and rarely did anyone venture out this far, but eventually the car would be found.

Just leave it. Don't risk getting caught trying to move it.

Winded, her arms and back aching from the effort it had taken to bring Jane Anne to the pond, she released her ankles, stood up straight, and breathed deeply. She didn't want to go into the water and chance getting her clothes wet. If anyone saw her before she could change, what explanation could she give them? Instead of dragging the body into the pond, she lifted her foot and nudged it; then gradually, one shove after another, she managed to ease Jane Anne into the pond.

Suddenly she heard someone humming.

Searching in every direction, she didn't see anyone, but the soft humming grew louder. After giving the body one final push into the water, she hurried away, running in the opposite direction.

Halfway back to the house, she paused to catch her breath. No one had seen her. She knew how to cover her tracks, figuratively speaking. She'd done it many times before, hadn't she? Even though she hadn't been able to make Dan's ex-wife's death look like an accident, no one would ever suspect her of the woman's murder.

And Jordan had an alibi, didn't she? She was with Rick Carson.

# Chapter 11

Rick found Jordan in her study, but she wasn't alone. She and Devon huddled together, his arm around her shoulders, her hand on his arm. They were whispering, so Rick couldn't hear what they were saying, but he surmised from the worried expressions on their faces that they were discussing Jordan's recent transaction with the senator's ex-wife. Whatever damaging information Jane Anne Price was using to blackmail Jordan, it was no secret to Devon Markham.

As if sensing his presence, Jordan glanced around Devon's shoulder and her gaze collided with Rick's. She lifted her hand from Devon's arm and pushed him gently to the side.

"Yes, Rick, what is it?" she asked.

"We need to talk," Rick said.

"All right, but can it wait?"

"No, it can't."

Her eyes widened. "Oh. All right. Come in and tell me what's wrong."

"I prefer to speak to you in private."

She glanced from Rick to Devon. "Would you mind?" she asked Devon.

"Are you sure?" Devon glowered at Rick.

Okay, so the guy didn't like him. No big deal. He wasn't fond of him either.

"I'm sure," Jordan said.

When Devon walked past Rick, he all but snarled at him. Rick shut the door. "He doesn't like me."

"He doesn't trust you."

"Do you?"

"Are you asking if I trust you?"

"Yeah, that's what I'm asking."

"I want to. There is no reason why I shouldn't, is there?"

Rick grunted. "Let's admit the truth. You don't know if you can trust me and I don't know if I can trust you."

She came across the room toward him, her movements like liquid silk, flowing smoothly and gracefully. She paused and smiled at him. His stomach muscles tightened. She laid her hand on his arm just above his wrist. His groin tightened.

Son of a bitch!

He eyed her small, slender hand, so soft and white against the sleeve of his brown jacket.

"What's this all about?" she asked. "Is there something I don't know about, something else that's happened?"

When he covered her hand with his, she clamped her fingers around his wrist.

"I want to be on your side," he told her. "I want to help you, but if we don't trust each other, that's going to be difficult."

"Tell me that you believe me when I say that I didn't kill Dan, that I've never killed anyone."

*Tell her what she wants to hear. Lie to her if you have to.* "I want to believe you, but when you do something like you did this afternoon, I have to wonder if I'd be a fool to believe you."

"What are you talking about? What did I—?"

"I followed you and saw you meeting with Jane Anne Price."

"Oh." She yanked her hand off his arm.

"You gave her a check, didn't you?"

"Yes."

"Is she blackmailing you?"

Jordan looked away, deliberately averted her gaze. "Yes."

He reached out and cradled her chin in the curve between his thumb and forefinger. "Look at me."

She lifted her head and stared right at him.

"How much did you pay her?"

"A hundred thousand," Jordan admitted. "It was a down payment. She wants a million."

Rick let out a long, low whistle. "She must know something awfully damn important. What the hell is worth a million bucks to keep secret?"

"My husband's reputation."

"Care to explain?"

"No, I can't. I . . . Oh, God, Rick, please, let it go. Don't keep digging. If you do, you're not going to discover that I killed Dan or Boyd or Robby Joe. But you could inadvertently pique someone's curiosity and if someone else found out . . . Please, for my sake, confine your investigation strictly to trying to discover whether or not Dan committed suicide."

"What are you so afraid of?" He grasped her by the shoulders. She looked up at him pleadingly. "Damn it, Jordan, you have to know that you're going to be crucified in the press. The kind of information they have about you is a reporter's wet dream. If what Jane Anne Price knows could make matters worse—"

"What she knows could hurt so many people, including my baby. Can't you understand that I had to pay her off?"

"Do you honestly believe that once you've paid her a

million that will be the end of it? A blackmailer always comes back for more. Whatever you pay them, it's never enough."

"Oh, Rick, what am I going to do?"

When he pulled her into his arms, she went into his embrace not just willingly, but eagerly. He stroked her back, trying to comfort her. "Does anyone else, other than you and Devon, know what Jane Anne knows?"

"Yes." She rested her head on his chest.

"Then she's not your only problem, is she?"

"No one else would ever—"

"Who knows?"

"Only a handful of people closest to Dan and me. Devon, of course, and Ryan and Claire."

"Anyone else?"

Before she could reply, a woman's screams, followed by shouting and the rumble of footsteps, echoed through the house. Jordan lifted her head from his chest. The study door flew open. Darlene gasped when she saw Jordan in Rick's arms.

Jordan lifted her head and pulled away from him. "What is it? What's happened?"

"That was Tammy screaming," Darlene said, her gaze jerking back and forth from Jordan to Rick. "She says there's a dead body in the south pond."

"What?" Jordan gasped.

"She's hysterical. She came running into the house screaming like a banshee. J.C. has gone with one of those Powell agents, that Mr. Keinan, to see if there really is a body in the pond and Roselynne is trying to calm Tammy."

Jordan looked at Rick. "You don't think—?"

He shook his head. "Stay here. I'll catch up with Holt and J.C. and find out what's going on."

She grabbed his arm, stood on tiptoe and whispered in his ear. "Please, don't say anything to anyone about what you saw earlier."

*Don't think it,* he told himself, but couldn't stop the thought from forming in his mind. What if there really was a body in the pond? And what if it was Jane Anne Price? If the check Jordan gave her was found on her . . .

There was a body in the pond, lying half in and half out of the water. After looking over the scene and discovering obvious signs that the body had been dragged from near the back gates to the pond, they agreed that the woman probably hadn't drowned. Without turning her over, Rick couldn't be a hundred percent positive that it was Jane Anne Price, but she was the same petite size, had the same dark hair, and her clothes were identical to those the senator's ex-wife had been wearing. They'd seen a small, leather shoulder bag by the gates. And the red sports car was still parked on the gravel drive. So, he was ninety-nine percent sure of the woman's identity.

Holt and J.C. stayed at the scene while Rick walked back to the house. On the way, he telephoned the sheriff first, and then he put in a call to Griffin Powell.

"Did Ryan Price fire you?" Griff asked when he answered the phone.

"No, I'm still on the job. And it looks like we'll need those extra Powell agents down here ASAP."

"What's happened?"

Rick filled Griff in on the situation, explaining about Jordan paying the former Mrs. Price blackmail money and it was a good possibility that Jordan's check was in Jane Anne's purse.

"You followed Jordan back to the house after her meeting, right, and there's no chance she could have doubled back and killed Jane Anne?"

"Yes, that's right."

"Then you're Jordan's alibi."

"It would seem that I am," Rick agreed.

"The police are going to be all over her once they find the check, and even if you can swear she wasn't out of your sight long enough to have killed Jane Anne, she'll still look guilty. They could accuse her of hiring someone to do the job or that she's in partnership with someone, like Devon Markham. They killed Dan Price and then they killed Jane Anne, only Markham did the actual deed."

"She's going to need a good lawyer."

"Yes, she is."

"Will you contact Cam Hendrix?"

"You're taking a lot on yourself," Griff told him. "Don't you think you'd better see what the lady wants to do before we—?"

"She needs someone to look out for her and that's what I'm trying to do. It's part of my job, right?"

"It's not like you to get personally involved with a client."

"I'm not getting— Okay, so maybe I am, but I swear, Griff, if not for bad luck, she wouldn't have any luck at all. She didn't kill Jane Anne Price, and I'm beginning to believe that she didn't kill her husband or anyone else for that matter."

"I'll call Cam," Griff said. "If Jordan gives you the okay, I'll do what I can to get Cam to drive over from Chattanooga right away."

"Thanks. And send at least half a dozen agents down here tomorrow. We're going to need them."

With his calls made, Rick picked up his pace on his walk back to the house. Jordan was standing on the back porch and when she saw him, she came running. Breathing hard and slightly winded, she stopped and looked at him, her eyes filled with questions.

"Is it—?"

"It's Jane Anne," Rick said.

"Oh, God."

He watched helplessly as Jordan struggled to maintain control. She clenched her jaw tightly.

"Holt and J.C. stayed at the scene to make sure nothing is disturbed. I called Sheriff Corbett. He's calling one of the guards at the front gate to go directly to the scene and he'll be here himself, along with the coroner within the hour."

"What happened to her? Could you tell how she died? Did she drown?" Jordan grabbed his arms.

Rick pulled her hands off his arms, brought them together, and held them as he looked into her eyes. "I want you to take a few deep breaths and get hold of yourself completely. Do it now."

She did as he requested, all the while never breaking eye contact.

"Good girl. Now, listen to me. I know you didn't kill her. I'm your alibi. But once they find your check in her purse—"

Jordan gasped. "Oh, dear God!"

He grabbed her shoulders and shook her gently. "It's going to be all right, but you have to prepare yourself for a few really rough days. The sheriff will have no choice but to question you and even if he goes easy on you, it still won't be pleasant. He's going to want to know why you gave Jane Anne Price a check for a hundred grand."

"I'll think of some reason, something believable. Maybe it was a loan or maybe—"

He shook her again. "How about telling him the truth?"

She stared at Rick as if he should have known telling the truth was out of the question.

"You're going to need a topnotch lawyer. And I don't mean Wallace McGee Airport. I mean a criminal defense lawyer."

"I'm sure Ryan will know of someone suitable."

"You know who Camden Hendrix is, don't you?"

She nodded.

"He's home-based in Chattanooga and is certified to practice in Tennessee, Georgia, Kentucky and Alabama. He's a personal friend of Griffin Powell's. Just say the word and—"

"Yes."

Rick released a relieved breath. "I'll talk to Ryan and see if he can't persuade his good buddy the sheriff not to officially question you until tomorrow morning. We'll use your being pregnant as a legit excuse to postpone things."

"People are going to think I killed Jane Anne, aren't they?"

"Some people will, just as some people think you killed Dan and possibly those other men, too."

"But you don't believe I killed any of them, do you?"

She looked at him as if his answer was the most important thing in the world to her, as if she would live or die depending on his response.

"Don't do this to yourself, honey," Rick said. "You're getting all worked up and it's not good for you or the baby."

"You—you think I'm capable of murder." Her voice quavered.

He shook his head. "No. No, I don't."

She shivered.

"You're cold." He slipped his arm around her shoulders. "We need to get you inside so you can sit down and rest."

"The others are going to want to know what happened. We'll need to get Dr. Carroll out here to sedate Tammy. And Darlene will need consoling. She'll be worried sick about me. And Devon!"

Rick tightened his hold on her shoulders as they walked toward the back porch. "You're going into your study and staying there. I'll have Vadonna bring you some hot tea and I will deal with everyone else, including Devon."

"I can't ask you to—"

"You didn't ask," he told her. "Once I get you situated in your study, I intend to stay with you and block the door while I call Ryan and then Griff. If anyone tries to get to you, they'll have to go through me first."

Jordan sat in her favorite chair in her study, her feet propped on the matching ottoman. A half-empty teacup rested on a floral coaster on the tea table to her right. Sitting at her desk, Rick talked softly to someone on his cell phone. She closed her eyes and sighed.

It hadn't been easy to relinquish control to someone else, but Rick all but forced her to let him take care of everything. She didn't know what he'd said or done, but no one had entered her study since Rick brought her in here. She had heard rumblings outside the door, but apparently no one had been brave enough to go against Rick's orders.

Her head throbbed with the tension created from stress. The day had started off with a bang and steadily gotten worse, ending with the horror of Jane Anne's body being found in the pond. She hadn't killed Dan's ex-wife, but even Rick swearing he knew her whereabouts when Jane Anne was killed wouldn't stop people from speculating about her. That alone was bad enough, but what worried Jordan far more was knowing that someone who had access to the estate grounds was the murderer. With the gates locked and guarded, it was highly unlikely that someone had breached the security. If no one had entered the estate unseen, that narrowed the list of possible suspects to those who were still here at the time of Jane Anne's death.

Claire and Ryan had gone home. Sheriff Corbett and Lt. McLain had been gone for quite some time. Other than Rick and the two Powell agents, that left only members of her family, which included Tobias and Vadonna. She simply couldn't believe that any one of them had killed Jane Anne.

Devon was a gentle soul, violence of any kind abhorrent to him. Rene would kill in self-defense, but for no other reason. J.C. was capable of just about anything, but what possible motive could he have had to kill Jane Anne? Tammy was mentally unstable and was prone to hissy fits, but Jordan refused to believe she was capable of murder. Roselynne would kill to protect those she loved and Darlene was incapable of cold-blooded murder.

A sudden wave of nausea hit Jordan from out of the blue. *Not now, please, not now. The last thing she needed to deal with was a bout of vomiting.*

She wasn't aware that she had made a sound, but undoubtedly she had moaned because Rick paused in his private telephone conversation to ask her if she was all right.

She started to say that she was okay except for being a little sick at her stomach, but before she could say anything, a piercing pain sliced through her lower body.

Oh, God, no!

She clutched her belly.

Not the baby.

"Jordan, what's wrong?" Rick asked, then spoke to the person on the other end of the line. "Look, I'll have to call you back later. Just get the ball rolling."

"Rick. Rick!"

"I'm here," he told her as he ran across the room. "What is it? Are you sick?"

"Yes, but . . . but I'm cramping. Oh, Rick, I think something's wrong with my baby."

# Chapter 12

When Jordan woke, she remembered very little after Rick had lifted her into his arms and carried her to the car. She vaguely recalled everyone talking all at once, their voices blending into one gigantic cry of concern. What had begun as mild nausea had quickly progressed into severe abdominal pain and culminated with vaginal bleeding. Rick had wasted no time with calling an ambulance or trying to soothe anyone else's concerns. He probably broke the speed limit by twenty or thirty miles per hour getting her to the hospital. Apparently she'd lost consciousness soon thereafter because she remembered nothing else, except . . .

The feel of Rick holding her hand. And the sound of his voice telling her that she was going to be all right.

When she opened her eyes fully, she glanced around the sterile room and realized she was at the small clinic/hospital in downtown Priceville. The room was semi-dark, illuminated only by the light from the hallway and the security lights shining through the slats in the closed window blinds. Darlene sat in a chair beside the bed, her head bowed, her eyes closed.

*She's praying. Praying for me and my baby.*

*My baby!*

Jordan's soft moan interrupted Darlene's prayer and brought Devon, who had been standing in the corner of the room, to Jordan's side.

Flanked by Darlene and Devon, she glanced from one to the other, but in the darkness she couldn't see their expressions clearly.

"The baby?" she asked.

Darlene sniffled and turned away.

Devon took Jordan's hand. "There was nothing they could do. You miscarried in the emergency room only minutes after you arrived here."

"No, no . . ." Jordan jerked her hand out of Devon's and turned over, burying her face in the pillow. This wasn't real. It couldn't be.

Devon rubbed her back. "I can't bear to see you like this. Please, Jordan, please . . ."

"Leave her alone," Darlene said. "She needs time to grieve."

"Why did this have to happen?" Devon's voice trembled. "Why did—?"

"Come on, let's go get some coffee and leave Jordan alone so she can rest," Darlene told him, and then touched Jordan's shoulder. "Sweetheart, we won't go far. We'll be back shortly."

She didn't reply. She couldn't. Emotional pain radiated through her, cutting her heart to ribbons. Knowing that her child was gone, lost to her forever, she felt horribly empty and so very alone. If Dan was alive, he would know what to do, what to say. He'd had such a way with words, always saying just the right thing. That was one of the things that had made him such a good politician.

"Oh, Dan, I wish you were here to help us . . ."

Losing track of time as she mourned the loss of her
child, she hadn't been aware that someone had entered
her room, not until he reached out and brushed the damp
tendrils of her hair off her cheek. Although his touch was
soft and gentle, his fingertips were rough. Not Devon's
hand, not his manicured fingernails.

"Rick?"

"Yeah, it's me."

"I lost my baby."

"I know. I'm sorry."

Without lifting her head from the pillow or turning to
look at him, she reached for his hand that lay on her
shoulder. He threaded his fingers through hers.

"Is there anything I can do for you?" he asked.

"No, there's nothing to be done now." She had lost the
child that she had waited a lifetime to have, a child who
would have been greatly loved.

"The nurse said you could probably go home tomorrow afternoon."

"Hmm . . ."

"The entire bunch has been here," he told her. "They've
taken turns looking in on you. I think everyone has gone
home except Devon and Darlene."

"How is Devon?"

"I'm not sure."

"Would you take them home . . . please?" She turned
over and looked up at Rick. "But first I need to see Devon
again."

"Are you sure you want to be alone tonight? Devon
could stay or I—"

"No, there's no need for anyone to stay. They'll keep
me doped up so I should be able to sleep. I just need to
say good night to Devon."

"I'll get him."

A few minutes later, Devon stood in the doorway and
waited for her to motion to him. When she did, he came

over and sat down on the bed; then he took both of her hands in his and kissed her knuckles. "I'm so sorry. It's not fair. We lost Dan. We shouldn't have lost the baby, too."

Teardrops fell from his big blue eyes and spattered across their clasped hands. When he put his head down on her chest, she forked her fingers through his dark hair and petted him as a mother would comfort a child. "Hush, now. Hush."

"I had imagined what the baby would look like." Devon told her. "I thought it was a girl and I knew she'd look just like you, only she'd have my dark hair and blue eyes. Dan would have loved her. He'd have spoiled her. All of us would have spoiled her."

She soothed him with her touch, hating to see him suffering so. "I thought our baby would be a boy. Dan would have loved having a son, and if he'd looked just like you, nothing would have made Dan happier."

Rick didn't make a habit of eavesdropping and the only reason he had overheard Jordan and Devon's conversation was because Devon had only partially closed the door. In a way, he wished he hadn't heard a damn thing. But he couldn't forget what he'd heard—Devon Markham had fathered Jordan's baby and apparently Daniel Price had known.

Something was screwy about this whole thing. It didn't make sense. But there had to be some kind of logical explanation. A top secret explanation? Apparently Jane Anne Price had known the secret, and possessing that knowledge had gotten her killed.

While Rick's mind whirled with unanswered questions and tried to form scenarios that solved the puzzle, Devon came out of Jordan's room.

"There's no need to tell her that Darlene is going to

stay here tonight, just in case she needs her," Devon said. "Jordan will probably be asleep before Darlene comes back from the snack bar."

"Whatever you think is best."

"If Jordan didn't insist that I go home, I'd stay." Devon glanced at Rick. "Even now, after all she's endured, she's thinking of me."

"Yeah, she is."

As they walked down the corridor toward the elevator, Devon asked, "You don't like me, do you, Mr. Carson?"

"I figured the feeling was mutual," Rick replied.

"We're very different types of men, aren't we?"

Rick punched the elevator's DOWN button. "I've got nothing against your type—fancy dressing pretty boys who get manicures and pedicures and know more about choosing a good wine than they do about sports and cars. I don't like you because I dislike men who have affairs with other men's wives and I can't stand to see a man lean on a woman when he should be taking care of her, not the other way around."

The elevator doors opened. Rick entered first, then Devon. Rick hit the GROUND LEVEL button.

"I don't like you because you actually think that Jordan is capable of murder," Devon said. "You aren't very perceptive about people, are you? You've misjudged Jordan terribly. And as for me . . ." Devon laughed. "You're half right about me, the part about my getting manicures and pedicures and knowing more about good wine than sports. And you're right about my leaning on Jordan. We've been friends since we were kids and she's always taken care of me. Don't let her looks fool you. Beneath that small, fragile façade, she's a strong, powerful lioness. She takes care of those she loves."

The elevator hit the ground level; the doors opened. Devon exited first, then Rick.

As they made their way to the parking lot, Rick asked, "So I've misjudged Jordan, but got you pegged, is that right?"

"Would you believe me if I told you that, although Jordan and I love each other and have loved each other since we were seven years old, we didn't have an affair?"

Rick unlocked the Jeep and waited until they were both seated inside before he responded. "Answer one question for me."

"All right."

In the semi-darkness, Rick looked at Devon and asked, "Were you the father of Jordan's baby?"

Dead silence.

"No."

"You're lying," Rick said.

"There are things you don't know, things you wouldn't understand. Jordan and I have never been lovers."

"Whatever the big secret is, it's only a matter of time before I find out. Secrets, no matter how well hidden or deeply buried have a way of coming out sooner or later."

"You're right, but it's not my place to . . . Only Jordan has the right to tell you."

"Whether you believe me or not, I really am on her side. I don't want her to be hurt any more than she already has been." Rick started the engine and backed out of the parking place.

"If you mean that, then believe in her and help her. She's beginning to trust you. Don't betray that trust."

Keeping his gaze fixed on the dark road ahead, Rick didn't continue their conversation. A strained silence developed between them. But oddly enough, Rick believed what Devon had told him—that he and Jordan had never been lovers.

Their baby's sweet little soul was in heaven now. Gone to be with the Lord. Perhaps it would also be with Dan and with Robby Joe and others in the family who had gone on before them. She knew for sure that that tiny, innocent spirit would never be alone or feel sorrow the way they did.

Jordan's heart was broken. Her heart was broken. But in time they would both heal. They would go on, as they had done time and time again. Together. And someday their lives would come full circle, back to the beginning. He was waiting for them, waiting for them to be reunited.

She sat in the darkness, alone and sad, wishing she could rewind time and bring back their baby. Devon had thought it would be a girl, but they had known it was a boy.

How many times had she dreamed of him, had almost been able to feel him in her arms? He would have been the center of their universe. They would have loved him, nurtured him, and protected him at all costs.

*God took away the baby to punish you.*

She jerked upright.

Who said that?

I did.

Her heartbeat accelerated. "Where are you?" she asked aloud.

*I'm inside you. I'm your conscience.*

She breathed a deep sigh of relief.

Oh, is that all? Hush up then. Go away and leave me alone.

She plumped the pillow behind her head and pulled the blanket up to her neck.

*God took the baby to punish you for killing all those people. You didn't think you'd get away with all those murders, did you? You had to know that eventually you'd have to pay for your many crimes.*

I said hush up. That's nonsense. The Lord knows that I've never killed anyone who didn't deserve to die.

*What about Dan? Did he deserve to die?*

No, maybe not, but the Lord had issued him a death sentence. All I did was send him to his Maker a little ahead of time. But the others deserved what they got. They would have hurt us. I couldn't allow that to happen.

*Perhaps you're right. I didn't like Jane Anne Price. She wasn't a nice woman. I'm glad you killed her.*

*She shouldn't have tried to blackmail Jordan.*

No, she shouldn't have. But I took care of her. She won't ever bother us again.

Ryan phoned Rick at eight the next morning and asked him to come to his house. "Steve's on his way here. He needs to question Jordan about Jane Anne's murder, but he's willing to speak to you now and wait to talk to Jordan after she gets out of the hospital."

Claire met Rick at the front door and took him straight to Ryan's home office. She knocked on the closed door.

"Yes, come in," Ryan said.

Claire offered Rick a token smile. "Go on in. He didn't sleep more than a couple of hours last night after we left the hospital. We're both very concerned about Jordan."

"It'll take time for her to get over losing her baby," Rick said.

"That child meant so much to her . . . to all of us really."

When Rick entered the office, Ryan rose from the brown leather chair-and-a-half near the double windows. He placed his nearly empty coffee mug on the side table and held out his hand to Rick. The two exchanged a cordial shake.

"Come on in and sit down. I expect Steve in the next fifteen or twenty minutes."

Rick took the brown-and-green plaid wing chair opposite Ryan's chair. "We need to persuade the sheriff to postpone talking to Jordan as long as possible. She's nowhere near ready for an interrogation."

"I agree, but he's doing me a personal favor not questioning her while she's still in the hospital."

"There's nothing Jordan can tell him that I can't. We were together when—"

"Can you tell him why Jordan gave Jane Anne a check for a hundred thousand dollars?"

Shit! He shouldn't be surprised that they'd found Jordan's check in Jane Anne's purse. "Jane Anne was blackmailing her."

"Damn that woman! I figured as much when Steve told me about the check."

"You know why she was blackmailing Jordan, don't you?"

Ryan's gaze darted about nervously before settling on Rick. "She knew things about Dan, about his marriage to Jordan, that could have ruined Dan's reputation."

"Did she know that Dan didn't father Jordan's baby and that Devon Markham did?"

Ryan's facial muscles tightened. "How did you find out? Did Jordan tell you?"

"Then it's true?"

Ryan nodded. "It's true. My brother was sterile, something he found out during his marriage to Jane Anne. But he very much wanted a child and so did Jordan. Naturally, Devon was the obvious choice for the biological father."

"Jordan was artificially inseminated?" Rick asked, a few of the puzzle pieces falling into place.

"Yes, of course."

"And Devon was the obvious choice because he and Jordan had been best friends since they were children."

"Yes, there was that, but also because of Dan and Devon's relationship."

Click, click, click. The rest of the puzzle pieces fell into place.

"Your brother was gay," Rick said, astonished that it had taken him this long to figure out the obvious. "He and Devon were . . ."

"Secret lovers, secret partners. That's why he ended his marriage to Jane Anne. He gave her a generous divorce settlement to buy her silence."

"And who else knows the truth about your brother and Devon?"

"Only immediate family."

"Who knew Jordan's child wasn't Dan's?"

"Claire and I, Jordan, Devon, Dan, and Jordan's doctor."

"No one else?"

"Not that I know of. Those who knew about Devon and Dan were told that Dan was the biological father, that it was his sperm that was used to impregnate Jordan."

"Son of a bitch! Why the hell did Jordan marry a man she knew was gay?"

"I think that's a question only Jordan should answer," Ryan said.

"Why didn't y'all tell me the truth to start with?"

"We should have, I know. But we've guarded Dan's secret for such a long time that it became second nature to do so. And we had hoped that it wouldn't be necessary to share the information with you or anyone else. The more people who know, the more likely it is to become public knowledge."

"The senator's dead. What difference would it make now?"

"Dan's reputation meant more to him than anything. More even than his love for Devon. He could have gone public and lived openly with Devon, but he was afraid of what might happen. He doubted the good people of Georgia would re-elect him to the senate if the truth came out and he'd have had no chance of running for the presidency. After Dan died, we all wanted to protect what he held dear. And with Jordan pregnant . . . Think what the truth about Jordan's baby's paternity might have done to the child."

A light rap on the door quieted Ryan and silenced Rick.

"Ryan, Steve's here. He's waiting in the living room," Claire called through the closed door.

"Thanks, honey. Ask him to come on back."

"He doesn't know?" Rick asked.

"Good God, no!"

A couple of minutes later, Claire opened the door, smiled lovingly at her husband, and stepped aside to allow the sheriff to enter. "Would you like for me to bring in a fresh pot of coffee?" She eyed the silver coffee pot on Ryan's desk.

"Not now, thank you," Ryan told her. "Come on in, Steve."

Corbett, dressed in brown slacks and a tan sport coat, held his hat in his hand. "I hate like the devil to cause your family more grief, but I've got to do my job."

"I understand," Ryan said. "I'd appreciate it if you could wait a day or two before questioning Jordan, considering she just lost her baby."

"I sure wish I could do that, but I can't," Corbett said.

"Why not?" Rick asked.

"I guess Ryan told you about the check we found in Jane Anne Price's purse."

Rick nodded. "I'm sure Mrs. Price has a simple explanation for the check."

"Sure hope so," Corbett said. "And I sure hope she can explain why the scarf tied around Jane Anne's neck, the scarf the coroner is pretty sure was used to strangle her, belongs to Jordan."

# Chapter 13

"It's a damn shame that the sheriff's wasting his time looking at Jordan for Jane Anne Price's murder when we all know she didn't do it," Roselynne said, then popped the last bite of buttered biscuit into her bright red mouth.

Tammy watched as her mother washed down the biscuit with her liberally sweetened coffee. Her mother was a beautiful woman despite being nearly sixty. She was slightly overweight, but her skin was flawless, her hair silky blonde, and her makeup and clothes impeccable. Of course, Roselynne's style was perhaps a bit too flamboyant for most women, but it suited her exuberant personality. Oh, how she wished she was half as attractive as her mother. It wasn't fair that J.C. had inherited their parents' good looks while she was the ugly duckling in the family.

"Somebody's sure got it in for our Jordan," J.C. said.

"What do you mean?" Roselynne asked.

"Well, somebody gave the *Daily Gazette* the information about Boyd and Robby Joe and Mr. Farris and Daddy Wayne. And my bet is that same somebody killed Dan's ex-wife and deliberately used Jordan's scarf to strangle the bitch."

"Now who on earth would hate our Jordan enough to try to frame her for a murder?" Roselynne asked, a totally baffled expression on her face.

"I agree with your mother," Darlene said. "Everyone loves Jordan and I can't imagine anyone trying to implicate her in a murder. Perhaps the scarf that was used to kill Jane Anne Price wasn't Jordan's and instead simply a scarf just like Jordan's."

"Don't y'all think it's odd that the information about the scarf was released to the press," Tammy said. "Now everyone who read the morning paper knows about it."

J.C. snorted. "For once you're right, Miss Straw-for-brains. You'd think the sheriff's department would have kept that tidbit under wraps."

Tammy both loved and hated her brother. Although he often was unmercifully cruel in the way he kidded her about her nervous condition—such as calling her Miss Straw-for-brains—he was equally nice to her some of the time. He would buy her little presents: a new music CD, a pretty sweater, a pair of earrings, her favorite candy. And when they'd been children, before Mama had married Daddy Wayne and she'd had to work nights, J.C. had taken care of Tammy. He'd fixed her meals and helped her with her homework and if she had a nightmare, he had sat beside her bed until she'd gone back to sleep.

"I hope Jordan isn't putting her trust in the wrong person." Darlene folded her linen napkin and placed it to the side of her plate. "Although I admit that Mr. Carson seems to be a good man and he's been genuinely concerned about Jordan, we don't really know him."

"He isn't one of us," J.C. said. "Not part of the family. Of course, that could be a plus for him. By now, Jordan's got to be damn sick and tired of the whole lot of us."

"Don't talk nonsense." As she pushed back her chair and stood, Darlene gave J.C. a belittling glare. "We are Jordan's family and she loves us as we love her. However, you have, no doubt, tried her patience almost beyond endurance and embarrassed her with your vulgarity and crudeness."

"You're not family, not the way we are." J.C. smiled that cocky, devilish grin that meant he was up to no good. "You're not Jordan's mother. Hell, you're not even her stepmother. You're just some pitiful old woman Jordan feels sorry for."

"J.C., you apologize to Darlene right this minute," Roselynne said.

"No need to waste your breath," Darlene told him. "Your hateful words mean absolutely nothing to me nor would your apology."

Tammy didn't especially like Darlene, although the woman had never been unkind to her. Actually, she mostly ignored Tammy, as if she didn't exist. But Darlene despised J.C., probably because he took every possible opportunity to rile her.

There was something sad about Darlene. When she'd mentioned this, her mama had said it was because Darlene had lost her only child and when a mother loses a child, she never quite gets over it.

Did that mean that Jordan would never get over losing her baby?

She wished she could think of something special to do for Jordan. Make her a cake or buy her a present, anything that would show her how much she was loved. And Tammy did love Jordan, who had always been the best sister in the world. Oh, she knew they weren't truly sisters, that they didn't have the same mama and daddy. But Daddy Wayne had been Jordan's real daddy and he had adopted her and J.C., so that meant she and Jordan were sort of real sisters, didn't it?

Jordan did so much for everyone. She supposed the others thought she didn't have sense enough to realize that without Jordan they would be destitute. She'd heard Mama say that to J.C. once when he'd been complaining that Jordan wouldn't lend him a thousand dollars.

"Boy, you'd try the patience of a saint." Their mama had shaken her finger in his face. "It's not enough for you that Jordan puts a roof over our heads, food in our bellies, and clothes on our backs, is it? No, you expect her to pay off your gambling debts. Why, that girl is a saint, I tell you. Without her, we'd be destitute."

Tammy and Mama agreed that there wasn't anything they wouldn't do for Jordan. They owed her more than they'd ever be able to repay.

"When Daddy Wayne died, she could have washed her hands of us," Mama had said. "But she didn't, did she?"

Sometimes she loved hearing J.C. laugh, but other times, like now, when he was laughing at someone, she hated the very sound of it. His laughter followed Darlene as she left the dining room. Holding her head high, she completely ignored J.C.

"That old biddy's got a cob stuck up her ass," J.C. said. "I swear, she's the snootiest old heifer I've ever known."

"I wish you'd learn to keep your mouth shut," Roselynne said. "But you're just like your father. He had a smart mouth, just like you. That man could cut a person to pieces with his sharp tongue. But mind what I tell you, boy, that mouth of yours is going to get you killed one of these days."

J.C. got up, leaned over their mama's chair and kissed her cheek. "But you love me, just like you loved him. And you're glad I got his handsome face and his sweet-talking charm, aren't you?"

Roselynne slapped him on the arm. "Just behave yourself. Jordan's coming home this morning and it's going to be rough enough for her, what with losing the baby and being a suspect in Dan's ex-wife's murder, without your adding to her problems."

"She's a person of interest, Mama, not a suspect," J.C. corrected her. "And you don't have to worry about our Jordan. She's got the Price millions at her disposal. Ryan's brought in half the Powell agency to keep the old homestead locked down. And I overheard Rick Carson and Ryan talking about bringing in Camden Hendrix. That guy's made a fortune defending rich folks like Jordan and getting them off scot-free whether they're innocent or guilty."

"Well, Jordan is most certainly innocent."

"You really think she's not capable of murder?"

"Most certainly not."

J.C. shrugged.

"Don't you be mean to Jordan," Tammy said. "Don't you dare be mean to her."

"Now, look what you've done." Roselynne huffed. "You've gone and upset your sister."

J.C. came over to Tammy and ruffled her hair. She stared up at him. He smiled down at her.

"I won't be mean to Jordan. I promise. So don't you worry, kiddo."

She smiled. "Okay." She liked it when J.C. called her kiddo. "I know you mean it because you've never broken a promise to me. Not ever."

The hordes descended on them the moment they slowed down to wait for the electronic gates to open. They pounded on the SUV's doors, jumped on the hood, and pressed their faces against the windows. All of them were shouting questions, their voices combining to create a horrendous roar like the sound of a monstrous beast. Devon, who was sitting in the backseat with Jordan, wrapped her protectively in his arms.

"My God, they're like a pack of mad dogs," Devon said.

"Hold on," Rick ordered. "I'm going to gun it and get away from them."

Jordan held her breath. The Jeep lurched forward, sending the people hanging onto the SUV flying off onto the ground. Rick barely managed to maneuver his Jeep through the front gates and onto the private drive without running over a reporter.

"The Powell agents at the gate will gather up anyone who came through with us by hanging onto the Jeep," Rick said. "And they'll escort them out."

Devon grasped Jordan's hand. "Don't worry. You're safe."

"Yes, I know. I'm safe for now." She looked at the back of Rick's dark head and broad shoulders. She instinctively knew that as long as she was in Rick's capable hands, she would be all right.

"You like him," Devon whispered in her ear, so softly that she barely heard him.

She squeezed his hand, looked right at him, and nodded.

Rick pulled up at the front of the house, hopped out of the Jeep, and opened the back door. By the time he helped her out and he and Devon escorted her to the veranda, her family poured through the front door. Flanking Jordan, Rick and Devon formed a protective shield between her and the others.

As she looked among smiling, concerned faces and heard murmurs of "welcome home" and "we love you," Jordan's gaze connected with her brother-in-law's. Ryan stood in the open doorway, his somber expression warning her of what was to come.

When she caught a glimpse of Sheriff Corbett standing in the foyer, behind and to Ryan's left, her steps faltered. Rick slid his arm around her waist to steady her. She closed her eyes for half a second and prayed for strength.

"Y'all need to let Jordan get through and into the house," Devon said. "Everyone can talk to her later."

The sea of friendly, loving faces parted, clearing the path to the front door. When they reached the entrance, Devon paused, kissed her cheek and then relinquished his position at her right side.

Once in the foyer, Ryan reached out and took her hands in his. "I'm so sorry about the baby."

Although she prided herself on being able to control her emotions, losing her child had punched holes in her steel armor.

She looked past Ryan and stared at Steve Corbett. Suddenly she noticed that the sheriff was not alone. A deputy, whom she recognized as Lt. Haley McLain, stood at his side.

"Steve's not going to question you until after you've spoken to your lawyer," Ryan said. "And Mr. Hendrix will be with you during the questioning."

"Has Cam gotten here yet?" Rick asked.

"He arrived about ten minutes ago," Ryan replied. "He's waiting in Dan's study."

"Take all the time you need, Mrs. Price," Sheriff Corbett told her.

"Thank you." She glanced around, searching for Tobias. When she caught a glimpse of him near the rear of the foyer, she motioned to him. "Tobias, please see that Sheriff Corbett and Lt. McLain have anything they need. Coffee or tea and sandwiches and cakes. And ask Vadonna to prepare lunch for everyone."

"Yes, Miss Jordan." He looked at her with a combination of sympathy and worry. "Do you need anything? Just tell me and—"

"Thank you, no."

Ryan fell into step alongside Jordan as Rick led her toward Dan's study. Ryan opened the door and entered first.

An attractive, sandy-haired man rose from the sofa and came toward her. He wore a tailor-made, dark blue, pin-striped suit that fit his broad shoulders to perfection. His silver-dotted yellow silk tie lay neatly against his white-and-pale-silver-striped shirt. The man's attire proclaimed him as a person of wealth and good taste. His closed-mouth smile and the cunning sparkle in his light blue eyes attested to his self-confidence.

He held out his hand to her. "Mrs. Price, I'm Camden Hendrix."

Keeping her gaze on his handsome face, she shook his hand. "Thank you for coming, Mr. Hendrix."

"Yes, ma'am. Now, we can speak alone, just the two of us, or your brother-in-law may stay with us, whichever you prefer."

"I prefer to speak to you alone."

Mr. Hendrix glanced from Ryan to Rick. "Gentlemen, if you'll excuse us, please."

She sensed that both Ryan and Rick were reluctant to leave her. But when she walked over and sat down in the chair behind Dan's desk and placed her hands in her lap, Ryan motioned for Rick to follow him. After they closed the door behind them, Mr. Hendrix turned and looked at her.

"You understand that anything you tell me will be—"

"Confidential," Jordan said. "Client-attorney privileged information."

He grinned. "Yes, ma'am. That's correct."

"Am I to assume you think I might be guilty?"

"We're all guilty of something, Mrs. Price. But if you're asking if I believe you killed your husband's ex-wife, then the answer is simple—I don't know. You tell me."

"I didn't kill Jane Anne."

"All right. Let's say I believe you. Tell me why you gave her a check for a hundred thousand dollars."

"She was blackmailing me." She kept her gaze focused on his face. "I thought perhaps you'd already spoken to Rick Carson and knew all of this."

"I asked Rick not to tell me anything."

"I see. Then I need to fill you in on the whys and wherefores, don't I?"

"Right to the point," Cam Hendrix said. "I like that. You and I are going to get along just fine, Mrs. Price."

"Please, call me Jordan."

Twenty minutes later, Cam invited Sheriff Corbett and his deputy into Dan's study and the official interrogation session began.

"First, I need for you to clarify something for me, Sheriff Corbett," Cam said. "Is my client a suspect in the murder of Jane Anne Price?"

Steve Corbett looked downright uncomfortable and after shifting about and heming and hawing, he finally replied, "No, sir, but Mrs. Price is considered a person of interest."

Cam leaned back against the side of the desk, resting his hips leisurely on the edge as he crossed his arms on his chest. The sheriff pulled up a chair and positioned it in front of where Jordan sat behind the desk. Lt. McLain remained stationed by the closed door.

"Did you see Jane Anne Price the day she was murdered?" the sheriff asked.

"Yes."

"When and where?"

"At the gates of the back entrance to the estate. And I believe it was around five o'clock."

"Why were you meeting secretly with—?"

"My husband's former wife was blackmailing me," Jordan said. "I had arranged to pay her a hundred thousand dollars and meet with her away from Price Manor.

But once my home was surrounded by reporters, I arranged to meet with her at the back of the estate. I gave her a check and I returned to the house. When I left her, she was very much alive."

"Why was she blackmailing you?"

There it was, the one question she didn't want to answer. She looked at Cam. He nodded.

"Having been married to Dan, she had certain information about his health that I preferred not to become public knowledge."

"And what was that information?"

Jordan placed her hand over her belly, swallowed hard and said, "Dan and I very much wanted a child, but my husband was sterile, so we agreed to try artificial insemination. Jane Anne knew that Dan was not the biological father of the child I . . ." She curled her hand into a fist and lifted it off her stomach. "I paid her to stop her from revealing this personal information to the world."

"But keeping this information secret certainly wasn't important enough to kill someone to keep them quiet, was it?" Cam injected the comment into the interrogation process.

Sheriff Corbett gave Cam a hard glare, then turned back to Jordan. "The scarf used to strangle Jane Anne Price belonged to you. It has your initials on it and was purchased for you by your late husband at a specialty shop in Priceville."

"The scarf is lavender silk and my initials are in dark purple," Jordan said. "I haven't worn the scarf since this past fall. I kept it in the top drawer of my dresser along with other scarves and several pairs of gloves."

"Then anyone in the house could have taken the scarf," Cam said.

Sheriff Corbett's face turned beet red as he glowered at Cam.

"I think what you're leading up to asking me is if I

killed Jane Anne," Jordan said, "and the answer is no. I met her, gave her a check, and returned to the house. Rick Carson, the Powell agent Ryan and I hired to privately investigate my husband's death, saw the entire transaction. He followed me back to the house and we spoke in my study. We were still together when Jane Anne's body was found."

"I'd say you have all the information you need from my client." Cam unfolded his arms, eased his hips away from the desk and stood. "I believe your next step is to verify what Mrs. Price just told you. I'm sure Rick Carson will corroborate her statement."

"I'm sure he will." Sheriff Corbett frowned, then glanced over his shoulder at his deputy. "Well, there's no easy way to say this, so I'm just going to spit it out—it looks like we're going to be reopening the investigation into the senator's death."

Jordan felt as someone had sucker-punched her.

"Since Mrs. Price and her brother-in-law hired a private firm to investigate Dan Price's death, then I'm sure they welcome this news." Cam gave Jordan a sideways glance, as if checking to make sure she was reacting properly.

"Yes, of course we do." Jordan rose to her feet slowly and rounded the desk to stand beside her attorney. "I assume your department now has reason to believe that my husband did not commit suicide."

"District Attorney Anderman has consulted with the GBI and they're in agreement that there is now reasonable doubt concerning your husband's death. In light of new . . . er . . . uh . . . new information, they believe that further investigation into the senator's death is called for."

"What new information?" Jordan asked, but she knew. Dear God, she knew.

"Mrs. Price, I don't know what to say." Sheriff Corbett shook his head and then rubbed his jaw. "It wasn't my decision and I don't want you or Ryan to think for one minute that I believe any of it. I don't. But . . . considering your past and all, the suspicious deaths of your first husband and your fiancé and—"

"Both deaths were accidents," Jordan said.

"Yes, ma'am, I'm sure they were."

"If you've finished questioning my client, Sheriff Corbett, then may I show you and your deputy out?" Cam Hendrix glanced at Jordan, his gaze silently ordering her to stay put. Then he walked the sheriff to the door and ushered him and Lt. McLain out into the hall.

Jordan stood glued to the spot, her body frozen in place, her emotions numb. *This isn't happening. It can't be. I'm innocent. I didn't murder Dan or Boyd or Robby Joe.*

Cam returned quickly and slammed the door shut.

As she stared at him, shivering inside, the only outward sign of her distress was a slight tremble in her hand.

"One question, Mrs. Price—have you ever killed anyone?"

"No," she croaked the single word, barely managing to get it past her lips.

"I didn't think so. But not everyone is going to believe you, which means that in all likelihood, you're going to be considered guilty until we can prove you're innocent."

# Chapter 14

After Sheriff Corbett questioned Rick about where Jordan was when Jane Anne Price was killed and seemed satisfied with his answers, he excused himself. "I need to speak to Ryan. I want him to know that I didn't have any choice in this matter. I'm just doing my job."

When Rick started to leave the room, Haley called his name. He paused and looked back at her. During the sheriff's questioning, she had stood silently in the corner. He'd caught a glimpse of her in his peripheral vision more than once and each time she had been studying him closely, gauging his reactions.

"Would you stay for a few minutes?" she asked.

He hesitated, then nodded and turned to face her. "What do you want?"

"You still believe that I called someone at the *Daily Gazette* and told them about Jordan Price's past, don't you?"

"I can't figure out who else it could have been," Rick said. "And I know Sheriff Corbett didn't leak the info that the scarf used to kill Jane Anne Price belonged to Jordan. You wanted the investigation into Dan Price's death reopened. Now, you've got what you wanted. The way I look at it, you're the only one who possessed the information and had a reason to leak it to the press."

"Why do you believe her when she tells you she's innocent and yet you won't believe me?"

Rick smirked. If he didn't know better, he'd think Haley was jealous of Jordan. "Who says I believe her?"

"You're backing up her story about your being able to vouch for her whereabouts when Jane Anne Price was strangled and dragged into the pond. You wouldn't do that unless she'd been able to convince you that she's innocent."

"I backed up her story because she was telling the truth," Rick said. "She didn't kill the senator's ex-wife. She couldn't have because she was with me when it happened."

Haley sucked in her cheeks, then huffed loudly. "Okay, so maybe she didn't kill the former Mrs. Price. She could have had someone else do it. Devon Markham or that stepbrother of hers or—"

"Or she could have had nothing to do with it." He examined Haley closely, noting the flare of her nostrils, the color in her cheeks and the way her eyes narrowed to slits. "You want her to be guilty. Why?"

"If you weren't infatuated with her, you'd see the obvious, as almost everyone else does. Damn it, Rick, you can't let her sucker you this way. You're too smart for that. Look at the evidence. You know as well as I do that the odds of a woman losing that many men in her life to so-called accidents are highly unlikely. She killed Dan Price and managed to make it look like suicide. She didn't want to get stuck taking care of a sick husband, or maybe he found out she was fooling around and he was going to divorce her or just possibly she wanted his money, so she—"

"You went to the DA with this theory, didn't you? You pressed him to order the case reopened. And you probably called the boys at the GBI, too. After the article ran in yesterday's paper, it would have been fairly easy to stir things up."

"Okay, so what if I did? I struck while the iron was hot. I did what Sheriff Corbett wouldn't do because he's a friend of the family."

"Yeah, and you did it while Jordan Price was in the hospital miscarrying a baby that meant everything to her."

"My God, would you listen to yourself! She's got you so snowed you don't know which end is up."

"I know that like every other U.S. citizen, Jordan Price is innocent until proven guilty." Rick needed to hit something, but he sure as hell couldn't hit Haley. He'd never struck a woman in his life. And he couldn't ram his fist through the living room wall without breaking his hand. This old house had hard plaster walls that were probably at least a foot thick.

"Just how much proof do you need?" Haley asked.

"A hell of a lot more than you've got. Even if you could prove that Dan Price and the men in Jordan's past were murdered, it doesn't mean she killed them."

"When we dig deeper into her past and unearth more information about those deaths, we'll be able to prove beyond a reasonable doubt that no one other than Jordan had motive and opportunity and—"

"While y'all are doing all that digging, just remember that Powell's will be doing our own digging."

"Oh, I won't forget and I won't forget that you're working for Mrs. Price."

"The Price family wants to learn the truth and that is what we'll be trying to find out. But you're not interested in the truth, are you? You've already tried and convicted Jordan. You and the DA are on a witch hunt."

"I really hoped you were smarter than other men. Smarter than Ryan Price and Sheriff Corbett and Devon Markham and the late senator and all the others Jordan Price has

charmed. But you're as big a fool as the rest of them." She
walked to the door and opened it, then paused and looked
back at him. "Let's just hope you don't regret trusting her
and wind up paying with your life like at least four other
men have."


Haley's words echoed in Rick's head as he stormed out
of the house. Was Haley right? Was he letting Jordan play
him for a fool?

"They're not going to arrest Jordan, are they?"

Only when she spoke did Rick realize he wasn't alone
on the veranda. Rene Burke was standing at the end of the
porch. She took a last drag on her cigarette, crushed the burn-
ing end between her hot pink nails, and flicked the butt
into the yard.

"No," Rick said.

"Things don't look good for her, do they?"

"She's being crucified in the press right now."

"She's tough. She'll survive."

Rick concentrated on Rene's face, scrutinizing her expression, trying to discern what emotions provoked her
comment. "I thought you were her friend."

"I am," Rene said as she walked toward him. "We met
in college, hit it off right away, and after college, when
she helped me get a job at the Peachtree Agency, we became best friends. There's nothing I wouldn't do for her.
What I said about her being a survivor is true. It's one of
her many admirable qualities."

"You knew her first husband, Boyd Brannon, didn't you?"

"Yeah, I knew Boyd and I knew Robby Joe Wright, too.
I've known all the men in Jordan's life." Rene smiled at
him. "Go ahead. Ask me."

"Ask you what?"

"Ask me if I think she killed them."

"Okay. Do you think she killed them?"

"No. Jordan's a caretaker, not a killer."

"You knew Dan Price pretty well, didn't you? Do you think he committed suicide?"

"I suppose it's possible, but Dan never struck me as the type. I'd come closer to believing that he was murdered."

"If that's true and Jordan didn't kill him, then who did?"

"How should I know? Everybody liked Dan."

"Not everybody."

"Almost everybody," she corrected her statement.

"What if someone killed him for Jordan, someone who either knew or suspected the senator had Alzheimer's and wanted to save Jordan from the agony of having to look after a slowly dying husband? Who do you know who would kill for her?"

Rene cocked her head to one side, cut her eyes in his direction and stared up at him. "That's some theory you've concocted, Mr. PI. Point the blame at someone else. Hmm . . . Who do I know who would kill for Jordan? The first person who comes to mind is Devon Markham, but he never would have harmed Dan."

"Anyone other than Markham?"

"Sure, several people. Darlene Wright for one. She all but worships the ground Jordan walks on. And then there's the Harris threesome, Roselynne and her two kids. They'd do anything in the world for Jordan because she's their meal ticket."

"What about her stepchildren?"

"I don't see either of them as a killer, but they're devoted to Jordan, so yeah, I suppose if push came to shove, they'd kill for her."

"And what about you, Rene?"

"What about me?"

"You said yourself that there's nothing you wouldn't do for Jordan. Would you kill for her?"

"Sure I would, if I had to."

* * *

Jordan escaped to her study and locked the door, something she never did. But she desperately wanted a few minutes alone without anyone hovering over her, asking her if she needed anything, if she was all right. No, she was not all right. She had lost her husband and her baby. She was being vilified in the press. They were calling her a black widow. She was also being labeled "a person of interest" in Jane Anne Price's murder. Her brother-in-law had hired one of the most famous criminal lawyers in the South to represent her. She found it difficult to believe how quickly her contented life had spiraled out of control, beginning with Dan's death.

When a woman suffered a miscarriage, she should have her husband at her side, someone to share the grief, to mourn the loss. Right now, she should be lying in her husband's arms, being comforted and consoled by the one other person whose loss was as great as hers.

But even under the best of circumstances, Jordan's life was far from normal and it hadn't been since she was a child of ten.

She sat in the comfortable armchair, leaned her head against the cushioned back and closed her eyes. If she had only herself to consider, she would have the luxury of shutting herself away to mourn for days on end. She could wallow in self-pity. She could let the world pass by until she was once again ready to participate in life.

But she could no more put her own needs first now than she'd been able to when Dan had died. Then she'd had to think of Devon, who had lost the love of his life. And she'd had to think of the child she'd been carrying.

When Boyd had died, she'd had to take care of his children and prepare them for a life without their father. It had been her responsibility to see to it that they not only had a home and the necessities of day-to-day living, but she'd had to think of their futures.

When Robby Joe had died, she had thought she would die, too. She couldn't imagine her life without him. But she hadn't been alone in her grief. Darlene had lost her only child, the son who had been her whole world. She'd been left with no one except Jordan.

Her father's death had changed her life, but not for the better, his legacy the burden of a stepfamily that anyone else would have abandoned to fend for themselves. Rose-lynne had a good heart, but she was lazy and incompetent. Tammy had emotional and mental problems that required medication and counseling, neither of which was cheap. And J.C. was a charming, good old boy who, as Devon so aptly put it, wasn't worth shooting.

*Dear God, give me the strength I need.*

Jordan wasn't sure how long she sat alone in her study without being disturbed. At some point, she had drifted off to sleep and dreamed about her baby. She awoke to the sound of someone calling her name.

"Jordan, are you all right?" Rick called to her through the locked door. "Tobias tells me you've been in there for nearly three hours. Shouldn't you go upstairs and lie down for a while?"

"Rick?" She came awake, groggy and slightly disoriented. "I—I'm okay." She rose from the chair on slightly unsteady legs, her whole body limp with physical and emotional exhaustion. "Please wait. I want to talk to you." She walked slowly across the room and unlocked the door.

After she opened the door, she looked up into a set of dark brown eyes filled with concern.

"You should be in bed," he told her. "You've just been released from the hospital. You shouldn't have had to deal with all this insanity. Not today."

"Come in. Please."

When he entered the study, she closed and locked the door. "The only way I can prevent people from just walking in here to check on me is to lock them out."

"Are you sure you don't want me to leave you alone?"

"No, I want to talk to you, to explain something."

"Whatever it is, can't it wait?"

"Ryan told you about Dan," she said. "That he was gay and he and Devon were lovers."

"Yeah, he told me. It would have made my job a lot simpler if y'all had just explained the situation when you first hired me."

"Those of us who loved Dan are very protective of his reputation and his legacy. The fewer people who know the truth, the safer his secrets are."

"The man's life was a lie and your marriage to him was a lie."

"I suppose in a way, you're right," she said. "But politics being what they are even in this day and age, especially here in Georgia, people are not very open-minded. Dan had to choose between being honest about his personal life and giving up his career or hiding his personal life and maintaining his career."

"So he chose his career over honesty."

"Dan grew up in a family and in an era that didn't approve of homosexuality. He did what he thought was best for himself and his career and for his family."

"And what about you, Jordan—why did you marry a man you knew was gay?" Rick waved his hand in a never-mind gesture. "Forget I asked. It's none of my business."

"No, I want to explain. I want you to try to understand."

When she turned and walked over to the sofa, Rick followed and sat beside her. She faced him, her chin up, her shoulders straight.

"Dan and I made a bargain," Jordan said. "We both got what we wanted from our marriage. He had decided that he wanted to seriously consider his party's plans for him to run for president. He was told that he needed a suitable wife at his side. Devon and I had been friends since we were children and I'd known Dan for years, ever since he and Devon became a couple. Devon knew that I didn't intend to ever marry again and that I certainly had no illusions of ever being in love again, so he and Dan came to me with a proposition."

Rick watched her carefully. She knew he was trying to evaluate her honesty. He wanted to trust her, wanted to believe her, and yet he still had doubts. She couldn't blame him.

"I had a family to support and even though I'd received a handsome insurance settlement when Boyd died, it wasn't nearly enough to raise Wes and Kendra and give them college educations and the start in their careers that they both deserved. And I had the family I'd inherited from my father. My stepmother and stepsister were and still are totally financially dependent on me, and even though J.C. works from time to time, he always needs money."

"Dan Price offered to take care of your family if you married him?"

"Not only that, but he promised me one-third of his estate upon his death, which I assumed wouldn't be for at least twenty or thirty years. I never dreamed . . ."

Rick narrowed his gaze in a hard, pensive stare. "You made a bargain that excluded love and sex from your life. Unless Dan agreed for you to—"

"I could have taken a lover, if I'd chosen, and if I'd been discreet as Dan and Devon were. But I've never met a man who tempted me."

"Did everyone know that you'd inherit a third of Dan's millions?"

"By everyone, you mean—?"

"Family and close friends."

"Yes, I suppose so. What are you thinking?"

"I'm thinking that it's possible someone dependent on you might have killed Dan so you would inherit a third of his estate now instead of sometime in the future."

She shook her head. "No, you're wrong."

"Am I? Someone inside the estate walls murdered Jane Anne. They probably killed her either because they were trying to protect the senator's reputation or because they were protecting you."

"But no one knew about Jane Anne blackmailing me, except Devon. And before you say another word, let me assure you that Devon is incapable of killing another human being."

"Okay, let's rule out Devon. But you said yourself that you have no privacy in this house, which means you have no idea who might have overheard you talking to Devon or even heard you speaking on the phone with Jane Anne."

"You're asking me to agree with you that someone I know and love killed Jane Anne. I can't do that."

"Are you willing to take the blame for a murder you didn't commit?"

"No, of course not."

"By ruling out other possible suspects, that's exactly what you're doing," he said. "Right now, the only reason you're a person of interest in Jane Anne's murder instead of a suspect is the fact I'm your alibi. But that alone won't keep you safe. If they think they can prove that you persuaded someone else to kill her for you—"

"Is that what you believe?" She glared at him, anger and frustration evident in the sound of her voice and the pinched expression on her face.

"All that matters is what the police believe. It doesn't matter what I believe."

"It matters to me."

He saw the truth in her eyes. What he thought did matter to her. But why? For what reason? With Jordan, he couldn't be sure. If she had asked Rene Burke to eliminate Jane Anne, would Rene have done it? And what about J.C.? Rick felt certain that that low-life SOB was capable of just about anything, especially if there was money involved. Had Jordan promised him a sizeable payoff if he did her dirty work for her?

Jordan's breathing quickened. She glared at Rick. "You're not sure, are you? Once again, it all boils down to a matter of trust. You don't trust me."

"I don't know you," he told her. "The real you, the Jordan Price hidden behind that thick protective shell. Inside, you could be anyone."

"Even a murderer, a woman who has killed over and over again."

"We shouldn't be discussing this. Not now. You should be upstairs in bed resting." Rick rose to his feet.

She reached out and grabbed his wrist. He looked down at her as she gazed up at him. "Find out the truth for me. Find out who killed Jane Anne. Find out if Dan was murdered."

"You really mean that?"

"Yes."

"Then there can't be any more secrets between us. From here on out, you need to be totally honest with me about everything. Agreed?"

She hesitated for only a moment, then released his wrist and said, "Agreed."


When she had put on her sweater before going outside yesterday afternoon and following Jordan, she had known she would probably have to kill Jane Anne. The woman had posed a threat that couldn't be ignored. There had been no time to plot and plan, to execute a crime that could have been mistaken for an accident. She hadn't meant to make things worse for them. Her intention had been to rid them of a nuisance. And God knew that when she'd pulled the scarf from her sweater pocket, she'd never thought about it being one she had taken from Jordan's dresser drawer weeks ago. She often borrowed Jordan's things.

Jordan didn't mind. Jordan was generous to a fault. She would have given her anything she wanted.

But her thoughtlessness had gotten Jordan in trouble. Next time she wouldn't make that kind of mistake.

Thank goodness Rick Carson had stepped in to defend Jordan. Perhaps she'd been wrong about him. Maybe he really would turn out to be their friend. She certainly hoped so. They needed a strong, caring man to look after them for the time being and Rick certainly seemed to fill the bill.

And as long as he was good to them . . .

But if he hurt them or betrayed them or posed a threat of any kind, she would take care of him just as she'd taken care of all the others.

# Chapter 15

Rick watched Jordan and Tammy. From the kitchen window, he had a partial view of the porch and the back-yard. He had come in here looking for Vadonna, to ask her to prepare fresh coffee and bring it into Dan Price's study, but the housekeeper was nowhere to be seen. After preparing lunch and cleaning up, she had probably gone to her room to rest. And it wasn't as if he wasn't perfectly capable of preparing the coffee himself. Even if no one else wanted coffee, he figured he and Cam might need a little fortification and hard liquor was out of the question. He didn't look forward to the meetings they had arranged for this afternoon, interviews with members of Jordan's extended family. Ryan and Claire, who had asked to be questioned together, had arrived straight from church and were waiting in the den with Cam.

Darlene Wright had informed him this morning, as if she thought an explanation was necessary, that the family usually attended Sunday church services together.

"Roselynne and I, though we often disagree, were in complete agreement that, considering the circumstances, we should stay at home today. And our dear Jordan really isn't well enough to attend."

He couldn't say he blamed Darlene and the others. Who wanted to hear people whispering behind their backs and or staring at them curiously, even accusatorily?

Feeling somewhat like a voyeur, Rick called himself a fool. He stood there gazing at Jordan as if he had nothing better to do. His interest in her went beyond the fact that she was a client, even beyond the fact that she was a beautiful woman. She fascinated him in a way no other woman ever had. He had seen definite signs of her cool, emotionless control; and yet he'd seen glimpses of her softness and vulnerability. Which was the real Jordan Price? Both? Neither? A combination? He had begun wondering if perhaps there were two Jordans, the gentle, charming woman he wanted to comfort and protect and her evil twin, the cold, unfeeling widow he had seen at the senator's graveside.

Holding Jordan's hand as they strolled toward the house, Tammy was smiling while she listened to whatever Jordan was saying. Tammy laughed, then pulled on Jordan's hand and led her to the glider on the porch. They sat together and continued their conversation.

Jordan Price was an enigma. A puzzle he couldn't quite figure out. It was obvious that she cared about other people, that she was capable of kindness and even sacrifice. And yet there was a coldness about her that seemed in direct contrast to her maternal nature. Not once had he seen her cry. Not at her husband's funeral or afterward and not even when she lost her baby.

"Those two love each other," Roselynne said as she entered the kitchen and came up behind Rick.

He glanced back at her, but said nothing.

"Some people don't have any patience with my Tammy, even me on occasion. And some folks are unkind to her because she's different. But not Jordan. Never Jordan. Not from the very beginning when Wayne brought me and my kids home with him."

"How old was Jordan then?"

"She was only twelve, and it had been less than two years since she lost her mama. She didn't like me much back then, but she didn't take out her feelings for me on Tammy. She rearranged her bedroom to share with Tammy and made Tammy feel welcome. It was like she adopted her for her little sister that first day and it's been like that ever since."

"You really are fond of Jordan, aren't you?"

"I love the girl because she's got a good heart and she's been better to us than we had a right to expect." Roselynne came around and stood at his side, her gaze following his to where Jordan and Tammy glided back and forth as the afternoon breeze tousled their hair.

"She seems to be doing all right, doesn't she? Aren't you concerned about the fact that she hasn't shed a tear since she lost her baby?" Rick asked.

Roselynne sighed, her large breasts rising and falling with the heavy breath. "Jordan doesn't cry. Oh, her eyes might get a bit misty, but that's all. As far as I know, she hasn't shed a tear since Robby Joe. I guess once she got done mourning for him, she didn't have any tears left."

Could the reason be that simple? But what kind of woman doesn't cry when she loses a child she claimed she wanted more than anything?

"I hate to disturb them," Rick said. "But I promised Jordan to let her know when Cam Hendrix and I started our interviews."

"Who's up first?" Roselynne asked.

"Ryan and Claire."

"And Tammy and me, we're after them, right?"

"Yes, unless you prefer to wait."

"No, next is fine with me. I just appreciate your understanding why I want to be with Tammy when y'all question her. She's liable to get upset and if I'm there, I can calm her down."

"We will try not to upset her. We just need to ask her a few questions."

"I see the way you look at Jordan." Roselynne placed her hand on his shoulder. "You could make things worse for her if anyone gets the wrong idea and I don't think you want that to happen."

"You're seeing something that's not there. Mrs. Price is a client. That's all."

"If you say so." She patted his back. "Why don't you let me go tell her that Claire and Ryan are here and save you the trouble?"

"Sure, why don't you do that? And when we finish talking to Ryan and Claire, either I'll find you or I'll have Tobias let you know when we're ready."

Rick waited until Roselynne left the kitchen before he breathed easily. From now on, he'd have to be careful about the way he looked at Jordan. Better yet, he needed to stop looking at her altogether.

After their interview, Cam shook hands with Claire and Ryan, thanking them for their cooperation. They had been open and honest; admitting they both had intensely disliked Jane Anne Price. Although they regretted that she was dead, they were relieved that she wouldn't be able to expose the late senator's well-kept secrets. But not only had they been together at the time of Jane Anne's murder, they had been on their way home and had been seen leaving by the deputies at the front gate.

Cam glanced at Rick where he sat with his feet propped up on the ottoman and a file folder spread out across his lap.

"They're both big fans of Jordan's," Cam said.

"Hmm . . . Who isn't?"

Cam chuckled. "You don't know if the lady is guilty or innocent and it's worrying the crap out of you. Well, join the club. I'm her lawyer and I've got my doubts."

"How could so many people love her if she's a cold-blooded murderer?" Rick asked.

"Serial killers—and that's what a black widow is—can often be charming and deceptively nice. But they're manipulative. They use their charm to captivate before they strike a deadly blow and destroy."

"She didn't kill Jane Anne. That much I know for a fact."

"Then we need to find out who did and if they worked alone or with a partner. But the bottom line is that I've been hired to protect Jordan's rights, not render a judgment concerning her guilt or innocence. You're the investigator. It's your job to uncover the truth."

Rick tapped the file folder. "Jordan isn't the only one who knew all the victims, if all the men in her life were indeed victims. Roselynne, J.C., and Tammy, as well as Darlene, Rene, and Devon knew every man in Jordan's life. Any one of them could have killed Dan or possibly all four men and Jane Anne, too."

"And their motive would have been?"

"Love, jealousy, hate. Take your pick."

"Why don't you find Mrs. Harris and her daughter while I read over the new information you received from Powell's this morning? That way, I'll be better prepared to question them."

"Take special note of the info about Mrs. Harris's first husband." Rick rose to his feet and handed Cam the file folder.

Questioning Roselynne and Tammy went pretty much as Rick had expected, both of them staunchly defending Jordan. Roselynne was relaxed and replied immediately to every question. Tammy was nervous and reluctant. Before responding to each question, she looked at her mother. When Roselynne nodded, Tammy replied. A few times, Roselynne interceded and answered for her daughter.

"I like to take walks. Sometimes Mama comes with me and sometimes Jordan does, but I can go anywhere around here I want to go all by myself, can't I, Mama?" Tammy looked to Roselynne for affirmation.

"That's right. Walking is good exercise and Tammy loves the outdoors."

"And you were taking one of your usual walks when you saw Jane Anne's body in the pond?" Cam asked.

Tammy's eyes widened and glazed over as if she could see the pond and the body in her mind's eye. "I didn't know who it was. I didn't know the woman. But I knew she was dead. Dead just like Dan was."

Roselynne patted Tammy's hand. "It's all right. It's all right."

"Did you see anyone else on your walk?" Rick asked.

Tammy thought for a couple of minutes, and then shook her head.

"She can't tell you anything else." Roselynne glanced from Rick to Cam. "I think she's had enough of this."

"I agree." Rick looked at Tammy. "Thank you, Tammy, for answering our questions. We appreciate it very much."

"Did I help Jordan?" Tammy asked. "I want to help Jordan."

"Yes, you helped Jordan," Rick told her.

Roselynne motioned to her daughter. "Then if y'all are finished with us, we'll—"

"Tammy can go tell Jordan how well she did," Rick said. "And while she's doing that, we have a couple more questions for you, Mrs. Harris."

"Can I, Mama? Can I go tell Jordan how good I did, how much I helped her?"

"Yeah, go on, honey. Go tell Jordan." Roselynne spoke

to her daughter, but her gaze remained on Rick's face. As soon as Tammy left, Roselynne's smile disappeared. "I guess you've dug up some trash on me. I figured it was only a matter of time before you did. I sowed a few wild oats in my younger years and I've messed around with some married men and . . . Whatever you found out about Tammy and J.C. having different daddies, I'd appreciate your keeping that to yourself. They don't know and I don't want them to know."

Rick and Cam exchanged glances, and then Rick said. "The only information that interests us right now is concerning your first husband."

"What does Andy Terry have to do with anything? He's been dead more than twenty-five years."

"How did Mr. Terry die?" Cam asked.

Roselynne's eyes widened as realization dawned. "Andy killed himself. Blew his brains out." Her face went chalk white.

"Just like Senator Price did." Rick scrutinized her reaction.

"Now, you look here. I didn't have nothing to do with Andy's death. We weren't even living together when it happened."

"No one is accusing you of anything, Mrs. Harris," Cam told her. "We simply thought it an odd coincidence."

Roselynne jumped up out of her chair. "Well, that's all it is—a coincidence. I didn't kill Andy and I sure didn't kill Dan. Not no more than Jordan killed him." She stomped across the room, yanked open the door and stormed out into the hall.

"What do you think?" Cam asked.

Rick shrugged. "I think the more people we can cast suspicion on, the better it is for Jordan."

\* \* \*

J.C. Harris was a cocky asshole. Rick wouldn't put anything past him. But the man had an answer for every question and used his mother and sister as alibis for the times of both Dan's death and Jane Anne's murder. He was slick. Maybe just a little too slick.

Devon Markham's hands trembled throughout the entire questioning process and a couple of times his voice quavered and tears trickled down his smooth, pretty boy cheeks. His love for Dan Price and his friendship with and love for Jordan seemed completely genuine. Rick couldn't picture this gentle man killing anyone.

Darlene Wright possessed an air of superiority that rankled Rick, but the lady was cooperative and her devotion to Jordan was obvious.

"I do have a small apartment in town, but whenever Jordan and Dan are at home, I often stay here and I was staying here at Price Manor the weekend when Dan killed himself," Darlene said. "And I'm glad I was. Jordan needed me."

"So, you still believe the senator killed himself?" Rick said.

"Well, I thought so until . . . If Dan was murdered, I can assure you that Jordan did not do it. She's the sweetest, dearest—"

"What about you, Mrs. Wright?" Cam asked. "Would you have killed Senator Price for Jordan's sake? Or what about Jane Anne? You'd do anything to protect Jordan, wouldn't you?"

"Yes, you're quite right. I would do anything for Jordan," Darlene admitted. "But if you're implying that she asked me to kill Dan or his ex-wife, then you're mistaken. Jordan abhors violence, just as I do."

"I have one final question for you," Rick said.

"Yes?"

"Do you believe, without even the slightest doubt, that your son's car accident really was just that—an accident?"

With her hands folded neatly in her lap and her ankles crossed in a ladylike fashion, Darlene Wright looked him directly in the eye. "Yes, I most certainly do."

Later, when they were alone in the study, Cam said, "The only clear picture I'm getting is one that shows Jordan Price in a favorable light. Not even that sleazy stepbrother of hers said a single word against her."

"What did I tell you? They all love her. Her family and friends, the senator's family, even the servants."

"It would appear so. And except for the Harris clan, who conveniently are one another's alibis, no one has an alibi for the time Jane Anne was killed. Any one of them could have done it."

"We still need to talk to Rene Burke," Rick reminded Cam.

Cam checked his wristwatch. "It's after five, so let's wrap things up before six, if possible. I'm driving back to Chattanooga this evening."

Rene cooperated fully, answering their questions quickly and succinctly. She had been asleep when Dan Price either killed himself or was murdered and alone when Jane Anne was strangled. She pointed fingers at everyone else, stating reasons why each might be the murderer.

"Have y'all ever considered the possibility that the person who killed Dan, if he didn't kill himself, isn't the same person who killed his ex-wife?" Rene asked.

"Sure," Rick replied. "We could easily have two murderers on our hands, but if we do, then it's highly likely they're working together. Maybe the cohorts are Rose-lynne and Tammy or Devon and Jordan or even you and either Darlene or J.C."

"You've left out Ryan and Claire."

"They weren't here at Price Manor the night the senator died and they had already left here when Jane Anne was murdered."

"That narrows down your suspects by two, leaving how many—seven? Nine if you count the servants."

"Who do you think killed Jane Anne?" Cam interjected a question into the conversation.

"I have no idea," Rene said.

"Do you think Dan Price killed himself or—?" Rick asked.

"I don't know. You tell me." She fidgeted in her chair. "Look, this is the second time you've asked me these questions. I don't know who killed Dan or his ex-wife. I don't believe Jordan killed either of them. And yes, under the right circumstances, I'd kill for Jordan, but I didn't kill Dan or his ex."

"What about Robby Joe Wright?" Rick leaned over her chair and made direct eye contact.

"Robby Joe?" Rene blinked repeatedly. "What the hell are you talking about?"

"Did you kill Robby Joe Wright?"

"You're nuts. Robby Joe died alone in a one-car accident. He wasn't murdered and most certainly not by me."

"How well did you know Robby Joe?"

"I told you yesterday that I've known all the men in Jordan's life, including her father and Robby Joe."

"You didn't answer my question—how well did you know him?"

She clamped her teeth together and glared at Rick.

"Didn't you know Robby Joe before Jordan met him?" Rick moved out of her face and stepped away from her.

"Yes, I did. I introduced them."

"Were you dating Robby Joe at the time?"

Rene snorted. "You dug pretty deep to get that information, didn't you? Yes, Robby Joe and I dated for several months, but it was never serious. Once he met Jordan, that was it. He fell for her like a ton of bricks."

"Were you in love with Robby Joe?"

Rene hesitated, then swallowed hard and said, "Yes, but he didn't feel the same and I don't think he ever knew how I felt."

"Did Jordan know?"

"No, she didn't. She wouldn't even date him until she cleared it with me. That's the type of person she is. She had no idea how I felt about Robby Joe and I really hope you won't tell her. Not now, after all these years. What would be the point?"

Her father had been a hunter. Once, when she was seven, he had taken her with him on her first hunting trip, disregarding her mama's pleas not to take a little girl with him to kill animals. But she had loved every moment of the experience. She had learned to use a rifle on that trip, experienced the thrill of the hunt and the triumph of the kill. After that, she had often gone duck and quail hunting with her father, as well as deer hunting. Those grand adventures were now treasured memories. If not for those hunting trips, she wouldn't have become an expert marksman.

On that cold November morning seven years ago, she had taken a rifle from the locked case in the basement of their home, dressed warmly in camouflage gear, and followed Boyd. After he had parked his truck and joined a group of friends, she had parked a good distance away, on a dirt lane, just outside the hunting area, and walked into the woods alone.

The memory of that morning came back to her as vividly as if it had happened yesterday, almost as if she were watching the scene unfold at this very moment.

He had made promises that he hadn't kept. They had believed they could be happy with him, that he would give them a child of their own to love. But he had disappointed them time and time again. Boyd Brannon had not been the man they had thought he was. They had overlooked his faults for as long as they could.

His infidelity was the proverbial last straw. An unforgivable sin.

Making the decision to remove him from their life had not been an easy one. After all, they loved his children and Wesley and Kendra had already lost their mother. But in the long run, they, too, would be better off without him.

She adjusted the heavy rifle she carried as she crept softly through the woods. Considering that it was so cold she could see her breath in the frigid air, she was glad she had worn long johns as well as two pairs of socks and a hat that covered her hair. If by any chance someone caught a glimpse of her all bundled up, she doubted they would even realize she was a female.

As the morning wore on and not one hunter had made a kill, she began to worry that Boyd might become discouraged and go home early. But she couldn't strike too soon. She had to wait until the time was right, the moment perfect.

Soon. Very soon.

She spied him, not more than a few yards away.

Her breathing quickened.

Steady. Stay calm. Mustn't miss.

She had only one shot. One chance to do the job right.

It had to look like an accident, a tragic hunting accident. Those things happened all the time. No one to blame. Just a matter of being in the wrong place at the wrong time.

Should it be a shot to the head or the heart? Which would seem more accidental? It probably didn't matter.

She watched closely as he propped his rifle against a tree and unzipped his pants. What was he doing? Good grief, he was relieving himself.

She smiled.

Now was the moment.

Without another thought or a second of hesitation, she brought the rifle up into position, got him in her sights, aimed, and fired. As the bullet zoomed toward its target, she held her breath.

Waiting with eager anticipation.

Wham! The bullet entered Boyd's forehead.

As he dropped to the ground, she felt that unequalled flush of exhilaration achieved only in a moment such as this. The moment of the kill.

# Chapter 16

After breakfast, Griff asked Nic and Sanders to join him in his study. She had wondered just how long it would take Griff to tell her and Sanders the details of his recent trip to England. Knowing her husband as she did, she had not pressed him about the matter. Griffin Powell made his own rules and had lived as he pleased for far too long for anyone to try to change him. Not even his wife. Oddly enough, Nic wouldn't change anything about him, even if she could.

He had been home since Thursday and all he'd said about his visit with Yvette Meng was that when he'd left London, Yvette had been well and had sent her regards.

"She'll be coming for a visit later this year," Griff had added. "And possibly staying quite a long while."

There had been a time, early on in their relationship, when Nic had been jealous of the beautiful Yvette, a rather mysterious and exotic woman from Griff's past. But now, knowing the truth about Griff's past and his unbreakable bond with his assistant Sanders and with Yvette, she understood the threesome's devotion to one another. Nic also understood that there were things about her husband she might never know and was, as he had told her, better off not knowing.

Except at night, when they made love, Griff had all but ignored Nic since his return home. He had been on the phone in his home office for hours on end, day after day, totally absorbed in God only knew what. And even though she didn't want to resent him for not including her in whatever was going on, she did. More than once in the past few days, she had come very close to demanding an explanation. Patience was a virtue she was trying to cultivate.

She and Sanders had spoken briefly about her concerns. "I suspect that he is dealing with something important," Sanders had told her. "He will explain everything to us in his own good time."

She hated the fact that Sanders understood Griff in a way she didn't and probably never would. But confident of her place in Griff's life and in his heart, she had learned to accept the importance of Sanders' and Yvette's relationships with her husband.

Once congregated comfortably in the study, Griff glanced from Nic to Sanders and back to Nic. "I'm sorry that I've been reticent about discussing my recent trip to visit Yvette, but first I had to work through everything in my own mind and set the wheels in motion for a joint project with Yvette."

Sanders remained silent. Nic decided to follow his lead.

"I didn't mean to shut you out." His gaze locked with Nic's. She saw the sincerity of his words reflected in his eyes and also a plea for her understanding. "I was a confirmed bachelor way too long. Be patient with me and in time, I'll do better about sharing things with you."

She smiled. "It will take time for both of us to get used to being married and coming to terms with what that means for each of us."

He returned her smile, then looked at Sanders. "Yvette is going to be sending a young woman to stay with us for a while. She will arrive next week."

"Someone special to Yvette?" Sanders asked.

"Yes, someone she has been working with," Griff replied. "I met her while I was in London. She's an American who has been living in Europe for a number of years."

"May I ask why Yvette is sending her to us if she's undergoing psychiatric treatment with Yvette?" Nic asked.

"What I'm going to tell you goes no further, except you may tell Barbara Jean," Griff said. "For some time now, people who have similar special gifts to those Yvette has have been going to her. At present, she is working with five. Four women and one young man."

"People who claim to be psychic?" Nic asked.

Griff's lips lifted in a tentative, indulgent smile. "You're still my little skeptic, aren't you?"

"I have an open mind, but—"

"I need you to be on board with our plans," Griff said. "Yvette wants to move here to the U.S., to Griffin's Rest. She wants to send Meredith here immediately and put her in charge of the construction of a house and a sort of small office complex."

Nic wasn't sure how she felt about Yvette moving to Griffin's Rest and bringing along a group of strange people. But if doing this was important to Griff . . .

Apparently sensing her reluctance, Griff added, "The building site I've chosen is not near our house and we won't be a part of what Yvette and her—" he paused "—her students will be doing. She simply needs a safe haven to work with these young people and help them." He looked directly at Nic. "Yvette was concerned about your reaction. She told me that she would come here only with your permission."

*Oh, great. Put me in the position of looking like a jealous, heartless shrew if I say no.*

*Don't do this to yourself, Nic. You like Yvette. You respect her. You have no reason to be jealous of her. She is Griff's friend and she has made it clear that she wants to be your friend, too.*

"If you want Yvette here at Griffin's Rest and are okay with her building a home and a school or an office or whatever she wants to call it for people with all kinds of psychic gifts, I have no objections."

"Thanks, Nic."

She took in a deep breath and released it.

No one had ever said being married to Griffin Powell was going to be easy, especially for her.

Nic stood. "If that's it, I have work to do."

"We'll talk more later," Griff said.

"Sure." She made it out the door, down the hall and into the sunroom before she screamed with frustration. "Damn, damn, damn!"

"Are you all right?" a voice asked.

Nic gasped and jumped simultaneously.

"I'm sorry," Barbara Jean said. "I thought you knew I was in here."

Taking a steadying breath, Nic faced one of Powell's many employees. But Barbara Jean was special. Not only did she live here at Griffin's Rest and kept their home office running smoothly, but she was "the" lady in Sanders' life.

"I didn't pay any attention," Nic said. "I just needed a place where I could let off a little steam without sounding an alarm through the whole house."

Barbara Jean, who had been crippled in a car accident years ago, maneuvered her wheelchair up to Nic. "Want to talk?"

"Yvette Meng is going to build a house here at Griffin's Rest and move here, probably permanently."

"Ah, I see."

"Well, I don't. I don't understand why she has to move

here and I don't understand why the idea of it upsets me so."

Barbara Jean reached out and grasped Nic's hand. "Will it make you feel any better if I tell you that I'm jealous of her, too?"

Nic and Barbara Jean exchanged knowing glances, then they burst into laughter.

Barbara Jean squeezed Nic's hand. "She shares a past with them, our men. And there's nothing we can do to change that. But their love for her is no threat to either of us. You know that, don't you?"

"Yes." Nic tapped her head. "In here, I know." She laid her hand over her heart. "It's in here that I'm having a problem."

"Then we'll just have to work on—"

Nic's cell phone rang, interrupting Barbara Jean midsentence.

Nic pulled the phone from her blouse pocket. "Excuse me."

"Sure. Go ahead and take the call. We can talk later if you want to."

"I'll probably need to." Nic flipped open the phone, noted the caller ID and said, "Hi, Rick, what's up?"

"I want to run something past you," he said.

"Shoot." Nic opened the French doors leading to the patio and walked outside.

"I need some information that's going to be tricky to get hold of."

"Info about the Daniel Price case, I assume?"

"Yeah. Actually, it's personal information about Jordan."

"What kind of personal information? I thought we had dug up just about all her old skeletons."

"I need to find out if Jordan has ever been under psychiatric care or if she's ever had a nervous breakdown or suffered any type of mental problem."

"Hmm . . . Interesting. Why do you think she might have—?"

"I don't know. Let's just say that I'm playing a hunch. Since I started working this case, I haven't been able to get a handle on Jordan. It finally hit me that she's like two different women."

"You're not saying you think Jordan Price has multiple personalities, are you?"

"No, no," Rick said. "None of that bullshit. But how normal is it for a woman to not shed a tear when she has a miscarriage and then to carry on as if she's perfectly all right?"

"I don't know, but maybe it's just Jordan's way of dealing with such a devastating loss."

"To my knowledge, she hasn't cried once since she buried Dan Price. The strange thing is that half the time she acts like a normal, caring person, but the other part of the time, it's as if she's little more than a robot."

"Getting access to a person's medical records is difficult," Nic said. "And illegal without their permission."

"So, you're saying—"

"I'm saying that I won't authorize doing anything illegal, but Griff might."

"Before we go that route—into the illegal zone—do you think Claire might know anything about Jordan's mental history?"

"Ah, so that's why you called me and not Griffin." Nic laughed. "Sure, I'll call Claire and see what she knows. Give me a couple of hours and I'll get back to you."

"Nic?"

"Yes?"

"Before you hang up, I thought you should know that I'm going to move out of Price Manor and into The Priceville Inn where the other Powell agents are staying."

"Any special reason you're moving out?"

"Let's just say that I was getting a little too personally involved with the case."

"With Jordan Price?" Nic asked.

"Something like that."

"Want me to pull you off this assignment?"

"No, I need to see this thing through to the end."

"Okay. I'll call Claire and get back to you."

"Thanks, Nic."

Jordan was spending the morning resting, mostly to pacify Darlene and Roselynne, who had been hovering over her as if she were a helpless invalid ever since she came home from the hospital. Darlene had brought her breakfast upstairs on a tray and sat with her until she'd eaten a little of everything on her plate.

"You have to rebuild your strength, dear," Darlene had told her.

Now, half an hour after Jordan had persuaded Darlene to leave her alone, Roselynne and Tammy breezed in. Tammy carried a bouquet of spring flowers, no doubt picked from the gardens here at Price Manor. While Tammy put the flowers in a vase, Roselynne plumped Jordan's pillows and straightened the covers.

"You're looking much better today. You have more color in your cheeks." Roselynne kissed Jordan on the forehead and patted her shoulder. "It'll take time, but you'll get over this." She lowered her voice so that only Jordan could hear. "None of you children ever knew this, but I had a miscarriage only a few months after your daddy and I got married. It broke our hearts."

Jordan hadn't known, had never even suspected that her stepmother had been pregnant. Was that the reason her father had married Roselynne, because she'd been carrying his child? If so, that certainly explained a lot of things.

After placing the bouquet on the nightstand to Jordan's right, Tammy sat down on the side of the bed. "Mama says you're going to be just fine and one day you'll get married again and have us another baby."

"Tammy!" Roselynne scolded.

Tammy's eyes flooded with tears. "What—what did I do wrong?"

Jordan grasped Tammy's hand. "You didn't do anything wrong." She glanced up at her stepmother. "Really, Roselynne, it's all right."

Roselynne shook her head and grunted. "When will I learn to keep my big mouth shut? I was just thinking out loud when I said that about your getting married again. I should know better than to do that around our Tammy."

"Then Mama was right?" Tammy asked. "You will have us another baby someday, won't you? We really were looking forward to having a baby to love. I had started knitting her a little sweater."

Roselynne's brow wrinkled. "Tammy, sweetie, maybe we should go and let Jordan rest now."

Jordan hugged Tammy, who hopped off the bed and, smiling brightly, waltzed out of the room. Roselynne followed, but paused at the door.

"If I could give you what you deserved, I'd pick you out a man worthy of you, somebody who'd love you the way you should be loved. And I'd wish you a good marriage and a bunch of children. Maybe someday."

Before Jordan could even think of a reply, Roselynne left. The last thing on Jordan's mind was remarrying and having children. She had tried marriage twice and both had ended in tragedy. As for a child . . . Her hand automatically went straight to her stomach. Her baby was gone. Devon's baby. Odd how she hadn't really thought of her child as Devon's. She supposed in her heart, she had thought of the child only as hers, even though she would have shared her son or daughter with both Dan and Devon.

She had been so preoccupied with herself and the investigation into Jane Anne's murder that she really hadn't given Devon the support he needed. He, too, had lost a child directly on the heels of losing Dan. Instead of allowing self-pity to overtake her, she should be concentrating on helping Devon.

Absorbed in her thoughts, Jordan barely heard the soft rap on her door.

"Jordan, may I come in?" Rene asked.

"Yes, of course."

Rene cracked the door, peered inside and smiled. "Are you sure?"

Jordan tossed back the covers and slid to the edge of the bed, then motioned to Rene. "Absolutely sure. I'm going crazy cooped up in here."

Rene carried a stack of envelopes in her hand. "Morning mail. I thought you could look through it and decide what you wanted to open yourself and what you want me to take care of."

"Give me five minutes for a quick shower." Jordan stood, slid her feet into her house shoes, and walked toward the bathroom. "We'll stay here and not go downstairs so that Darlene and Roselynne will leave me alone."

"They're worried about you. That's why they're smothering you with attention."

"I know, but they shouldn't be so concerned. I'm going to be just fine."

"Sure you are," Rene said. "But you know, honey, no one would blame you if you fell apart. Just this once."

"I can't."

"Yeah, I know."

Fifteen minutes later, Jordan and Rene sat in the side chairs flanking the tea table in Jordan's sitting room. Rene had poured them coffee from the silver pot left on Jordan's breakfast tray and they were ready to start going through the mail. After Dan's death, she had been flooded with sympathy cards and letters and even now a few still trickled in. Rene took care of most of her correspondence, but she usually went through the mail first, choosing what to handle personally.

"Have you talked to Rick Carson this morning?" Rene asked.

"No, why?" Jordan noted a hint of concern in her assistant's voice.

"Then he didn't tell you that he's moving into town, did he? He's going to stay at the Priceville Inn where the other Powell agents are staying."

Where Rick stayed, where he spent his nights, shouldn't matter to her. But it did. Why had he decided to leave Price Manor so suddenly? And why hadn't he come to her and explained?

"No, he didn't tell me."

"Look, I wouldn't know either except I ran into him as he was leaving, suitcase in hand."

"What did he say? Did he give you an explanation or—"

"Nope. He just said if you asked about him, to tell you he'd be in touch."

"I see."

"Damn men! Every last one of them. They're nothing but big, hairy, horny apes, the whole lot."

Jordan laughed. That was one of the things she loved about her friend. Rene could always make her laugh.

"You like him, don't you?" Rene asked.

"I've known him a week. I met him for the first time at Dan's funeral. He thinks I may have killed both of my husbands and my fiancé. I have no reason to like him."

"I'm talking about that other kind of liking. The kind that has nothing to do with the length of time you've known someone or the reasons why you should or shouldn't like them. I'm talking about hormones. Rick Carson lights your fire."

"If that's your none too subtle way of saying you think I'm physically attracted to him, then if I'm completely honest, I'd have to say yes, I suppose I am. And I hate it. I don't want those feelings. Not ever again. And especially not now. Not when my life is in utter chaos."

"If it'll make you feel any better, you should know that I think he feels the same way. He's attracted to you and doesn't want to be. Despite what he might tell you, I believe that's the reason he's moving out of Price Manor."

"Then he's done the right thing for the right reasons. Rick has to know that for us, it's definitely a matter of the wrong time, wrong place, wrong everything." Jordan tapped the three-inch stack of mail. "Let's get started on these."

She flipped through the envelopes quickly, sorting them into three stacks: trash, Rene, and handle personally. So far, she had only one that she would have to deal with herself. An invitation of some sort.

Jordan stopped halfway through the stack and stared at the plain white envelope. The address had been hand printed, in pencil. No return address. Postmarked Priceville, Georgia.

"Something interesting?" Rene asked.

"Take a look at this." She handed the envelope to Rene.

"Hmm . . . Looks almost like a child's handwriting, doesn't it? Want me to open it?"

"No, I'll do it." Jordan's hand trembled as she took the envelope from Rene and ripped it open with her silver letter opener.

Why her heartbeat had accelerated and her palms were suddenly moist, she didn't know. As if guided by a sixth sense that forewarned her, Jordan carefully removed the single sheet of nondescript white lined notebook paper and unfolded it. The message had been written in pencil in the same childlike printing.

**They think you are a killer. We know you are
not, don't we? What do I have to do to prove
to them that you're innocent—kill you, too?**

Jordan stared at the succinct message, her pulse pounding, roaring in her head like a runaway train.

"Jordan? Jordan, what's wrong? What is it?"

Rene's voice sounded as if it were coming from a great distance. Without saying anything, she handed the letter to Rene, who read it quickly.

"What the hell is this?"

"You tell me."

"Some nut-job." She laid the letter on the table. "We need to call Sheriff Corbett."

"No," Jordan said.

"But you don't know if this person is a sicko or just a prankster."

Jordan got up, dumping the mail off her lap and onto the floor. She found her cell phone lying on her nightstand where she'd put it before going to bed last night. She flipped it open, paused to recall the memorized number, then dialed.

"Who are you calling?" Rene asked.

She held up her hand in a please-wait gesture as she listened to the phone ringing.

"Hello, Jordan," Rick Carson said.

"I need you to come back to Price Manor right now."

"I take it that Rene told you I'm moving into the Priceville Inn."

"Yes, but that's not why I'm calling. You certainly can stay wherever you want to stay. That's up to you. But I want you back here immediately. Someone has threatened to kill me."

# Chapter 17

"Is this the only threatening letter you've received?" Rick asked.

"Yes, it is."

"Then I think we can chalk it up to the fact that the loonies were bound to crawl out of the woodwork considering the press coverage since Jane Anne's murder."

Jordan released a relieved breath. "That's pretty much what Rene said. But I have to admit I was shocked when I read it and . . ."

"And what?"

"And frightened, too."

"Unless someone on the estate wrote this letter, you don't have anything to be afraid of here at home. Or is that what has you so upset—you think someone you know and thought you could trust wrote the letter?"

"No, of course I don't think that. Surely you don't believe—"

"I know you don't want to accept the very real possibility that someone close to you and Dan killed him. But facts are facts. It's looking more and more like Dan was murdered and if you didn't help him pull the trigger, then who did? Only a certain number of people had access to your home."

"You're asking me to believe that a member of our family killed Dan. I can't accept that. No one, not even J.C for all his faults, would have harmed Dan."

"Believe what you will," Rick told her. "But right now, you're the number one suspect, even if the sheriff's department is referring to you only as a person of interest. Unless you're willing to take the blame for a murder someone else committed, you'd better accept some hard truths."

"I can't. You're not only asking me to believe that someone I love and trust murdered Dan, but if they sent that letter—" she glared at the piece of paper Rick held in his hand "—they might actually try to kill me, too."

"Whoever wrote the letter seems to believe in your innocence, but they certainly have an odd way of showing it." Rick waved the letter at her. "Either someone with a limited education wrote this or someone deliberately printed the message and used a pencil and lined paper for a reason."

"Rene wanted me to phone Steve Corbett. If someone is actually threatening me, he should know about it."

"I'll tell him if and when I think it's necessary," Rick said. "For now, I'll put the letter and envelope in a plastic bag and keep them with me. There are probably numerous fingerprints on the envelope, but only yours, Rene's and mine should be on the letter and possibly the person who wrote it. If you get another letter, I'll send them both to Powell headquarters and our lab can test them. If you don't receive another one, then we'll chalk this up to some harmless kook."

"All right. We'll hope for the best." She held out her hand. "Thank you."

Rick hesitated, then shook her hand quickly.

Despite his reassurance, Jordan looked worried. He

hated to see her like this, pale and jittery and gazing at him as if he had the answers to all her problems. The vulnerability she projected brought all his protective instincts into play.

*Get out of here before you do something stupid.*

He had moved to the Priceville Inn this morning for a damn good reason, one he shouldn't forget.

"I'll be around for a few more hours, if you need me for anything," he told her. "When the shift at the front gate changes, I'm giving a couple of the agents a ride back into town."

She stared at him with those soulful blue-gray eyes and he got the oddest feeling that she could see right through him, that she knew what he was thinking.

"Why did you move to the Inn?" she asked.

"All the other Powell agents are staying there. It seemed the right thing to do. I didn't want it to look like just because I was heading up the case that I was getting preferential treatment."

It was a lie and they both knew it, but she didn't contradict him.

"Is there anything new about Jane Anne's murder?" Jordan asked.

"No, nothing."

"And what about the investigation into Dan's death?"

"Like I told you, now that the sheriff's department has reopened the case, we can assume your husband was murdered."

"Yes, of course."

"The only questions that remain to be answered are who killed the senator and who killed his ex-wife," Rick said.

She was making idle chitchat, asking him questions when she already knew the answers. It was obvious that she wanted something from him. His time? His understanding? What exactly?

*Admit it, Carson, you're as guilty as she is. You've been stalling because you want more time with her, even if it's just a few extra minutes.*

Damn, he was a fool. He and Jordan were deliberately making conversation. Any excuse to stay together just a little while longer. Was her reason the same as his? Hell, what did it matter? This was a lose-lose situation for both of them.

When his cell phone rang, Rick hesitated. "Excuse me." He removed his phone, flipped it open and said, "Carson here."

"Rick, it's Nicole."

"Can you hold a sec?" He looked at Jordan. "I need to take this. It's business."

She tried to smile, but the effort failed. "Certainly. I need to speak to Vadonna about the grocery list for next week."

He watched her leave the den, which was actually one of the front parlors that had been transformed from a formal living room into an informal family room. He didn't return to his phone until she had closed the door behind her. "Yeah, Nic, I'm back. Sorry about that, but I was with Jordan."

"I spoke to Claire."

"And?"

"She really didn't know anything much about Jordan's life before she married Dan, other than a few things Jordan told her."

"Did she mention to Claire anything about having mental or emotional problems in the past?"

"No, not really, but it's hardly the thing you'd want to discuss, is it?"

"So, Claire didn't know anything that—?"

"Claire said that if you want to know anything about Jordan's personal history, you should ask Jordan herself."

"And you think she'd confide in me?"

"Probably not," Nic said. "Is there anyone there who has known Jordan for a long time who might be persuaded to help you help Jordan by giving you some insight into what's made her the woman she is today?"

"You're saying pretend that I'm asking about Jordan because by understanding her better, I can possibly do more to help her prove she's completely innocent."

"It's worth a try. And who knows, you just might discover that she is just that—completely innocent."

Rick had tried the persuasive tactic that Nic had suggested, but unfortunately it hadn't worked with a single person. He'd thought that if anyone would fill him in on Jordan's past, it would be Roselynne, but apparently the lady had seen through his ploy. Devon, Tammy, Darlene and J.C. had sung Jordan's praises, but had given Rick no new information. Rene was his last hope.

"Are you still here?" Rene asked when he cornered her outside on the patio where she'd gone to smoke. "I thought you'd be back at the Inn by now."

"I'll be heading out in about thirty minutes, when the shift for the agents at the front gate changes."

She sucked in a deep draw and blew out a spiral of smoke. "Do you really think that moving into the Priceville Inn is going to change anything?"

He shrugged. "I don't know what you mean."

"Sure you do. Out of sight, out of mind. Only it won't work. Once Jordan's in your system, you can't get her out. I've seen it happen time and time again." Rene laughed. "You don't think you're the first man to fall victim to Jordan's charm, do you?"

"I thought you didn't harbor any resentment about Robby Joe Wright."

She took another puff on her cigarette. "I don't. Believe me, I'm glad I wasn't the one engaged to him when he died. By that time, I was pretty much over him. If you could have seen what Jordan went through . . ."

"She took it pretty hard, huh? I guess that was to be expected. She was in love with the guy, right?"

"They adored each other. God, they were so in love." Rene took a final drag on the cigarette, dropped it onto the stone patio floor and ground it out with the tip of her black, three-inch heels.

"Did she undergo any grief counseling?" Rick asked the question as casually as possible.

"Yeah, sure. She and Darlene actually went together. They'd been close before Robby Joe's accident, but afterward they became inseparable. I don't know that they'd have made it through such a tragedy without each other."

"I'm surprised that, considering Robby Joe was her only child, Darlene didn't go off the deep end."

"Well, she didn't. I think she held it together for Jordan's sake. Jordan was the one who—" Rene stopped abruptly as if she'd suddenly realized she was on the verge of revealing something that was none of Rick's business.

"Jordan was the one who went off the deep end?"

Rene glared at him. Did she suspect him of having an ulterior motive for probing?

"Look, I'm asking because I want to help Jordan. If she's had emotional issues or mental problems in the past, it might explain why she's the way she is now."

"And how is she now?"

"I swear to you that I don't want to hurt Jordan," Rick said. "I want to help her."

Rene studied him for a couple of minutes. "You know, I actually believe you. You don't trust her. You don't understand her. You're not a hundred percent sure she hasn't killed several people, but you still want to help her." With a perplexed smile lifting the corners of her mouth, Rene shook her head. "I swear, I don't know how she does it."

"How she does what?"

"Wraps guys around her little finger. Devon, J.C., Robby Joe, Jay, Boyd, Dan, Ryan, and now you."

"Ryan?"

"Oh, there's never been any hanky-panky between them. That's not what I meant. It's just that Ryan thinks she's wonderful, just the way every man has her entire life."

"Who's Jay?" Rick asked.

"Jay? Oh, Jay Reynolds. We worked with him at the Peachtree Agency. He had a thing for Jordan, but she was still mourning Robby Joe and although they dated a few times, nothing ever came of it. When she stopped dating him, he took it pretty bad. They had an ugly scene at work one day."

"What kind of ugly scene?"

"Jordan never did elaborate, but I think he stepped over the line, you know, got aggressive, and she slapped him."

"What happened after that? Were they able to continue working together?"

"Uh, for a while, but Jay wound up leaving Atlanta. I think he got a job in another city," Rene said. "Look, I've enjoyed our little chat, but I have a few phone calls to make and some e-mails to send out before dinner."

When she turned to go, he reached out and grasped her wrist. "Exactly what happened to Jordan after Robby Joe died?"

Rene hesitated. "Look, I'll tell you because I know that you'll find a way to dig up the information on your own." Her gaze locked with his. "Jordan tried to commit suicide."

How did he reconcile the information Rene had given him about Jordan's attempted suicide with his firsthand knowledge of the woman Jordan was now? The Jordan he knew would no more try to take her own life than he would. If he'd learned nothing else about her in their brief acquaintance, he'd learned that she was incredibly strong and resilient. As a general rule, strong, resilient people didn't take their own lives. Had Rene lied to him? If so, why? Or had Jordan been an entirely different kind of person twelve years ago when she'd lost her fiancé?

Had she loved Robby Joe so deeply that she thought she couldn't live without him? And if that was the case, it was highly improbable that she had murdered him.

Could Robby Joe's death have triggered a mental breakdown that led to a suicide attempt and altered her personality so greatly that she became a cold-blooded murderer?

Now that he had this information about Jordan, did it answer his questions about her? No. All it did was create more questions. And the only person who could provide the answers was Jordan herself.

Rick checked his wristwatch. Ten minutes until the front gate shift change. He flipped open his cell phone and called Holt Keinan.

"I'm going to be held up here at Price Manor for a while. Can you arrange for transportation for the guards back to the Inn?"

"No problem," Holt said. "I'm bringing in the second shift and then heading back into town. The guys can ride with me."

"Thanks."

When Rick went in search of Jordan, he found her where she apparently spent most of her time—in her small, isolated study at the back of the house. The door stood partially ajar, so he simply knocked once and shoved the door wide open. Standing by the windows overlooking the yard, she merely glanced at him when he entered.

"I thought you'd already left," she said. "Have you changed your mind about staying at the Inn?"

"No, I got held up," he told her.

What was the best way to broach the subject? He could hardly come right out and ask her if she had tried to kill herself, could he? How would she react if he told her that he suspected she might have mental and emotional problems that could possibly make her capable of murder?

"Did you need to speak to me about something?" she asked.

He walked over to her. "You know, don't you, that I don't want you to be guilty of murder."

She smiled at him, then looked away, focusing her gaze on some far distant object outside. "If I were guilty of murdering anyone, Dan or any of the other men who have died, don't you think someone would have figured it out before now?"

"Not necessarily."

"I've told you the truth time and again. I've proclaimed my innocence repeatedly. I don't know what else I can say or do to convince you or the sheriff's department or even my own lawyer that I have never killed anyone."

"Have you ever tried to kill anyone?"

She snapped her head around and glared at him. "No, I've never—"

"You didn't try to kill yourself?"

All color drained from her face. She stared at him as if he'd suddenly grown a set of horns. "What—what did you say?"

"I asked you if you tried to kill yourself not long after Robby Joe Wright died."

"Who told you that I—?"

"It doesn't matter how I found out," Rick said. "Is it true?"

"No, it isn't true."

"So, you're saying that you didn't OD on sleeping pills and didn't have to have your stomach pumped?"

Color returned to her face, anger brightening her cheeks. She clenched her teeth tightly.

"You know that I can double check the facts," he said.

"After Robby Joe died, I had a problem sleeping. And when I did sleep, I had nightmares. My doctor prescribed sleeping pills for me. I lived from day to day in a hazy fog, feeling nothing but pain and loss. I went through the motions of living, but I was hardly alive."

"So you tried to—"

"No! I did not deliberately try to kill myself. At least, I don't think I did. I don't remember taking the entire bottle of pills." She closed her eyes, the memories of that long ago event no doubt still painfully unsettling. "But apparently I did swallow the entire prescription or at least most of it. If Darlene hadn't found me and called 911 . . ."

Jordan swayed toward him, the movement so subtle that he didn't think she was even aware of what she was doing.

*Whatever you do, don't touch her.*

Her breathing deepened as if she were trying to force herself to stay calm and in control.

"Did you get some psychiatric help?" Rick asked, his voice low and soothing.

"Yes, I was under psychiatric care for three months. I came out of that experience with a determination that nothing would ever push me to the edge of sanity ever again."

That explained it, Jordan's cool, unemotional discipline. She had lost control and almost died as a result. Loving too deeply, feeling too much, made her vulnerable. And even if she sometimes appeared to be vulnerable, she wasn't. She wouldn't allow herself to be.

A ringing telephone broke through Rick's thoughts. It wasn't his ring.

"That's my phone." She reached over to the desk where her phone lay, picked it up, and flipped it open. "Hello."

She didn't say anything else, just listened, then suddenly, she gasped.

"Who is this? How did you get my private number?"

Rick's gaze silently questioned her. Jordan flipped the phone closed.

"What was that all about?" he asked.

"I don't know. He . . . or maybe she . . . I couldn't tell because they were talking so quietly and the voice sounded muffled."

"What did they say?"

Jordan's phone rang again. She clutched it with white-knuckled ferocity.

"Give it to me." Rick held out his hand.

She placed the phone in his palm.

He checked caller ID—Unknown. He flipped open the phone and placed it to his ear, but didn't say anything.

"Don't hang up on me," the strange voice said. "I'm doing you a favor. I'm giving you fair warning and that's more than I did for the others. Watch your back. Don't trust anyone. Someone close to you is your worst enemy."

"I'll relay the message," Rick said. "Now let me give you fair warning. You come anywhere near Mrs. Price and I'll take you apart, limb from limb. She's under twenty-four-hour-a-day protection. Got that?"

Silence.

The bastard had hung up.

# Chapter 18

One brief letter and one phone call wouldn't be enough to convince them that Jordan was in danger. The only way to convince everyone—the sheriff's department and the Powell agents, Rick Carson in particular—that Jordan was innocent was to threaten her life. If she were a victim, she could hardly be the killer, now could she?

In the beginning, she had been unsure what role, if any, Rick would play in their lives; but now she knew, without any doubt, that Jordan needed him. Temporarily. To see her through this rough patch in their lives. And she intended to see to it that Jordan got what she needed. Hadn't she always?

Keeping Jordan safe was a matter of self-preservation. Jordan could not survive without her, even if she didn't realize it. Nor could she survive without Jordan. If one died, the other died, so strong was their bond.

Everything she'd done, she had done for both of them.

She glanced down at the lined notebook paper and the

number 2 pencil on the desk. She would have to write more letters and make more phone calls, using the prepaid cell phones that couldn't be traced. One letter and one phone call each day. That should be sufficient. And she would have to be careful not to get caught.

She tapped the pencil against her cheek. Perhaps the letters and the phone calls would be enough, but if they weren't . . .

She unlocked and opened the bottom left drawer, glanced down at the scrapbook she kept hidden away and decided that perhaps, in a few days, she should mail Jordan a little surprise package.

Alone in her study, Jordan gasped when she heard the knock on the door. Hurriedly, she closed the old photo album, tossed it into the bottom desk drawer and as she rose from the chair, she shoved the drawer closed with the tip of her foot. She knotted her hands into loose fists to keep them from trembling and faced Maleah Perdue, who had opened the door and now stood waiting for Jordan to invite her into the study.

"Mrs. Price, Rick asked me to—"

"Where is he? Where's Rick?"

"He left a few minutes ago. That's what I was trying to tell you—he's put me in charge of guarding you. He felt that it would be easier for you if your bodyguard was a woman."

"Oh, yes, I—I suppose he's right."

*But I don't want you. I want Rick.*

"I'll be staying here at Price Manor," Maleah explained. "And I'll need a bedroom close to yours. You won't go anywhere outside the house and certainly not off the estate without me."

Jordan nodded. "I understand."

"Even if the person who sent you the letter and made the phone call isn't dangerous to you, it's better not to take any chances. From now on, I'll open all mail that is the least bit suspicious and I'll answer all calls on your cell phone unless you know the identity of the caller."

"Surely that doesn't mean you intend to be with me all the time, that I won't have any privacy at all."

"We'll get together once a day and open the mail," Maleah said. "And I suggest that whenever you're alone you either turn off your cell phone or simply let any calls that come up on caller ID as Unknown go straight to voice mail."

"Yes, certainly. That makes sense."

"I'll try to be as unobtrusive as possible, but it's my responsibility to keep you safe."

Jordan looked at the attractive woman Rick had assigned to protect her from an unknown enemy. Maleah Perdue didn't look like Jordan imagined female bodyguards looked. She was average height and had a slim but nicely rounded figure. With her blue eyes, blonde hair and creamy complexion, she epitomized the All-American beauty of decades past.

Maleah dressed sensibly in tan twill slacks, navy blue blazer, white shirt and low-heel navy shoes. As Jordan studied her, she noted a bulge beneath the left side of the blazer.

"You're wearing a holster." Jordan spoke aloud without realizing what she'd done until it was too late.

"Yes, ma'am. It's mandatory whenever I'm on guard duty."

"I don't like guns."

"I assure you that I won't use it unless it's absolutely necessary.

"Yes, of course." Jordan cleared her throat. "At dinner this evening, I'll introduce you to everyone and explain the situation, but until then I'd like to be alone. I promise

I won't leave the house and I won't answer the phone unless I know the identity of the caller."

"All right. I'll see you at dinner then."

"Dinner is at seven this evening."

"Yes, ma'am."

As soon as Maleah left, Jordan slumped down in the nearest chair. Just when she'd thought things couldn't get any worse, this had to happen. A threatening letter, followed by a threatening phone call. And instead of staying on at Price Manor to personally see to her safety, as she had hoped he would do, Rick had put someone else in charge.

*You don't need him. You don't need anyone. You can take care of yourself. You know better than to rely on another person. People disappoint you. They let you down. They die and leave you all alone.*

Darlene seldom slept past five-thirty. She had been a creature of habit all her life. When the weather permitted, she took a long walk every morning. When she stayed at her apartment in Priceville, she'd walk downtown and usually stop at the small coffee shop on Main Street where she bought a cup of her favorite espresso and a morning newspaper. When she visited Price Manor, as she was doing now, she often walked around the grounds, sometimes following the drive to the front gates and back or occasionally taking the path that led through the woods. And when she returned to the house, she always prepared her own coffee, using the espresso machine Jordan had purchased especially for her.

Although springtime was in full bloom, there was a definite chill in the air this morning and that's why she'd worn a lightweight jacket. When she opened the back door, the morning breeze's cool breath fanned her face. She buttoned her jacket and headed out, intending to shorten the usual length of her stroll so that she would be back before Jordan woke. When she had stopped by Jordan's room this morning and peeped in, she'd found her sprawled sideways in the bed, without even a sheet over her.

Jordan had been having difficulty sleeping since Dan's death and even more so since she'd started receiving threatening letters and phone calls five days ago, on Monday. Darlene had made her a cup of hot tea every night and taken it to her before bedtime.

"I know Dr. Carroll prescribed some sleeping pills for you, but I don't think you should take them," Darlene had told her.

"I haven't even had the prescription filled," Jordan had said. "I put it in the desk in my study. If it'll make you feel better, I'll tear it up and throw it away."

"There's no need to do that. If you continue having problems sleeping, I can get the prescription filled for you and keep the medication in my room and give you one tablet each night."

Jordan had hugged her. "Thank you, Darlene. What would I do without you?"

This morning, she had tiptoed into Jordan's bedroom and covered her with the down comforter crumpled at the foot of the bed. As she had crept silently out of the room, she'd met that female Powell agent at the door.

"Is everything all right?" Maleah Perdue had asked.

"Yes. Jordan's asleep."

Such a dreadful shame that Jordan needed a bodyguard, but under the circumstances, it was necessary. Darlene had wondered why Rick Carson hadn't taken the job himself, but when Jordan had explained that Rick believed a female bodyguard was more appropriate, Darlene had agreed.

With her mind deep in thought about and concerned for Jordan, Darlene hadn't realized she'd taken the path that led past Roselynne's cottage at the back of the mansion. Jordan certainly had more patience with her step-family than most would have. She had tried to tell her years ago that no one would blame her if she cut the lot of them loose to fend for themselves.

"But that's just it—they can't fend for themselves," Jordan had said. "If it was only J.C., I'd have tossed him out on his ear after Daddy died. But I don't think Roselynne could have provided properly for Tammy and in order to take care of Tammy, I had to take care of Roselynne, too. Besides, Roselynne has a good heart."

Hogwash. The woman was a leech, plain and simple. Jordan was the one with the good heart, not her worthless stepmother.

As Darlene rounded the curve in the path that went behind the cottage and into the woods, she noticed the back door of the cottage open and two people walk out on the porch. Intending to hurry away before they saw her, she stepped up her pace, but when, in her peripheral vision, she caught a glimpse of the two people, she stopped dead still, turned around, and gaped at them.

Wallace McGee, with his shirttail hanging out, his leather belt draped around his neck, and his shoes in his hand, stood there grinning like a lovesick fool. Roselynne, wearing nothing but a sheer nightgown, wrapped her arms around Wallace's neck and kissed him. On the lips.

Hussy! The woman was nothing but a slut. How could a man such as Wallace be seduced by bleached hair and large breasts? She had thought better of him. But then again, he was just a man, with a man's weaknesses. No, she didn't blame dear, sweet Wallace. She blamed that worthless piece of trash.

Darlene inched her way slowly into the outer fringes of the wooded area at the back of the cottage, keeping out of sight while she watched as Wallace slipped into his shoes and put on his belt.

She understood loneliness all too well and knew that

Wallace had been terribly alone since his dear wife, Glenda, passed away two years ago. But of all the women in the world he could have chosen to assuage his loneliness, why had he chosen Roselynne? They could hardly have anything in common. Wallace was, after all, a highly intelligent, well-educated, cultured gentleman.

Sex. That's all it was between them. Just sex.

When Wallace came to his senses and decided he wanted to remarry, he would look elsewhere. Not that she wanted him for herself or would marry him if he got down on his knees and begged her. But she wouldn't be opposed to seeing him socially.

She should have continued on her walk instead of watching Wallace kiss Roselynne again and then blow her kisses just before he got in his car and drove away.

*No fool like an old fool.*

"Good morning, Darlene," Roselynne called loudly. "Why don't you come on in and have a cup of coffee with me."

Damn the woman. She'd seen her.

*Did she know all along that I was watching them?*

"No, thank you. I'll wait and have coffee after my walk."

"Suit yourself." Roselynne smiled like the proverbial Cheshire cat as she looked skyward. "It's a beautiful morning, isn't it? Of course any morning is a beautiful morning after you've spent the night making love. Don't you think so?"

"Do you have no shame?" Darlene took several hesitant steps toward the back of the cottage. "You had a man spend the night while both of your children were sleeping under your roof."

Darlene had always detested Roselynne's loud, throaty laughter, but never more than at that precise moment.

"Lordy, the way you talk, you'd think Tammy and J.C. were little kids. They're adults and not the least bit shocked to know their mama has herself a gentleman friend."

"You won't keep him, you know," Darlene said. "He's just using you for sex. Once he tires of you, he'll find someone more suitable, someone worthy of sharing his life."

"Maybe. Maybe not. But don't think for one minute that you've got a chance with him. A dried-up, old, prune-face like you won't interest him, so I suggest, if you're looking for a man, you look elsewhere."

The ugliness of Roselynne's words hurt her, but it was only a temporary pain, much like being slapped. Darlene tilted her chin and stuck her nose in the air. She was too much of a lady to continue exchanging insults.

"You have yourself a nice walk," Roselynne said. "I'll see you up at the house later this morning for breakfast."

Without replying, Darlene walked away quickly, but Roselynne's coarse laughter followed her. Mocking her.

When Rick stepped out of the shower, a towel wrapped around his waist, his cell phone rang and someone knocked on his door. He grabbed the phone, saw that Nicole was the caller, and as he flipped open the phone, he walked to the door.

"Yeah, Nic, what's up?" He peered through the peephole in the door. Lt. Haley McLain, dressed in jeans and long-sleeved T-shirt, stood in the hallway.

"You asked us to try to find out where a man named Jay Reynolds who used to work for the Peachtree Agency is now," Nicole said.

"Yeah. Hey, wait up just a minute. There's someone at my door." He cracked the door a couple of inches and looked at Haley.

"Good morning," she said. "May I come in?"

What the hell! "Sure, come on in."

When he opened the door and walked toward the bathroom, Haley entered. She eyed his state of undress, letting her gaze travel from his damp hair to his bare chest, over the white towel covering him from waist to upper thighs, and down to his feet.

"Like what you see?" he asked.

"Rick, who are you talking to?" Nicole's question reminded him that his boss was on the phone.

"Sorry. Give me another minute, will you?" He held the phone against his bare chest. "Sit down," he told Haley. "I need to take this call and put on some clothes."

"Take your time. I can wait. I'm off work today."

He closed the bathroom door. "Lt. McLain's paid me an early morning visit."

"Business or personal?"

"I'm not sure, but I can assure your that as far as I'm concerned it's business." Rick turned on the sink's faucets to create background noise, then lowered his voice and asked, "Now what's the news about Reynolds? Have you located him?"

"In a matter of speaking."

"Meaning?"

"Jay Reynolds, former employee of the Peachtree Agency, the man who worked with and dated Jordan Price, is dead."

A cold lump of dread formed in Rick's chest. "When did he die?"

"Ten years ago."

"After he left the Peachtree Agency and moved from Atlanta?"

"Nope. He was still in Atlanta and still employed by the Peachtree Agency when he died."

Rene Burke had lied to him. She'd told him Jay Reynolds had left Atlanta. And there was no way she wouldn't have known the guy had died. "How old was Reynolds?"

"Thirty. Want to know how he died?"

"Something tells me that it was an accident of some sort."

"Not exactly. He was beaten to death in the parking deck of his apartment complex. The murder weapon was never found, but the ME felt certain it was either a baseball bat or something similar in size and shape. The report we received states that he was hit over the head repeatedly. After the person killed him, they robbed him. They took his wallet, his watch and two rings."

"Did the police ever find his killer?"

"No. There were no witnesses. Nobody saw a thing."

"In cases such as that, the killer is usually male, but not always."

"You read my mind. We both know that if Reynolds was taken by surprise, a woman could have easily knocked him out first and then beaten him to death."

"I know what you're thinking," Rick said. "You're thinking this is just one more nail in Jordan's coffin. How many men does this make? Six, if you count her father. It was hard enough to believe that five was a horrible coincidence, but six. Damn, Nic, it can't be a coincidence."

"I agree and so does Griff. It would seem that the person who killed Dan Price and possibly his ex-wife may have systematically killed five times before, all of the victims men closely associated with Jordan."

"But that doesn't mean she's the one who killed them."

"Again, I agree. But if not Jordan, then it has to be someone close to her, someone who has known her for at least a dozen years or more."

"That includes everyone in her close-knit little family, her stepmother, stepbrother and stepsister. Then there's Devon Markham, Rene Burke and Darlene Wright."

"We know for certain that Jay Reynolds was murdered and so was Jane Anne Price. We and the Dade County sheriff's department believe Dan Price was murdered. What we need to know is, if there's any proof Jordan's father, her former boss or her fiancé were also murdered. And if we believe Jordan is innocent, then we should start looking for a motive or motives for the murders. It would certainly help if there had been autopsies performed on all those men."

"We'd need a court order to have a body exhumed," Rick said. "And for that we either need some kind of evidence to substantiate our suspicions or permission from the next of kin."

"Powell's will send someone to talk to Donald Farris's widow," Nic told him. "You're there in Priceville, so I'll leave it up to you to talk to Roselynne Harris and Darlene Wright."

"And say what to them? Tell them we've discovered another of Jordan's men was possibly murdered and we believe that Robby Joe and Wayne Harris were also victims? Believe me, if they think we're implying that Jordan killed these men, they'll circle the wagons around her."

"I see your dilemma. If they think you're accusing Jordan, they'll defend her and refuse permission to exhume the bodies. But if you present it differently, say that someone in Jordan's life has been murdering these men, then they may think they're a suspect and refuse to cooperate."

"Either way, we're still working with the only information we have to date and that information is all but screaming serial killer, and certainly not your usual garden-variety serial killer at that."

"We have another problem," Nic said.

"And that would be?"

"We have new information that might relate to two active murder cases. Griff and I disagree whether we're obligated to share this info with the Dade County sheriff's department."

"Let me guess. You believe we should notify Sheriff Corbett and Griff thinks we shouldn't."

"I don't have to ask you which one of us you agree with, do I?"

"Jordan Price is our client and this information can only hurt her," Rick said.

"What's that old saying about the truth not hurting anyone unless it should?"

"Do you think she's guilty, that she really is a black widow who has killed man after man?"

"The evidence points us in that direction, doesn't it?" Nic said. "But the way I look at it, we have three possibilities: Jordan is indeed a black widow. Or someone close to her has been killing the men in Jordan's life who have, in some way, harmed her. Or someone close to her hates her and by killing these men has been punishing Jordan, maybe even laying the groundwork for our black widow theory."

"Maybe Griff should contact Derek Lawrence and ask him to look over the information and draw up a profile on the type of person who could have killed all six men."

"And Jane Anne Price, too," Nic reminded him.

"Her killer could be someone else," Rick pointed out the obvious. "The former Mrs. Price was definitely killed in order to keep her quiet, but whether it was done to protect Jordan or to protect Dan Price or both, we don't know."

"Speak to Darlene Wright and Roselynne Harris. Griff and I will duke it out over whether or not to contact Sheriff Corbett."

"Just remember one thing—you're not an FBI agent now. You're in the private detective business. That changes things. Your first allegiance is to your client."

"Didn't you forget all about that allegiance when you shared information with Lt. McLain?" Nic reminded him.

"Yeah, I did, and I've lived to regret that decision." The mention of the deputy reminded Rick that the lady in question was waiting for him just beyond the closed door.

"I'll keep an open mind and not make a hasty decision," Nic said. "I promise."

Rick laid his cell phone on the back of the commode and turned off the faucets. He whipped off the towel around his waist and grabbed his briefs from the vanity. His shirt and jeans hung on the door hook. He dressed hurriedly, grabbed his phone, stuck it in his pocket, and then walked into the bedroom.

Haley sat in one of two chairs facing the coal-converted fireplace. When he entered the room, she smiled.

"I'd begun to think you'd forgotten about me," she told him.

He had almost forgotten about her. "Like I said, the call was business. If you had a problem waiting, maybe you should have considered phoning ahead of time instead of just dropping by."

"The news must not have been good," she said. "You seem to be in a bad mood."

"Why are you here, Haley? If it's in a professional capacity—"

"Only in a way. Actually, I came by to invite you to breakfast."

He stared at her, trying to figure out what she was up to. Although he couldn't be a hundred percent sure that Haley had been the one who leaked the info about Jordan to the press, his gut instinct warned him that he couldn't trust the lady.

"Breakfast is provided here at the Inn," he told her as he put on his socks and shoes. "It's part of the B&B deal."

"Then invite me to join you."

"Why so friendly all of a sudden?"

"I want to bury the hatchet. I thought the best way to start was to share some information with you, just as you did with me, to prove that I trust you."

He eyed her suspiciously. "Why would you do that? What's in it for you?"

She grinned at him, her expression flirtatious. "We both want the same thing—to find out the truth. Who killed the senator and his ex-wife? The way I look at it, that puts us on the same side. We should be working together, not against each other."

"Steve Corbett didn't send you here, so who did?"

She laughed, but it was a nervous, I'm-hiding-something laugh. "We're not asking you to betray your client, but if we could share information, wouldn't that help us both?"

"I'll ask you again—who sent you?"

She huffed, obviously disappointed that her let's-be-friends tactic didn't work. "Cy Anderman thought I could talk sense to you."

"Cyrus Anderman, the DA?"

She nodded. "Cy has contacted the FBI and asked them to look into the possibility that the murders of Senator Price and his ex-wife are the work of a serial killer who murdered Boyd Brannon, Donald Farris, Robby Joe Wright, and Wayne Harris."

"Good," Rick said. "Maybe if the FBI gets involved, they can prove that none of those men were murdered."

"Do you really believe that?

"Whatever you thought you'd get from me, forget it. You're wasting your time fluttering your eyelashes at me. It's beneath you, Lt. McLain, to use your feminine charms to try to worm information out of me."

"Is that what you think I'm trying to do?"

"Isn't it?"

"Maybe."

"What do you think I know that's so important?"

"You tell me."

"Any information that Powell's collects for our client belongs to the client," he said. "If we come across anything that we believe the police should know, Griffin and Nicole Powell decide how to handle it."

"Okay. I tried. I failed." Haley shrugged.

"Giving up so easily?"

She sauntered over to him, stopping when only inches separated their bodies. She looked up at him, then ran the tip of her tongue over her lips. "I thought you weren't interested."

He grunted. "I'm not. I was just curious to see how far you'd go."

She glowered at him. "You son of a bitch."

"Don't let the door hit you on the way out."

She shook her head as if stunned that he'd turn down her unspoken offer. Then she turned and walked away. When she reached the door, she paused and said, "Watch your back, Rick. If you aren't careful, you could wind up as dead as all the other men who trusted Jordan Price."

# Chapter 19

"It was a relief when I drove up to the gates to see only a handful of reporters," Ryan said as he entered the foyer at Price Manor. "I believe all the hullabaloo is finally dying down."

"We can only hope," Jordan said.

Ryan leaned over and kissed her cheek. "How are you holding up?"

She laced her arm through his. "By sheer will power alone."

"If not for this damn investigation, I'd suggest you and Devon take off to the house in Key West for a few weeks. Some sun and sand and complete privacy would do you both a world of good."

"I'm afraid running away from our problems isn't an option."

He searched her face, his gaze sympathetic and caring. Ryan was a fine man, so like Dan in many ways. Claire was a very lucky woman.

"Has Rick Carson arrived yet?" Ryan asked.

"Yes, he arrived about five minutes ago. Tobias told me

that he showed Rick into my study and took him some coffee. I was dealing with an unpleasant family matter that held me up."

"Anything I can do to help?"

"No, not really. It's nothing serious. Just one in a long line of squabbles between Darlene and Roselynne."

"I thought those two had called a truce for the duration," Ryan said. "What on earth are they at each other about now?"

When Jordan tugged on his arm, he fell into step alongside her as she led him out of the foyer.

"Would you believe they're quarreling over a man?"

Ryan chuckled. "You're joking."

"No. It seems that Darlene saw Wallace slipping out Roselynne's back door this morning and she is livid."

"Why should Darlene care? It's not as if it's news to anyone that Roselynne's morals are questionable."

"I'm afraid Darlene may have a little crush on Wallace. I have noticed that whenever he has come to Price Manor during the past year or so that she's managed to be here, also, and always wearing a new outfit and her hair and makeup perfect."

"Of all the things for you to have to deal with now—a romantic triangle involving your two mothers."

"Actually, in an odd way, having something that trivial to focus on is a relief. It takes my mind off other things. Serious things."

Ryan didn't reply, he simply gazed at her with understanding in his eyes.

When they reached the open door to her study, Jordan released Ryan's arm and entered first. Standing to the right of the fireplace, Rick held a cup and saucer in his hand. He took a sip of coffee, then eyed Jordan over the rim of his cup.

"Good morning." Rick glanced from Jordan to Ryan.

"You sounded dead serious when you phoned and asked me to meet you here," Ryan said. "You mentioned that something has happened that will directly affect Powell's investigation into Dan's death."

Rick placed the cup and saucer on the mantel. "Cyrus Anderman has contacted the FBI and asked them to come on board with the investigation into the senator's death."

"Why would the FBI be interested in Dan's death?" Jordan asked. "Even if Dan was murdered, it's hardly a case that falls under federal jurisdiction."

"Serial killers fall under federal jurisdiction," Rick said. Jordan's blood went cold. "Serial killers?"

"This is ridiculous," Ryan said. "I'll call Steve and see—"

"There's not much Steve can do," Rick told them. "The DA's calling the shots." He looked at Jordan. "Anderman's bought into all the news hype about your being a black widow."

She couldn't tell from Rick's expression what he was thinking. She wanted to cry out to him, "I'm innocent. I swear to you, I have never killed anyone." But she simply stared at him, her heart aching for him to believe her.

"So, what can we do?" Ryan asked. "Have you notified Camden Hendrix about this latest development?"

"I called him before I did you," Rick said. "He's not overly concerned at this point because asking the Bureau to come in on an investigation and their actually doing it are two different things."

"You must believe that the FBI will take over," Jordan said. "Otherwise you wouldn't be so worried." She held up a restraining hand. "And please, don't try to tell me . . . us . . . that you aren't worried."

"I've spoken not only to Cam, but to Nicole and Griffin Powell. We're all in agreement that what is needed now are some preemptive measures."

"Such as?" Ryan asked.

"Before we get into that, there's something else." Rick seemed reluctant, as if he dreaded burdening them with this new information.

"For pity's sake, just say it." Jordan braced herself, knowing that whatever happened, she had to remain strong. "It couldn't be any worse than the FBI stepping in to investigate Dan's death and—"

"Why didn't you tell us about Jay Reynolds?" Rick asked.

Jordan's heart stopped for a millisecond. "Jay Reynolds? Why would anything I had to say about Jay be of interest to you or anyone else?"

"Oh, I don't know, Jordan, maybe because you worked with this man and even dated him several times and he, too, wound up dead, just like so many other men in your life."

Jordan felt as if he'd backhanded her.

"See here, Carson, I object to your speaking to Jordan in such a manner." Ryan stepped between Jordan and Rick.

"No, it's all right." Jordan gently pushed her brother-in-law aside and walked right up to Rick. "Jay Reynolds was mugged in the parking deck of his apartment building. How on earth could his death have any connection to me whatsoever?"

"It wouldn't, if five other men in your life hadn't also died. Bam, bam, bam—" Rick snapped his fingers "—one right after the other. Reynolds makes six. Nobody, including the FBI, is going to believe that all those deaths were mere coincidence."

"Oh, my God!" Feeling suddenly lightheaded, Jordan swayed ever so slightly.

Rick and Ryan both reached for her, but Rick moved faster and slipped his arm around her waist. He helped her to the nearest chair.

"Do you need some water?" he asked. "Or a stiff drink?"

She shook her head. "No, thanks."

"Should we call Dr. Carroll?" Ryan asked. "Or perhaps your obstetrician? What's his name—Lamar? You're not fully recovered from the miscarriage."

"No, really, I'm okay. It's just that I believe Rick is right. It couldn't be just a coincidence that six men who were a part of my life died, one after the other, over the past dozen or so years." She closed her eyes and prayed for strength. "It's possible that two or three deaths could be a coincidence, but not six. Unless we can prove that each death was either from natural causes or truly was an accident, then we have to assume that some, if not all, of them were murdered."

"And if the same person killed some or all of them," Rick said, "then the FBI has a serial killer case."

"I know that I didn't kill Dan or Boyd or Robby Joe or anyone else," Jordan said. "So if they were all murdered and I didn't do it, who did?"

J.C. eased his red Thunderbird off the two-lane county road and onto the gravel path that dead-ended halfway into the woods. The brick chimney and cinder block foundation was all that remained of the old house that had burned down years ago. He got out of the car, leaned against the closed door, and retrieved a pack of cigarettes from his shirt pocket. Just as he flipped open his lighter and lit his cigarette, he heard the gravel crunching as another car pulled up behind his. He took a long drag on the cigarette as he waited for her. He didn't have to turn around to see who it was. He knew. She had called him half an hour ago and asked him to meet her. Actually she hadn't asked, she'd ordered.

"Morning, sugar." The smoke from the cigarette he held in his hand curled upward into the bright morning sunlight. He glanced at her and grinned. She was a damn fine looking woman and an even better piece of ass. His only complaint was that she liked being the aggressor, liked to be in charge when they fucked.

When she approached, he reached out, grabbed her around the waist and hauled her up against him. But when he lowered his mouth to hers, she shoved him away.

"Business first," she told him. "Pleasure afterward."

"Sure. Whatever you say." He brought the cigarette to his lips and took another deep draw.

"Would you like to make a quarter of a million?" she asked as easily as a waitress would ask if he wanted fries with his burger.

"Who do I have to kill?"

She laughed. "You don't have to kill anyone, just tell me the secret about Jordan's marriage that you claim to know. You can get big money if what you know is really scandalous, and I mean the more scandalous the better."

"I thought I'd already butchered Jordan's reputation when I did what you wanted me to and made a phone call to that reporter on the *Daily Gazette* and filled him in on all the dirt the Powell Agency dug up on her."

"You already knew everything Rick Carson told me," Haley McLain said. "You're her stepbrother. You could have shared that info with me right after the senator's murder and I could have gotten the ball rolling before the GBI declared his death a suicide and before Ryan Price hired Powell's to do a private investigation."

"Until you came to me, I'd never put two and two together," J.C. admitted. "I still find it difficult to believe that Jordan might have killed six people."

"Make that seven. Or are you forgetting about Jay Reynolds?"

"Who is Jay Reynolds?"

"You really don't know?"

"I don't have a clue."

"I've been doing some digging of my own and discovered that a guy she used to work with at the Peachtree

Agency was mugged and beaten to death about ten years ago. It just so happens that he and Jordan had dated a few times."

"And you think she killed him?"

"I don't know," Haley said. "I really don't care. As long as we can convince the FBI that there's a possibility she killed him and six others, that's all that matters."

"The FBI is getting involved?"

"Not yet, but after you contact The Chatterbox and tell them all the sordid details of Jordan's life, including the secret about her relationship with the senator—"

"Hold on just a damn minute. You actually want me to out Dan and Devon's relationship? You want me to—"

"Dan and Devon?" Haley's eyes sparkled as realization dawned. "Are you saying what I think you are?"

"Yeah, I'm saying Dan was gay and Devon was his boyfriend. Does that surprise you?"

"A little," she admitted. "But I suspected there was something odd about Jordan's marriage and I'd heard rumors about Devon. Now, it all makes sense." Chuckling wickedly, she danced her fingertips up J.C.'s chest. "You could use two-hundred-and-fifty-thousand dollars, couldn't you? That's what this story is worth. Probably more."

"You're a heartless bitch, you know that, don't you?"

She slipped the cigarette from between his fingers, tossed it onto the gravel, and then wrapped her arms around his neck. "The Chatterbox isn't going to dish out big money just to learn that there's another corpse in Jordan's past. You're going to have to go all the way and make the news as dirty and juicy as possible."

"Why do you hate Jordan so much?" He looked deep into her eyes, trying to figure out what made her tick.

"I don't hate Mrs. Price. She doesn't matter to me one way or another." Haley brushed her lips against his. "She's merely a means to an end for me and for Cy. If we can nail Jordan Price for her husband's murder, it'll be a feather in my cap and in Cy's. I want Steve Corbett's job and Cyrus has political aspirations that could take him to the governor's mansion."

"If Jordan is convicted of Dan's murder, she won't inherit, will she?"

Haley pulled away from him, her mouth downcast in a frown. "No, she won't. But that shouldn't matter to you. It's not like you'll ever see a dime of that money. She and the senator washed their hands of you, didn't they? This way, you come out ahead, with at least a quarter million in the bank."

"Yeah, you're right about me, but what about my mother and sister? Jordan takes real good care of them."

"If you invest your money the right way, you won't need anybody to support your family. You can do it." Haley ran her fingertips over his belt buckle. "And who knows, there could be a book deal in your future, even a made-for-TV movie. Think of all the money you'll make." She tapped her fingers up and down the fly of his pants.

J.C. grabbed her hand, spread it over his erection, and pressed it down hard against his crotch. He grinned. "You've almost persuaded me."

She undid his belt and unzipped his pants, then reached inside his shorts and freed his sex. Their gazes clashed. She knew what he wanted, what he expected in a non-monetary down payment.

Haley pulled him over into the grass, leading him there by his dick; then she dropped to her knees, took him into her mouth and gave him one of the best damn blow jobs he'd ever had.

Rick walked Ryan to his Mercedes and saw him off with reassurances that Powell's would continue do all they could to find out the truth. He intended to leave Price Manor himself as soon as he talked to Maleah. He wanted an unbiased opinion about Jordan's state of mind. This case was simply a job to Maleah. She wasn't emotionally invested in the outcome.

*And you shouldn't be either.*

But he was and there wasn't much he could do about that fact except maintain a barrier between Jordan and himself.

Jordan looked pale and drawn, almost haggard. He wondered if she'd been sleeping poorly and eating very little. Giving her more bad news this morning certainly hadn't helped any.

When he started up the steps to the veranda, the front door opened and Jordan walked out, her gaze searching the drive.

*Was she looking for him?*

"Rick, you aren't leaving yet, are you?"

He met her halfway in the middle of the veranda. They each stopped suddenly.

"Is there something you need?" he asked.

"I—yes, I was hoping you'd stay for a while."

"I need to speak to Maleah, then I should—"

"Don't go. Not yet."

"I realize you're probably upset and wondering what's going to happen next, but I promise you that Powell's will protect you and do everything possible to find out the truth, not only about the senator's death, but the others, too, if their deaths affect you or the Price family."

She reached out and touched him, her fingers gripping his arm tentatively, as if she were uncertain how he would react. "Do you think I'll be arrested for Dan's murder?"

"No, not unless they come up with more evidence than they have now. All the suppositions in the world aren't evidence. Even the most logical theory isn't evidence."

"But what about circumstantial evidence? You know people have been convicted—"

He clutched her shoulders. She gasped.

"Trust us to do our jobs. Trust me."

He shouldn't have put his hands on her. The temptation to comfort her overruled his common sense. Damning himself for a fool, he pulled her into his arms. As she rested against him, her head touching his chin, she released a quavering sigh and wrapped her arms around his waist.

He pressed his jaw against her temple as he held her. Protectively. Possessively.

"I feel as if I've finally lost everything," she whispered. "Even my sanity. Nothing makes sense anymore. I thought I had reached a point where nothing and no one could ever hurt me, but . . ." She burrowed her face deeper into his chest and clung to him as if he were her only lifeline.

Was she crying? Had her strong dam of reserve finally broken? God, he hoped so.

But when she lifted her head and looked up at him, her eyes were dry, her expression somber. He sensed her pain, felt it acutely, and would have taken it from her if he could have.

*Cry, damn it, cry.*

As he held Jordan, he caught a glimpse of movement behind her and looked across the veranda to the front door. Rene Burke stood in the open doorway watching them. When her gaze connected with his, she held up a package and waved it in the air.

Rick slid his hands up the outer edges of Jordan's arms until he reached her shoulders. "I think Rene needs to speak to us," he said softly.

Jordan lifted her head and pulled out of his arms, then turned to face her assistant. "Yes, what is it?"

"I've been looking through the morning mail and discovered a package—" she held out the small yellow padded envelope "—addressed to you. The label is printed in pencil."

Rick reached down and grabbed Jordan's hand. She threaded her fingers through his and gripped tightly.

"Where's Maleah?" Rick asked Rene.

"She's waiting for us inside," Rene replied.

Jordan looked up at Rick. "You'll stay, won't you? At least until after I open the package."

His nonverbal reply of squeezing her hand seemed to be all the reassurance she needed. She released his hand and followed Rene into the house. Just as he started to enter the foyer, his sixth sense warned him that he was being watched. He looked right and left, behind him and then up. A shadow of movement caught his eye. Someone standing in an upstairs window had moved away quickly.

Whoever had been there was gone now.

A weird vibe crept up his spine.

He went into the house and quickly caught up with Jordan and Rene. Not once on the walk from the foyer to her study at the back of the house did Jordan glance over her shoulder to see if he was still there.

Was she that sure of him?

Maleah met them as they entered the study. She eyed Rick inquisitively, but she didn't say anything.

"Do you want me to open it?" Rene asked.

"No, I'll do it," Jordan replied.

Rick held out his hand. "Give it to me and you two step back. I doubt there's a bomb inside or anything deadly, but it's better to be safe than sorry."

After his comment, Rene couldn't hand him the package fast enough. Rick took it and examined it thoroughly. With all eyes on him, he ripped open the envelope, up-ended it, and then shook it. Sheets of white paper held together with a large paperclip slid from the padded container and dropped onto the desk.

Rick picked up the small bundle and looked at the top sheet. It was a copy of Jane Anne Price's obituary.

After removing the paperclip, he shuffled through the other pages.

"What is it?" Jordan came toward him.

"Copies of obituaries," he told her.

"Whose?" Rene asked.

Rick went through them, one by one. "Jane Anne Price." He laid the sheet on the desk. "Daniel Price, Boyd Brannon, Donald Farris, Jay Reynolds, Robby Joe Wright, and Wayne Harris." He held one final sheet in his hand.

"Who else?" Jordan asked.

He handed the sheet of paper to her. She read it slowly, carefully, then reread it aloud.

*"Jordan Helene Price, thirty-four, of Priceville, Georgia is dead. Funeral arrangements will be announced by Benefield Funeral Home. Mrs. Price was a native of Valdosta, Georgia, the only child of Wayne and Helene Harris. She was preceded in death by her parents, her fiancé, Robby Joe Wright, her first husband, Boyd Brannon, and her second husband, Daniel Price."*

Rick snatched the paper out of her hand. "That's enough."

Jordan stared at him, a detached look in her eyes.

He grabbed her by the shoulders and shook her. "Jordan. Jordan!"

She continued staring at him, not moving, not speaking.

"Damn it, Jordan, snap out of it." He shook her again.

"Am I dead?" she asked half a second before she fainted.

# Chapter 20

After parking her car a block from his apartment, she removed the wooden baseball bat from the trunk, slipped it beneath her all-weather coat and held it close to her body. She had followed him from the Peachtree Agency, keeping a discreet distance behind him the entire way. Once she realized that he was going home, she had relaxed, knowing that tonight would be the night. If she could catch him alone in the parking garage, she would put her plan into action.

The autumn air was crisp, the half moon semi-bright, the stars twinkling dimly in the black sky. As she hurried along the sidewalk, rushing to reach the entrance to the basement parking garage, her heartbeat raced as excitement rushed through her body.

She had worn rubber-heeled athletic shoes that she had purchased at the Dollar Store, just as she had bought the cheap all-weather coat and the bat at Wal-Mart. None could be easily traced, certainly not back to her.

She would burn everything she wore tonight, including her underwear, and also, the weapon.

Breathless, her face warm, her adrenaline high, she paused for a moment when she saw him standing by his BMW, his back to her as he leaned into the front seat. He had no idea that tonight was his last night on earth. Within a few minutes, he would be dead, punished for his sins. She removed the baseball bat from under her coat and held it up, both hands wrapped tightly around it. With quiet, catlike movements, she came up behind him just as he removed his briefcase from the car.

She lifted the bat as high as she possibly could, then with one hard, fast lunge, brought it down on the back of his head. He yelped, then staggered, unsteady on his feet. Before he could turn on her, she hit him again, this time landing a blow to the side of his head. As blood trickled from his scalp in two places, dampening his sandy hair and freckled face with red streaks, he slumped forward, his flailing arms reaching out. His knees buckled. She hit him again. Harder. He fell to his knees. She repeated the blows over and over again until he lay flat on his face, sprawled out on the concrete floor.

He wasn't moving, wasn't breathing. He was dead. And yet she couldn't stop hitting him, bringing the bat down on his head repeatedly until only a raw, bloody mess remained.

Breathing hard, the triumph of the moment obliterating everything from her mind, she stood over his body, proud of her kill, as any hunter would be.

After enjoying her moment of glory, she propped the baseball bat against the side of the BMW, knelt beside him and searched his pockets. She removed his wallet and shoved it into her coat pocket. Then she took off his watch and rings and put them in her other pocket.

After she picked up the bloody baseball bat, she swiped it back and forth over his legs to clean it off, then she slipped it under her coat. Before leaving, she looked down at him one final time.

"You will never harass another woman, never frighten anyone again. You weren't a nice man, Jay Reynolds. You got just what you deserved."

The memory of that long-ago night flashed through her mind as if it had been captured on film and was now re-playing.

"She's coming to," Rene said. "Her eyelashes are flut-tering and she's moaning."

Rick, who had caught Jordan when she fainted and brought her to the sofa, huddled beside her. He ran the back of his hand over her face. "Jordan? Jordan, wake up."

She opened her eyes and stared up at him. "What happened?"

"You fainted," Rene said.

When Jordan tried to sit up, Rick put his hand high on her chest and gently pushed her back down. "Stay still and relax."

She grabbed Rick's hand. "Please, don't mention this to anyone else. I don't want them worrying about me."

"*I'm* worried about you," he said. "I sent Maleah to get your doctor's phone number from Tobias."

"No, please, I don't need a doctor."

"You fainted," he reminded her. "People don't faint without a reason."

"Seeing my own obituary written out like that unnerved me," she told him. "That's all it was."

"I'm not buying it. You didn't faint when you found your husband's body, did you? I don't think reading a mock obituary would—"

"I need to sit up." She looked at him pleadingly.

He slid his arm beneath her shoulders and helped her into a sitting position.

"I didn't eat much breakfast," Jordan said. "I don't have any appetite and I'm not sleeping well at night. Please, believe me. I do not need a doctor."

The door flew open and Darlene Wright stormed in. "What happened to Jordan? Is she all right?" Darlene looked Jordan over thoroughly, then slumped down on the sofa beside her. "Oh, thank goodness, you're all right. I heard that woman . . . Ms. Perdue . . . asking Tobias about calling Dr. Carroll. She said that you fainted."

Jordan took Darlene's hand in hers. "I'm all right. I was just a little lightheaded."

Darlene stared at Rick. "Did something happen to upset her?"

"No, no, nothing," Jordan said.

"There's no use trying to hide it from her," Rene said as she gathered the stack of obituaries and handed them to Darlene. "Someone's tormenting Jordan. First that damn letter, then the phone call and now this."

"Oh, my, my." Darlene's eyes glistened with tears as she looked through the papers in her hand. "Whoever this person is, he or she may well be the one who killed Jane Anne. I'm afraid you may be in real danger."

Devon tore into the study. "Are you all right? I overheard Tobias telling Vadonna that you had fainted." He looked at Rick. "Shouldn't we call Dr. Carroll?"

"No, we shouldn't." Jordan shoved everyone aside and rose to her feet. "I am perfectly all right. I forbid anyone—" she glared at Rick "—to call Dr. Carroll."

The distinctive ring of Jordan's cell phone silenced any protests that might have been made. Everyone froze.

"That's my phone," Jordan said. "Rene, it's on the desk. Would you get it for me, please."

Before Rene had a chance to move, Rick reached the

desk and picked up the phone. Caller ID read Unknown. He flipped open the phone. Everyone looked at him.

He listened as the caller rattled off something about being chosen for a special service to pay off credit card debts. With the recorded message still playing, he closed the phone and placed it back on the desk.

"It was a solicitor," he told them.

They released a collective sigh of relief.

"I think you should go upstairs and rest until lunchtime," Darlene suggested. "I'll bring you up a pot of tea and—"

"Actually, what I think I need is some fresh air," Jordan said.

Rene, Devon and Darlene all spoke at once, each offering to go for a walk with her.

She held up her hand in a STOP gesture. "You're all very sweet to offer, but I need to discuss some things with Rick." She looked at him. "Do you have time to go for a short walk with me before you leave?"

He nodded. "If you think you feel up to it."

After hugs all around and verbal reassurances that she really was all right, she shooed everyone out of her study, except Rick and Maleah.

Rick bundled up the obituaries and gave them to Maleah. "Secure these," he told her. "Then call the sheriff and fill him in on what's happened—the letter, these obituaries, the phone call yesterday. Don't speak to anyone else, only to Steve Corbett."

Maleah nodded, then left Rick and Jordan alone in the study.

"Do you think it's necessary to involve the sheriff?" Jordan asked.

"Yeah, I think it's time."

"Darlene and Devon and even Rene are upset and worried about me. I'm sure one of them will tell Roselynne and then the whole family will know."

"A lot of people care about you," Rick said.

"I keep asking myself when this nightmare will end, but I'm beginning to think it never will. First Dan's death, then all the ugly publicity, followed by Jane Anne's murder and now this—someone harassing me."

"Do you really feel up to a walk?" Rick asked.

"Yes, I do." She smiled. "Fresh air and sunshine is a remedy for almost any ailment."

"Do you need a sweater?"

She shook her head.

They walked in silence for at least ten minutes, strolling through Dan's rose garden, Vadonna's herb garden, and then past the greenhouse and onto a dirt path that led to the pond at the front of the property. In the distance, he caught a glimpse of the drive and the massive front gates. But within seconds, a row of evergreen hedges blocked the view. Noonday bright and warm, the sun poised directly overhead in the clear, blue sky. A hint of a breeze stirred, ruffling the treetops and caressing the high grass. Wildflowers grew in abundance in the fields, their scent delicate and subtle. This was one of those rare, springtime, perfect weather days.

But Jordan Price's life was far from perfect.

She broke the silence by asking, "When you were in your late teens or early twenties, did you think you knew exactly what your life was going to be like?"

Rick broke a small dead twig off a low-lying tree branch. "I'm not sure if I can remember back that far."

Jordan smiled. "You say that as if you're an old man now."

"I'm thirty-nine," he told her.

"That's not old."

He tossed the brittle twig through the air and watched it hit the ground a good ten feet away. "I'm old enough to know better than to reminisce about boyhood dreams."

"Then you did have dreams."

"Sure. I guess everybody does." Rick kept in step with Jordan as she continued walking.

"When I met Robby Joe and fell in love with him, I thought I would have a perfectly wonderful life." She didn't pause or look at Rick. "If he hadn't died, we'd be married now and have a home in the suburbs, a couple of children, a dog and an SUV. I'd be teaching school and running my kids from soccer practice to ballet lessons. In the evenings, after the kids were asleep, we'd sit alone together and talk about our day."

Rick glanced at her and the look on her face rattled him. Not once in the time he'd known Jordan had he ever seen happiness on her beautiful face.

"You were very much in love with him, weren't you?"

"Very much." She paused and smiled at Rick. "Haven't you ever been in love?"

"I've been in lust a few times, but not in love. Not the real deal."

"My life didn't turn out the way I'd planned. After Robby Joe died . . . I don't know, everything changed. I changed."

"We all change as we grow older and wiser," Rick said. "The rose-colored glasses come off and reality slaps us in the face."

"When did that happen to you?"

He didn't reply.

When she started walking again, he followed along beside her.

Maybe because she didn't press him for an answer, he chose to be honest with her. "By the time I was a senior in high school, my widowed father, who'd been raised dirt poor, had built up a construction business from scratch. When he met Sharon, he was worth a couple million. She took one look at him and saw dollar signs. It had been my dad's dream for me to go into business with him. Carson and Son Construction." Rick hadn't talked about his father in years and he'd never told anyone about how his stepmother had driven his father to an early grave and had stolen Rick and his sister's inheritance.

And he wasn't sure why he was telling Jordan.

They came to a clearing near a spring-fed brook not more than fifteen feet wide. The water flowed slowly over the rocky bed, sunlight reflecting off the surface. Birds chirped from their perches in nearby trees. Bees buzzed as they flew from one plant to another.

Jordan sat down in the grass near the stream, pulled her knees up, and circled them with her arms as she stared dreamily into the rippling water.

Rick sat beside her. "Sharon was fifteen years younger than he was. She convinced him that she was madly in love with him. He believed her, married her, and she made his life a living hell. She spent money as if it grew on trees. She flirted with other men like the tramp she was. But my father was crazy about her and forgave her God knows how many times. Their marriage lasted six years, until the day he died. He was only forty-eight years old. And when she buried him, she never shed the first tear."

Jordan reached out and laid her hand over his.

He felt her touch to the marrow of his bones.

"By the time he died, Dad and I were barely speaking. He left everything to Sharon and within a year, she'd gone through every cent the old man left her. She sold the business for half of what it was worth and I heard that a couple of years later, when she was flat broke, she found herself another sucker."

Jordan squeezed his hand.

"My dream of going into business with my dad after college, the two of us working together, growing Carson and Sons into the biggest and best construction firm in the state of Mississippi . . ." Rick snorted. "It was a kid's dream."

"I don't have any more dreams," Jordan said, her voice whispery soft. "My last dream died with my baby."

Rick flipped her hand over and held it. "You haven't had a chance to mourn. You need to cry."

"Did you cry when your father died?"

"Damn right, I cried," he admitted. "Not at the funeral, but a week later when I was alone. I cried like a little boy."

"I cried when my father died and when Robby Joe died."

"Not since then?"

She eased her hand out of his, then brought her chin down to rest on her knees. "I wish I could cry. I can't. The tears just won't come. I couldn't cry when Boyd died or when Dan died. I can't even cry for my baby."

"Jordan?"

She closed her eyes.

Rick put his arm around her shoulders. "I'm sorry about the baby."

She leaned her head on his shoulder and they sat there, with the sun shining, the birds singing, and the breeze blowing. Rick wasn't sure whether five minutes or five hours had passed. It was as if time had stood still. Somehow the only thing that seemed to matter was comforting Jordan, helping her find a few stolen moments of peace.

She turned her face toward him and gazed into his eyes. He had never seen anything more beautiful in his entire life and had never wanted anything as much as he wanted to taste her mouth. Without conscious thought, he lowered his lips to hers, taking them with tender hunger. She responded, her mouth parting on a sigh.

Suddenly as if only then realizing what she was doing, she ended the kiss and pulled away from him. He stared at her, slightly dazed by the way he'd reacted to the kiss. She jumped up, brushed the grass from her slacks and turned away without saying a word.

"Jordan?"

She walked off, leaving him sitting there staring at her back.

He rose to his feet and followed her.

"Jordan, wait."

She walked faster and faster. He called her name again. She ran away from him without a backward glance.

# Chapter 21

Devon hated seeing Jordan so unhappy, so stressed, so in need of something he could not give her. From childhood, she had been his best friend, his champion when he was persecuted, his confidante when he needed someone with whom he could share his innermost secrets, his comforter when his heart had been broken. He had relied on her unwavering friendship and had depended upon her strength to lend him support whenever it was needed. But what had he ever done for Jordan? Even in the worst times of her life, he had been able to do little except hold her hand and mouth platitudes, promising her a better tomorrow.

He had wept with her when her father died, but had been unable to help her when she'd asked him, "What am I going to do about Roselynne and Tammy? How can I take care of them?" But in true Jordan fashion, she had found the answer within her generous heart.

He had watched her fall apart when she lost Robby Joe. He had held her, wept with her, slept alongside her, stayed with her day and night for weeks. And when she had overdosed on sleeping pills, he and Darlene had taken turns sitting at her bedside twenty-four/seven. And once again, Jordan had rebounded because she had focused on helping Darlene instead of drowning in self-pity.

In the beginning, he had been opposed to her marrying Boyd Brannon. Not that he hadn't liked Boyd. He had. But Jordan had been in love with Boyd's children and the dream of having a child of her own, not with Boyd. When Boyd had been killed in a tragic hunting accident, he had flown in from D.C. and stayed two weeks. But she hadn't needed him, not the way she had when she'd lost Robby Joe. He and Darlene had realized that Jordan's only concern had been Kendra and Wesley. She loved them then and loved them now as if they were her own. Darlene had moved in with them and stayed for over a year, and he and Dan had visited as often as possible.

Sadly, helplessly, Devon had watched Jordan's metamorphosis as she changed from a sweet, happy, optimistic young girl into a lonely, guarded, emotionally restrained woman. She had given up her youthful hopes and dreams and focused on her caretaker duties to her adopted family: Roselynne, Tammy, J.C., Darlene, Kendra and Wesley. And then three years ago, Dan had been approached by leaders in the party and asked to consider running for president. They had pointed out that in order to project the proper image to the public, he would need a wife.

Neither he nor Dan had wanted to share their personal relationship with a third party. Dan's first marriage had ended badly when he had admitted to his wife that he was gay and in love with someone else. Even though Devon had known that a second marriage would have been a marriage in name only, he'd hated the thought of sharing Dan, of giving up even a few of the precious stolen hours they shared. But he understood how politically ambitious Dan was and he hadn't wanted to be the reason the man he loved wouldn't be able to fulfill his lifelong dreams.

He actually couldn't remember whose idea it had been for Dan to marry Jordan. When she'd come for a weekend visit to Price Manor, as she often did, the three of them had been sitting around one evening after dinner and the subject of Dan running for president had come up. During the course of their conversation, Jordan had joked about how Dan should marry her because she had no intention of ever falling in love and marrying again and she knew and loved both Devon and Dan. By the time Jordan drove back to Atlanta that Sunday night, they had formed a plan for Jordan and Dan to marry. By week's end, the arrangements had been made for a private ceremony, and by the end of the month, Jordan became Mrs. Daniel Price.

Oddly enough, the marriage had been a blessing for all three of them, or so they had thought. Even their decision to have a child had seemed like the right thing to do. In retrospect, Devon wondered if they had been ridiculously naïve to believe that the three of them could continue living a lie indefinitely.

As he gazed out his bedroom window, his thoughts in the past with Dan, he was brought abruptly back to the present when he saw Jordan running toward the house, running as if she were being chased by the devil.

Where the hell was Rick Carson? Hadn't he been with Jordan? And if he had left Price Manor, why wasn't Maleah Perdue keeping tabs on Jordan?

Devon left his room and rushed into the hall and down the back staircase, intending to meet Jordan when she entered the house. Within minutes, she raced through the back door, her face flushed, her eyes overly bright.

He called her name. She ignored him.

As she passed him, he reached out and grabbed her arm. She glared at him, then jerked free of his grasp and dashed up the backstairs.

"Jordan?"

"I need to be alone for a while," she called to him from halfway up the stairs. "Please, Devon, please."

What the hell had happened to her? She was obviously upset, but why? Or should he wonder who had upset her?

He would give her some time alone, but later, he would go to her and find out what was wrong.

Suddenly the back door flew open again and Rick Carson bounded into the house. "Where is she?" Rick asked.

"I assume you're referring to Jordan."

Rick nodded.

"She went upstairs to her room," Devon said. "And she doesn't want to be disturbed."

"That's too damn bad."

When Rick headed for the backstairs, Devon stepped in front of him. The two men stared at each other, both knowing that this confrontation could end badly.

"She's upset," Rick said. "I need to make sure she's all right."

"What happened to upset her?" Devon asked.

"That's between Jordan and me."

"Why don't we give her some time alone, then I'll go check on her and if she wants to talk to you—"

"Go check on her now," Rick told him.

Devon hesitated, then said, "All right, but only if you promise to stay here and if she doesn't want to see you, you won't insist."

"Agreed."

They didn't shake on it, but Devon sensed he could trust Rick, that he was a man of his word.

When Devon reached the closed door to Jordan's bedroom suite, he paused, uncertain whether or not he was doing the right thing, but then he lifted his fist and knocked. She didn't respond. He knocked again. Not a sound. He grasped the knob and tried the door, suspecting she might have locked out the world. But she hadn't. The door opened easily. He peered inside, but didn't see her. He walked into the room and looked around, but Jordan wasn't there. Maybe she'd gone to the bathroom. The door leading through the dressing room and into the bathroom stood partially ajar. When he entered the dressing room, he noticed that the louvered doors to the walk-in closet were wide open.

Jordan sat on the floor inside the closet, a garment bag draped over her body as she held it to her chest. He stopped outside the closet, his gaze traveling the length of the unzipped garment bag, and looked at the heavily beaded, white satin wedding gown.

"Jordan?"

She didn't seem surprised by his presence, didn't gasp, didn't call his name or even glance up at him.

"What are you doing in here?"

Sitting there calm and still, she asked, "Do you remember going with Darlene and me to look for my wedding dress?"

"Sure, sweetie, I remember."

"The moment I put this dress on and walked out of the dressing room, you and Darlene both laughed and said this was the one."

"You looked like a princess, beautiful and regal." And happy. God, she'd been so very happy. He'd give anything to see her like that again.

"Robby Joe never saw this dress." She caressed the lace bodice, dripping in crystal beads and pearls.

Devon entered the closet, eased down slowly, and sat beside her. "I didn't know you still had the dress. I thought maybe—"

"I haven't looked at this dress in years." She hugged it to her chest.

"Then why are you looking at it today?"

When he reached out to take the garment bag from her, she held it all the tighter.

"Jordan, give me the dress and let me hang it back up."

"I've never really loved anyone else, only Robby Joe. In all these years, I've never met another man who . . . who . . ." She stroked the beads, but Devon could tell that her fingers worked on their own, separate from her thoughts.

"What happened between you and Rick Carson?"

She snapped around and stared wildly at Devon, but didn't answer his question.

"He followed you, you know. He's waiting downstairs. He wants to talk to you."

"I don't want to talk to him."

Devon laid his hand over hers and lifted it up and away from the dress; then he speared his fingers through hers. "Let me put the dress up."

She looked at him through glazed eyes and when he tugged on the garment bag, she released it. He sighed with relief. He had seen Jordan like this only two other times—shortly after Robby Joe died and the morning she discovered Dan's body. She had snapped out of it fairly quickly that morning, unlike in the past when Devon had feared for her sanity.

He stood, carried the garment bag with him, and placed it deep in the back of the closet.

Why on earth had she kept the damn dress?

He held out his hand to her. "Come on. Let's go."

She put her hand in his and rose to her feet. He slid his arm around her shoulders and guided her into the sitting room, but she didn't want to sit. Instead, she paced back and forth, while he watched her, feeling totally helpless.

"I've made so many mistakes, so many." Her voice trembled with emotion. "I've tried to do the right thing, tried to take care of my responsibilities, done the best I could." She stopped and looked right at him. "I have done my best, haven't I?"

He grabbed her gently by the shoulders. "I don't know what's going on, but you have to get hold of yourself. I haven't seen you like this since—"

"Since Robby Joe died," she finished the sentence for him. "I think I went a little crazy after I lost him. Even now, there are things I can't remember clearly. I think I've blocked out some of the memories."

"It's better that you have."

She nodded. "I remember being in love, how it felt . . . I remember what it was like to want someone until I ached with the wanting. I've never wanted anyone else the way I wanted Robby Joe, not until . . . It's wrong to feel like this. I know it's wrong. Wrong time, wrong place, wrong man. Wrong, wrong, wrong."

"It's Rick Carson, isn't it?"

She grabbed Devon's hand. "I just lost my husband and my baby. My life is being put under a microscope because I'm suspected of killing half a dozen people. And I've known Rick for less than two weeks and the man doesn't even trust me."

"The heart wants what the heart wants," Devon told her.

She smiled weakly. "I'm not sure it's what my heart wants, maybe just what my body wants."

"Tell me what happened between you and Rick."

"He kissed me. I don't think he meant to kiss me, but he did. And it wasn't one-sided. I kissed him back."

"And it scared the hell out of you."

"Maybe he's just a really good kisser. Maybe because of the miscarriage, my hormones are all screwed up. Maybe I'm just freaking nuts!"

Devon brought her hands to his mouth and kissed each one, then released her. "You're not nuts. At least not any nuttier than the rest of us. You've been through hell lately. Just like me, your world has been turned topsy-turvy and you don't know what's going to happen next. Add to that scenario a big, strong macho guy with broad shoulders to lean on. Hell, if he wasn't straight, I'd be tempted to—"

Smiling broadly, Jordan tapped his lips with her right

index finger. "No, you wouldn't. It's going to take you a long time to get over losing Dan."

He heaved a deep sigh. "Dan was the love of my life, just as Robby Joe was the love of your life. But that doesn't mean that someday I won't meet someone else and fall in love again. And even if what's happening between you and Rick isn't love, it's not wrong."

"Maybe not, but it feels wrong." She closed her eyes, tilted her head back and breathed deeply. "I feel as if I'm being unfaithful to Robby Joe." She opened her eyes, held up her hand in a STOP signal and said, "I know that doesn't make any sense."

"You need to talk to Rick. Tell him that you're not ready for any kind of a relationship, emotional or physical. I have a feeling that he'll understand and probably agree with you."

"I acted like such an idiot when he kissed me."

"He's downstairs just waiting for a word from me to come up here."

She nodded. "Okay."

"Okay, you'll talk to him?"

"Yes, I'll talk to him."

Devon tickled her under her chin. "You scared me there for a few minutes, back in the closet, sitting there clinging to that old wedding dress."

"It was just a moment of weakness," she said. "We all have them occasionally, right?"

"Right."

Leaving her alone to sort through her feelings and hopefully, to steady her nerves, Devon took his time going back downstairs. He wasn't completely convinced that Jordan really was all right.

He found Rick alone in the kitchen, his cell phone pressed against his ear.

"Talk to you later," Rick said, then turned to Devon.

"She wants to see you," Devon told him.

"Is she okay?"

"Yeah, I think so."

"What did she tell you?"

"That you kissed her and she kissed you back," Devon said.

"It wasn't planned. It just happened."

"She knows that."

Rick nodded, then took the backstairs two at a time.

*Why couldn't Rick Carson have shown up in Jordan's life sooner, before she married Dan or Boyd?* Devon wondered.

Rick knocked on the closed door.

"Yes?"

"May I come in?"

"Yes."

He eased the door open and paused for half a second when he saw her standing in the middle of the room looking right at him, head held high, shoulders squared. Battle ready.

"About what happened," he said.

"Come in and close the door."

He responded to her request, then hesitated before approaching her.

What the hell had happened to him out there? He wasn't the type of man who mixed business with pleasure or had ever had trouble keeping his dick in his pants. What had he been thinking, kissing a woman in such a vulnerable state, someone who so obviously needed only the utmost tender, loving care.

"I'm sorry," they spoke simultaneously, both expressing the same sentiment.

Her lips curved upward in a fragile smile. "I overreacted to a simple kiss."

There was nothing simple about the kiss they'd shared

and they both damn well knew it. "I shouldn't have kissed you."

"It had been a long time since a man kissed me that way."

"You just looked so damn beautiful." He huffed, releasing some of his frustration. "I know that's no excuse. I didn't realize I was going to kiss you until it actually happened."

"We're both making far too much of this. It was just a kiss and that's all it was."

"Yeah, that's all it was."

"Sometimes physical attraction just happens. If we look at the situation for what it is—"

"It won't happen again," he assured her.

"No, it won't happen again."

"Then we're good?" he asked.

"Yes, we're good."

"I'm going to head back to the Inn, make a few phone calls, wrap up the copies of those obituaries and send them off to the Powell lab in Knoxville. I'll let Maleah know I'm leaving."

When he turned and walked to the door, Jordan followed him. He stepped into the hall, then paused for a minute and faced her.

"Will you be back tomorrow?" she asked.

"Probably not."

"Monday, then?"

"Yeah, I'll be back Monday." Come Monday morning, he intended to speak to Roselynne about exhuming Wayne Harris's body and Darlene about exhuming her son's body. If the doctor employed by Powell's to do independent autopsies could verify that Wayne Harris did indeed die of a heart attack and Robby Joe Wright died as a result of injuries sustained in a car wreck, then they could blow holes in the DA's theory that Jordan was a black widow.

And right now, proving Jordan innocent was more important than anything else.

# Chapter 22

Rick had kept busy Sunday, going over every tidbit of information Powell's had gathered on Jordan and those closest to her. He had studied the copies of the police reports on the deaths of Jay Reynolds, Donald Farris, Boyd Brannon, Dan Price and Jane Anne Price. Only two deaths had been ruled homicide: Jane Anne's and Jay Reynolds's. Farris's and Brannon's deaths had been classified as accidents; and Dan Price's as suicide. He had read and reread the hospital files on Wayne Harris and Robby Joe Wright, everything detailed from the minute they entered the ER until they were pronounced dead. Harris, who had been only 49 when he died, had been a heavy smoker, overweight and dealing with a stressful job as a plant manager. The night Robby Joe had died, he'd been driving on a rain-slick highway during a thunderstorm. His small sports car had hydroplaned and landed head-on into a massive oak tree. He had received severe head trauma in the accident. Even if the paramedics had arrived seconds after the crash, there would have been no way to save him.

How could anyone believe that either Harris's death or

Wright's had been murder? The facts were right there, in the files. But neither man had been autopsied because there had been no reason to perform the procedure. Autopsies hadn't been necessary and if performed now would serve only one purpose—to substantiate the doctors' original opinion as to cause of death.

As he drove his Jeep up to the front gates at Price Manor, Rick noticed that the horde of reporters swarming around the entrance to the estate had dwindled to only a few. The newspaper and television reports were no longer front page news. But how long would this lull last if and when the FBI became involved?

The Powell guards opened the gates and Rick waved at them as he entered. If it were possible to avoid seeing Jordan this morning, it would make things easier all the way around. Not that he couldn't handle seeing her, but they were both better off spending some time apart. Physical attraction could be a tricky thing.

After parking his Jeep near the garage, he got out and walked to the cottage where Roselynne Harris lived. He had phoned her an hour ago and made an appointment, telling her only that he wanted to speak to her about a way she could help Jordan.

"You name it," she had said. "Anything on God's green earth I can do for that girl, I'll do."

Rick had no more than raised his fist to knock on the door, when Tammy yanked it open and stood there staring up at him.

"Good morning," he said.

She bounded out the door. He stepped aside to give her ample space to get by him.

"I'm going to sit out here in the swing and wait for Jordan," Tammy said. "We're going for a walk together while you and Mama talk."

"I see. That's nice. You and Jordan are great friends, aren't you?"

"We're more than friends, silly. We're sisters."

"Yes, I know."

"Mr. Carson?" Roselynne called from the doorway. "Come on in."

He entered the living room, a warm, welcoming area filled with a mix of antique and new furniture and decorated in a style that he'd call homey.

"Would you care for some coffee?" she asked. "I just put on a fresh pot."

"No, thanks, nothing for me."

"Well, sit down and take a load off."

He sat on the sofa. Roselynne sat beside him. He noticed that despite the early hour—eight-fifteen—she had already applied a thick layer of makeup, fixed her hair, and put on a pair of skin-tight jeans and a low-cut, knit sweater. Two pairs of large gold hoops dangled from her ears.

"I appreciate your agreeing to talk to me this morning."

"You said there was something I could do to help Jordan. I told you that I'd do anything I could to help her. Just name it."

"I'm sure you would." When Rick turned to face her, he realized she was right there, less than a foot away from him. He eased down to the end of the sofa, all the while smiling as he said, "You know what's being said about Jordan, that quite a few men in her life have met untimely deaths."

"It's a tragedy, but that's all it is," Roselynne said. "That girl could no more kill somebody than I could."

"We need to try to prove just that—that she didn't kill anyone. And we can start by proving that she didn't kill her father, that he actually did die of a heart attack."

"Well, of course, he did. My Wayne was a chubby-chubby. Cute as a button, mind you, but roly-poly. That man loved fried food and I cooked him what he liked.

And it didn't help that he smoked like a chimney. I quit smoking after Wayne died. I didn't want to drop dead before I turned fifty the way he did."

"Very wise decision, Mrs. Harris."

"Well, what exactly can I do to help you prove for sure and certain that Wayne died of a heart attack?"

"You can give us permission to have his body exhumed," Rick said, wishing there had been a gentler, less direct way of saying it.

"What?"

"The Powell agency can have an independent autopsy done to corroborate the cause of death stated on Mr. Harris's death certificate."

"You want to dig Wayne up and cut him open?"

"Everything would be done in a respectful manner and—"

Roselynne jumped up. "No. Absolutely not!"

Rick stood. "Mrs. Harris—"

"I said no. I'm not going to let anybody dig up my Wayne and cut him up in little pieces. He had a heart attack. The doctor said so. Nobody killed him. Certainly not Jordan."

"I believe that," Rick said. "But an autopsy should be able to prove the cause of death beyond a reasonable doubt."

"No, no . . ." She shook her head. "It's just not right to dig a person up after all these years. It's indecent, that's what it is."

The screendoor swung open and Tammy entered, her eyes wide, her small hands clenched like talons. "Don't you upset my mama. Leave her alone."

"Tammy, honey, it's all right. Mr. Carson didn't mean to upset me."

"I'm sorry, the last thing I wanted to do was upset anyone," Rick said.

"I think maybe you'd better go," Roselynne told him.

"I'm sorry I can't help you, but I honestly don't think Jordan would expect me to agree to such a thing."

Rick sensed her presence before he glanced at the doorway again and saw Jordan standing on the other side of the screendoor. Tammy must have sensed that she was there, too, because she turned around and called out Jordan's name.

"Is there something wrong?" Jordan asked.

Tammy opened the screendoor, grabbed Jordan's hand and dragged her into the living room. "He—" she pointed at Rick "—has upset Mama. He told her he wants to dig up Daddy Wayne and cut him up in little pieces."

Jordan's gaze clashed with Rick's, her eyes filled with questions.

Roselynne shook her head. "He asked me for permission to have your daddy's body exhumed and an autopsy performed. I told him I couldn't agree to it. You know I can't."

"That's a bad thing, isn't it, Jordan?" Tammy looked to her stepsister for agreement. "Digging up dead people is a sin."

"Roselynne, see if you can explain to Tammy that nothing bad is going to happen to anyone, that everything is all right." Jordan didn't break eye contact with Rick. "We need to talk. Outside."

He should have known better than to think this would be easy. Nothing about this case had been simple, easy, or cut-and-dried from day one.

Once on the porch, Jordan walked out into the yard. He followed her. She glanced at the house and when she saw that Roselynne had closed both the screendoor and the wooden front door, she turned on Rick.

"What possessed you to ask Roselynne for permission to exhume Daddy's body?"

"Nothing sinister, I assure you. If Powell's could conduct an independent autopsy that corroborated the cause of death stated on your father's death certificate, and we could do the same with Robby Joe, then that would prove two of the six men you're suspected of killing were not murdered."

"My God! You haven't approached Darlene about exhuming Robby Joe's body, have you?"

"No, not yet," Rick said.

"Don't you dare suggest such a thing to her. Do you hear me? The very thought of exhuming his body would tear Darlene apart. He might have died twelve years ago, but the loss is as much a part of her now as it was then, and she loves—"

"Are we talking about how Darlene feels or are we talking about how you still feel about Robby Joe?"

Jordan tensed.

"Maybe exhuming Robby Joe's body would not only enable us to prove he died from injuries sustained in a car wreck, but it just might allow you to crawl out of that grave you buried yourself in when he died."

She slapped Rick.

He knew he deserved it. He'd had no right to say such a thing to her, even if he'd meant every word.

She cried out in shock at what she'd done. "I'm sorry. I—I didn't mean . . ." Her voice quavered. "I don't want to you say anything to Darlene. And please don't approach Roselynne again. We will not agree to have Daddy's or Robby Joe's body exhumed."

"You do realize, don't you, that by being so adamantly opposed to autopsying their bodies, you make it look as if you're trying to hide something?"

"What you mean is that you think it makes me look guilty, that people will believe I really did kill my father, whom I loved dearly, and my fiancé, who meant everything to me."

"This information goes no further than right here," Rick told her. "It stays between you and me. But I'm telling you that the more proof we have of your innocence in any of the past deaths, the better it will be if you're charged with Dan's murder. Cam Hendrix is a great lawyer, but he needs—"

"Do you think I'm going to be arrested for killing Dan?"

"I didn't say that. I just said if."

"I thought things were improving. The reporters aren't setting up tents outside the gates and neither Steve nor any of his deputies have questioned me again. Things seemed to be dying down, so I assumed—"

"Assume nothing," he told her. "Prepare for the worst."

"Yes, of course, you're probably right. Past experience has taught me that lesson well. I can't expect my luck to change now, can I?"

"I won't bother your stepmother again and I won't say anything to Mrs. Wright."

"Thank you."

"I had planned to speak to you after meeting with each of them this morning," he told her. "I wanted you to know that I'm going back to Knoxville today. Maleah's here to act as your personal bodyguard and Holt Keinan will lead the case from here on out."

"But why? I need you here."

"What you need is an agent in charge who hasn't allowed himself to become personally involved. I can't be objective when it comes to you, and in the long run, that could hurt you instead of help you."

"Oh, I see. So you're saying that you're taking yourself off this case permanently. You're leaving and you won't be coming back."

"I think it's best, don't you?"

She didn't reply for several minutes and a part of him wanted her to disagree, wanted her to ask him to stay on the job.

Finally she said, "Yes, I agree. You've made the right decision."

# Chapter 23

On his return to Knoxville, Rick had hoped Powell's would send him out of town on a new assignment, but as luck would have it, his turn came up in the rotation of agents at Griffin's Rest. He figured Nic might have maneuvered the list in order to bring him here, but he hadn't questioned her judgment. For the past nine days, while on duty at what many referred to as the Powell Compound, he had been included in agency conferences concerning the Price case. The guards at the front gate of the Price estate had been reduced to three, who rotated on eight-hour shifts. Except for an occasional straggler, the reporters had all but disappeared, making life easier for everyone, but especially for Jordan.

The harassing phone calls and letters had continued almost daily until this past Friday, and then stopped abruptly. But they were no closer to discovering the culprit's identity than they'd been fourteen days ago. All the letters had been postmarked Priceville and from cell phone records, the calls, too, had come from the Priceville area, transmitted through a tower halfway between the town and Price

Manor. And fingerprint analysis of the letters showed no prints other than those expected. Donald Farris's widow had died three years ago and they'd had no children. His next of kin, a second cousin, had adamantly refused Powell's request to exhume his body for an autopsy.

Maleah remained as Jordan's bodyguard at Ryan and Claire Price's insistence. If it had been up to Jordan, Maleah would have been dismissed at least a week ago.

Taking himself off the Price case had been the right thing to do. Even now, with more than a week and hundreds of miles separating them, Rick couldn't get Jordan off his mind. But he sure as hell was trying to; and keeping busy during the day helped. But at night, she invaded his dreams. Sometimes those dreams turned scary, with Jordan trying to kill him. Other nights, the dreams were erotic, with the two of them making wild, passionate love.

Rick turned off Highway 129 and headed for the airport. As he pulled his Jeep into the short-term parking area at McGhee Tyson, he checked his watch. He'd made the trip from Griffin's Rest to Alcoa in record time, which left him about half an hour to wait. Nic had sent him to pick up a lady named Meredith Sinclair, who was flying in from London where she had been staying with the Powells' friend, Dr. Yvette Meng. Rick had met the gorgeous doctor several times during his years with the Powell Agency and although he knew nothing about Griff's past, he did know that Dr. Meng had been a part of those ten missing years of Griff's life, as had Sanders. And he knew something else—Nic didn't seem overly thrilled about the arrival of their guest. Not that she'd said anything negative, but he'd been around Nic enough since she married Griff to know when she wasn't happy.

While he waited, Rick picked up a newspaper and a cup of coffee, settled in and was up to date on world, national, and local news by the time Ms. Sinclair's plane landed.

Along with at least a dozen others, he waited for the disembarked passengers to appear in the baggage claims area. He had been told to look for a redhead in her late twenties.

With a name like Meredith Sinclair, he wasn't sure what he'd been expecting—a tall, leggy, model-thin beauty maybe—but the only redhead he saw was short, curvy and rather plain. She wore loose-fitting black slacks and matching jacket, with a white blouse, no jewelry that he could see other than a wristwatch, and her thick, curly, carrot-red hair had been pulled away from her face and secured in a bushy ponytail.

As he approached her, he noted that she wasn't wearing any makeup, which exposed her pale skin and an abundance of freckles. "Ms. Sinclair?"

"Yes?" She looked at him, her face expressionless.

"I'm Rick Carson. I'm from the Powell Agency. Mrs. Powell sent me." He held out his hand in a cordial greeting.

"Oh, yes. Thank you, Mr. Carson." She glanced at his offered hand for half a second, and then ignored it completely.

Overlooking her rudeness by not shaking his hand, he said, "If you'll describe your bags to me, I'll get them for you."

"I have only one bag," she told him. "It's a large black suitcase. There's a bright green circle painted on the center of both sides."

He grinned. "I assume the suitcase didn't come that way."

"Oh, no. I added the circles to help for easy identification. I certainly hope the bag hasn't been lost or misdirected, but the inefficiency at airports these days has become par for the course, hasn't it?"

"Yes, I guess it has."

When he ventured toward the conveyor belt that was

only now beginning to make its slow journey around and back again, Ms. Sinclair followed him.

"Did you have a good flight?" he asked, simply trying to make conversation.

"Yes, thank you. I slept on the flight from London. It was quite nice traveling first class."

"Nothing but the best for any friend of Griff and Nic Powell."

"Oh, I'm not a friend of theirs, Mr. Carson."

He shrugged. "Maybe not, but you're a good friend of their good friend, Dr. Meng. Right?"

"I wouldn't say that Dr. Meng and I are good friends. Our relationship is quite complicated and not something I discuss with strangers."

Rick was torn between laughing and telling Ms. Sinclair to lighten up, that he didn't give a rat's ass what her relationship was with Dr. Meng. All he'd been doing was making an effort to be polite. And he was finding that with her, it was becoming more and more difficult.

Finally, after the empty conveyor belt made a couple of rounds, a variety of luggage emerged from the chute. A large black suitcase with a green circle painted in the middle was the fourth piece to appear. Rick yanked it off the conveyor belt and set it upright. God, the thing must weigh seventy pounds. What the hell did she have in there? Lead? Gold?

She reached for the suitcase. "I've got it," he told her.

"All right. Thank you."

"If you'll follow me," he said as he lifted the handle and dragged the suitcase behind him.

Ms. Sinclair didn't say another word until they left the airport and were on Highway 129. "I've never been to Tennessee. Dr. Meng says that it's quite beautiful here. I believe she especially likes the mountains and the lakes."

Rick nodded, keeping his eye on the road. "Being an old Mississippi boy, I grew up where the land was mostly flat. I remember the first time I saw the Smoky Mountains. I was about seven and I was awestruck."

"Is it a long drive to Griffin's Rest?" she asked.

"No, not long."

He had thought by telling her he was from Mississippi, she might mention where she'd been born and raised. He heard a definite southern drawl in her speech, but he couldn't imagine anyone from the South never having visited some area of Tennessee since it bordered eight other southern states.

"I hope it didn't inconvenience you having to pick me up at the airport so early this morning," she said.

"No, ma'am, not at all. It's just part of my job."

"Oh, yes, of course."

He briefly cut his eyes in her direction and noted that she sat stiff as a board, her feet flat on the floor and her hands resting in her lap. There was something prim and proper about her, like an old-fashioned schoolmarm or a strict governess. It was on the tip of his tongue to ask her about her profession, but why should he feel compelled to carry on a conversation with this odd, somewhat unfriendly lady? If she wanted to talk, he'd talk. If not, that was fine with him.

Jordan took her morning coffee outside, sat in the swing beneath the canopy of budding trees and sighed with a contentment she hadn't felt since before Dan died. Her life had returned to something resembling a normal routine, although she hadn't ventured beyond the gates of the estate. Claire and Ryan had visited several times, bringing little Michael with them. The child was an adorable, auburn-haired, blue-eyed imp, with Ryan's coloring and Claire's beauty. His presence at Price Manor was always like a breath of fresh air. Although being with Michael reminded her of what she had recently lost, of the child that wasn't meant to be, the joy his lively presence brought into their lives far outweighed any sorrow she felt.

With Rick Carson out of her life and the craziness surrounding the black widow news reports all but stopped now, a semblance of peace had settled over Jordan and everyone at Price Manor. The harassing phone calls and letters had also stopped, as of this past Friday. If not for remaining under Maleah Perdue's watchful eye, Jordan could almost convince herself that everything was going to be all right.

Last week, she had spoken to J.C. When she had asked him to leave, he hadn't seemed surprised nor had he put up a fuss.

"Yeah, I figured I'd overstayed my welcome this time. Even Mama's been hinting that she thinks it's time I went back to work. Of course, she still thinks I've got my job at a casino in Biloxi Mississippi."

Jordan had handed her stepbrother a check for $10,000.

"What's this for?"

"For a fresh start."

"Why so generous?"

"Because you're family," she'd told him. "But the handouts end with this check. Understand?"

"Sure thing, Sis."

First he had kissed her cheek, then he'd grinned and winked at her.

When he left sometime Thursday, she'd been glad to see the last of him. At least for a while. She didn't kid herself. Like a bad penny, he'd eventually show up again.

Devon had flown to D.C. Friday and gone to their townhouse in Bethesda to pack up Dan's personal items. They would eventually put the place on the market, but there was no rush. With Dan gone, neither she nor Devon had any desire to ever live there again. He had phoned every evening, but they had kept their conversations short. Devon was still highly emotional whenever he spoke of Dan. She hoped that during his stay at the townhouse, he could find a way to finally say goodbye to the man he had loved.

Only yesterday, she had persuaded Darlene to return to her apartment in Priceville. As much as she loved Darlene and appreciated her staunch support, there were times when she felt smothered by her attention. She understood that Darlene had no one else, that she had become Darlene's substitute child, and was her only remaining link to Robby Joe. Also, with the little romance between Roselynne and Wallace heating up, Jordan felt it was better if Darlene wasn't around to see the lovey-dovey couple on a daily basis.

With everything relatively calm, Jordan found that she had way too much time on her hands, for thinking, for brooding, for mourning, and even for daydreaming. Considering the sizeable fortune she would inherit from Dan, she didn't have to worry about supporting Roselynne and Tammy and she certainly didn't have to return to the work force. But she couldn't spend the rest of her life as a member of the idle rich set. Eventually, she would have to find something to fill her days. She could broaden her participation in various philanthropic organizations or she could open her own PR firm or even renew her teaching degree.

Finding a new purpose in life would take time, but it would happen. She could fill her days with work, but what about her nights?

She would never remarry, of course. She did not want or need . . .

Liar!

She did want. She did need. She longed for something that had always been just beyond her reach, the kind of happiness so many people took for granted.

*Don't think about Rick. He's gone. Out of your life forever. Whatever you thought you felt for him, it wasn't love.*

"Mind if I join you?"

Rene's request brought Jordan out of her thoughts about Rick Carson.

She looked up and smiled at her friend. "Not at all." She patted the cushioned seat.

Rene held an empty coffee mug, which she placed on the ground beside the swing after she sat down with Jordan. "You know, I think May is probably my favorite month of the year. It's usually warm, but not hot yet. And everything is in full bloom."

"I'd love to drive into Priceville later today and go to Elmore's and buy some bedding plants and see what their selection of ferns looks like. Would you go with me?"

"Of course, I will, but do you think your jailer will allow you to leave Price Manor? She keeps a close watch over you." Rene inclined her head toward the house where Maleah Perdue stood by the back door, doing her best to allow Jordan some personal space while at the same time guarding her.

"We'll take her along," Jordan said. "But I feel as if I don't leave this place, at least for a few hours, I'm going to lose my mind. I'm beginning to feel like a prisoner in my own home."

"Then let's go and make a day of it. If people stare at you, we'll just make funny faces at them."

Jordan chuckled. "I think I can deal with a few people staring at me. But I hope most of the people in Priceville have come to know me well enough not to believe everything they've been hearing about me lately."

"I'm sure you're right," Rene said. "Oh, while we're out and about, let's go to Ruff's Barbeque for lunch and pig out on ribs and onion rings." Rene smacked her lips. "Just thinking about that delicious food makes me practically orgasmic."

Jordan laughed. "As much as I love Ruff's ribs and onion rings, I don't think even eating them, let alone thinking about them, has ever brought me close to an orgasm. But I have to admit that eating their fried pies has curled my toes a few times."

They sat together, laughing, appreciating the warmth and beauty of an early day in May. Just two girlfriends, acting silly, and planning a little excursion into town. Life's simple pleasures.

For the first time since she had found Dan's lifeless body six weeks ago, Jordan sensed that eventually she would be able to enjoy living again.

Rick had intended to drop Ms. Sinclair off, fully expecting someone to meet her, so it didn't surprise him when, as they pulled up in front of the house, Sanders approached the Jeep. But instead of opening the passenger door, he rounded the hood and motioned for Rick to lower his window.

"Yeah, what's up?" he asked.

"Griffin and Nicole would like for you to come into the house with Ms. Sinclair. I will park your Jeep and bring in the luggage while you escort her to Griffin's study."

Rick shrugged, left the motor running and keys in the ignition, then opened the door and got out. By the time he made his way to the other side of the Jeep, Ms. Sinclair stood on the sidewalk waiting for him.

"If you'll come with me." He held out his arm.

"Please, lead the way and I'll follow."

"Sure." What was it with this woman? Did she have an aversion to touching other people or just to touching him?

Although she tried not to gape, Rick noticed the way she stared at the house and even paused in the foyer, her eyes wide and her mouth slightly parted as she took in the understated splendor of Griff and Nic's home.

"They're waiting for us in Griff's den," Rick said as he led her down the hall. "You'll like staying here. Nic and Griff know how to make their guests feel welcome."

She didn't reply, didn't smile, didn't even blink an eye.

Meredith Sinclair was an odd one, no doubt about it.

The den door stood wide open. As they entered, Griff came forward from where he'd been standing beside Nic in front of his massive antique desk. Rick noticed that Griff didn't offer his hand in greeting to their guest. That told Rick that his boss obviously knew something about the peculiar Ms. Sinclair that he didn't.

"Meredith, I'm Griffin Powell. This is my wife, Nicole." Nic smiled and nodded. "And this is Barbara Jean Hughes, one of the Powell Agency's most valued employees."

Barbara Jean rolled her wheelchair toward their guest, a warm, friendly smile on her face. "Have you had breakfast, Ms. Sinclair?"

"I ate on the plane quite early this morning," she replied.

"Please, come to the kitchen with me. We have coffee-cake and I can prepare fresh coffee or make you a cup of tea. Sanders will join us after he takes your luggage upstairs and then he can show you to your room so you can freshen up."

Ms. Sinclair looked at Griff. "Am I to stay here, in this house, with you and your wife?"

"For the time being, yes," Griff said. "You'll have all the privacy you need and if you prefer to have your meals in your room, you may."

"I had hoped I would have separate accommodations."

"All in due time," Griff said, effectively dismissing her.

Apparently Ms. Sinclair, just as the rest of them, understood that the subject was closed. Decisions had been made on her behalf and Griffin Powell would brook no arguments.

"Tea would be nice, Ms. Hughes," Meredith said.

"Then come along, Ms. Sinclair. You can tell me all about London and how Yvette is doing these days." When Barbara Jean guided her wheelchair into the hall, Ms. Sinclair followed and they heard Barbara Jean say, "We want you to be comfortable here at Griffin's Rest, so if there's anything you need or anything we can do for you, please let me know."

Griff closed the door.

An uneasy feeling took root in Rick's gut. Something was wrong, something he was pretty sure had nothing to do with the Powell's recently arrived houseguest.

"Whatever it is, just tell me." Rick looked from Griff to Nic.

"There's been a new development in the Price case," Griff told him.

"What sort of new development?"

Nic reached out on the desk behind her, turned Griff's open laptop around so that Rick could see the screen, and said, "Take a look at The Chatterbox Web site. They've posted the headlines that appear on this week's issue that hit the stands today."

Rick grunted. What had that sleazy gossip rag printed about Jordan now? He moved in closer and leaned down, scanning the screen. The headlines jumped out at him.

"Son of a bitch!"

Pam and Jim Elmore had inherited Elmore Feed and Seed from Jim's daddy and he from his daddy before him. In Priceville, now as in the past, businesses tended to be handed down from one generation to the next. Ted Payne, who owned the local drugstore, had taken over as drug-gist when his maternal grandfather retired. Wages & Odell Insurance Company had been in the Odell family for more than 100 years. A Mr. Wages had married into the family 50 years ago. And a member of the Ruff family had been barbequing pork since the late 1800s.

Pulling an empty supply cart behind her, Pam took Jordan, Rene and Maleah into one of the greenhouses at the back of the Feed and Seed.

"Take your time, Jordan," Pam said. "When you find

something you want, we'll load it on here—" she tugged on the cart's long, adjustable handle "—and Jim can deliver your order this afternoon."

"Oh, there's no need for him to bother," Jordan said. "Tobias can have Mr. Poole bring everything out to the house tomorrow when he comes to do the yard work."

"Good, good." Pam noticed new customers entering the greenhouse. "Just look around. I'll be right back."

As they wandered through the rows of plants, Jordan chose several of her favorite summer annuals. Within fifteen minutes of strolling leisurely through the large greenhouse, half a dozen other customers had entered and were milling around inside. All of them were staring at Jordan and whispering among themselves.

"Ignore them," Rene told her. "Damn bunch of busybodies!"

"I suppose I should have expected it," Jordan said. "I've been trying to ignore them, but I don't think that's possible. Let's get out of here. It's a little early for lunch, but we could stop by Cream and Sugar for iced tea or coffee and if we have to, we can sit in the car and drink it, then pick up lunch later and take it home."

As Jordan passed by one middle-aged woman who'd been inspecting a rose bush, the lady sneered and mumbled under her breath, "Murderess."

Maleah moved to Jordan's side and deliberately nudged open her jacket, just enough to give everyone a glimpse of her gun. Her action made it plain to the other customers that she was Jordan's bodyguard. The sudden silence that fell over the greenhouse was far more disturbing than the whispers had been.

On the short walk from the greenhouse to the sidewalk, three other customers stopped dead in their tracks and gaped as Jordan walked by.

"Take a picture," Rene hollered at one man. "It'll last longer."

"I should have known this was a bad idea," Jordan said. "Apparently there are people in Priceville who actually believe I killed Dan."

"Why don't you go to the car," Rene said. "I'll run up the street to the Cream and Sugar and get us something to drink. What do you want?" She glanced from Jordan to Maleah.

"Iced tea," Jordan said.

"Sounds good to me."

"When I get back, why don't we drive over to Chattanooga and spend the day?" Rene suggested. "Not as many people will recognize you in a big city."

"Why not?" Jordan forced a smile. "I'll wear my sunglasses all day and look mysterious." Her words projected a bravado that she didn't possess. But she'd be damned if she'd let these people force her back to the prison that Price Manor had become.

While Rene went up the street to the Cream and Sugar, Priceville's alternative to Starbucks, Jordan slid in behind the wheel of her Navigator while Maleah opened the back door and took the seat behind the passenger side. People passing on the street glared at Jordan, some even stopped, stared, and pointed fingers. A few actually hurled insults at her. She yanked down her sunglasses from where she'd hung them over the visor, put them on, and slouched down in the bucket seat.

The sooner Rene returned with their drinks, the better. Escaping to Chattanooga for the day couldn't happen soon enough.

Suddenly, Rene reappeared, a frantic expression on her face, and without their drinks. Clutching a folded magazine of some sort in her left hand, she grabbed the door handle with her right hand, yanked open the door, and hurled herself into the front seat beside Jordan.

"God, just when we thought things had finally settled down," Rene said, practically shouting. "Now this!" She snapped open the newspaper and slapped it across the steering wheel in front of Jordan. "No wonder the whole town is staring at you and whispering behind your back. While I was waiting in line to order our tea, I saw this on the magazine rack."

Jordan's heart hammered turbulently as she read the headlines on the front page of this week's issue of The Chatterbox.

"Oh, Lord, have mercy."

MÉNAGE À TROIS: SENATOR DAN PRICE, HIS WIFE AND HIS MALE LOVER.

Rick hurriedly read the titillating short article on the Web site, its purpose to induce readers to rush out and buy the weekly newspaper-style magazine.

*Find out all the details in this week's issue of* The Chatterbox, *on sale today. Just what went on behind closed doors at Price Manor? Who was the father of the child Jordan Price recently lost? Did the senator's wife and his lover plot his death?*

"How the hell did this happen?" Rick asked.

"I've placed some phone calls," Griff told him. "It's apparent that someone close to Jordan Price sold this story about the private details of the senator's life, including the well-kept secret of his homosexuality."

"We need to find out who betrayed her confidence and deal with them," Rick said.

"Unless she and Devon Markham can prove this—" Griff pointed to the computer screen "—is slander and not a word of it is true, neither the person who sold this story nor the magazine are liable. You can't sue someone for telling the truth. Our main concern now is some type of damage control."

"Does Jordan know about this?"

"Not that we know of," Nic said. "We haven't heard

from her or from Maleah. We didn't know ourselves until about five minutes ago when Cam Hendrix phoned Griff."

"We have to warn her," Rick said.

"I'll call Maleah," Griff said, "while Nic contacts Claire and Ryan. Do you want to call Mrs. Price, or should I—" Griff's phone rang interrupting him mid-sentence. He checked caller ID, then flipped it open. "Maleah?"

Rick could tell by the frown on Griff's face and the way he nodded his head that more than likely Maleah was telling him that she knew about the article in The Chatterbox; and if Maleah knew, then Jordan knew.

"Call the sheriff and have him send some deputies to clear the road for you," Griff said. "I'll send as many agents as we have available right away." Griff closed his phone, pocketed it, and turned to Rick.

"Maleah went with Jordan and her assistant into town this morning. They didn't know anything about The Chatterbox article. As soon as they found out, they headed back to Price Manor, but it seems word leaked out that Jordan was in downtown Priceville. They're now being chased by a horde of reporters."

"Are they all right?" Rick asked.

"For now."

"Exactly where are they?"

"About halfway between Priceville and Price Manor."

"If I find out who did this, I'll break their neck. If anything happens to Jordan, I'll . . ." Rick took a deep breath. "I want to take one of the choppers. It'll get me to Priceville faster."

"Is your license up to date? If it's not, get Jonathan to take you."

"It is."

"Then what are you waiting for? Go."

# Chapter 24

Fear surged through Jordan as she sped down the country road, at least five vehicles in hot pursuit. The one riding her bumper was a van carrying a news crew from a Chattanooga television station. An SUV behind the van kept careening over the yellow line, trying to pass. Casting a glance in her rearview mirror, Jordan noted the logo on the SUV and knew it belonged to a local Dalton, Georgia TV station. The other cars, vans, and SUVs following behind these two were probably reporters from various newspapers and maybe even someone from The Chatterbox.

"This is total insanity." Rene turned as far around in her seat as the safety harness would allow and watched the caravan of vehicles following them. "They're like a pack of vultures that got a scent of rotting flesh."

Maleah was on her cell phone, her voice low, so that Jordan could make out only a word or two now and then, but she got the impression that her bodyguard was speaking to someone at the sheriff's office.

"Of all days, I chose today to venture out and go into town as if all was right with the world," Jordan said.

"You had no way of knowing that The Chatterbox was going to print an exposé on your and Dan's personal life." Rene gasped. "Oh, God, Jordan, what about Devon? He'll be absolutely devastated when he finds out."

"Call him," Jordan said. "Tell him what's happened and what's going on here. Explain that I'll talk to him as soon as I can."

One horn honked, and then another and another, creating a godawful racket that only added to Jordan's stress level. Just as Rene placed the call to Devon, a small, black sports car behind both the van and the SUV swerved onto the opposite side of the road, sped past them, and then came up alongside Jordan's Navigator.

"Crap!" Rene muttered under her breath. "That guy's crazy."

"Gun it," Maleah ordered. "Put some distance between us and them."

"If I go any faster, I don't know if I can control—"

"Do it!" Maleah practically shouted. "If you don't get ahead of them, they're going to try to surround you and block us in." Then into the phone, she said, "Yes, damn it, we need help now!"

Jordan gripped the steering wheel with white-knuckled fierceness, pressed her foot down on the gas pedal, and prayed. The Navigator charged into high gear and shot down the road like a small rocket.

When her cell phone flew out of her hand and landed on the floorboard, Rene grumbled an unladylike obscenity. "Hell, just let it lay there. Devon didn't answer. It went straight to voice mail."

"He may have his phone turned off," Jordan said, her gaze riveted out of the windshield, the scenery zipping by at lightning speed as she pushed the Navigator up to ninety.

The massive gates of Price Manor loomed in the distance. She could just barely make them out, but even a long-range glimpse offered her hope that they could make it to the estate before being overrun by their pursuers. Once behind the gates, they would be safe.

"We're almost there," Jordan said.

"Good," Maleah replied. "That black sports car is gaining on us."

As Jordan approached the entrance to the estate, her heart in her throat and her pulse pounding like war drums inside her head, she all but cried out when she saw what lay ahead—four vehicles effectively blocking her path. The Powell agent whose name she couldn't remember was talking to the woman who had parked her Toyota Camry directly in front of the closed gates.

"Now what?" Jordan knew their choices were limited to two, stop at the gates and be overrun by reporters or keep going and hope she could outrun them.

"Is there a side road somewhere around here?" Maleah asked.

"Yes, there's an old gravel road that leads to the back entrance of the estate, but it's at least a mile from here," Jordan said, then suddenly drew in a gasping breath. "Wait, there's a dirt road that cuts through the Landaus' cotton field or what used to be a cotton field. We'll have to go through the woods and I'm not sure how clear that old lane is."

"Keep going," Maleah told her. "Turn off on that road and disappear as quickly as possible. There are two sheriff's deputies on their way here right now. They're not more than three miles away. We just need to buy some time."

Jordan didn't even slow down as she passed the entrance to Price Manor. The Navigator shimmied just a little when it reached ninety-five. She didn't ease her foot off the gas pedal until she saw the partially hidden dirt lane where she would have to turn.

*Dear God, help me turn this truck off the road without wrecking us.*

"Hold on," Jordan yelled.

She turned the steering wheel sharply, almost fishtailing the SUV, but she got it under control just before running over several small shrubs that lined the grassy path into the woods.

"Dear God!" Rene clutched the dashboard.

When they were through the woods and on the old road leading into what had once been a cotton field, Maleah alerted them to bad news.

"The black sports car is behind us."

"Only the one car?" Jordan asked.

"As far as I can tell."

When the path abruptly ended, Jordan stopped and slowly, carefully turned the SUV around, heading out.

"What are you doing?" Rene asked.

"I'm going to run over that damn little sports car, if that's what it takes," Jordan said.

"Who do you think you are, Mrs. Rambo?"

"No, I'm Jordan Price and I'm sick of being hounded, of being made to feel like a prisoner in my own home, sick of being tried and found guilty in every newspaper, magazine and television newscast in the country."

Rene laughed. "You get 'em, girl."

The tension inside Jordan boiled over, released like steam from an overheated kettle. She laughed and laughed; then she buried her face in her hands.

"Are you all right?" Rene punched Jordan's shoulder.

She lifted her head and smiled. "I'm okay. We're all alive and that's a miracle, don't you think?"

"Before you run over this guy, let me see if I can talk to him." Maleah opened the back door and stepped down and out of the SUV.

"Now *she's* playing Mrs. Rambo," Rene said.

As Maleah walked toward the approaching car, she dialed her cell phone and spoke to someone. The sports car pulled to a halt a good twenty feet from the front of the Navigator and the driver opened his door and got out to face Maleah. The man was tall, slim and dark-haired, probably in his early thirties. He wore tight jeans, a cotton knit sweater, and a pair of aviator sunglasses. From the way he moved, it was obvious that he was more than comfortable in his own skin.

Jordan and Rene waited while Maleah carried on a conversation with the man. He kept shaking his head and looking toward the Navigator. Once, when he tried to sidestep Maleah, she reached out and put her hand on his shoulder. They squared off, as if on the verge of fighting.

"Listen," Rene said. "I hear a siren."

Jordan heard it, too, and within minutes she saw the sheriff's car driving up behind and to the side of the sports car. Two uniformed deputies emerged. Maleah spoke to one of the deputies while the other talked to the reporter. After arguing heatedly with the deputy, the guy finally gave up and got in his once clean and shiny, now filthy, black sports car. He shifted into reverse, backed into the field, turned around, and sent a cloud of dust into the air as he ripped off toward the highway. Maleah walked over to the Navigator and opened the driver's side door.

"I want you two to go with the deputies," she told them. "They'll take y'all home. I'll follow in the truck."

Jordan gladly did as Maleah suggested, relieved to have a police escort. But her relief was short-lived. When they arrived back at the entrance to the estate, they found not only more news people in their cars, trucks, and vans, but a small crowd of what she assumed were curiosity seekers. The deputy driving stopped in the middle of the road and the other deputy got out and shouted orders to the horde assembled in the road, along the road, and even across the road. Some people were actually standing in the shallow ditch. A few of the onlookers carried binoculars.

Clearing all the vehicles out of the way took at least ten minutes, but eventually, they unblocked the route to the entrance. One deputy remained at the gate with the Powell agent while the other eased the patrol car up to the entrance, and then gave the signal for the Powell agent to open the gate. The minute he did, the deputy sped through and onto the drive, but not before some idiot threw himself onto the hood. With his face pressing against the windshield, he glared at Jordan and shouted a string of damnations. As the gates closed behind the car, the deputy stopped, got out and peeled the man off the hood.

"Murderess! Whore! Infidel!" he shouted. "There is a special place in hell for women like you."

The deputy handcuffed the man, marched him to the guardhouse, and handed him over to the other deputy.

Rene draped her arm around Jordan's shoulders. "Don't let what he was saying bother you. He's obviously crazy."

"Yes, but there are people who aren't crazy who think the way he does. And there are others who believed in my innocence before today, who will now condemn me, just as they'll condemn Dan and Devon."

"Then they're cold, heartless bastards. They have no right to judge you. Your arrangement with Dan and Devon was nobody's business. You three were happy with the way things were."

"Were we?"

Jordan hadn't realized she had voiced her thought until Rene stared at her, obviously surprised by her comment.

Thinking back over the past few years, Jordan admitted to herself that she had not been happy. Not really. Nor had Devon and Dan. They had each settled for less than they should have. She had escaped into a bogus marriage believing it could protect her from ever being hurt again.

Devon had loved Dan enough to give him what he'd wanted—a secret love affair and a marriage to Jordan that had been in name only. In the beginning, their arrangement had seemed quite logical and it had worked for all of them. But only for a while. Their having a child together, her undergoing artificial insemination, her being pregnant with Devon's baby, had been a mutual decision, one they all thought would cement the cracks in their unique three-way relationship.

Rene didn't say a word; she simply sat there in the backseat of the patrol car and kept her arm around Jordan's shoulders. By the time the deputy drove up in front of the house, Maleah was right behind them in the Navigator. Before either vehicle came to a full stop, the residents of Price Manor swarmed around them.

Jordan emerged to arms reaching for her and voices clamoring their concern. She hugged Tammy, who had shoved her way to the forefront, then came Roselynne and then Darlene, each in need of comfort and reassurance.

"How long have you been here?" Jordan asked Darlene.

"I got here before the hordes descended," Darlene replied. "Oh, my dear girl, are you truly all right? Just when we thought things were finally getting better, this had to happen."

"I'm fine or I will be. I just want to go inside, get a stiff drink and pull myself together."

"Yes, of course. Just know that I'm here and I'm staying. I won't leave you again no matter what you say."

Maleah came up behind Jordan, curved her hand over Jordan's shoulder and said, "I want y'all to step back and give Jordan a little breathing room. I'm sure she'll want to see y'all again later, but right now, I'm taking her inside where she can catch her breath."

Grateful to have Maleah as a buffer between her and her loved ones, Jordan allowed the Powell agent to lead her into the house.

"Would you like to go up to your room or—"

"I wasn't joking about that stiff drink," Jordan said.

Tobias and Vadonna stood in the foyer, both staring at Jordan, each obviously concerned. She turned to them and smiled.

"Miss Jordan, if there's anything Vadonna or I can do for you . . ." Tobias said.

"Thank you. The only thing I need right now is some time alone. And, Tobias, would you bring me a bottle of that fig vodka I like so much? I'll be in my study."

"A whole bottle, ma'am?"

"Yes, the whole bottle."

His eyes widened, but he nodded and said, "Yes, ma'am."

While the others entered the foyer and watched her as she escaped down the hall and into her study, Jordan realized that only Maleah's hard glare kept her distressed family at bay.


Half an hour and several drinks later, Jordan had spoken to Devon, who was an absolute basket case. She hated that he was there in Bethesda, all alone, when the news of his true relationship with Dan became public knowledge.

"Just stay put for the time being. Hole up there in the townhouse until you hear from me. I'll arrange with Powell's to send an agent to D.C. to escort you home."

"Who would have done such a thing? Only a handful of people knew the truth about Dan and me."

"As much as I hate to even think it, we both know it was someone in the family."

After a lengthy conversation with Devon, she sat quietly, trying to make sense of what had happened, and not just what had happened today with the vicious story in The Chatterbox, but with the events in her past as well.

Just as she was considering pouring herself another drink

and dulling her senses even more with alcohol, someone knocked on the locked study door.

"Yes?"

"It's Maleah."

When she stood, she realized she was slightly tipsy. Steadying herself, she walked to the door, unlocked it, and said, "If it's bad news, I don't want to hear it."

"One off Powell's helicopters has just landed in the south field behind the house," Maleah said. "Rick Carson has come back."

Jordan couldn't breathe for a couple of seconds. Every cell in her body responded to the thought of her seeing Rick again.

"If you'd like, I'll go with you to meet him."

"Yes, I'd like that very much," Jordan said.

# Chapter 25

The helicopter created a thunderous roar and a rotating wind surge that flattened the grass and swayed the nearby bushes and treetops. Maleah and Jordan watched from a distance as Rick landed the chopper in a wide open field on the Price estate. Sunlight danced off the blades as they slowed and finally stopped. The quiet stillness of the green meadow, the only sounds those of nature, seemed all the more pronounced once the chopper engine shut off. Jordan raised her hand as a visor to block the blinding sun. The chopper door swung open and Rick emerged.

Jordan's heartbeat accelerated with anticipation.

She wanted to run to him. She didn't. Instead, with Maleah at her side, she walked briskly toward Rick as he threw up his hand and waved at them.

With her thoughts centered on Rick's return, on what it would mean to have him back in her life, Jordan didn't hear, see, or sense anything else. Her entire being was centered on this one moment and this one man.

And then, without warning, the distinctive resonance of a rifle shot rang out, terrifyingly clear. Before Jordan had a chance to react, Maleah shoved her forward behind a clump of tall bushes and then onto the ground, coming down over her like a protective shield. It took Jordan half a minute to realize that someone had shot at them and a full minute to realize that she had screamed.

Maleah grunted. "Are you all right?"

"I—I think so."

"Stay down," Maleah told her.

Jordan felt something wet and sticky dripping onto her neck. She managed to maneuver her hand up so that she could run her fingers over the substance. She looked at her fingertips and gasped when she saw that they were smeared with something red. Oh, God. She had blood on her fingers, blood she had wiped off her neck. Had she been hit? She hadn't felt the impact of a bullet entering her body.

"You two all right?" Rick shouted.

"Jordan's okay," Maleah replied. "But I'm hit."

"Stay put," Rick told her.

"You've been shot?" Jordan asked her bodyguard, who at that precise moment was literally protecting Jordan's body with her own.

"It's a shoulder wound," Maleah said. "It won't kill me."

Jordan managed to turn her head just enough to peer through the bushes and get a glimpse of Rick, gun in hand, carefully canvassing the area as he made his way toward them.

Fully expecting to hear more gunfire, Jordan uttered a prayer. *Please, God, don't let the shooter fire again.*

With her pulse pounding rapidly, the sound drowning out everything else, all sense of time and place distorted by fear, she wasn't sure how long it took Rick to reach them. He hunched down, reached out, and hauled Maleah away from Jordan. When Maleah rolled over onto her side, Jordan did the same, so the two faced each other. It was then that she saw the hole in Maleah's blood-soaked blouse. She clamped her teeth together to keep from crying out.

"Did you see where the shot came from?" Rick asked as he visually examined Maleah's wounded shoulder.

"From the left," Maleah told him. "Left, into the woods, and a little in front of where we were, not from behind."

"We need to get you to the hospital." Still holding his gun in his right hand, he used his left hand to pull his cell phone from his pocket. He hit a pre-programmed number. "Yeah, Maleah's been shot. Put in an emergency call and get some men over to the field where I landed the chopper ASAP."

Jordan watched as Rick ripped apart Maleah's blouse and checked the entry wound, then looked for an exit wound. He frowned. "The bullet went straight through, but it left a hell of a mess."

She grunted. "Yeah, and it hurts, too."

Rick grinned at her, then still holding the gun, shrugged off his jacket and tossed it to Jordan. "Fold this into a thick, compressed square and use it to apply pressure to Maleah's shoulder. We need to stop the bleeding."

Silent and dazed, Jordan followed his instructions.

He glanced at her. "How are you holding up, honey?"

She couldn't manage to speak, so she simply nodded.

"Help's on the way," he told them, but his attention was focused elsewhere. He watched and listened, apparently preparing for a second attack.

"Don't pass out on me," Maleah told Jordan. "You're white as a sheet."

"I—I'm okay. Just—just worried about you."

Maleah grimaced. "It's probably not as bad as it looks."

If only she could stop trembling, but she couldn't. Jordan knew without anyone saying it—the bullet Maleah took had been meant for her. *She* had been the target, not her bodyguard.

\* \* \*

Jordan had wanted to go to the hospital with Maleah, but Rick had quickly nixed the idea. He knew that Jordan was concerned, that she cared, that she felt responsible for what had happened to her bodyguard; but her staying put was the safest course of action.

"You'll be easier to protect, here, inside the house," he had explained. "Since we have no idea who the shooter was or what his or her motive was, you'll need twenty-four/seven personal protection. I'm taking over as your bodyguard and the only time you'll be alone is in the bathroom. Got that!"

When he had landed the Powell Agency helicopter, he'd been anticipating seeing Jordan again. Although he'd done his level best to put her out of his mind the past nine days, she had never been far from his thoughts. The rifle shot had rung out only moments after he left the chopper, and in that defining moment, all that had mattered to him was Jordan.

Once they arrived back at the house, he'd had a hell of a time keeping Jordan's leeches off her. He supposed thinking of family and close friends as bloodsucking sycophants said something about his view of the world. A negative view. Even if they all truly loved Jordan and their concern for her well-being was genuine, why didn't they realize that they were drawing the life out of her with their need for constant reassurance? Why couldn't they see that their concerns were self-centered, that each of them was imagining what would happen to her without Jordan?

Once they had convinced everyone that Jordan was unharmed and simply needed some breathing room, he took her to her study, which seemed to be where she felt the most comfortable. He closed the plantation shutters and ushered her away from the windows.

"Sit down. I'll get you a drink."

"No. I don't want to sit down and I don't want a drink."

She looked at him. "I had several drinks earlier. I want a clear head right now."

"You're trembling."

"I know. I can't help it. I guess realizing that someone actually tried to kill me shook me up just a little."

"Jordan . . ." When he reached out to her, she side-stepped him, avoiding his touch.

"Don't try to convince me that whoever shot Maleah wasn't aiming at me."

"I won't," he said. "Whoever shot Maleah may have been aiming at you. But if they wanted to kill you, they weren't much of a shooter. They not only missed you, but they didn't fatally wound Maleah."

"Thank God."

"Yes, thank God. And thank Maleah's quick action."

"She saved my life."

"Possibly."

"What do you mean possibly?"

"Come on, honey, sit down before you fall down." He reached for her and once again she avoided him. "You look like you might pass out any minute now."

"I'll sit down like a good little girl, if you'll tell me what you're thinking."

"Agreed."

She chose one of the chairs instead of the sofa. Had she chosen the sofa to prevent him from sitting beside her? Why didn't she want him to touch her? Was she angry with him or afraid she'd fall apart in his arms?

"Talk," she said.

He pulled a ladder-back chair away from the wall, dragged it across the room and placed it in front of Jordan. She eyed him suspiciously as he sat.

"We don't have long to talk, just the two of us," he told her. "Your brother-in-law and Sheriff Corbett are on their way here now. When they arrive, we're going to discuss a couple of theories about what might be going on. Why someone outed Dan and Devon. Why someone shot at you today. Who really killed Dan and possibly killed the other men in your past."

She stared at him, her eyes round with surprise and interest. "Do you finally believe that I'm not a killer?"

His instinct was to reach out for her hands in a reassuring manner, but considering how she'd been avoiding his touch, he kept his hands to himself.

"Yeah, I guess so," he said.

"You don't sound very certain."

"Chalk it up to my pessimistic, negative view of people in general," he told her. "A psychiatrist would probably say that I have trust issues."

"Probably. And more than one therapist has told me that I have fear-of-abandonment issues."

"Wonder why?"

Although her lips didn't lift upward, her eyes smiled. "Life experiences have a way of molding us, don't they? If we're lucky, we start out as happy, carefree children with loving, protective parents. We're little soft, sweet lumps of clay. And then somewhere along the way, we get our first hard knock and the process begins."

He searched her face, looking deep into her eyes. "You know that I want to hold you right now, don't you?"

She took a deep breath. "Oh, boy, is my life screwed up or what? I want you to hold me, but I'm afraid. Maybe it's just a matter of knowing you might be the right guy, but this is definitely the wrong time."

A loud rap on the door interrupted any further personal admissions.

"Yeah?" Rick called.

"It's Ryan Price. And I have Steve Corbett with me."

Rick got up, walked to the door, and undid the lock. He shook hands with Ryan, who then hurried to Jordan. Rick and the sheriff nodded cordially.

"Before we get started, I need your word that this discussion won't go beyond these four walls and the four of us," Rick said.

"I've given Ryan my word that everything short of a confession to a crime will be strictly off the record," Steve said.

Ryan pulled Jordan to her feet and hugged her. Rick felt a tinge of what he figured was jealousy. She would let her brother-in-law give her a comforting hug, but she wouldn't let him touch her. Yeah, sure, he understood her reasoning, but the primitive male in him didn't give a damn.

Jordan pulled away from Ryan. "I really am all right."

"Claire sends her love. She said to tell you if you need her, need anything . . ."

"Please, thank her for me, will you," Jordan said.

"Why don't we all sit down," Rick suggested and waited until the others were seated before he explained why he'd initiated this gathering.

"I'm going to toss out some theories. One is possibly the right one, but we won't know which. I need everyone to listen without getting on the defensive. Just hear me out. And if we're going to find Dan Price's killer, you need to keep an open mind."

"What sort of theories are you talking about?" Ryan asked.

"Theories about why someone might have wanted to kill your brother and several other men in Jordan's past."

"Then you believe all those deaths are linked to Dan's?" Steve asked.

"All of them, maybe. Some of them, definitely."

"Let's hear your theories," Steve said.

"Okay, the first and presently most popular theory is that Jordan is a black widow who murdered both of her husbands and her fiancé for profit. Also, it's likely she killed her father, her former boss and a co-worker. Her father for profit, her former boss so she could get his job, and a co-worker because he sexually harassed her. DA Anderman and your deputy, Lt. McLain, prefer this theory and either one or both of them is behind the leaks to the press, first Jordan's past and then about Dan Price and Devon Markham's relationship."

"Do you have any proof that Haley was involved?" Steve asked.

"No proof," Rick admitted. "Remember, I'm theorizing."

"Since we know that Jordan is not a killer, then I assume your other theories point to someone else as the murderer." Ryan, who sat on the sofa beside Jordan, reached out and took her hand in his.

"Someone close to Jordan, someone who has been in her life for a long time, possibly since her teens, has killed all of these men or perhaps only some of them." Rick paused, allowing them time to absorb the suggestion before he continued. "This person has killed for one of two reasons, either because they hate Jordan and wanted to punish her or they love her and see the murders as a way of protecting Jordan, of somehow doing what's best for her."

"I can't believe that anyone close to me is capable of such a thing," Jordan said.

He looked directly at her. "Yeah, I know, but if you're not the killer—and I think we're all in agreement that you're not—then the only alternative is that it's someone near and dear to you."

Jordan shook her head. "No, no . . ."

Ryan squeezed her hand. "Let's hear him out. I know it's not easy."

"Since recently someone has been threatening Jordan and tried to kill her today, let's hear the they've-killed-over-and-over-again-to-punish-Jordan-because-they-hate-her theory," Steve said.

"Sure." Rick stood, giving himself the freedom to move

around the room. "Who would hate Jordan enough to want to hurt her? Remember, whoever it is would have pretended love and devotion all these years."

"Devon Markham," Steve said the name under his breath.

"No!" Jordan instantly jumped to Devon's defense.

"We're going to accuse everyone close to you," Rick reminded her, "at least in theory. Don't waste our time defending each of them."

She glared at Rick, frustration and even a tinge of anger in her eyes. Okay, so let her get pissed off at him. It didn't matter. All that mattered was finding out the truth and if she wound up hating him in the end, so be it. At least, he'd have done his job.

"I'm sorry." Jordan jerked her hand from Ryan's, threaded her fingers together, and nervously rubbed first one thumb and then the other against her palms. "I'll do my best to play along."

"Let's say that Devon, for some unknown reason, hates Jordan. He's known every man in her life who has died and he has been a part of Jordan's life since second grade," Rick said.

"But Devon has no reason to hate me. We've been best friends since we were children." Apparently Jordan found it impossible to remain objective.

"I agree," Rick said. "Devon doesn't hate Jordan. He would never do anything to hurt her."

"Thank you." Jordan smiled.

"But we have several other suspects. Roselynne might actually be a wicked stepmother and despises Jordan. Tammy, who we know is mentally unbalanced, might secretly hate Jordan and be jealous of how much Roselynne loves Jordan. J.C. could have killed not because he hates Jordan, but because any profit she made off those deaths was money he could beg, borrow or steal from her. Then there's Rene Burke, who has known Jordan since college.

Maybe she never forgave Jordan for taking Robby Joe Wright away from her. Maybe she's been punishing Jordan again and again. And last but not least, there's Darlene. What if for some reason she blames Jordan for Robby Joe's death?"

"She doesn't blame me," Jordan cried. "Darlene loves me. She's been a . . . like a mother to me all these—"

"Once again, I agree," Rick said. "In the hate-Jordan theory, I'd ruled out Devon and Darlene first thing."

"What about your other theory?" Ryan asked.

"It's the theory I prefer," Rick told them. "It's the one that makes sense. It not only explains why he or she killed some of the men in Jordan's life, it explains why they've been threatening Jordan."

"I'm afraid I don't understand," Ryan said.

"Let's say someone close to Jordan is fanatically obsessed with her. Is this person in love with Jordan and doesn't want to share her with anyone else? Or does this person believe it is his or her duty to eliminate any man he or she sees as a threat of any kind to Jordan?

"Tammy seems to adore Jordan. She looks up to her, almost worships her. Roselynne is grateful to Jordan and repeatedly tells anyone who will listen that she thinks of herself as Jordan's mother. J.C.? Could he secretly be in love with Jordan? And what about Rene? She could be bisexual and in love with Jordan. It's a stretch, I admit, but it's possible. Or Rene could simply love Jordan as a dear friend. And Darlene sees Jordan as her one link to her dead son. She's transferred much of her motherly affection from Robby Joe to Jordan. Then last but not least, there's Devon, who possibly loves Jordan more than any of the others."

"You actually think one of these people killed Dan and possibly Jordan's first husband and fiancé?" Ryan asked, doubt in his voice. "How would this theory tie in with the threats to Jordan and the attempted murder today?"

Steve snapped his fingers. "Damn, I get it. He or she is threatening Jordan to take suspicion off her. They know Jordan is innocent, but short of confessing, making Jordan look as if she's a victim is the only way to help her. Right?"

"Right," Rick said. "If this theory is the correct one."

"But someone tried to shoot me today. No one who loves me would—"

"We assumed they were shooting at you. What if Maleah was the intended victim all along, but the shooter wanted it to appear to be a mistake? They didn't shoot to kill, unless they're a terrible shot." Rick wasn't sure Jordan would be able to accept the fact that she had not been the target. To give her something hopeful to hang on to, he added, "The shooter couldn't have been Devon since he's out of town."

"If this theory is true, then apparently anyone acting as my bodyguard could be in danger, as well as anyone this person sees as a threat to me." Jordan's gaze met Rick's and he immediately knew what she was thinking.

"If his theory is right," Steve said. "And I'll be damned if it doesn't make sense. Someone killed Dan, believing it was what was best for you."

"Where do we go from here?" Ryan asked. "What do we do next?"

"Our first priority is to protect Jordan." Rick forced himself to look away from her and glanced first at Ryan and then Steve. "And next, we need to find out who among our suspects knows how to use a rifle. If I'm right about this, then the person we're looking for has some serious mental problems. They're capable not only of murder, but of rationalizing their reasons for killing. They believe whatever they do is always done in Jordan's best interest. In each instance, they did what they believed had to be done for Jordan's sake."

"And if you're wrong?" Steve asked.

"Let's work under the assumption I'm right, at least for

the time being. The Powell Agency has a former FBI profiler on the payroll. Nic and Griff have asked him to consider my theories and give us a profile of the killer to fit each scenario."

"Okay, let's say I go along with your theory, at least unofficially, how do you suggest we go about proving it?" Steve rose to his feet. "This person has gotten away with murder more than once without leaving any evidence to link him or her to the crimes."

"We set a trap," Rick told them.

"What sort of a trap?" Steve asked.

"I haven't had time to figure that one out yet," Rick admitted. "But I'm working on it."

Someone pounded loudly on the closed door. "Jordan, it's Rene. Devon called me when he couldn't reach you on your cell phone. He's desperate to talk to you again. I'm concerned about him. He wouldn't tell me what was wrong, but he didn't sound like himself."

"Thanks, I'll call him right now."

"Okay. If you need me, I'll be in Dan's study," Rene said.

Jordan felt in her pockets, then a puzzled look crossed her face. "I don't have my phone. I must have lost it outside in the field somewhere."

The house phone in Jordan's office had been unplugged to prevent being bothered with its incessant ringing. When she got up, heading for her desk, Rick darted in front of her.

"I'll reconnect the line," he told her.

"Thank you."

He opened the middle drawer of the desk and retrieved the plastic line. After plugging it into the back of the phone on Jordan's desk, he dropped down on his haunches and inserted the other end into the wall-jack.

She picked up the receiver and hurriedly punched in the telephone number. Rick watched her, hating that worried look on her face. Ryan and Steve waited, neither of them saying a word.

"Devon, it's Jordan, sweetheart. What's wrong?"

She listened, nodding her head, a frown creasing her brow. "Listen to me. When we hang up, call the police, and then unplug the phones through the whole house. After that, answer your cell only if you recognize the caller." She paused, listening to Devon. "I want you to go into the den and turn on the CD player or the TV, anything to block out the sound of the doorbell ringing and the shouts coming from outside. I'll catch the next plane out of either Chattanooga or Atlanta and be there as soon as possible." She sighed. "I love you, too. Just hang in there and don't do anything stupid."

She replaced the receiver and turned to Rick. "I have to go to Bethesda right away. Devon's holed up in our townhouse there and he's being bombarded with phone calls and the press is outside ringing the doorbell and beating on the door and there's a group of protestors of some kind throwing things at the windows."

"I'll send a Powell agent," Rick told her. "There's no need for you to expose yourself to—"

"You don't understand. Devon needs me. He's there all alone."

"He's a big boy, honey. He can handle things without you this time. I'll send two agents, if that will make you feel any better. And as soon as things die down just a little, they'll bring him back here to Priceville."

"No, you won't send Powell agents. I'm going to Bethesda and this is not up for discussion. So, either you go with me or choose another agent to go with me."

He saw the determined look in her eyes and realized he couldn't win this argument. Short of tying her down and gagging her, she was going to D.C.

"I'll take you," he said. "We'll need to make arrangements for me to land the Powell helicopter and then have ground transport ready to take us to your townhouse in Bethesda. Give me ten minutes to get everything set up."

"Thank you."

That look of gratitude in her eyes said it all. She could count on him. He wouldn't let her down. Neither of them had to say a word. Whatever she needed from him, it was hers.

# Chapter 26

The Powell Agency had arranged for a car to pick up Rick and Jordan at the airstrip where Rick had landed the helicopter. The driver, a six-four, muscular guy with a military bearing, introduced himself only as Hart. Rick knew that Griffin Powell had friends in high places, both in D.C. and around the world and therefore the agency had advantageous contacts just about everywhere. Other than informing Rick that he would be at their service while they were in D.C., Hart didn't say much else, simply opened the rear door of the black Lincoln and stood at attention while they slipped into the backseat and settled in for the drive to Bethesda.

Jordan was as nervous as the proverbial cat on a hot tin roof. She had fidgeted on the flight to D.C. and even now she anxiously worked her hands together and glanced from one side window to the other. When her cell phone rang, she nearly jumped out of her skin. Luckily, before they'd taken off from Price Manor, one of the sheriff's deputies had found her phone not far from where Maleah had been shot. Rick figured that Devon Markham was calling her again.

"It's not Devon," she told Rick, as if she'd known what he was thinking. "It's Wesley." She frowned. "I knew it was only a matter of time before he called once he saw this week's issue of The Chatterbox."

"Want me to talk to him?" Rick asked.

She shook her head, flipped open her phone, and said, "Hi, Wes."

Rick could figure out what Jordan's stepson was saying by listening to her responses. She assured him that she was all right and for Kendra and him not to worry.

"Rick—Mr. Carson—and I are in D.C. and on our way to the townhouse to pick up Devon and take him back to Priceville," Jordan said. "No, absolutely not. You and Kendra are to stay in school."

She listened to his reply, and then told him, "I know you'll both have to endure some unpleasant comments from ignorant people, but—what!" She held her phone to her chest as she turned to Rick. "Wes and Kendra are being harassed by reporters. I don't know why I didn't re-alize that would probably happen."

Rick held out his hand for her phone. She hesitated, and then turned it over to him.

"Wes, this is Rick Carson. I'm going to arrange for a Powell agent to come down there to Auburn for you and another to go to Athens for Kendra. They'll serve as your bodyguards and handle the press."

"Send someone to Kendra first," Wes said. "She's holed up in her dorm room, afraid to even go to classes."

"Call her and tell her that we'll get a female agent to her ASAP, someone who can be with her twenty-four/seven. The agency will contact the proper authorities at your school and hers."

"Yes, sir. Thank you. And thank you for looking after Jordan."

"No problem," Rick said. ""Do you want to talk to Jordan again?"

"Yes, sir. Please."

He handed Jordan the phone. She offered him an appreciative smile.

Immediately, he put in a call to Griffin and requested two agents for Jordan's stepchildren and explained the situation. Griff assured him that Powell's would take care of everything. Just as he ended his conversation with his boss, he heard Jordan finishing hers with Wesley.

"Everything is going to be okay. We'll weather this storm together, as a family. Just stay put. Help's on the way. And call me as often as you want, and tell Kendra to do the same."

Jordan closed her phone, opened the side flap on her small shoulder bag, and dropped the phone inside. "This is going to be difficult for the kids. You have no idea how much I hate that they have to go through this nightmare with me. It was bad enough when my good name was slandered in the press, but now this. The kids have always adored Devon. He's been like an uncle to them. And they thought the world of Dan."

"They knew the truth, didn't they?" Rick asked.

"Yes, of course. Before Dan and I were married, Dan, Devon, and I sat down with the children and explained the situation. They weren't babies. Kendra was fifteen and Wes seventeen at the time. Young people these days know a lot more about the world and its complexities than we did at their age."

"Didn't anyone in your little family circle voice a few objections? Wasn't anyone concerned that you were making a mistake?"

"You don't approve of what I did, do you?"

"What you did is really none of my business, is it? But you've got to admit that your arrangement with Dan and Devon was unorthodox to say the least."

"It suited us," she said.

"Did it really?"

She stared at him, the look on her face a mixture of surprise and resentment. "I don't expect you to understand."

"Good, because I don't. Daniel Price might have been a great guy, but his whole life was a lie. And before you jump down my throat about not understanding what it was like for him to be politically ambitious and know that him being gay would prevent him from running for president, I'll admit that I don't understand. But I do know that for whatever reason a person tells that first big lie, they have to continue lying. There's no escape. They're trapped. And Dan Price trapped Devon and you along with him."

Jordan didn't reply immediately, she simply looked at him with those beautiful blue-gray eyes as if searching inside him for something she needed. That look rattled him. Had his soapbox speech done more harm than good?

"You're right," she finally said. "I married Dan for Devon's sake and also because I hoped that a marriage in name only would protect me. I had been in love and I had been married before and both times, I had been deeply hurt. I never wanted to experience that kind of pain again."

He didn't know how to respond. He'd spent most of his life avoiding commitment, determined to never let a woman do to him what his stepmother had done to his father. If you didn't love, you weren't vulnerable. You didn't make stupid mistakes.

Damned if he and Jordan didn't share a common fear. Neither of them wanted to be hurt.

"Actually, I get it," Rick told her.

"I thought you might." She leaned her head back against the leather seat and closed her eyes.

For the remainder of the ride to the Price townhouse, neither he nor Jordan said a word. After all, what was there to say?

* * *

Her mind drifted back to another time and place, to a man who had posed a threat to them. She had done what was necessary and she had no regrets.

Donald Farris was a very unpleasant man. She had disliked him the first time they met, but she had made allowances for him for Jordan's sake. After all, he was her boss and her future at the Peachtree Agency had been in his hands. Why Jordan had chosen to forgo her dreams of teaching was something only she knew. Jordan would have been a wonderful teacher, just as she would have been a wonderful wife and mother. But now that she was working her way up the ladder at the PR agency, she seemed content—almost happy—for the first time since Robby Joe died. And then that nitwit Farris had done the unthinkable and promoted Paul Dueitt to junior VP, a job everyone knew should have been Jordan's. Even the owner of the agency questioned his choice, but had upheld his decision, then promised Jordan she was next in line.

Well, next in line was not good enough. Jordan deserved that job as junior VP. Actually she should have Farris's job. Getting rid of Paul was an option she had quickly dismissed. He was a very nice young man with a wife and two children. Besides, Jordan's unhappiness wasn't his fault. It was Donald Farris's fault. He had hurt Jordan. He stood in the way of her happiness. There was only one thing to do—get rid of him.

She had spent weeks studying his daily routine and forming a plan. Farris was thirty-five, vain and arrogant. He was health conscious to the point of being obsessed with staying fit. Morning and evening, when everyone else at the Peachtree Agency took the elevator to the fifth floor suite, Donald Farris took the stairs. On Wednesday evenings, he usually worked late and was often the last to leave the office. And that's why this Wednesday evening, she lay in wait, intending to follow him. Once she knew for sure that they were alone, she would make her move.

There he is. Look at him. Such a cocky son of a bitch. Mr. Aren't-I-Important written all over his swagger and smirking grin. If she had her way, after today, he wouldn't swagger or smirk ever again.

As soon as he opened the door that led to the stairwell, she checked the hallway to make sure no one else was anywhere around. Not a soul in sight. She made her way to the door, opened it, and went inside. Inhaling and exhaling a deep breath to steady her hands and calm her nerves, she followed him. The sound of her footsteps was drowned out by Donald Farris's expensive leather loafers tapping rapidly against the concrete stairs. She had to make her move soon before he reached the lower levels. And it had to be a sneak attack or as close to a sneak attack as she could achieve.

She all but ran from the fifth floor to the fourth, catching up with him halfway between the fourth and the third. He had to know he wasn't alone, but he didn't slow his pace or even look back to see who was following him. Although he was, as far as she knew, the only Peachtree Agency employee who regularly used the stairs, he wasn't the only person in the building who did. Apparently he was accustomed to others occasionally taking the stairs.

When she came up directly behind him, practically breathing down his neck, he glanced over his shoulder and gave her an odd look, no doubt recognizing her. He started to say something, but she didn't give him the time to speak. With him staring at her, she lifted her palms and, using them as weapons, shoved them into his chest with all her might. Losing his balance, he stumbled backward.

She had caught him off guard. She had the advantage.

When he stared at her, his eyes wide with shock, she smiled.

When he tried to grab the railing to steady himself, she gave him another hard shove, hoping to push him down the stairs. But instead, his feet slipped out from under him and he hit the guard rail. Grasping in thin air for something—anything—to break his fall, he panicked. She used his fear against him and as his back hit the rail and one foot remained in the air, she pounced on him. He tried to latch on to her, but his hands slipped away from the leather jacket she wore and he toppled backward and over the railing.

His terrified scream echoed through the enclosure, but she was the only one who heard his dying shriek. She stood on the stairs, looked down over the guard rail and watched him as he soared, head first, down, down, down . . . His body hit the concrete floor at the first level with a resounding thud.

She smiled, brushed her hands together in a that's-that gesture, and walked down the stairs. She maneuvered around his splattered body, being careful not to step in the blood or gore, and without a moment's regret went down to the basement parking deck. Once safely in her car, she glanced at herself in the rearview mirror above the console. Her cheeks were flushed, her eyes bright and she was still smiling.

What an exhilarating experience! She had just killed a man and no one would ever know. She laughed. The bastard deserved exactly what he got. He had made the mistake of making an enemy of them, her and Jordan.

Hart slowed the Lincoln to a standstill a block away from the townhouse.

"The police have cordoned off the street," Hart said. He tapped the earphone in his left ear. "I'm being told that there will be no easy way to get you into the house. The police are keeping the news crews away from the front door and there's a police officer posted at the back entrance, but front or back, we're facing making our way through a mob of reporters and protestors."

"Protestors?" Jordan asked.

"A group of right-wing religious fanatics," Hart explained. "I'm told there are about twenty of them, half of them carrying signs. They're an independent group not affiliated with any of the major churches in the area."

Jordan didn't need to ask what types of hate-filled slogans were on the signs. She knew the rhetoric all too well. Having been Devon's best friend most of her life, she had been exposed to this kind of hatred and ignorance before. She had been raised as a Christian and she believed in most of the basic, old-fashioned values that had been observed by generations of her family. She also believed strongly in love, understanding, and tolerance. At the very heart of Christianity and every other great religion in the world was one core belief—God is love. God loved. People hated.

No wonder Devon was half out of his mind. He had seen the protestors, read the signs, knew he was despised.

"You can stay here in the car," Rick told her. "Let me go in and get Devon."

"No, he won't leave unless I go in and get him. You have no idea how fragile he is. Ever since Dan died . . ." She laid her hand on Rick's arm. "The townhouse holds a great many happy memories for Devon. It's been difficult for him to say goodbye. But he isn't safe here and he will be at home with me in Priceville."

"It's going to get ugly out there," Hart warned her, then looked right at Rick. "It'll take both of us to get her through."

Rick nodded. "Yeah."

Once out on the sidewalk, Rick and Jordan waited while Hart finished a brief conversation with someone, probably a member of the police force. Then Rick and Hart flanked Jordan, Rick to her left and slightly behind her and Hart to her right and one step in front of her. Their path remained clear until approximately thirty feet from the townhouse. Suddenly one of the reporters spotted Jordan and called out her name. He came running toward her, microphone in hand and a cameraman racing along behind him.

"Brace yourself," Rick whispered.

The police barricade prevented vehicles from entering or exiting the city block, but the official manpower was concentrated at the front and back of the townhouse. It would have taken a riot squad to keep the horde of reporters and protestors at bay.

"What type of relationship did you have with your husband, Mrs. Price?" a reporter shouted. "Did you have sex with both the senator and Mr. Markham? Or did you simply watch while they had sex?"

Jordan felt Rick's muscles tense. "Ignore them," she told him.

"I can, if you can," he replied.

A barrage of questions followed, each one bouncing off Jordan like water off a duck's back. She had no intention of dignifying the lurid questions with answers. Neither the heartless paparazzi nor the pit-bull legitimate reporters could harm her anymore than she'd already been harmed. Her reputation was in shreds, her personal life past and present exposed for the world to see, her children hounded, her best friend harassed unmercifully, her family hiding away at Price Manor, and her bodyguard shot.

"Did you sleep three to a bed?" someone else called out to her.

"Whose baby were you carrying?"

"Are you a lesbian, Mrs. Price? Do you hate men?"

"Just how many men have you killed?"

"Who are the guys with you, Jordan?" Another reported yelled. "Have you moved on and formed a new threesome?"

"You'd better watch out," someone else hollered. "One of you could be her next victim."

Snide laughter clashed with the damnations chanted by the sign-carrying bigots, the resulting sound a loud echo of voices that didn't blend.

The ugly questions and the vicious taunts continued as Rick and Hart plowed a path through the crowd lining the sidewalk and covering the street. Jordan didn't know if it was their formidable size, both men being tall and muscular, or the steely determination in their eyes combined with auras of sheer masculine strength that parted the reporters, hecklers and onlookers. But they all fell away, one by one, as Jordan and her protectors marched toward the front entrance of the townhouse.

"Got your key?" Rick asked her.

"It's in my pocket."

"I want you to walk up the steps and unlock the door," he told her. "Hart and I will guard your back and then follow you inside."

Hart spoke to one of the policeman at the foot of the front steps and the officer stepped aside to allow them to pass. Jordan followed Rick's instructions, ignoring the barrage of new questions and insults propelled at her and the rocks hitting and cracking the windows and bouncing off the brick walls. A few golf ball size stones barely missed her head. Despite her hands shaking, she managed to insert the key in the lock and open the door. Not glancing back, she entered the marble-floored foyer. Within seconds, Rick came in behind her and then Hart, who closed and locked the door.

She didn't wait for her companions. She hurried down

the hall, calling Devon's name. If she knew Devon, and she did, he would be waiting for her in the cozy den, a room in the center of the house with one window that opened onto the small screened back porch. There, he was more protected from the ugliness going on outside.

Just as she reached the den, the door opened and Devon stepped out. He rushed into her open arms. She hugged him to her, rubbing his back, and whispering soothingly to him.

"It's all right. I'm here now."

"You practically risked your life coming through that pack of wild animals out there," Devon said as he hugged her and then lifted his head from her shoulder. "How are we going to manage to get out of here?"

"We're going out the back and through your neighbor's yard," Rick said as he approached. "Hart has a distraction planned out front in approximately"—he glanced at his wristwatch—"ten minutes. We don't have much time, so don't bring anything with you. Whatever you want can be picked up later. Powell's is sending a couple of agents to guard the townhouse."

"What if the distraction doesn't work?" Devon asked.

"Then we'll face them down," Rick said.

"Ignore the reporters and feel sorry for those poor, misguided people who misuse the Bible to justify their hatred," Jordan told him. "We used to stand up to people like that when we were just teenagers, remember?"

Devon nodded. "That seems like a lifetime ago. Before I met Dan and started living a double life."

"You did what you did to protect Dan. No one can fault you for that." Jordan eyed Rick, her gaze daring him to contradict her.

"I denied the truth for so many years that lying started seeming like the normal thing to do," Devon said. "I lied and said anyone who claimed I was gay was misinformed. I pretended to be straight. I even dated a string of lovely women until finally I couldn't stand the subterfuge any longer and Rene agreed to go to social functions with me after you and Dan married." He hung his head. "Those reporters have every right to have a heyday with this news. I wouldn't blame them, no matter what they said or did."

"Stop feeling sorry for yourself," Rick told him. "Think about Jordan and what your and Dan's secret has done to her."

"Rick!" Jordan glared at him. "How dare you say such a thing."

"No, he's right," Devon said. "I'm the one who pulled you into our web of lies. It's all my fault."

"We can discuss who's at fault, who's to blame, and who's guilty of what later," Rick told them. "We need to be out back and ready to make a run for it as soon as Hart calls me. He'll meet us down the block where he left the car."

Ten minutes and one teargas explosion later, Rick, Jordan and Devon made it halfway down the street when Hart caught up with them.

"Keep going," he shouted. "Time's a-wasting."

They managed to get to the car before some reporters on the fringes of the crowd, coughing, wheezing and crying from the teargas, caught sight of them and ran toward the car. Just as Hart backed up the Lincoln, two men hurled themselves onto the hood, but when Hart whipped the big black car around, the intruders sailed off into the street.

Sitting in the front seat with Hart, Rick glanced in the rearview mirror and his gaze met Jordan's.

That singular moment of silent communication ended practically before it began when Rick's phone rang. Jordan grasped Devon's hand, gave it a squeeze, and then closed her eyes as she said a prayer, asking for the strength to see this nightmare through to the end.

When Rick answered his phone, Griff Powell said, "Maleah's going to be all right. She's out of surgery. Nic

and I are at Erlanger in Chattanooga. We're staying overnight and plan to see Maleah in the morning."

"That's good news," Rick replied. "Now if we can figure out who shot her and why—"

"That's one of the other reasons I'm calling. The deputies
arrested a guy about an hour ago. They found him and his
high-powered rifle in the woods. He shot Maleah from
outside the estate."

"Are you sure they've got the right person?"

"Reasonably sure. The man confessed. We'll know for
sure once the bullet is examined, but this nut-job claims
he meant to shoot Jordan. It seems he considered it his
duty to act on God's behalf and mete out punishment. As
far as we know, he's not connected with her or her family
or the late senator in any way, other than the fact he lives
in Priceville."

"If this turns out to be on the up-and-up that means
people we eliminated from our suspects list have to go
right back on it."

"By people, you mean Devon Markham, don't you?"
Griff said.

"Yeah."

"While we're on the subject of suspects, I talked to
Derek Lawrence and he's promised us a profile to fit each
of your scenarios by Thursday. Maybe one of those profiles will fit one of the suspects to a T."

"If only," Rick said.

"In the meantime, be careful. If we're right, there is a
serial killer among Jordan Price's family and close friends,
someone who has possibly killed seven people. He or she
won't hesitate to kill again. You're not just investigating
Dan Price's murder now, you're guarding Jordan." Griffin
paused. "And even though I know you don't want to en-
tertain the possibility that Jordan herself is the killer,
you'd be a fool to totally discount her as a suspect."

# Chapter 27

Rick landed the helicopter at the Price estate Tuesday evening. A couple of Powell agents and a sheriff's deputy met them when they disembarked.

The deputy spoke to Rick. "Sheriff Corbett wants to talk to you, privately. He's waiting down by the pond." He hitched his thumb in the general direction. "Mr. Price and Mr. Keinan are with him."

"Sure thing," Rick said. "As soon as I get Mrs. Price settled." He motioned to one of the two agents, a fairly new Powell Agency recruit named Nix Elliott. "I want you to stay with Mrs. Price until I relieve you. Stay close to her and know exactly where she is and who's with her at all times."

Elliott nodded.

Rick explained the situation to Jordan, who simply said, "I'll be fine. I'm home now. We're safe." She had slipped her arm around Devon's waist and hugged him to her side.

The poor guy looked as if he'd been through a physical and emotional wringer. But oddly enough Jordan was cool, calm, and totally together. Rick marveled at her ability to keep herself in check while taking care of others, in this case, looking after Devon.

If only he could believe that she was safe here on the Price estate. But he couldn't. If his suspicions were correct, someone she loved and trusted was a killer. The only thing he didn't know for certain was whether this person loved Jordan or hated her.

When they reached the house, Rick pulled Jordan aside. "I just need a minute, okay?"

She looked back at Devon. "Go on in. I won't be long."

Agent Elliott waited on the veranda while Devon and the other agent went inside the house.

"Everything that I discussed with you, Ryan, and Steve Corbett this morning is to stay among the four of us," Rick told her. "Understand?"

"Yes, of course." Her eyes widened. "Oh, you mean now that we know the man who shot Maleah isn't personally connected to me or Dan or the other deaths, then Devon is a suspect again."

"I'm sorry. I know you love him and trust him, but—"

"But you don't trust him. You don't even trust me. Not really."

He grabbed her arm. "Damn it, Jordan, why can't you understand that if you trust the wrong person, it could cost you your life."

Trembling, she stood there and stared at him, but didn't respond to his warning.

"Honey, don't do this," he said.

"Do what?"

"Make me the bad guy."

"I know you're one of the good guys," she told him. "But so is Devon. I trust him as much as I trust you."

*She trusts me.*

*I want to trust her. And I do. Almost.*

When he released his hold on her, she walked away

and went inside the house. Rick waited until Nix Elliott followed her before he left to find the sheriff.

The late afternoon sunlight glistened off the pond's smooth surface. Several geese floated leisurely, paying no heed to the humans. Thick, rich grass grew along the bank and wildflowers had recently sprouted in the field nearby. May in the Georgia countryside was fresh and green and vibrant.

Steve Corbett threw up his hand and motioned for Rick to join them where they stood near the pond, obviously waiting for him.

"Thank you for bringing Jordan and Devon home safely." Ryan extended his hand to Rick and the two men exchanged a cordial shake.

"You know that we found the man who shot Maleah Perdue, don't you?" Steve asked.

"Yeah, I know. Griff called me."

"That puts Devon Markham back on the suspects list," Holt said. "Until we get those profiles from Derek Lawrence, we can only speculate about who we think killed Senator Price."

"Even with the profiles, we'll be speculating," Steve said.

"I find it difficult to accept that any one of the people closest to Jordan may have killed my brother." Ryan grimaced. "And I refuse to even consider the possibility that Jordan is guilty of any crime other than perhaps being too self-sacrificing."

"We've been working on a plan." Holt glanced at his two co-conspirators. "I've run it by the boss and he's in agreement, but Griff said the final decision would have to be yours and Mrs. Price's."

Just what sort of plan had these guys come up with? "Well, spit it out."

"If either of your scenarios about why someone has killed numerous men in Mrs. Price's life is correct, then whoever our killer is, he or she goes after anyone, men in particular, whose death benefits Jordan in some way. She benefits either by eliminating a perceived threat or by her inheriting large sums of money," Holt explained. "Our killer isn't going to make another move unless he or she is presented with someone new who fits either description."

"It doesn't really matter why this person kills, does it? If he or she has killed in order to punish Jordan or in order to protect her, the end results have been the same," Steve added.

"The plan is to present the killer with a new victim," Ryan said. "Someone they would believe capable of harming Jordan."

A tight knot formed in the pit of Rick's belly. He wasn't sure exactly what the game plan was, but he figured he had been chosen as the killer's next target.

"Okay," Rick said. "I'm the new victim, right? Just what am I going to do to threaten Jordan?"

"Jordan will know from day one what the plan is," Ryan said. "You have to believe in her innocence, but pretend otherwise."

"If our plan is to work, it will require some acting on your part and Jordan's." Steve shuffled his feet nervously, as if he wasn't sure how Rick would react to the details of their plan. "On the surface, you'll be Jordan's champion. You believe in her. You know she is completely innocent. She sees you as her knight in shining armor. The two of you exhibit some personal interest in each other. But while you're supposedly playing up to Jordan, you're going behind her back trying to prove she murdered Dan and the others."

"The plan's too complicated," Rick told them. "Besides, I don't think Jordan will agree to it."

"Don't shoot it down. At least not yet," Steve said. "Once we get the profiles from Powell's expert and get a better idea of who our killer could be, we'll know whether to follow through with the plan or try another tactic."

"My brother's reputation is ruined," Ryan said. "Everything that Jordan and Devon sacrificed for Dan was for nothing. Now Jordan's life could well be on the line. How can she ever move past what's happened unless the killer is found? We have to find the real killer and prove Jordan's innocence."

"Okay, we'll talk to her." Rick glanced at Ryan. "Just the two us. If she agrees, we'll put this convoluted plan into motion. But God help us if we screw this thing up."

"No!" Jordan was adamant. "You're asking me to lie to the people who mean the most to me. By taking part in this plan, I'm as good as admitting that I believe someone near and dear to me is a murderer."

"On the other hand, it could do the exact opposite," Rick pointed out to her. "If no one takes the bait, it could convince us that we're wrong."

"I can't do it." Shaking her head, she turned away from him.

"Jordan, I don't want to believe it's possible any more than you do," Ryan told her. "But even if there is the slightest chance that Rick is right—"

"He's not." She turned on them, her gaze darting from Ryan to Rick and back to Ryan. "Do you honestly believe that Devon could have killed Dan? My God, he all but worshipped your brother. He would have moved heaven and earth for him."

"No, not Devon, but—"

"Darlene? She's like a mother to me. She's gentle and kind and I love her dearly."

"I admit that Darlene doesn't have the disposition you would expect a cold-blooded killer to have," Ryan said.

"And Rene is my best friend. She's ambitious and aggressive, but good grief, she cries when she sees a dead animal in the road. She couldn't kill anyone. What about

Roselynne? Do you honestly think she's a killer? And
Tammy? Do you think she's actually smart enough to get
away with murder and not just one murder, but six or
seven? And even J.C., for all his faults, doesn't have it in
him to kill."

"I know and I agree," Ryan said. "But someone killed
Dan."

Jordan closed her eyes, obviously wanting to shut out
the ugliness of that undeniable truth. Someone with access to their home, someone who had known where Dan
kept the gun he'd bought her, had killed Dan. As horrible
as the thought was, she had to accept the facts—if Jordan
didn't kill her husband that meant someone else did.

She opened her eyes and looked at Rick. "All right. I'll
go along with this, but only if the profile you receive from
Powell's actually points to one of your suspects."

"We shouldn't wait," Ryan told her. "The sooner—"

"You have a deal." Rick glanced from Jordan to Ryan.
"We can wait a couple of days if that makes this any easier for Jordan."

"I'm agreeing to this only to prove to both of you that
you're going to have to look beyond the obvious and find
other suspects."

Ryan frowned sympathetically, then walked over to
Jordan and hugged her. "I'm sorry to put you through this
and I truly hope you're right. But you must understand
how important it is to me, now more than ever, to prove
that Dan didn't commit suicide. And we all want to prove
that you have never killed anyone."

She hugged him and kissed him on the cheek. "I do
understand. I want Dan's killer caught and punished just
as much as you do. And Devon wants the same thing."

Ryan released her and then turned to Rick. "Take good
care of her. She's a special kind of lady."

Rick nodded.

When Ryan closed the study door behind him, Rick

made a quick decision. He intended to leave Jordan in peace, at least for the rest of the evening. "Agent Elliott will be posted outside the study," Rick told her. "He'll stay with you for a few hours while I take care of some other things."

"What things?"

"Nothing you need to worry about. If I learn anything new, I'll share it with you immediately."

"Promise?"

"Yeah, I promise."

He hated leaving things this way, with Jordan exhausted, emotionally raw, and worrying about everyone except herself. But he needed to put some distance between them— even if it was only a few rooms inside the house.

"You realize that from here on out, I need to be with you around the clock," he said. "Maybe you could see if Tobias can round up a cot of some kind and put it outside your bedroom."

"Do you actually think someone might—"

"Work with me, okay? I know your feelings. You know my thoughts. It's my job to keep you safe. I need you to cooperate with me."

"There's no reason for you to sleep on a cot. There's a daybed in my dressing room. You can sleep there." She looked him over, from head to toe. "The bed may be a little too short for you, but it will be far more comfortable than a cot."

"Do you trust me that much, to let me sleep in your dressing room?"

"I believe you're the type of man who would never do anything I didn't want you to do." She offered him a wavering smile. "You see, I trust you far more than you trust me."

"Don't assume you know what I think."

"I assume nothing where you're concerned."

"If I sleep behind closed doors with you, what will your family think? Aren't you concerned about—?"

"No, I'm not the least concerned. You're my bodyguard. It's expected that you will stay close to me at all times."

Despite his better judgment, he moved toward her, narrowing the space between them to mere inches. "That's the problem. I want to be close to you."

He reached out, clamped his hand on the back of her neck and drew her to him as he lowered his head down far enough so that they were staring directly into each other's eyes. Her mouth opened on a startled gasp.

"Rick?"

"Damn!"

He covered her mouth with his, his tongue circling her lips, tasting her before he thrust inside. She swayed toward him, her breasts brushing against his chest. Holding her head in place, he deepened the kiss. Just as he realized that she wasn't responding and started to end things, she laid her hands on his chest and moaned as she kissed him back. It was then that he knew she was as hungry for him as he was for her.

Taking full advantage of the opportunity, Rick kissed her until they were both breathless. As they broke apart slowly, his hand still gripping the back of her neck and her hands still on his chest, he lifted his head and looked at her.

When she closed her eyes, he pressed his forehead against hers.

"You make me feel things I haven't felt in years," she said. "Not since . . ."

He ran his index finger up and down the back of her neck in a caressing gesture. "Not since when?"

She opened her eyes, smiled at him and said, "Not since I was young and foolish and believed in happily ever after."

"Not since Robby Joe?"

"What I had with Robby Joe, I'll never have with anyone else. But I didn't expect this. I don't even know what to call it."

"Sexual attraction."

"That's all it is," she said. "It's all it can be."

"Don't discount the power of lust in a relationship."

Neither of them realized someone had seen the kiss and overheard their conversation; not until Rick heard the door close and caught a glimpse of Rene Burke as she hurried away.

"What is it?" Jordan lifted her hand to his face, cupped his chin, and turned his face to hers. "Did you hear something?" She glanced at the closed door.

"The door was open," he told her. "Rene was there, but when she realized she was interrupting something between us, she left."

"Oh."

"Does it bother you that she saw us?"

"No. And I suppose it plays right into the little charade you have planned to trap Dan's killer, doesn't it?"

Rick cupped her face and forced her to look directly at him. "That kiss had absolutely nothing to do with the plan. It was something just between you and me."

"I know."

"Good." He kissed her forehead and her cheeks.

"We can't act on our baser impulses again."

"You're calling the shots. We'll go as fast or as slow as you need to and we can stop with this one kiss, if that's what you really want."

"What I want—"

Rick's cell phone rang. He cursed under his breath. "I'd better get it."

She stepped back, moving away from him, while he retrieved his phone and checked caller ID.

"It's my boss." He flipped open the phone. "Yeah, Griff, what is it?"

"We've unearthed a piece of information I think Mrs. Price should know about as soon as possible," Griff said. "Our sources have uncovered the identity of the person who sold the story about the senator to The Chatterbox."

"Was Haley McLain involved in any way?" Rick asked.

"I don't know," Griff replied. "But you can ask J.C. Harris. The Chatterbox paid Mrs. Price's stepbrother three hundred thousand dollars for the info they used in the exposé about Daniel Price."

"Do you know where Harris is now?"

"He's in Vegas spending his ill-gotten gains."

"How about sending someone to question him?" Rick suggested. "Someone who knows how to get the truth out of him."

"If Haley McLain was involved, she could lose her job."

"Yeah, I know. If she put Harris up to this, she shouldn't be in law enforcement."

"Agreed. I'll send Luke Sentell to Vegas."

"Thanks." Rick slipped the phone back into his pocket and turned to Jordan, who had waited quietly while he spoke to Griff. "Your stepbrother sold the story about Dan and Devon and you to The Chatterbox. They paid him three hundred thousand."

"Oh, God. This news will kill Roselynne when she finds out. And Tammy. Rick, I don't want either of them to know. Please."

He stared at her, stunned by the fact that instead of being outraged that her stepbrother could have betrayed her in such a blatant and hurtful way, she was worried about his mother and sister.

"Honey, are you for real?"

Before she could do more than stare at him, he pulled her into his arms and kissed her again.

# Chapter 28

For the past two nights, Rick had slept on the daybed in Jordan's dressing room. He had made a point of being up and out of the room before she awoke both mornings and had waited until she was in bed each night before he walked quietly through her bedroom. After sharing some hot kisses Tuesday evening, they had agreed not to allow things to progress any further. Rick wanted more and was sure she wanted more, too, but exactly what that more involved he didn't think either of them knew for sure. Yeah, okay, so he did know he wanted sex. That went without saying, didn't it? But did it go beyond that for either of them? After all, they had known each other less than a month and had met the day of her husband's funeral. But Dan Price had been Jordan's husband in name only, so it wasn't as if she were in mourning for a man she'd been in love with.

*Don't forget about her baby.*

Jordan hid her grief for her child. Since the miscarriage, she'd barely had time to come to terms with the loss. She'd been forced to deal with being suspected of murder and having the truth about her marriage revealed to the world. And it seemed that as usual, she'd had no choice but to put everyone's needs before her own. He wasn't going to do that to her. Instead, he was going to do what he knew was best for Jordan and keep his hands off her. She needed his protection, needed the Powell Agency to find out who murdered her husband, and needed to be exonerated of any guilt in the deaths of the others.

Taking care of Jordan sure as hell didn't include screwing her.

Rick checked his wristwatch as he finished his brisk morning walk around the estate. Ten-fifteen. He had left Nix Elliott in charge of Jordan while he escaped. Being with her twenty-four/seven was proving to be more difficult than he'd thought. If she were any other woman and this was any other case, he'd have already bowed out and handed her over to another agent. Permanently. He had never allowed himself to become personally involved with a client and knew he was playing fast and loose with his own code of ethics.

*If you think things are difficult now, just wait until you two set "the plan" into motion.*

As he came up the drive, he heard an approaching vehicle. He turned just as a silver Corvette drove past him and pulled to a stop in front of the house. Rick recognized the tall, lanky guy who emerged from the sports car. Derek Lawrence, former FBI profiler, now an independent contractor, the author of half a dozen true crime books, and a part-time Powell Agency employee.

Derek threw up his hand. "Hey there."

"I thought you were going to call," Rick said.

"I'm on my way to Atlanta, so Griff suggested I stop by and give you my report in person." Derek glanced around, his gaze sweeping over the antebellum mansion and the broad expanse of lawn. "Quite a place."

"Have you had breakfast?" Rick asked.

"Yes, thanks. I stopped in Chattanooga for a bite on the way here."

"Come on in. I'll get Jordan and we can—"

"Let's talk, just you and me. You can share whatever information you think Mrs. Price needs to know with her later."

Rick eyed Derek questioningly. "What's going on?"

"Do you feel like showing me around the place? I wouldn't mind taking a stroll around the property."

"Sure. Come on."

They left the veranda, side by side. Rick waited for Derek to continue the conversation, his gut warning him that he wasn't going to like whatever this renowned profiler had to say.

"After going over all the information Griff sent me, I've come to the conclusion that your killer is probably either Jordan Price or someone who would do anything for her."

Rick had figured as much. Hadn't he, early on, suspected Jordan? She was the logical choice.

"I know all the reasons why she would head the list of suspects. But ruling her out completely, who's our second choice?"

"Don't rule her out," Derek said. "That would be a mistake."

"You were supposed to work up a profile of our killer, not—"

"Just because you don't want the lady to be a killer doesn't mean she isn't." Focusing on Rick as if he were trying to solve a puzzle, Derek scowled. "Your interest in Mrs. Price goes beyond the professional, doesn't it?"

"No." Rick huffed. "Yeah, okay, it does. And I know she's the prime suspect in her husband's murder and if the other deaths were murder, then she's the person who had the most to gain from killing each of them. But if you knew her, you'd know that Jordan is not a killer."

"All right, let's work under the premise that someone

other than Mrs. Price killed her husband and his ex-wife and possibly her first husband and fiancé and the others." Derek glanced back at the house. "Let's keep walking. We'll have more privacy that way."

Rick chose the path, one that led away from the mansion. When they were no longer within earshot of anyone in or near the house, he paused and confronted Derek. "Who's your number two suspect?"

"You know enough about profiling to know it's not an exact science."

"Yeah, but it's a notch above looking into a crystal ball."

Derek grinned. "If we actually have a serial murderer on our hands, then we start with the basics. Most serial killers can be divided into categories based on how they interact with their victims. Some rape or sexually torture. Some mutilate. I'd say your killer executes. He or she may get a thrill from the murder itself, but killing appears to be a means to an end."

"Yeah, I got that. The killer believes he—or she—is taking care of Jordan, punishing those who hurt her or eliminating those who stand in the way of her happiness."

Derek nodded. "If we assume that all or at least most of the men, and the first Mrs. Price, were murdered, then we look at each death. Was each murder premeditated, was it planned? Yes, each seems to have been, at least to some degree. What did the victims have in common? Jordan Price. What was the method of murder? It varied from person to person, but in each case, except for Jane Anne Price and Jay Reynolds, the other deaths appeared to be from natural causes, accidents and suicide. It all boils down to one fact—this person is no ordinary, run-of-the-mill, serial killer."

"You're giving me a Beginner's Lesson in Profiling. Why?"

Derek chuckled. "Sometimes I just like to impress people with my knowledge."

"Or maybe you don't have a clue as to who might have killed Dan Price or any of the others."

"Let me paint you a picture and see if you recognize anyone. Our killer is mission oriented. The murders occurred whenever our killer perceived that the victim was harmful in some way to Jordan. That fact dictated when the murders took place. As for where and by what method, where depended on being able to isolate the victim and the method seemed to be whatever could be disguised as anything other than murder."

"With two exceptions," Rick said.

Derek nodded. "Our killer is rational and calculating. He or she doesn't have a specific MO except their single motive of protecting Jordan. These murders, be it two murders or seven, were all about Jordan."

"The killer loves Jordan."

"The killer is obsessed with Jordan," Derek said. "My educated guess is that this person loves Jordan to the point of obsession. She is the beginning and end of their world. They need her the way they need the air that they breathe. If Jordan isn't the killer, then find the person who thinks of the two of them as one. The killer has no life without Jordan and probably believes that Jordan has no life without him or her."

"Crap! That tells me two things—you haven't narrowed down the suspects list by much and we're dealing with someone who is completely mental."

"Our killer probably appears normal," Derek said. "He or she lives a relatively ordinary life just like the average person. A person can be evil without being abnormal."

"You've read over the files on each possible suspect. Does anyone send up a red flag?"

"The people in Mrs. Price's life seem to be extraordinarily devoted to her. Her stepmother and stepsister, and to some extent her stepbrother. I wouldn't rule out J.C. Harris, but I'd put him at the bottom of the list. Tammy

Harris could be obsessed with Jordan. She loves being her sister and possibly identifies closely with her, but she wouldn't head my list either simply because I don't believe she's smart enough to have gotten away with murder numerous times. Of the three members of the Harris family, Roselynne is the most likely."

"What about Rene, Devon, and Darlene?"

"Rene is smart, calculating and one of Jordan's best friends. I'd keep her on the list, along with Roselynne and Darlene Wright. Mrs. Wright appears to be totally devoted to Jordan. It's possible that her devotion turned to obsession at some point along the way."

"You're forgetting Devon Markham."

Derek shook his head. "I didn't forget Devon, I simply left the best for last. I'd place him at the top of the list. He has known Jordan longer than any of the others. He loves her like a sister, like a best friend, perhaps loves her as the other half of himself. She has loved him, protected him, defended him, and sacrificed for him since they were children. It wouldn't be a stretch to believe that he would do anything for her, just as she would for him. Even kill."

Of all the possible suspects, Devon headed Derek's list, just as he did Rick's. And of all the suspects, Devon was the one Jordan loved more, trusted more, and would never believe guilty.

"I agree," Rick said. "But why would Devon kill Dan Price? They were lovers. They had been in a committed relationship for twelve years."

"For the same reasons men kill their wives and women kill their husbands. Infidelity. Money. Freedom. And there are always incidents where a spouse kills a terminally ill mate who is suffering. If Devon Markham knew about his lover's Alzheimer's—"

"He didn't. Supposedly no one knew, except the senator's doctor."

"Supposedly," Derek said. "All you have is each person's word that Dan Price didn't share that information. If the senator would tell anyone about the diagnosis, don't you think it would be his partner?"

Rick nodded. He had really hoped that Derek's profiles would point the finger of suspicion at someone other than Devon. If any one of her family and close friends turned out to be the murderer, it would break Jordan's heart; but if it was Devon, Jordan would be devastated.

"Did Griff tell you anything about the idea of our setting a trap for the killer?" Rick asked.

"He mentioned it."

"And?"

"It might work. But on the other hand, you have to know you could be risking your life. And there's always the chance that he won't take the bait. That is assuming Devon is the killer."

"You think he is."

"I think it's possible, especially if he thinks like a woman."

"What do you mean?"

"My initial conclusion was that the killer is female, but I altered that assumption when I saw that Devon Markham fit all the other criteria. I think he's the most likely suspect out of the six that you offered me. But you cannot rule out any of the others, especially not Roselynne, Rene, and Darlene."

"When I asked Roselynne for permission to have her husband's body exhumed, she refused. Maybe she didn't want anyone to find out that his heart attack wasn't really a simple heart attack, but actually murder."

"You'd think she'd want to do anything to help prove Mrs. Price innocent of past crimes, wouldn't you? What about Darlene Wright? Did she refuse to give you permission to have her son's body exhumed?"

"No. Actually Jordan told me, in no uncertain terms, not to ask her."

"Ask her anyway and see what she says. If she's willing to have his body exhumed and an autopsy performed, I'd say that means she believes her son's death was an accident and neither she nor Jordan has anything to hide."

"I should have asked her. But Jordan is our client and as a general rule, Powell's does what the client wants."

"I believe Ryan Price actually hired you, didn't he? If I understood correctly, Jordan Price joined him in the request after the fact."

"That's right, but she's been as determined as Ryan to find out the truth."

"What about Ryan Price?"

"What about him?" Rick asked.

"He's not among the suspects you listed. Why not?"

"As you said, he hired us to prove the senator's death wasn't suicide. If he'd killed his brother, he wouldn't have questioned the ME's findings, would he? Besides, his relationship with Jordan doesn't go back far enough for him to have had anything to do with any of the deaths before the senator's."

Derek nodded, apparently agreeing with Rick.

"If you want details in writing, I can send you everything by e-mail," Derek said. "I need to get going. I'm supposed to be in Atlanta by one. Griff's got me on speed dial, so if there's anything else I can do, just let me know."

Rick walked Derek to his car, shook his hand, and thanked him. Now that he had a professional profiler's opinion, which just happened to match his own, Rick felt more confident about their plan to trap Dan Price's killer. All he had to do was convince a ruthless murderer that he, Rick Carson, was a threat to Jordan.

Rick set things in motion later that day by questioning each suspect individually, masking his inquiries under the guise of wanting to help Jordan. He'd said the same things, asked the same questions, made the same observations with each of them, beginning with Roselynne. She had defended Jordan and even scolded him for questioning her innocence; then practically in the same breath, she had encouraged Rick to romance Jordan.

"You've got a thing for my girl," Roselynne had said. "And as her mama, I'm giving you permission to make your move. I know it doesn't seem like the right time, but Lord knows Jordan's been in need of a real man for quite some time."

Apparently, despite the fact that he'd all but come right out and told Roselynne he believed Jordan might be a murderer, she saw him as a potential lover for Jordan, not her captor.

He had fared a little better with Rene, who had told him off in no uncertain terms. "How can you possibly still think Jordan killed Dan? And Boyd? And even Robby Joe? I thought you knew her better than that by now. I thought you honestly cared for Jordan. What's going on? Are you pretending to be her friend so you can trap her into confessing? Well, forget it. Jordan is not a killer!"

Questioning Devon had been like walking a tightrope. Rick wanted him to believe that he suspected Jordan had killed Dan, Dan's ex-wife, her first husband and all the others, too, while the truth was that he actually thought Devon could be the murderer.

"I've seen the way you look at Jordan," Devon had said. "And the way you are when you're with her. You care about her and I don't believe it's an act. So how can you possibly believe that she's capable of murdering seven people?"

"I don't want to think it," Rick had told him. "But all the evidence points to her. No one else has a motive for each murder. Only Jordan. If she did kill Dan and the others, she needs help. As her oldest and dearest friend, you should want to know the truth and if she's guilty, get her the help she needs."

"Does Jordan know that you still suspect her? My God, she trusts you and you're betraying that trust!"

His talk with Devon had ended abruptly when Devon, eyes flashing with outrage, had walked out on him. If he'd wanted to make Devon angry, he had achieved his goal.

Three down and one to go.

He found Darlene alone in the kitchen, sitting at the table by the windows, a cup of what he assumed was tea in her hand.

"Good afternoon," he said as he approached her.

She glanced at him and smiled. "Good afternoon, Mr. Carson."

"May I join you?" he asked.

"Would you like a cup of tea?"

"No, thanks. But I'd like to talk to you, if you have time."

"Won't you sit down."

He joined her at the table, taking the seat across from her. "You want to help Jordan, don't you?"

"Yes, certainly."

"You know that she's considered the most likely suspect in Dan Price's murder."

"Yes, I know, and it's absolutely ridiculous."

"Some people believe she not only murdered the senator, but also her first husband, her father, a former boss and even your son."

Darlene eyed him speculatively. "I think I know where this is going. Roselynne told me that you asked her for permission to have Wayne Harris's body exhumed and an autopsy performed."

"She refused," Rick said. "Powell's thought if an autopsy proved Mr. Harris died of natural causes—"

"I'm sure he did. And I know, without a doubt, that Robby Joe died from injuries he received in the car wreck and that the wreck was an accident."

"If we could prove—"

"You can," Darlene told him. "I had what was left of the car inspected thoroughly at the time. I had planned to sue the manufacturer if the accident had been caused by any type of default. There was none. So you see, if your theory is that there might have been tampering, there wasn't."

"Do you still have that report?" Rick asked.

"Yes, I do. And if you believe that it's possible Robby Joe was drugged or poisoned and his condition either caused the wreck or the wreck was a cover-up, then an autopsy might prove otherwise. Is that right?"

"Yes, ma'am."

"Then you have my permission to exhume Robby Joe's body and have an autopsy performed."

"No!" Jordan cried.

They turned and stared at Jordan standing in the doorway, a stricken expression on her face.

"Yes," Darlene said. "You didn't kill Dan or anyone else. Certainly not Robby Joe. If allowing them to do an autopsy will prove he wasn't murdered, then let them do the autopsy."

"No. You don't have to do this." Jordan came into the room, her gaze searing Rick with her barely restrained anger. "I thought I told you not to ask her. I believed you understood—"

"Don't blame Mr. Carson." Darlene rose to her feet and held out her hand to Jordan. "He didn't ask me. I made the offer because I want to help you, because it's what Robby Joe would want me to do."

# Chapter 29

During the next few days, Rick came to understand something important about Jordan, something he had sensed about her for weeks now. The lady had an uncanny ability to hide her true emotions. Although she had been angry with him since this past Thursday and was still upset with him, she played her part in their public charade. But in private, she barely spoke to him. He could deal with her coldness even if it did piss the hell out of him. What he had real difficulty dealing with were his doubts. Jordan's reluctance to have Robby Joe Wright's body exhumed worried him. Did that mean she had something to hide, that if an autopsy was performed on Robby Joe, it would reveal that he had been drugged or poisoned?

When Devon had learned that Darlene had given Powell's permission to have her son's casket unearthed, he had reacted just as Rick had thought he would, with a great deal of hostility, all of it directed at Rick. But committed to their plan of trapping Dan's killer, Jordan had defended Rick to Devon and the others, pretending she agreed with Rick.

Considering Jordan's reluctance to have her former fiancé's body exhumed and her devotion to Devon, was it possible that Jordan either knew or suspected that Devon had killed Robby Joe? And Dan? Would she really have covered up for him over the years, time and time again? Rick didn't want to believe that she was capable of either murder or of protecting a friend she knew was a killer.

It was possible that she opposed the exhumation only because, as she had told him, she thought it would be a difficult ordeal for Darlene.

He wanted to believe her. God, how he wanted to believe her.

With Darlene Wright's permission, Powell's had set the legal wheels in motion to have Robby Joe's casket removed from the cemetery and taken to the Powell agency's lab in Knoxville. Darlene's only requests were that she be present for the exhumation and that before the reburial, they would have a private ceremony at the local funeral home chapel.

Rick didn't understand why she would want to watch while her son's casket was dug up and removed from the burial plot. But if that's what she wanted, so be it. He suspected that Jordan didn't want to be there, on the scene, but she wouldn't allow Darlene to go to the cemetery without her.

If he had thought he could talk Jordan out of going, he would have tried; but when it came to family obligations, she always stood firm. There had been no use wasting his breath.

While Jordan and Rene went over Tuesday morning's mail, Rick left Nix Elliott at the study door to keep watch while he took a break. Although he had come to the conclusion that Jordan was in no real danger, that all the phone calls and letters had merely been attempts to take suspicion off Jordan, guarding her twenty-four/seven was now part of the deadly game they were playing.

The cold, silent wall that Jordan had erected between them when they were alone bothered him more and more each day. And Jordan damn well knew it.

Just as he opened the door to the kitchen, intending to get a cup of coffee, his phone rang. When he noted the caller—Griff Powell—he answered immediately.

"Everything is set for the exhumation," Griff said, not bothering with any preliminary greetings or small-talk. "This afternoon. Three-thirty."

"It's a forty-five minute drive," Rick said. "The cemetery is a private family place, out in the country, on land that's been in Mrs. Wright's family for generations."

"I take it that you haven't been able to persuade Mrs. Wright not to be there when they bring up the casket."

"Nope. I'll be driving her and Jordan and Devon Markham to the cemetery."

"The body will be taken directly to Knoxville, to our lab at headquarters. We're bringing in two retired medical examiners to oversee our doctor's autopsy. I'm asking for a rush job on this. Hopefully, we'll have some answers in days instead of weeks."

"The sooner the better," Rick said. "Mrs. Wright insists on a private ceremony before the reburial. She's already made plans with the local funeral home to provide a new casket. I think it's a bad idea having a second funeral, no matter how small and private. It'll be difficult for Jordan and for Mrs. Wright."

"If the autopsy indicates that any factors, such as drugs or poison, or an injury not likely to have occurred in the car wreck, led to Robby Joe Wright's death, Powell's will have to turn over that information to the proper authorities."

"Yeah, I know."

"Watch your back," Griff told him. "You're the bait in the trap. If the killer comes after you, you're at a disadvantage because you don't know for sure who the killer is or exactly when he or she will strike."

She watched him as he stood there on the patio, his cell phone to his ear. Who was he talking to? His boss? Or had someone from the hospital called to give him a report on Maleah Perdue, who was supposed to be released tomorrow? Perhaps the caller was a woman, someone he had known in the past? He was quite handsome and rather charming when he chose to be. There were probably numerous women in his past.

Even though she knew that Jordan would never find anyone to replace Robby Joe, she could be tempted by broad shoulders and piercing brown eyes. After all, she was only human. But surely Jordan realized that Rick Carson was no different from other men.

They couldn't trust him.

Knowing how untrustworthy he was, how could Jordan have allowed him to move into her bedroom? She said he slept on the daybed in her dressing room, and there was no reason not to believe her. But it was obvious, at least to her, that Jordan had strong feelings for Rick. Hadn't she learned anything from past experience? He was not her friend. Couldn't she see that? She was putting her trust in the wrong person, putting her life in the wrong hands.

She should know by now that I will take care of everything, as I always have. I'll protect her, no matter what the cost. I'll even protect her from herself.

He doesn't love you, Jordan. He may want your body, but sex isn't love. Why can't you see him for what he is? He's a user. He'll toss you aside once he's finished with you. He will break your heart.

If I don't stop him.

The Jernigan Cemetery, atop a hill outside the small town of Jernigan Crossroads, Georgia, looked down over green fields in three directions and thick woods to the north. The oldest headstone dated back to 1812. Darlene had informed them that the couple buried beneath the stone marker were her father's ancestors, one of the first families to settle in the area.

"Jernigan Crossroads was named for Ezekiel Jernigan," Darlene had told them, quite proud of her heritage.

On the drive over from Priceville, the sky had turned dark as rain clouds moved in, but not a drop had fallen. Jordan hoped that the rain would hold off until after the exhumation.

It had been a year since she and Darlene had been here at the family cemetery where Robby Joe was buried. They usually came once every year, on Mother's Day, which was Decoration Day at this cemetery and many others throughout the South. This year, they had arranged for flowers to be delivered, but had stayed away because the press had been following Jordan's every move. Even today, a couple of reporters had somehow found out what was happening and were already here waiting for them.

Jordan leaned over and whispered to Darlene, "Are you sure about this? If you've changed your mind—"

"I haven't. The autopsy will prove that Robby Joe's death was the result of an accident." She grasped Jordan's hand. "As for being here this afternoon . . . I have to be. I feel that if I'm here, Robby Joe will understand that I would never disturb his rest without a very good reason."

Jordan swallowed hard, determined to stay strong. When they made their yearly pilgrimage to Robby Joe's grave, Darlene always cried. Jordan didn't.

Rick pulled the Mercedes up behind the patrol car that was parked on the gravel drive circling the small cemetery. A spit-and-polished young deputy leaning against the side of the hood snapped to attention.

"If y'all will stay put, I'll see if I can get rid of those reporters." Rick opened the car door.

"Wait," Jordan called. "They aren't likely to leave just because you tell them to, and right now, they're not rushing toward us, so don't create a scene."

"Okay. Whatever you want."

*Whatever I want? I don't want to be here. I don't want to watch while that big, loud backhoe digs into the earth, going deeper and deeper with each lunge until Robby Joe's casket appears. I don't want to see the casket. I don't want to think about the day Robby Joe died or the day we buried him or the fact that he's not in that casket, not really. Only what remains of his body is inside the casket. He's gone from me forever. He's in a better place. Isn't that what the minister had said at his funeral? Robby Joe's soul is now in heaven.*

"They're waiting for word from you, Mrs. Wright," Rick told her as he opened the back door and held out his hand to assist her.

She looked up at him, her eyes damp with tears, and took his hand. "Thank you."

Jordan emerged from the car, but when Rick offered her his hand, she refused to touch him. Devon got out last and immediately slipped his arm around her waist. She could accept Devon's tender concern, but not Rick's. She couldn't explain why she felt the way she did, but somehow having Rick here today didn't seem right. Even though she wasn't sure how she felt about him, she did feel something— something powerful—and feeling that way seemed like a betrayal of her love for Robby Joe.

"I can go with Darlene," Devon told her. "You should stay here."

"He's right," Darlene said. "If you don't want to—"

"My place is with you," Jordan said. "I won't let you go through this alone."

In her peripheral vision she noticed Rick glancing her

way. She had gotten over her initial anger with him rather quickly, but she still held him at least partially responsible for their being here today.

"Please, tell them to begin," Darlene said to Rick.

He nodded and then spoke to the deputy who held up his hand and signaled the workers. The roar of the small backhoe's engine shattered the gentle stillness enveloping the cemetery. Flocks of birds perched in nearby trees, startled by the racket, fluttered into the sky and flew away.

Jordan moved to Darlene's side, then reached out and took her hand. They stood there together and watched as the machine dug into the grave, scooped up a shovel of earth and dumped it behind Robby Joe's headstone. As the process continued, shovel after shovel of dark, rich Georgia earth excavated, Darlene wept quietly, her slender shoulders quivering. Jordan felt immense pity for Robby Joe's mother. For Darlene, the agony of his loss always seemed as fresh and painful as the day they had buried him. But it wasn't like that for Jordan. Odd that she only now realized how on their visits to his grave the past few years, she had thought only of consoling Darlene, not once thinking about her own grief and her own great loss.

She had loved Robby Joe with youthful passion. So many of her dreams had been wrapped up in the fantasy of the life they would share. Their home. Their children. Their perfect happiness.

Emotionally buried in the past with her first love, she had married twice, both times to men she hadn't loved, not the way a woman should love her husband. She had gone into both marriages believing they could protect her from ever being hurt again. But by barricading herself against pain, she had also cut herself off from the joy of truly loving again.

*Oh, Robby Joe, I loved you. A part of my heart will always belong to you.*

The backhoe engine shut off. An eerie silence echoed on the warm spring breeze. Two men with shovels walked over to the gaping hole in the ground and removed the last few inches of earth covering the casket. Then they moved aside as the mini-crane wheeled off the gravel road, onto the thick, green grass, and pulled to a stop by the open grave.

Darlene keened softly. Jordan squeezed her hand.

Once the casket had been raised, four men who had been standing near the large dark truck parked in front of the backhoe approached the dirty, age-stained casket nestled in the grass.

"Those men will load the casket onto the truck and take it directly to the Powell lab in Knoxville," Rick explained.

Darlene broke away from Jordan and ran toward the casket. She laid her shaky hand atop the damp, faded lid. "We're doing this for Jordan. I've taken care of her for you and she's taken care of me. Forgive us for disturbing you. I promise that we'll bring you back here soon and then we'll all be at peace again."

Jordan walked slowly toward Darlene. Once at her side, she touched her back gently. "Are you ready to go now?"

Darlene lifted her hand from the casket, looked at Jordan, and nodded.

When she took Darlene's hand in hers, she felt the moist, gritty earth that had transferred from the casket to Darlene's palm and fingers.

A strange, foreboding tingle shivered along Jordan's nerves.

Before they reached the Mercedes sedan, which had been Dan's car, the two reporters, who had been taking photographs throughout the excavation procedure, made a beeline to Jordan. Rick rushed Darlene and Jordan into the backseat, then he and Devon faced the reporters.

"We'd like to ask Mrs. Price a few questions," one said.

"It's not going to happen," Rick told him.

"Then what about you, Mr. Markham?" the other reporter asked. "Now's your chance to tell your side of the story."

"Get in the car." Rick motioned to Devon.

"Are you running the show, Mr. Carson? Are Mrs. Price and Mr. Markham taking orders from you?"

"Leave us alone," Devon shouted. "You have no right to harass us this way."

Rick eased between Devon and the reporters. He turned his head sideways and reissued his initial order. "Get in the car. Now."

Devon froze for a millisecond, then backed up, opened the driver's side door and got in, leaving the door open behind him as he moved over into the passenger seat.

"How about you tell us what's going on, Mr. Carson?" the younger of the two reporters asked, a cocky grin on his face. "Why dig up Robby Joe Wright?"

"Is Powell's doing an independent autopsy?" The other reporter, middle-aged and stocky, lifted his camera and snapped a shot of Rick. "Tell me, what's it like guarding a black widow? With her track record, aren't you worried about becoming one of her many victims?"

"Is there a problem?" The young deputy walked toward the reporters.

"No problem," they replied in unison, then backed away from the car.

"I have no statement," Rick said. "Nor does Mrs. Price or Mr. Markham." He slid behind the wheel and shut the door.

The reporters continued snapping shots of the car, of the empty grave, of the backhoe, and of the casket as it was loaded onto the truck.

Rick started the engine, backed up, and drove around the squad car and equipment blocking his way.

"Please, get us out of here," Devon said.

"Y'all can take it easy," Rick told them. "The worst is over."

*No, it's not. He only thinks it is. Jordan knew that, at least for her, the worst was yet to come.*

# Chapter 30

Jordan didn't realize she had left her bedroom door wide open until she heard Rene's voice.

"What are you doing?"

Clutching the see-through dress bag she had just taken from the closet and folded over her arm, she whipped around to face her friend. "I'm doing something I should have done a long time ago."

Rene walked into the bedroom. "Isn't that your wedding dress?"

"It's one of them. Remember, I've had three."

"But only one like that, a real fairytale princess gown." Rene eyed the white satin dress. "You wore a simple, cream-white, knee-length dress when you married Boyd, and a beige suit when you married Dan."

"You have a good memory."

"I was your maid of honor when you married Boyd and again when you married Dan."

"So you were."

Rene crossed the bedroom and paused in the doorway. "Want to tell me what's going on?"

"I'm just doing a little closet cleaning and thought I'd start with this." She held up the clothes bag. "I should have packed it away or given it away or even thrown it away years ago."

A loud gasp from the doorway gained their attention. Darlene stood there, her eyes wide with surprise. Rose-lynne, who stood behind Darlene, patted her on the back and urged her to move.

"I ran into Darlene in the hall," Roselynne explained. "I was on my way up here to see how you were doing. We're all concerned about you, you know, every last one of us."

"I'm fine," Jordan said. She looked directly at Darlene, then glanced at the wedding gown she held. "I'm sorry. I don't want you to think that this dress doesn't mean something special to me. It does. It has since the day you helped me pick it out. But . . . don't you see, that's the problem. It has meant too much to me all these years. I've held on to it the way I've held on to Robby Joe."

"There's nothing wrong with holding on to good mem-ories," Roselynne said. "That boy was the love of your life. You should keep the dress."

"Maybe she shouldn't." Rene reached out and fingered the zipper on the garment bag. "Maybe it is time she packed it away." She held out her hands. "Want me to take it and put it in a box and store it in the attic for you?"

Jordan hesitated. *Do it. Take that first step, no matter how difficult.*

She looked at Darlene.

"It's all right, dear. I knew today, at the cemetery."

"What did you know?" Roselynne asked.

Jordan smiled. "Thank you, Darlene."

"I'm confused," Roselynne said. "Did something hap-pen at the cemetery today when they dug up Robby Joe's coffin?"

"Nothing you would understand," Darlene said before she turned and walked away.

Jordan handed Rene the garment bag. "I appreciate your doing this for me. It makes it a little easier that I don't have to do it."

"No problem." Rene took the bag, folded it over her arm, and leaned in to give Jordan a quick kiss on the cheek. "Don't let the fact that the timing couldn't be worse stop you from grabbing happiness with both hands."

When Rene hurried out of the room, Jordan rushed after her, but Roselynne grabbed Jordan's arm, stopping her at the bedroom door.

"Don't," Roselynne said.

Nix Elliott, who was standing guard outside the bedroom, glanced their way. "Is everything all right, Mrs. Price?"

"Yes," Jordan replied. She watched as Rene stopped in the hall, lifted the bag and pressed it to her face.

"All these years, Darlene and I haven't been the only ones mourning Robby Joe," Jordan said.

"I never knew for sure who she loved the most, you or Robby Joe." Roselynne wrapped her arm around Jordan's shoulders and led her back into the bedroom.

"She pretended that she was all right with my dating Robby Joe and even threw us an engagement party. God, how hard that must have been for her. She was in love with him and I didn't have a clue. And when he died . . . Why couldn't I see it at the time?"

"For two reasons. One, you were so wrapped up in your own grief and in consoling Darlene, you weren't aware that anyone else was suffering. And two, Rene is almost as good as you are at hiding her true feelings."

"Apparently, she's better at it. I really had no idea that she was in love with Robby Joe, that she still—"

"She doesn't still love him, if that's what you think. What you saw just then with Rene was nothing more than a moment of 'what-if' going on." Roselynne gently clasped Jordan's chin between her thumb and forefinger. "You're not still in love with him either. You haven't been in a long time. You just didn't know it. But something's happened to make you finally realize it. That something wouldn't be Rick Carson, would it?"

"I'm attracted to Rick, but—"

"Be careful, baby girl." Roselynne squeezed Jordan's chin, then released her. "You've just buried a husband, miscarried a child, had your personal life exposed to the world, become a murder suspect, and finally said goodbye to your first love. Now's not the time to do anything stupid. Rick Carson is one fine-looking man and I daresay he knows a thing or two about pleasing a woman, but it wouldn't pay to trust him."

Jordan grabbed her stepmother and hugged her. "Have I ever thanked you?"

"For what?"

"For turning out not to be the wicked stepmother I thought you were when you first married Daddy."

Roselynne laughed, the sound as boisterous and bawdy as the woman herself. "You've thanked me a hundred times over by taking care of me and Tammy and even J.C."

"Have you heard from J.C. lately?" Jordan asked.

She never wanted Roselynne to find out that J.C. had sold the secrets of her marriage and Dan's homosexuality to The Chatterbox. It would break her stepmother's heart.

"He called from Las Vegas a few days ago. He's got a job out there and he likes it better than the one he had at the casino in Biloxi."

"That's good. I hope it works out for him."

Roselynne smiled. "Me, too." She nodded to the door. "I need to get home before the bottom falls out. I think we're in for some stormy weather tonight."

"See you tomorrow."

"Sure thing." Roselynne paused and looked back just

before reaching the open door. "You don't have to trust a man completely to enjoy what he's got to offer. Just don't go falling in love and get your heart broken."

Jordan didn't respond. There was no point in denying the effect Rick had on her. She never thought she'd feel this way again. All those smoldering feminine passions she had tried to bury with Robby Joe really hadn't died when he did. She had repressed them for twelve years out of fear. Her reasoning had been that living without the ecstasy of being in love protected her from ever again suffering the agony of losing that love.

Of course, she wasn't in love with Rick and didn't expect a future with him. Even if by some miracle he was the right man, not only was now the wrong time, it was the worst possible time. But perhaps someday . . . in the future . . .

If she had a future.


Jordan had identified his body to save Darlene from having to do it. As long as she lived, she would never forget the moment she looked down at the mangled lifeless body of the man she loved. Only hours before the accident, they'd had a stupid, senseless quarrel about Devon.

"Honey, I know he's your best friend, but it's unheard of to have a man as your maid of honor."

"Man of honor," Jordan had corrected.

"I've offered to let him be my best man. That's a far more sensible solution to our problem."

"We wouldn't have a problem if you weren't so narrow-minded. You're more concerned about what people will think than about how I feel."

"That's not true, sweetheart. But you have to admit that in the social circle we'll be a part of when we're married—"

"Maybe we won't get married!"

She had stormed out of Robby Joe's apartment, not listening to his pleas for her to come back, knowing that if she didn't put some distance between them, she might really call off the wedding. And that's not what she wanted. She loved Robby Joe. He loved her. And he was very fond of Devon. But sometimes he could be such an old-fashioned man. Of course, some of those old-fashioned masculine traits were part of the reason she loved him.

He had been on his way to her apartment later that evening for makeup sex. He had phoned her and apologized and told her that if she had her heart set on Devon being her man of honor, then so be it.

"You love me that much, huh?" she'd said.

"That much and more."

"Why don't you come over here and spend the night?"

"I'm hanging up right now," he'd told her. "Light some candles and put on some soft music. And wear that pink teddy I bought you for Valentine's Day. I'll be there in fifteen minutes."

Thirty minutes later, she had called his apartment. No answer. She had called his cell phone. No answer. An hour and a half later, when she was almost out of her mind with worry, she dressed in jeans and a sweatshirt and grabbed her shoulder bag on her way out the door. As she was locking up, she heard her phone ring. She managed to unlock the door, open it, and run back into her apartment by the time the phone rang the sixth time. At the precise moment her answering machine picked up and she heard Darlene's hysterical voice, she grabbed the phone off the hook.

"Darlene, what's wrong? Is it Robby Joe?"

"Oh, Jordan . . . Jordan . . ." Darlene had kept saying her name over and over again.

"What's happened? Is Robby Joe all right?"

"He's dead."

Everything that happened after that became a blur and

to this day was still a blur. Somehow she had managed to do all the things that were required, undoubtedly working on automatic pilot, her emotions thankfully frozen. She had identified Robby Joe's body, had made the funeral arrangements, had stayed at Darlene's side day and night, had held it all together from the moment she'd been told the love of her life was dead until over a week after they buried him.

She had awakened in the middle of the night, her body drenched in sweat, her heart racing alarmingly, her emotions hot with pain and anger. The agony she endured during the following weeks had nearly destroyed her.

And then she had accidentally overdosed on prescription medication.

While recovering in the hospital, she had made a solemn vow, a promise to herself that she had kept these past twelve years. She would never allow anyone or anything to ever hurt her that way again. Whatever she had to do to protect herself, she would do. If that meant never falling in love again, she had considered it a small price to pay. If it meant living half a life instead of a whole life, she had accepted that fact.

And not since that day when she'd walked out of the hospital, had she shed a single tear. Not for Boyd Brannon. Not for Dan Price. Not for her sweet lost baby. Not even for herself.

Rick had heard her when she got out of bed. He'd been lying there listening to her tossing and turning for the past hour. When he had come upstairs for the night and relieved Nix Elliott, Jordan had already been in bed and either asleep or pretending to be. He had grabbed a quick shower, put on the pajama bottoms he never wore when at home, and tried to get comfortable in the daybed. Eventually, he had fallen asleep, but he seldom slept soundly, not when he was on guard duty. He woke the minute Jordan began stirring.

Lying there in still silence, he watched as she walked across the bedroom, moving slowly toward the French doors that opened onto the balcony. He tossed back the covers, sat up, and reached for his wristwatch lying under the bed, alongside his holstered Smith & Wesson. He checked the lighted digital face and noted that it was three-eighteen.

*Don't get up. Don't follow her. She's safe.*

He sat on the edge of the daybed and listened. He heard rumbles of distant thunder, the tick-tock of the mantel clock in Jordan's bedroom, and then the distinct creak of the French doors opening.

*She's going outside for a breath of fresh air. She doesn't need you. She wants to be alone. Give her some space.*

Was she thinking about Robby Joe Wright?

Probably.

Rick rose to his feet, walked into the bathroom, and, in the dark, turned on the faucet. He cupped his hands together to catch the flow and threw cold water into his face.

A streak of lightning flashed, illuminating the small window in the bathroom and giving him a quick glimpse of his reflection in the mirror. His face was darkened with beard stubble and his hair was too long. He definitely needed a shave and a haircut.

He tried to talk himself out of checking on Jordan; but instead of crawling back in bed and leaving her alone, he entered her bedroom and halfway to the French doors, he stopped and looked at her. Both doors stood wide open. The wind blew the sheer curtains, billowing them into waltzing fluffs of fabric. Another rumble of thunder, louder and closer, followed the slash of lightning that momentarily brightened the dark sky.

Rick's breath caught in his throat at the sight of Jordan,

her slender body covered with a floor-length, silk gown. Pink. No lace. No ribbons. Pencil thin straps. Cut almost to her waist in the back, revealing her shoulder blades.

He gripped his hands into loose fists, opened them, and then repeated the movement a couple of times. He wanted to touch her, to put his hands all over her, to feel every creamy inch of her skin.

As if sensing he was watching her, Jordan glanced over her shoulder. Only the pale glimmer from the outside motion-sensor, security lights, activated by the high winds, prevented total darkness.

Rick swallowed hard.

Their gazes met and locked.

He moved toward her. She watched him until he was within a couple feet of her, then she turned her head and looked away. He came up behind her, almost touching her. He felt her heat. Smelled her sweet femininity. Sensed the need she couldn't hide.

When he touched her, his hands moving over her shoulders, she gasped, then sighed heavily. He slid his hands down her upper arms, slowly moving into her, bringing her back against his chest, her hips against his erection. As he slipped one hand across her waist and covered her breast with the other, she whimpered and leaned her head back against his collarbone. He rested his jaw against her temple and strummed his thumb across her tight nipple, stroking it through the thin silk.

He nuzzled the side of her face. He kissed her temple. And then he moved lower until his open mouth pressed against her neck. Moaning softly, she shuddered. While he toyed with her nipple, he trailed his other hand down over her belly. Slowly. Driving himself crazy with his hunger for more. He pressed his hand over her mound and shoved his fingers between her legs, plastering her gown against her inner thighs. When he rubbed her intimately, she covered his hand with hers.

He nibbled on her neck as he clutched the sides of her gown and drew it up. Bunching the shimmering silk in his hands, he lifted it high enough to touch the triangle of curls nestled at the apex of her thighs. When he inched his fingers through the soft dampness and discovered her sensitive nub, her breathing quickened with excitement. The edge of her gown draped his wrist as he fondled her.

She sighed. She whimpered. She moaned.

He loved every sound. He loved the feel of her beneath his hands and the taste of her on his tongue. Her moisture gushed around his fingers. She was slick and wet and hot. So very hot.

"Come for me," he whispered huskily, his lips against her ear. "Let go. Let me feel you falling apart."

Her entire body tensed. He increased the pressure and the tempo as he gently bit her shoulder. She cried out when her orgasm hit. Shuddering with release, she reached on either side of her and grabbed his thighs for support.

As she climaxed, the first hard, heavy drops of rain fell. But he didn't rush her into the bedroom. Instead he let her float down from the sensual high by slow degrees. When he eased his hand up and under her gown, caressing her belly, she shivered and he knew her skin was sensitive to the touch.

By the time her breathing returned to normal and the aftershocks of her orgasm subsided, they were both drenched. He draped his arm around her waist and turned her to face him. She looked up at him. Until the day he died, he would never forget how beautiful Jordan was at that very moment.

Without saying a word, he scooped her up in his arms and carried her into the bedroom. Leaving the French doors open, the rain blowing inside and the curtains fluttering, Rick put her on her feet when they reached the bed. When his gaze traveled from her face, down her throat, across her breasts, over her stomach and down her legs, she reached for him. Her fingertips caressed his face and then slid down his throat. When she spread her open palms flat against his damp, naked chest, he groaned. Her mouth opened with a surprised smile. He grasped her gown where it stuck to her hips, pulled at the wet material and brought it up and over her head.

He looked at her. Her full, round breasts high, her nipples peaked. A thatch of thick dark blond curls covered her mound.

"Are you sure?" he asked.

She nodded.

"It's not too soon after . . . the baby?"

"No. I—I . . . it's not too soon."

He looked in her eyes. "Then say it. Tell me what you want."

"I want you." Her voice was raspy with emotion.

He shrugged off his pajama bottoms, stepped out of them, and left them on the floor as he pushed her back, then lifted her up and onto the bed.

"I'll be right back," he told her. "I've got some condoms in my shave kit."

Smiling, she nodded, and then seductively slinked across the satiny cotton sheets and into the middle of the bed.

Rick made a mad dash into the bathroom, unzipped his shaving kit and upended the contents in his haste to find the three condoms. Clutching them in his hand, he returned to the bedroom, tossed two down on the nightstand and ripped open the other.

Jordan sat up halfway in the bed, her gaze on his penis, and watched him. Feeling her looking at him excited him. With the condom in place, he got in bed and came down over her, his knees on either side of her legs, his arms braced against the mattress, keeping his weight off her.

He hesitated, but only for a moment. He kissed her

hungrily, then began an assault on her body, covering every inch with his hands and mouth, leaving him trembling and her begging.

He lifted her hips, bringing her body up to his, and thrust into her. She clung to him, enthusiastically meeting each deep, hard lunge. They mated wildly. No pretense. No pretty words. Nothing, but the raw, animal pleasure they both craved.

Hours later, as early morning sunlight poured into the room, Jordan woke. She stretched languidly, her body aching and slightly bruised. But she had never felt more alive in her entire life.

Rick lay beside her, his dark head on the blush-rose pillowcase. She reached down and ran her index finger softly over his lips. He grunted. She jerked her hand away. He opened his eyes and smiled up at her.

"Good morning."

She leaned over him, her tangled hair falling about her shoulders, and returned his smile. During the night she had become as familiar with this man's body as he had with hers. They knew each other on the most physically intimate of terms. And yet in the cold hard light of day, she felt oddly shy with him.

As if sensing her timidity, he ran a finger down her throat and between her breasts. "It's all right. Neither of us made any promises."

"No, we didn't."

"Don't analyze what happened," he told her. "This thing between us is what it is."

*It isn't love. It isn't love.*

"You understand, don't you? The timing is all wrong."

"Wrong time, wrong place. Wrong man?" He tossed back the covers separating their bodies, then reached out and pulled her down over him.

She snuggled close, her naked body fitting perfectly on top of his. "Wrong time, wrong place, but there's nothing wrong about or with the man."

He skimmed her hips and buttocks with his fingertips. His touch set her on fire. When he urged her up enough to ease inside her, she shuddered, loving the feel of him, big and hard, sheathed within her.

They made love again, but this time with a tender passion, savoring each moment.


They have no idea that I opened the door and I'm watching them. They're too caught up in having sex. I had planned to surprise Jordan with fresh flowers from the garden and instead she surprised me.

You have no idea what you're doing. You don't love him. And he certainly doesn't love you.

Don't you know what kind of man Rick Carson is? He believes you're a killer. You can't trust him.

If only you hadn't lost our precious baby, we would be complete and neither of us would ever need anyone else.

I can't stay here any longer. I have to leave. I have to forget what I've seen. But I must remember that you're in danger, now more than ever.

I know what I have to do. I finally realize what will make you happy. And it's not Rick Carson or any other man. Why has it taken me all these years to understand that there is only one place on earth where you belong?

Don't worry, I'll take care of everything. I'll make all the plans for us and soon, very soon, Rick Carson will be out of our lives forever.

And you'll be happy again. Truly happy.

# Chapter 31

Rick figured everyone suspected that his relationship with Jordan had changed, which worked to their advantage in trying to force the killer to attack him. Although they weren't openly affectionate toward each other when anyone else was around, they often looked at each other, smiled at each other and sometimes even laughed as if they shared a secret.

He and Jordan were lovers. For the past four nights, he had shared her bed.

They had just finished breakfast in the dining room this morning, along with Darlene, Devon, Roselynne, Tammy, and Rene. He had felt their curious stares during the meal and sensed that each of them wanted to warn him that if he hurt Jordan, he'd be sorry. But on the surface, each of them was cordial to him; Roselynne and Rene were even friendly.

While walking Jordan to her study where she and Rene would go over the morning mail and attend to any other business matters concerning Price Manor and the loose ends of the late senator's life, Rick's phone rang.

"You two go on," he told them.

From where he stopped in the hallway, he could see the door to the study. He flipped open his phone. "Morning. I hope you have some news for us."

"Actually, I do," Griff replied. "First, I thought you'd want to know that J.C. Harris made a phone call to Sheriff Corbett last night."

"Is that right?" Rick snorted. "Not of his own free will, I'll bet."

"Let's just say that Luke Sentell persuaded him to tell the truth."

"Which is?"

"Lt. Haley McLain went to Harris and encouraged him to sell the information about Jordan and her marriage to the senator to The Chatterbox. She even set things up for him."

Rick wasn't surprised, but he was disappointed. He had hoped he was wrong about Haley. "I hate being right."

"She'll receive disciplinary action," Griff said. "More than likely, she'll lose her job, but that's what happens when you betray the people who trust you. Seems, according to Harris, the lieutenant had her eye on Sheriff Corbett's job."

"That doesn't surprise me either."

"I didn't call you last night to tell you about Lt. McLain because I was expecting a report from Dr. Hamilton this morning and hoped I'd have some good news for you."

"And?" Rick's gut tightened. He hadn't admitted to himself until this very second how important the autopsy report was to him.

"We did a rush job on the lab work," Griff told him. "Neither the autopsy nor the lab results show anything suspicious. Dr. Hamilton's opinion is that Robby Joe Wright was a healthy, drug-free young man and his death was caused by trauma from injuries sustained in the car wreck. Add these findings to the initial police report, which we went over with a fine-tooth comb, and there's only one logical conclusion."

Rick released a deep breath. "His death wasn't the result of murder. It was an accident."

"Out of seven deaths, that's two we know for sure Jordan wasn't responsible for. You were with her when Jane Anne Price was murdered and her former fiancé's death was an accident."

"How does this change the dynamics of the black widow theory?"

"It adds the element of doubt. If Jordan didn't kill her fiancé, then it's possible she didn't kill either husband number one or husband number two. Brannon's death could have been a hunting accident and nothing more. But Dan Price was murdered. At this point, I don't believe there's any doubt about it."

"Do you think it's possible the other deaths were just what they appeared to be and we're not looking for a Jordan-obsessed serial killer after all?"

"At this point, I don't know," Griff admitted. "I talked to Derek before I called you and, even knowing Robby Joe wasn't murdered, he still thinks some if not all of the others were murdered by the same person."

"Damn!"

"Are you willing to keep your head in the noose to see if somebody will try to tighten it around your neck?" Griff asked.

"Yeah. Absolutely. I want Jordan cleared and I want the real killer brought to justice."

"Do I take it that you now have no doubts about Jordan's innocence?"

He hesitated before replying. All of his adult life, Rick had gone with his gut instincts, which luckily had been proven right most of the time, but not always. One thing he'd never done was go on blind faith alone. This time, things were different. He was different.

"Let's just say that I know Jordan isn't a killer."

"All the same, don't take any stupid chances."

Rick grunted. "I'll do my best."

"By the way, you can tell Mrs. Wright that we'll send her son's body to the funeral home this afternoon. She can contact them and follow through with the arrangements."

"I think having a re-interment service is a bad idea. It's only going to make it more difficult for everyone involved."

"She's his mother. It's her right to do whatever she wants. Maybe having this second funeral is necessary for her peace of mind."

"Yeah, sure. Maybe you're right."

The last thing Rick wanted was for Jordan to be dragged back into that emotional black hole created by Robby Joe's death. She was alive again, truly alive, and he'd be damned if he would let her regress and disappear back into the passionless existence she'd lived in for the past twelve years.

The private service for Robby Joe took place the following day at Jernigan Crossroads Funeral Home, a small town operation that had been in business for nearly a hundred years. Rick and Nix Elliott had taken two cars. Jordan, Mrs. Wright and Devon rode with Rick. Roselynne, Tammy and Rene rode with Nix. The service had been postponed until three in the afternoon so that a quartet from one of the local churches could perform two songs, both chosen by Darlene.

Nix remained outside the chapel while Rick waited inside, standing at the back, close by in case Jordan needed him. But he wasn't one of the mourners. If he'd had his way, Robby Joe's casket would have been put back in the ground unceremoniously.

Jordan accompanied Darlene from the front pew to the casket which was draped in a full blanket of fresh spring flowers. Five large floral arrangements flanked the torchieres on either side of the casket. Recorded music, piped through the room from strategically placed speakers, provided an organist's rendition of an old spiritual. Darlene laid her hand on the side of the dark blue coffin. Weeping quietly, she dabbed her eyes with her lace handkerchief.

Rick noticed that Darlene said something to Jordan, who immediately broke off one of the red rosebuds from the blanket. When she walked Darlene back to their seats, Jordan handed her the flower.

Just as the minister, Reverend Crowell, from the church Darlene had attended as a young woman, approached the pulpit, Claire and Ryan Price entered the chapel. They paused beside Rick and both glanced his way. Ryan nodded at him, then he and Claire made their way forward and sat in the pew directly behind Jordan.

Rick could only imagine the effect today's events would have on Jordan, who sat ramrod straight, her arm draped around Darlene's hunched shoulders.

After the minister read several verses from the Bible, the quartet sang "The Lord's Prayer." When the good reverend spoke about Robby Joe in a kind, sympathetic voice, a chorus of sniffling and soft weeping filled the chapel.

Thankfully, the service was short. Twenty minutes from beginning to end. While Devon and Jordan helped Darlene into the car, Jordan pulled Rick aside.

"We won't be going on to the cemetery today," she told him. "There was some sort of mix-up about the backhoe to cover the grave and it won't be available until tomorrow. Darlene and I will drive back over to the cemetery in the morning."

"You can't go alone, just the two of you. I'll drive y'all."

"All right." She looked at him, her eyes dry, her expression solemn. "Thank you."

"For what?"

"For being here. For staying inside the chapel for the

service. I couldn't see you, but I felt you were there with me."

He wanted to pull her into his arms and tell her to cry and keep on crying. Instead, he cupped her elbow and helped her into the backseat of the sedan.

It hadn't been difficult to cancel the backhoe and re-schedule it for tomorrow morning. All it took was one little phone call pretending to be a new funeral home employee. But getting Rick Carson out of the way might prove to be more difficult. She had to find a way to distract him, if she intended to get Jordan alone. Of course, killing him was one solution. But she couldn't risk drawing attention to herself, so she'd have to find another way.

While waiting for the results of Robby Joe's autopsy, she had formulated her plan. She should have known all along that there was only one way to secure Jordan's happiness. All these years, she had done everything possible to keep Jordan safe, to protect her, to support her, love her, give her whatever she needed, and to share every sorrow with her. And yet she had only partially succeeded.

She knew she had a very brief window of opportunity to accomplish her goal and secure Jordan's happiness.

It had to be tonight.

Dinner had been a somber threesome that evening. Rene had been a no-show, using the excuse of a headache in order to escape. Darlene had requested hot herbal tea be brought upstairs to her guestroom. Roselynne had phoned to say that she and Tammy were going to have dinner at home. And even Devon had excused himself before Vadonna served dessert.

Jordan had moved her food around on her plate for the

past thirty minutes, but Rick noticed she hadn't eaten more than a bite or two.

When Vadonna placed the bowls of blackberry cobbler à la mode in front of Rick and Jordan, she frowned as she stared at Jordan's plate.

"If you don't start eating, Miss Jordan, you're going to dry up and blow away. I want to see you eat that cobbler. I picked those wild blackberries myself, off the bushes here on the estate."

"The cobbler looks delicious," Jordan said. "I promise I'll eat as much as I can."

Vadonna smiled as she cleared the table and returned to the kitchen.

"Is there any way I can persuade you not to go to the cemetery tomorrow?" Rick asked.

"I have to go. It's important to Darlene."

"Couldn't you talk to her, maybe convince her to wait and you two visit his grave in a few weeks?"

"No. She needs to see this through tomorrow and so do I."

He nodded. "Cam Hendrix called when you went upstairs to take Darlene her tea. He plans to meet with the district attorney and the sheriff tomorrow. With the proof that Robby Joe's death was an accident and with J.C.'s written confession that Lt. McLain was involved in The Chatterbox exposé, Cam believes he can persuade the DA not to pursue you as a suspect in your husband's murder."

Jordan's hand holding the dessert spoon shook so badly that she dropped the spoon against the glass bowl. She jerked her hand back, took a calming breath and pressed her open palm over her neck.

"I still find it difficult to believe that someone killed Dan," Jordan said. "And it seems our little plan to force someone to attack you hasn't worked, has it? Maybe your theory is wrong. Maybe no one—"

Tobias called, "Miss Jordan, you have to go over to

Mrs. Harris's right away." He stood in the doorway, concern etched on his face. "She just called and said Miss Tammy has gone crazy or something. She's screaming and crying and throwing things and Mrs. Harris can't do a thing with her. Miss Tammy keeps saying your name."

Jordan shoved her chair back and shot to her feet. Rick got up and followed her through the house and out the back door. When she broke into a run, he caught up with her halfway to the Harris's cottage. Even from that distance, they could hear Tammy hollering.

Roselynne, in her red satin robe and matching slippers, met them in the yard, a look of absolute fear on her face. "I've never seen her like this. Not ever. This isn't one of her usual temper tantrums. It's as if she's gone berserk. I can't get her to calm down and she won't tell me what's wrong." Roselynne grabbed Jordan's hands. "She keeps saying that she wants you."

"I'll go in and talk to her," Jordan said.

"She's locked herself in her room and told me to get out of the house and stay out, that she doesn't want to see anybody but you."

Jordan looked at Rick. "Please, stay out here with Roselynne and let me go in alone."

"I don't think that's a good idea," Rick told her.

"Tammy won't hurt Jordan, if that's what you're thinking," Roselynne said. "If she hurts anybody, it'll be herself."

"Stay out here, both of you," Jordan said. "If I need you, I'll let you know."

Rick didn't like the idea of Jordan going into the house alone, but short of using physical force, he knew he couldn't stop her.

He grabbed her arm. "Be careful."

She pulled away from him and went into the house.

They could hear Tammy screeching, the sound slightly muffled through the closed doors. Then suddenly a door slammed and Tammy quieted.

"Maybe just seeing Jordan has calmed her down," Roselynne said.

"You have no idea what caused Tammy to—"

"She was fine when I went into the bathroom to take my nightly bubble bath. I usually listen to some soothing music and relax for thirty minutes or so. I left Tammy in the kitchen, putting the supper dishes in the dishwasher. She'd been kind of quiet ever since the service for Robby Joe, but I didn't think anything of it. It was a sad day for all of us. And even though Darlene's not my favorite person, I felt so sorry for her. I guess it was kind of like losing her boy all over again."

"Were you already in the bathtub when Tammy started screaming?" Rick asked.

"Sure was. I'd been soaking a good fifteen minutes when I heard her wailing like a banshee and tearing through the house, stomping like a horse. Lord, you should see the mess she made in the living room. She knocked over lamps and tossed throw pillows on the floor and broke two of my snow globes."

"Exactly what did Tammy say?"

"Nothing that made any sense."

"Stop and think and then tell me, word for word, if possible."

Roselynne crossed her arms under her ample breasts and huffed. "Just a bunch of gibberish. Some nonsense about Jordan."

"What sort of nonsense?" Rick wanted to shake Roselynne and he would if he thought it might help the situation.

"Oh, she kept saying that she loved Jordan. Her exact words were 'I do so love Jordan. I do.' She kept repeating that over and over again. Then she said something about our having to help Jordan be happy."

"When Tammy gets upset, she doesn't usually rant and rave and scream and tear the house apart, right?"

"Right." Roselynne glanced at the closed front door. "She throws a hissy fit now and again, but nothing like tonight. I swear, if I didn't know better, I'd think she was putting on an act."

Rick grabbed Roselynne by the shoulders. "Why would she pretend to go berserk?"

"I—I don't know. I didn't say she did, but maybe she did it to get Jordan to come over here to the house and talk to her."

Rick loosened his hold on Roselynne. "Wouldn't Jordan have come if Tammy had just called her?"

"Of course she would have and Tammy knew she would. That's why none of this makes any sense."

Rick rushed past Roselynne, bounded up the front steps and onto the porch. As he opened the door, she called after him.

"What's wrong? Why are you going in there? Jordan told us she wanted to go in alone and we should wait out here."

Rick didn't respond. He went down the hall. Two doors stood open. A bedroom, obviously Roselynne's, and a bathroom. The third door was closed. Rick tried the knob. The door swung open and revealed a semi-dark room. The only illumination was a nightlight plugged into a wall outlet.

"Jordan?"

No response.

"Jordan?"

Roselynne came up behind him just as he felt along the wall and flipped on the light switch. Tammy sat in the middle of her bed, her legs folded as if she were sitting at a campfire. She looked at him and smiled.

"Where's Jordan?"

"Jordan's happy now," Tammy said, then repeated the phrase over and over again in a singsong fashion. "Jordan's happy now. Jordan's happy now."

Rick turned to Roselynne. "Talk to her. See if you can get her to tell you where Jordan is."

Rick visually searched the small bedroom. Twin beds. He peered under one and then the other. A dresser on one wall, a chest of drawers between the two windows on the other outside wall. The windows were closed and locked. He yanked open the closet. Small, no more than three feet wide and three feet deep.

"Tammy, honey, where did Jordan go?" Rick heard Roselynne ask as he ran through the house and searched, room by room. When he entered the kitchen he stopped dead still when he saw the back door standing wide open.

"Rick!" Roselynne screamed his name as she came running into the kitchen, all but dragging Tammy with her. "Somebody put Tammy up to that little wild girl performance." Roselynne shoved Tammy in front of her. "Tell him. Tell Rick what you told me."

"If I love Jordan and want her to be happy forever, then I should act crazy," Tammy said, smiling and cheerful. "And I should get Jordan to come in the house alone to talk to me. Everything will be all right then because Jordan can go away and be happy forever."

"Tell him where Jordan's going?" Roselynne looked at Rick, terror in her eyes.

"She's going to be with Robby Joe because she's never been happy except when she was with him."

# Chapter 32

Rick ran out the back door, all the while hoping and praying that Jordan was still nearby. But after a quick search, he realized that whoever had taken Jordan had planned well ahead. He couldn't waste precious time trying to search alone. He flipped open his phone, brought up the number, and waited impatiently for the phone to ring.

"Elliott here."

"Jordan's missing," Rick said. "She hasn't been gone more than five minutes. Contact the front gate to alert them. Get in touch with Holt and tell him to get out here to Price Manor. In the meantime, do a search of the house to see who's there and who isn't, then get back to me."

"Rick!" Roselynne yelled.

He looked back at the cottage. Waving her arms, Roselynne came running toward him.

He dialed Steve Corbett's private number.

"I can't get Tammy to tell me who took Jordan," Roselynne said. "She says it's a special secret and she can't tell anybody because we would try to stop Jordan from being with Robby Joe. She said that Jordan is going to wear her wedding dress and become Robby Joe's bride forever and ever, just like in a fairy tale."

"Good God!"

"What?" The voice on the phone asked. "Carson, is that you?"

"Yeah, it's me," Rick said. "Look, Corbett, we've got a bad situation here. Jordan's missing. Someone put Tammy up to tricking us. Jordan went into the Harris cottage alone to talk to a hysterical Tammy, but she never came back out the front door. Someone's taken her."

"Damn! Any idea who?"

"Nix Elliott is checking the house as we speak and he's alerting the front gate, but I'm pretty sure they left by the back entrance. I need you to get some men out here to do a search, but from what little we could get Tammy to tell us, I think whoever kidnapped Jordan is taking her to the funeral home in Jernigan Crossroads."

"I'll get some deputies out there to search the grounds at Price Manor and I'll send a couple of guys to the funeral home."

"How long will it take to get deputies to the funeral home?"

"I can't say for sure. I don't know if we've got anybody patrolling in the area tonight. If not, it'll take a good forty-five minutes or longer," Steve said.

"Put the word out that I'll be driving a black Jeep Wrangler, Knox County tag." He rattled off his license plate number. "I'll be breaking every speed limit. I'm not stopping for anyone or anything."

"Why are you doing this?" Jordan glanced in the rear-view mirror of her Navigator and caught a glimpse of the two figures in the dark backseat.

"Because I love you and I know now what I should have done years ago. I didn't realize what I had to do until we brought Robby Joe back to us."

"I don't understand," Jordan said. "Why do you want us to go to Jernigan Crossroads tonight? We could wait until tomorrow—"

"No! It has to be tonight."

Jordan glanced into the rearview mirror again and saw the sheer terror in Rene's eyes.

Dear God, she'd been such a fool. She should have listened to Rick and not rushed into the cottage to help Tammy. But then again, how could she or anyone else have suspected that the whole thing had been a setup, a trap to snare her. And poor Tammy had been a witless participant. By now, Rick had to know that she was missing. But he'd have no idea who was responsible.

"You don't want to do this," Jordan said. "You don't want to hurt me or anyone else. I know you don't."

"Oh, Jordan, I'd never hurt you. I love you. All I've ever wanted is for you to be happy. But you haven't been happy. Not since Robby Joe left us."

"I'm not unhappy. Actually, I think I have a chance to be truly happy with Rick Carson."

"You're wrong. He doesn't love you. He just wants sex. The only man who's ever truly loved you was Robby Joe."

"Rick loves me. He's told me that he does," Jordan lied. "We'll get married and we'll have a baby, maybe several babies and you can—"

"No! He won't make you happy. Why can't you understand that?"

"Rick will come after me." She knew he would turn the world upside down searching for her. "He loves me and he—"

"Don't worry, if he tries to stop us, I'll take care of him."

A flash of metal in the moonlight reflected in the mirror. Jordan swallowed. She hated guns. Always had and always would.

"You wouldn't kill Rick, would you? You wouldn't kill anyone."

*Please, dear God, please, let the answer be "no, of course, I wouldn't kill Rick or anyone else."*

"I think you know the answer to that question. Of course, I'd kill him. I'd kill anyone who posed a threat to you."

A surge of fear-induced adrenaline roared through Jordan's body, putting all her senses on high alert. If she had doubted whether or not her life was in danger, she no longer had any doubts.

"Did—did you kill Dan?" Jordan asked.

"Dan was a good man, but we couldn't be burdened with a sick husband, not when we were expecting a baby. I actually thought I had talked him into committing suicide, but he didn't have the guts to do it, so I just helped him along a little."

Jordan barely managed to stifle the scream vibrating in her throat. *Oh, Dan . . . Dan, I'm so very sorry.*

"Killing Dan was simple really," she said, her voice oddly calm as if she were talking about nothing more sinister than the weather. "He had left the gun on his desk. You know, the Glock he bought for you. I truly believe he thought about killing himself, but when I went to check on him, he was passed out drunk on the sofa. I put the gun in his hand, aimed it at his temple and pressed my finger over his to fire the pistol. He committed suicide, with a little help from me. I took care of your problem, just as I've done in the past. I always take care of you."

"Did—did you kill Boyd?" Jordan asked, dreading her reply and desperately needing to hear her admit the truth.

"Of course, I did. After the way he betrayed us, first by not letting us have a baby and then by having an affair with that awful woman, he didn't give me any choice, did he? He hurt you terribly. He had to pay for the way he had mistreated you."

"But the children . . . didn't you think about what killing Boyd would do to Wes and Kendra?" Jordan felt sick at her stomach.

"I did it for them, too. They were better off without him. We all were."

"How did you . . . ? I mean, everyone thought it was a hunting accident. The sheriff . . . the coroner. Someone shot him in the head. How could you have done that?"

"I'm an expert marksman, my dear Jordan; something I didn't think you needed to know. My father taught me how to use a rifle when I was only eight. I went hunting with him often. Since Boyd was an avid hunter, the solution to ridding ourselves of him was quite clear. I planned his death months ahead of time. I simply had to wait for deer season. You can't imagine the absolute triumph of the kill unless you've experienced it. It's quite exhilarating."

*She's insane,* Jordan thought. *Completely deranged. Why did I never suspect the truth? She has always seemed so normal.*

"Would you like for me to tell you about how I took care of all your other problems? I think about each of them fairly often and I always get such a feeling of satisfaction knowing how much I've helped you." She laughed softly, so obviously pleased with herself. "I was able to make several of the deaths look like accidents. Not Jane Anne's death, but then I had to act quickly when I killed her. I didn't have any time to make plans. It was pretty much spur of the moment."

She had admitted killing Dan and Boyd and Jane Anne. What about the others? Donald and Jay and her father?

As if she had read Jordan's thoughts, she said, "Donald

Farris should have given you the promotion you deserved. He was such a smug SOB. I knew that as long as he was your boss, he'd never do right by you. But I took care of him. I planned his death to look as if he had accidentally fallen down the stairs and broken his neck. He had no idea when he heard someone coming down the stairs behind him that I was going to shove him over the railing. Oh, my, my, the way he looked lying there on the concrete, his body broken, his head smashed. Not a pretty sight."

*Don't tell me anything else, please,* Jordan wanted to scream, but she managed to remain silent. For now, she had to do whatever it took to keep them alive. Rick would find them. That one single thought kept her from totally panicking.

"You know, I believe that I enjoyed killing Jay Reynolds far more than any of the others. He was such a nasty man, wasn't he, Jordan? He tried to rape you, but I showed him just what happens to a man when he hurts us. I followed him day after day, week after week, until I knew his schedule. That night I caught him unaware and hit him over the head with the baseball bat before he realized what was happening." She heaved a deep sigh. "I hit him over and over again, even after I knew he was dead. Beating him repeatedly was absolutely thrilling, probably because he, more than any of them, deserved to die."

*Jay didn't try to rape me,* Jordan thought. *He got fresh and I slapped him. That's all that happened. Why did ever I tell you about it? Why, why, why? He didn't deserve to die. And poor Donald Farris. The only thing he was guilty of was being a male chauvinist who was notorious for promoting men with families over single women.*

And Boyd. She had killed him, too. Shot him as she would have shot an animal, almost for the sport of it. Yes, he had betrayed their marriage vows, but so had she. Although she hadn't had an affair, she had been in love with another man. During her entire marriage to Boyd, she had still been in love with Robby Joe.



Rick sped along the highway, his Bluetooth headset in place, which allowed him to keep both hands on the wheel. Pushing the Wrangler to the limit, he focused on his objective—saving Jordan.

His phone rang.

"Yeah, what have you got for me?" Rick asked.

"I've tried several times to contact the funeral home," Nix Elliott told him. "There's no answer. Sheriff Corbett is getting the director's private number and calling him at home."

"Who's missing from the house?" Whoever was missing had to be the person who had abducted Jordan.

"Vadonna and Tobias are the only two people in the house. Markham, Rene Burke, and Mrs. Wright are all missing."

"Son of a bitch."

"I checked with the front gate. Actually, I'm there right now. O'Steen says that no one has come in or gone out through the front gates this evening."

"I figured as much. Jordan was taken out the back entrance. There had to have been a car there waiting."

"Mrs. Price's Navigator isn't in the garage. I gave this information to the sheriff when I spoke to him."

"Did either Tobias or Vadonna see anything?"

"Tobias said he saw Devon Markham leave the house by the front entrance shortly before you and Mrs. Price were summoned to the Harris cottage."

"What about Mrs. Wright and Rene?"

"No one has any idea where they are or when they left."

"Has Holt made it there, yet?"

"Not yet. He just checked in. He's ten minutes away,"

Nix said. "Hey, wait a minute. A couple of deputies are here. We'll get started searching the grounds right away."

"If you find anything—"

"I'll contact you immediately."

Rick stared at the dark country road ahead of him. It was two-lane highway all the way from Priceville to Jernigan Crossroads. If only he hadn't sent the Powell helicopter back to Knoxville, he could get to the funeral home before Jordan and her kidnapper arrived. He might have had a hell of a time finding a safe place to land in town, but he could have found a suitable landing area on the outskirts.

Hindsight was twenty-twenty. He had to deal with the reality of the moment. He didn't have the chopper.

What if I'm wrong? What if they're not on their way to the funeral home? What if I've misinterpreted the things Tammy said? But what else could Jordan wearing her wedding dress and becoming Robby Joe's bride forever mean? Whoever had Jordan—Devon? Rene? Mrs. Wright?—they intended to kill her.

Only in death could she be with Robby Joe forever.

As instructed, once they were within ten miles of Jernigan Crossroads, Jordan took a back road that she hadn't even known existed.

"Will this take us directly to the funeral home?" Jordan asked.

"We're not going to the funeral home."

"We aren't? Then where are we going?"

"We're going to meet Robby Joe. He's waiting for us at the cemetery."

"What! But—but I thought . . ."

"I arranged to have him taken to the cemetery. It cost me quite a bit to bribe one of the funeral home employees, but for five thousand dollars, he was perfectly willing to break the rules."

"You had Robby Joe's casket taken to the cemetery? But why?" Jordan asked, hopelessly confused and scared out of her mind.

"I was afraid we might be disturbed if we met Robby Joe at the funeral home. Meeting him at the cemetery will give us the privacy we need."

"Privacy for what?"

"For your wedding, of course."

Rick had left Price Manor twenty-five minutes ago. If his calculations were correct, he'd make it to the funeral home in another five minutes.

His phone rang.

"Yeah, let's hear it."

"We're still searching," Nix Elliott said. "We've covered over half the grounds."

"Nothing?"

"No sign of Mrs. Price, but we found Devon Markham."

"Alive?"

"Yes, alive. The guy had just taken an evening stroll. He was alone when we found him. He's pretty frantic now that he knows Mrs. Price is missing."

"Any sign of Mrs. Wright or Rene Burke?"

"No."

"We were too sure Markham was our killer," Rick said. "Looks like we were wrong."

"Yeah, dead wrong."

Afraid not to follow orders because she knew that she was not the only one whose life was in danger, Jordan turned the Navigator off the back road and onto the gravel drive that circled the cemetery.

"Pull off the drive and into the grass. Park so that the front of the car is facing Robby Joe's monument."

Jordan parked the SUV.

"Leave the headlights on. They won't be as beautiful and romantic as candlelight, but they'll have to do."

Jordan did as she was instructed.

"Now, take your wedding dress with you and get out. We'll wait here and give you some privacy while you change clothes."

Jordan glanced at the garment bag lying on the front passenger seat. "You want me to put on the wedding dress?"

The shrill laughter jangled off Jordan's nerves like ice daggers. "Of course, silly. You can't get married in what you're wearing now. You've waited twelve years to wear that beautiful dress. Now hurry up. And don't do anything stupid like trying to run away. If you do, I'll have to kill her, and you don't want me to do that."

"No, please, don't hurt her." Jordan grabbed the garment bag from the seat, clutched it to her chest and opened the driver's side door.

This couldn't be happening. Surely she was having a nightmare. If only . . . But this was no nightmare. This was real.

*Rick will find me. Somehow, some way, he'll figure out where we are and what's going on. I just have to buy us some time.*

*Put on the dress and play along with her. Pretend you agree with her, that you understand why she's doing this.*

Jordan glanced toward Robby Joe's headstone spotlighted by the Navigator's headlights. When she saw the casket resting on the grass beside the empty grave, she gasped. Why was the casket open?

*Oh, God. Oh, God!*

Her hands shook so badly that she had difficulty removing her blouse and slacks, but she somehow managed to strip down to her underwear. Glancing at the car, at the two women in the back of the SUV, one holding a gun to the other's head, she hurriedly unzipped the garment bag and removed the wedding dress.

She pulled the dress over her head, slipped her arms into the sheer lace sleeves and shivered when the thick, heavily beaded skirt fell about her hips and the scalloped lace edge skimmed the grass beneath her feet. She reached behind her and tried her best to maneuver the tiny pearl buttons into the buttonholes. Her fingers felt numb. Finally she managed to fasten three of the buttons, the ones closest to her waist.

The SUV's right side back door opened and the two women emerged. "Do you need a little help with the buttons?"

"Yes," Jordan replied.

"Then we'll be glad to help you."

Jordan forced a smile. "Thank you. I—I want everything to be perfect, especially my dress since I've waited such a long time to wear it."

Twelve years and what seemed like a million lifetimes ago, this had been her fantasy wedding gown. And now, it just might become her burial gown.


Rick whipped the Wrangler into the parking lot at the funeral home and skidded to an abrupt stop in front of the entrance. Just as he jumped out of the Jeep, the chapel doors opened and a man he recognized as the funeral director met him under the canopied portico.

"Mr. Carson, I'm Charles Farmer. Sheriff Corbett called me at home and explained the situation."

"Is Mrs. Price here?"

"No, sir. When I arrived, I checked the entire place and no one is here."

Rick shoved Mr. Farmer aside. "If you don't mind, I'll see for myself."

The director followed Rick inside as he went from room to room, from the chapel, through the offices, and back into the mortuary where the bodies were prepared for burial.

"Mr. Carson, please listen to me."

Rick kept moving, searching for any sign of Jordan and her abductor. "Talk."

"There's no one here. I promise you. But—but—"

Rick stopped as they reentered the chapel. "But what?"

"Mr. Wright's casket is missing."

"What do you mean it's missing?"

"I mean it isn't here," Mr. Farmer said. "I've checked the hearse, too, and it's not there. I have no idea where it is."

"Shit!" He grabbed Farmer by his jacket lapels. "How many people have access to the funeral home after hours?"

"You don't think one of my employees would—"

"Yeah, I think they would. For enough money."

"What possible reason would anyone have to steal Mr. Wright's casket? Who would do such a thing?"

"Someone who intends to put another body in the coffin."

Robby Joe Wright's bride.

Jordan looked from Darlene to Rene, keeping her wavering fake smile in place.

Holding Rene's arm with her left hand and clutching the gun in her right hand, Darlene forced Rene into position behind Jordan.

"Button her dress, please, won't you, Rene," Darlene said. "It's just one of those little things a maid of honor does for the bride."

*Do it, Rene, please do it. Don't argue with her.*

Rene struggled with the buttons and after several tries, she managed to accomplish the task.

"Good job," Darlene said. "Now, turn around, dear, and let us see how beautiful you look."

Jordan turned slowly. Her gaze locked with Rene's for one long, mutually terrified moment.

"I know you wanted Devon to be your man of honor, but that was just foolishness on your part. It's much more appropriate for Rene to be your maid of honor. After all, it's what Robby Joe really wants, isn't it?"

"Yes. Yes, you're right," Jordan said.

"You're going to make my son such a wonderful wife. The two of you are so perfect together. I only wish I had realized sooner that this was the only way you could be truly happy."

"You've always put me first, haven't you, Darlene? You love me as if I were your daughter. You've been at my side all these years, taking care of me."

Darlene smiled. "I knew you'd understand why I had to kill them."

"I do understand. I really do. You were protecting me from them, weren't you? Jane Anne and Dan and Boyd and—"

"And Donald Farris and Jay Reynolds," Darlene added the final two names to the list. "I had planned to get rid of J.C., but he left before I was able to finalize a plan."

"What about my father?" Jordan asked.

"Oh, my dear girl, I had nothing to do with Wayne's death. Undoubtedly living with that trashy whore he married finally became too much and he just keeled over with a heart attack."

"You—you're going to kill us, too, aren't you?" Rene's voice quavered with fear.

"I'm so sorry that I had to involve you, Rene. I've always liked you. But I wasn't sure Jordan would come with me without a little persuasion. I promise that I'll make it quick and painless."

"Darlene, please let Rene go. She doesn't need to be a

part of this. It should be just you and Robby Joe and me. We don't need her for the wedding. I'm all ready. See?" Jordan pivoted around slowly as if showing off her bridal gown. "Robby Joe has been waiting twelve years. Let's not keep him waiting any longer."

Tears glistened in Darlene's eyes. "Oh, my dear, dear Jordan. I knew you still loved my son."

"Please, let Rene go."

"All right. After the ceremony."

"Let her go now."

"Oh, I'm afraid I can't do that. But once you become Robby Joe's bride, Rene can leave."

When Rick rounded the last bend in the country road leading to the cemetery, he looked up ahead and to the right, directly toward the graveyard. Beams of two bright headlights broke through the darkness surrounding Robby Joe's burial site.

God in heaven!

He pulled the Jeep onto the shoulder of the road, turned off the lights, and killed the engine. His heartbeat drummed inside his head. His muscles tensed.

As he got out of the Jeep, he pulled his Smith & Wesson from his shoulder holster. Adrenaline rushed through his body as he quietly made his way down into the ditch, up the other side, and into the cemetery.

As he approached the parked SUV, he heard voices.

"Go to Robby Joe. He's waiting for you," Darlene Wright said. "Take your place at his side."

"Please, Darlene, think about what you're asking me to do." Jordan's voice was amazingly calm. "Robby Joe is dead. He's not in that casket. He's in heaven."

"Yes, of course, my dear. I know that. But soon you will join him and the two of you will be together forever."

"You don't want to kill me. You love me. Remember?"

"Of course, I love you. That's why I'm doing this. It's the only way you'll ever be truly happy."

"Please, please . . ." Jordan's voice grew panicky.

"If you don't go over there and get in the casket with Robby Joe, I'll be forced to kill Rene. You don't want me to do that, do you?"

"No, don't. Please. I'm going. I'll do what you ask."

"No, Jordan, don't! My God, you can't!" Rene cried out.

Rick crept closer, pausing directly beside the Navigator.

Darlene held a gun to Rene's head, the muzzle pressed against her temple. Even if he could get a clear shot at Darlene, he couldn't be a hundred percent certain her finger, which was a hairsbreadth from pressing the trigger, wouldn't react involuntarily. But what choice did he have?

Jordan walked slowly toward the open casket.

Rick slipped around the Navigator.

Jordan looked down into the coffin.

Darlene shoved Rene ahead of her and came up behind Jordan. "Get in. Don't keep Robby Joe waiting any longer."

Jordan lifted one foot and stepped into the coffin.

"Now, lie down beside your groom," Darlene said.

Jordan lay down inside the casket.

Holding the pistol with both hands, Rick took aim.

Darlene slammed the casket lid closed.

Rick fired.

Rene screamed.

# Chapter 33

Jordan shivered uncontrollably as she lay there in the darkness, her body resting on top of the recently autopsied corpse.

*Not Robby Joe. Not Robby Joe,* her mind screamed.

She gasped for air. Oh, God! There was no air. She was going to suffocate. Lifting her hands, she pushed on the padded satin lid.

Suddenly, as if from far away, she heard a loud noise. A gunshot? And then someone screamed.

*Oh, please, no, no. Darlene, you promised not to kill Rene. You promised.*

Was she going to die, too? Was it too late for anyone to save her?

*Where are you, Rick? Where are you? You won't let me die. I know you won't.*

Rene stood there shaking and screaming, her hands over her ears, her eyes wild with fear. Not bothering to check Darlene's body lying on the ground to see if she was dead, Rick shoved Rene aside, and grasped the edges of the coffin lid. As he tried to pry up the lid, he noticed half a foot of white satin covered with heavy beading hung out the edge of the casket, preventing it from sealing. He managed to get his fingers beneath the latch, then he shoved the lid up and open.

Jordan lay inside, her eyes wide, her mouth open. But she didn't move. She can't be dead. She can't be! She'd been in the coffin for only a few minutes. But in those few minutes, she could have suffocated.

He reached inside and slid his arm beneath her. His hand grazed the corpse as he lifted Jordan up and into his arms. She was limp and seemingly lifeless as he carried her away from the gravesite.

He went down on his knees and placed her on the ground, then he tilted her head back and listened to see if she was breathing.

She wasn't.

*Damn it, you're not going to die. I won't let you!*

He pinched her nose and then covered her mouth with his. After he blew into her mouth, he watched as her chest rose. He repeated the process.

*Come on, honey. Breathe for me.*

Just as he started to proceed to the next CPR step and begin chest compressions, Jordan gasped.

Rick felt as if he, too, had come back to life.

"That's it, honey. Breathe!"

She coughed. Rick helped her into a sitting position as she continued coughing. "Rick . . . Rick . . ." She sucked in deep breaths as tears streamed down her cheeks.

He wiped flyaway strands of her hair from her face and kissed her forehead, her cheeks, her chin and finally her mouth. She lifted her arms and wrapped them around him.

"I knew you wouldn't let me die."

Holding her close, he buried his face against her neck. Shivering and weeping, she clung to him.

"Rene? Darlene shot her. Is she—?"

"I'm all right," Rene said, her voice a fractured whisper.

Jordan lifted her head and looked up, then cried out when she saw her friend. "Oh, thank God."

"I shot Darlene," Rick said as he slowly rose to his feet and helped Jordan to stand.

"Is she dead?" Jordan asked.

"Probably." Rick glanced over at Darlene's still body.

He had shot her in the back of the head. He had intended to kill her.

"Oh, Rick, she killed Dan," Jordan said. "And Jane Anne and Boyd and Jay and Donald. She killed them all. And she believed she was killing them to protect me, to help me. Why didn't I see it? Why couldn't I—"

"It's not your fault." Rick clasped her face between his hands. "You had no way of knowing how mentally deranged she was and probably has been for a long time, maybe even before Robby Joe died."

Jordan glanced at the open casket and shuddered. "She made me . . . Oh, God, Rick, I was in that coffin with . . . with . . ." She sobbed.

Rick stroked her back tenderly. "That's it, honey. Let it all out. Cry until you can't cry anymore."

In the distance, police and ambulance sirens wailed, piercing the natural quiet of the country night.

Rick had stayed close by at all times during the past week, there at her side whenever Jordan needed him. But often she wanted to be alone and he and the others who loved her, gave her the right to mourn in private. He had slept on the daybed in her dressing room, but in the morning before dawn every day, she had called to him and he'd gone to her, simply to hold and comfort her.

This morning, six weeks to the day of Senator Daniel

Price's funeral, Darlene Wright had been laid to rest in the plot next to her son at the Jernigan Crossroads Cemetery. The ceremony at the graveside had been brief. Reverend Crowell had read from the Holy Scriptures and said a prayer beseeching the Good Lord to give Darlene eternal peace.

Only Jordan's nearest and dearest had attended the service and those same people were now sharing coffee and drinks at Price Manor. Everyone wanted to be there for Jordan, to offer her their support. Roselynne and Tammy. Devon and Rene. Claire and Ryan. Wesley and Kendra. Tobias and Vadonna.

Jordan came up to him there in the foyer where they'd first met. Had it really been only six weeks ago?

"We need to talk," she told him.

"There's no rush. It can wait."

"No, we need to talk now." She took his hand. "Let's go to my study."

He followed her to the back of the house and into her small, cozy hideaway. He closed the door behind them. He knew what was coming. It had been inevitable. And he'd told himself he was prepared, but he wasn't.

"I think I'm in love with you," she said.

"Jordan, I—"

She pressed her index finger over his lips. "If you love me, you'll give me time. I can't do this. Not now. I'm only half a person. I need to be whole before I can make any kind of emotional commitments."

"How much time do you need?"

"I'm not sure. Weeks. Months. Maybe a year."

"That's a long time to make a guy wait."

"I know I'm asking for a lot, but—"

He silenced her with a kiss.

She kissed him passionately, and then pulled out of his arms. "Will you give me some time? Will you wait?"

"Yeah, honey. I'll wait. Take all the time you need. And when you're ready, let me know."

Tears shimmered in her eyes. "Would you say it, just once."

He looked at her, but didn't touch her again. "I love you, Jordan." Then he walked out of her study and out of Price Manor.

He got in his Jeep and drove down the drive, through the front gates and onto the highway, leaving behind the one thing in the world that meant the most to him.

# Epilogue

*Ten months later . . .*

Rick rang the doorbell. Devon Markham opened the door and greeted him with a smile and cordial handshake.

"Come on in, Rick. I'm glad you could make it. Everyone is going to be happy to see you."

By everyone he sure as hell hoped Devon meant Jordan. He hadn't seen her or heard from her directly in ten months. The last time he'd seen her, the day of Darlene Wright's funeral, she had told him she loved him and then she'd sent him packing. He had been waiting impatiently for her to send for him. He had just about given up hope when he received an invitation to Roselynne Harris's wedding to Wallace McGee.

He had found out through Griff and Nic that the wedding would be a small, private ceremony, held at Price Manor, which Jordan had turned over to Ryan and Claire when she moved out six months ago.

"She's living in Chattanooga. She has an apartment there and is taking classes at UTC," Nic had told him.

"Claire said that Jordan's thinking about renewing her teaching certificate and getting a job teaching elementary school."

As he entered the foyer, he straightened his tie and swallowed hard. Weddings weren't his thing. Wearing a suit and tie wasn't his thing. If he wasn't halfway sure that he'd been invited to this shindig because Jordan was ready to see him again, he damn well wouldn't be here.

"I'm the only groomsman," Devon told him. "So, allow me to show you to your seat."

The house was decked with flowers and ribbons and candles, all tastefully done. He definitely saw Jordan's fine hand behind the decorations.

"I guess you heard that J.C. got in a bit of trouble a few months ago. I'm afraid he's serving jail time out in California and can't be here. Ryan's going to give the bride away and Tammy and Jordan are bridesmaids. It's a real family affair." Devon led Rick into the front parlor which had been stripped of eighty percent of its furniture to make room for white folding chairs, set up in two sections with an aisle, strewn with rose petals, between the double rows.

"How is Jordan?" Rick asked.

"She's well and moving forward with her life."

Rick paused by the chair at the end of the row, the seat next to Claire Price and her four-year-old son, Michael.

"Is she happy?" Rick asked.

"She will be when she sees you." Devon grinned, then winked at Rick before he turned and went back to his duties as the single groomsman.

Rick sat down beside Claire, who smiled at him. "It's so good to see you again. Jordan wasn't sure you'd come, but I told her that I knew you'd be here."

Before he could respond, either by commenting or questioning, the harpist in the corner began playing. A robed minister appeared in front of the altar set up by the fireplace; then Wallace McGee and a young man who looked so much like him that he had to be his son took their places on the left, directly in front of the altar. As the music changed, heads turned and the guests watched while Tammy Harris, in a knee-length pink satin dress and a single strand of pearls, walked down the aisle and took her place on the right. She held a small bouquet of pink roses. Devon followed Tammy and when he reached the altar, he walked over and stood by Wallace and his son.

And then, there she was.

Jordan entered, wearing an identical dress and pearls to those Tammy wore. Her ash-blonde hair was piled atop her head and wispy curls framed her face. She was the most beautiful thing he'd ever seen.

Twenty minutes later, after a traditional wedding ceremony, the guests were asked to join the new Mr. and Mrs. Wallace McGee in the dining room for refreshments. Rick waited in the parlor, hoping Jordan would make her way over to him, but she didn't, so he joined the others in the dining room.

He caught a glimpse of her talking to and laughing with Claire and Ryan. Suddenly she glanced his way. Their gazes locked instantly. She smiled at him and waved. He smiled back at her.

Just as he made his way across the room, he noticed Roselynne talking to Jordan and then the two of them left the room.

Devon clamped his hand down on Rick's shoulder. "She's going upstairs to help Roselynne change into her going away suit. She and Wallace are flying from Atlanta tonight for a two-week honeymoon in Hawaii, so they've got to get on the road right away."

Fifteen minutes later, Rick joined the others at the foot of the stairs in the foyer. How different things were today than they'd been nearly a year ago when he'd stood right here and shook hands with Daniel Price's widow.

"All you single ladies line up." Roselynne giggled as she waited for the four single ladies—Tammy, Rene, Kendra, and Jordan—to separate from the others.

Roselynne turned, glanced over her shoulder and tossed the bouquet. Tammy squealed with delight when she caught it.

Rick followed the crowd onto the veranda and, like everyone else, he threw birdseed at the couple as they hurried down the front steps and got into Wallace's vintage Jaguar.

Suddenly he sensed Jordan. He smelled her delicate perfume. Felt her heat. She came up to him and slipped her arm through his.

"I'm so glad you came to the wedding."

"I wouldn't have missed it."

"Are you staying overnight or are you heading home?" she asked.

"I'm heading back to Knoxville."

"Good. Would you mind giving me a ride to Chattanooga? I drove down with Devon, but he and Rene are going to take Tammy, Kendra and Wes on a vacation to Disney World while Roselynne is on her honeymoon. They're going to stay here overnight and head out first thing in the morning."

"Do you like living in Chattanooga?" he asked.

"Yes, I like it very much. I have my own place. One bedroom, one bath. It's cozy. Kind of like my study here at Price Manor."

"You're looking well." He laughed. "Damn, what am I saying? You look great. You look beautiful."

She smiled. "Thank you. You look beautiful, too." She laughed.

"God, honey, it's so good to see you."

Tears misted her eyes. "Rick Carson, if you don't kiss me, I'm going to—"

He yanked her into his arms, lowered his head and

took her mouth in a hot, hungry kiss. When they finally came up for air, she grabbed both of his hands.

"That's all I needed to know," she said. "You still love me, don't you?"

"Damn straight, I do."

"And I love you."

He slipped his arm around her. "So, am I moving to Chattanooga or are you moving to Knoxville after we get married?"

"Married?"

"You *are* going to marry me, aren't you? And if you need a long engagement—"

"I don't. I've wasted too much of my life. I don't want to waste another minute," she told him. "As for where we'll live—I don't care, as long as we're together for the rest of our lives."

Please turn the page for an exciting sneak peek of
Beverly Barton's *The Fifth Victim*
coming in 2009!

# Prologue

Dark. Cold. Predawn quiet. Wind whipped through the tall, ancient trees in the forest. Soon the sun would ascend over Scotsman's Bluff. He was prepared, ready to strike the moment the morning light hit the altar. Once the deed was done, once he had sacrificed the first victim, the ritual would begin anew. As soon as he tasted her sweet life's blood, he would no longer feel the winter's cold. Her blood would warm him, empower him, prepare him for the others who would lead him to the most important transposition of his life. All these years he had diligently searched for perfection, for the most powerful, all the while building his strength, bit by bit, with lesser mortals.

He gazed down at the naked girl tied to the wooden altar, her long blond hair flowing about her angelic face as the frigid wind caressed her luscious body. Her eyelids fluttered. Good. That meant the drug he'd given her was wearing off and she would be awake for the ceremony. He loved to see the look on their faces—the shock and horror—when they realized what was about to happen to them.

Flinging back his dark cape, he smiled. There was no need to hurry. He could take his time afterward, savor the kill for as long as he liked. No one in their right mind would be out in the woods at dawn in January. Only he and the girl.

He laid the ornately carved wooden case atop the girl's trembling body, opened it and removed the heavy sword, then placed the case on the ground. Gazing up at the sky, he waited.

She whimpered, but the gag in her mouth kept her from doing more. He glanced down at her, ran his hand over her naked breasts and lifted the sword toward the heavens.

A pale pink blush spread out over Scotsman's Bluff, only a hint of color in the dark sky.

"Soon, my little lamb. Soon."

Languidly, with tendrils of light reaching farther and farther into the sky, the sun welcomed the dawn of a new day. He jerked the gag from her mouth. She screamed. He brandished the sword and spoke the sacred words in an ancient tongue.

*From the depths of hell, hear me and do my bidding. Let this sacrifice please thee. I bid thee to accomplish my will and desire.*

He brought the sword down, down, down. From throat to navel, he split her open. Her sightless eyes stared up at the towering treetops overhead.

He wiped the sword with a soft cloth and returned the weapon to its bed, then stuffed the bloodstained cloth into a plastic bag and dumped the bag into the case. With her blood still warm, he lowered his head until his lips touched the gaping wound. He licked, then sucked, filling his mouth with her blood and energizing himself with her life force before it escaped.

Genevieve Madoc woke with a start, sweat drenching her body, soaking her flannel gown. Her heart beat at a dangerously accelerated pace as she shot straight up in bed.

"Oh, God! Oh, God!" she moaned as she recalled her dream, a shadowy, terrifying vision of death.

Uncontrollable tremors racked her body. She hated these moments directly following a revelation, when she was weak and vulnerable. Drained of all energy, barely able to move. She fell backward; her head hit the pillow. She would call Jazzy for help once she regained enough strength to reach out to the nightstand for the telephone. But for now she would lie still and wait. And pray the images would not return. Sometimes *the sight* came to her in dreams, but just as often she experienced it while wide awake.

Rising from the handwoven rug in front of the fireplace, Drudwyn's keen eyes searched the darkness, seeking his mistress. He uttered a concerned whimper.

"I'll be all right," she told him, her voice a delicate whisper. Then she spoke to him telepathically, assuring him that she was in no danger. The big, mixed-breed animal lumbered to the side of the bed, then slumped to the wooden floor. She sensed his mood and knew his protective instincts had automatically kicked in. The dog she had raised from a mongrel puppy considered himself her bodyguard. Like she, Drudwyn's heritage—the results of a wolf having mated with a German shepherd/Lab-mix mutt—made him unique. Her ancestry, comprised of Scots-Irish, English, and Cherokee might not be all that uncommon in these parts, but the gift of sight she had inherited from her grandmother was.

As she lay in bed, waiting for her strength to renew, she couldn't help thinking of the vision she'd had. Out there somewhere, a young woman had been murdered. Genny knew it as surely as she knew her own name. She had not seen the girl's face, only her flawless naked body and the huge sword that had sliced her open as if she were a ripe

melon. Bile rose from Genny's stomach and burned a
path up her esophagus to her throat.

*No, please, I can't be sick. Not now. I don't have the
strength to crawl out of bed.* She willed the nausea under
control.

Who could have committed such a heinous crime?
What sort of monster would sacrifice a human being?

Her cousin Jacob had mentioned that there had been
several animal sacrifices in the area—four since
Thanksgiving. Had those been nothing more than a pre-
cursor to the killing of a human?

After she called Jazzy for help, she would call Jacob. It
would be too late for him to do anything to help the
woman, but as the county sheriff, it would be his job to
investigate the murder.

*What will you tell him?* Genny asked herself. *If you explain that you've had another vision, only this one far
more gruesome than any you've had before, he'll understand. He's your blood-kin. He won't dismiss your vision
as nothing more than a dream.*

Fifteen minutes later, Genny forced herself to ease to
the edge of the bed. She lifted the telephone receiver and
dialed Jazzy's number. The phone rang five times before a
harsh voice answered.

"Who the hell's calling at this ungodly hour?"

"Jazzy?"

"Genny, is that you?"

"Yes. Please—"

"I'm on my way. Just stay put."

"Thank you."

The moment she heard the dial tone, Genny punched
in Jacob's home phone number. He picked up on the second ring. Always an early riser, as was she, her cousin
was probably in the middle of preparing his breakfast.

"Butler here," he said, his voice gruff and deeply bari-
tone.

"Jacob, it's Genny. Please, come to my house … now."

"What's wrong?"

"I've had a dream … one of my visions."

"Are you all right?"

"No, but I will be. I've called Jazzy. She'll be here soon. But I must tell you …" Her voice suddenly failed her.

"Tell me what?"

She cleared her throat. "Someone has been murdered. A young woman. I'm sure you'll find her body in Cedar Tree Forest, not far from here. I saw … through the killer's eyes … I saw—" She sucked in a deep breath. "He watched the sunrise over Scotsman's Bluff."

"Are you sure, Genny? Are you positive it wasn't just a nightmare?"

"I'm positive. It's too late to save her, but you can find her body and perhaps find some evidence of who killed her—if you can get there soon. I think I can guide you to the exact spot."

"Ah, shit …" Jacob murmured under his breath.

"Jacob?"

"Hmm?"

"He tied her to an altar of some sort and sacrificed her. I—I think he drank her blood."

"God damn son of a bitch!"

# THE MURDER GAME

## Beverly Barton

**If looks could kill . . .**

It's the ultimate game.
To win, you have to kill.
To lose, you have to die.
If he's chosen you to play, then it's Game Over . . .

A brutal serial killer is on the loose. Each victim is a former beauty queen, a single rose placed next to their mutilated bodies.

The scenes of unimaginable carnage have become familiar to Detective Lindsay McAllister. For the last 5 years, dozens of beautiful women have been slain and lives have been shattered, including Judd Walker whose wife was one of the first victims.

But when the killer strikes again Lindsey knows she needs Judd's help. The murderer is getting bolder, faster, and more ruthless. The game has escalated, the rules have changed, the body count is rising . . . and no one is safe.

ISBN: 978-1-84756-020-9

Out now.